THE
BEIJING BLUNDER

BOOK 4 OF THE ONE HUNDRED YEARS OF WAR SERIES

JAY PERIN

Publisher's Cataloging-In-Publication Data

(Prepared by Cassidy Cataloguing Services, Inc.)

Names: Perin, Jay, author.
Title: The Beijing blunder / Jay Perin.
Description: [New York, New York] : East River
    Books, [2022] | Series: One hundred years of war
    series ; book 4
Identifiers: ISBN 9781736468074 (paperback) | ISBN
    9781736468067 (ebook)
Subjects: LCSH: Presidents--United States--History--
    20th century--Fiction. | United States--Politics
    and government--1989---Fiction. | Petroleum
    industry and trade--History--20th century--
    Fiction. | Nineteen nineties--Fiction. | Heirs--
    Fiction. | Freedom of expression--Fiction. |
    Power (Social sciences)--Fiction. | LCGFT:
    Political fiction. | Thrillers (Fiction) |
    Historical fiction.
Classification: LCC PS3616.E7443 B45 2022 | DDC
    813/.6--dc23

Editors:
Chase Nottingham
Elizabeth Roderick http://talesfrompurgatory.com/
Cover: www.ebookorprint.com
Maps and illustrations: Murat Bayazit
Video (book trailer): Nauman Gandhi
Special mention: Marcus Jordan https://www.marcusjordanart.com/

www.EastRiverBooks.com

To the One They Called God;
To the Best of Men;
To That Goddess of Knowledge;
To the Chronicler.

Table of Contents

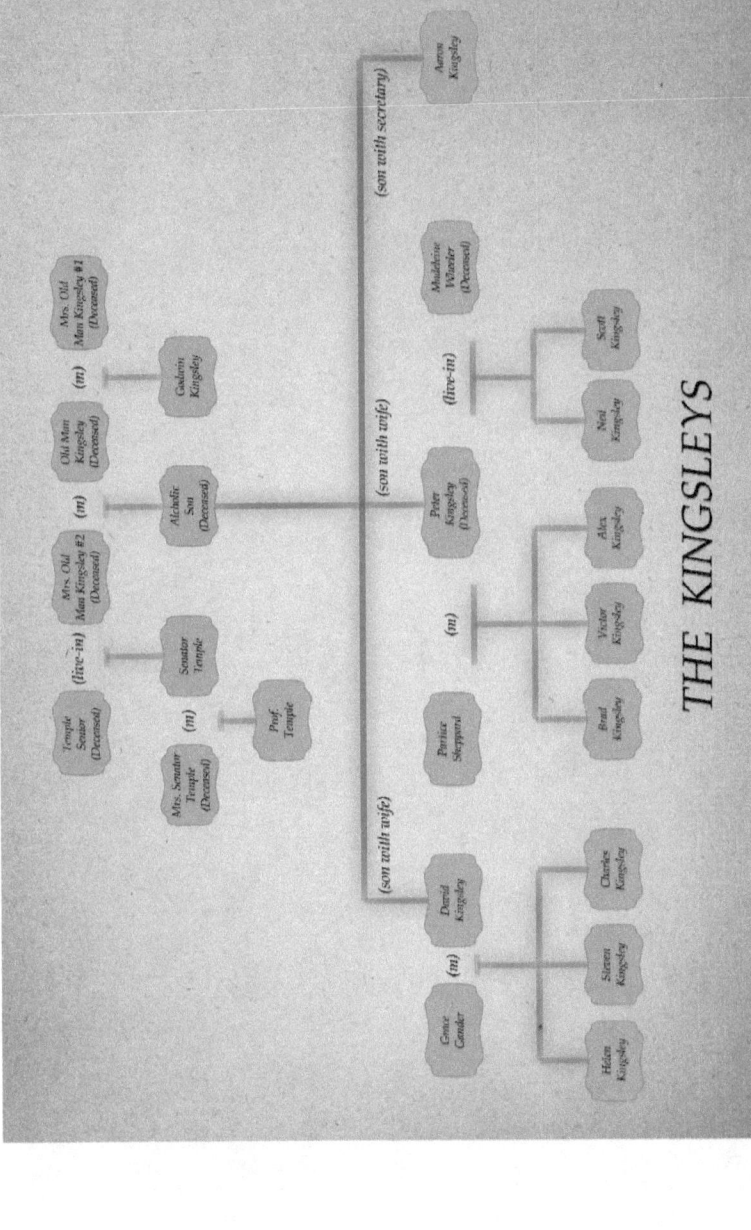

THE KINGSLEYS

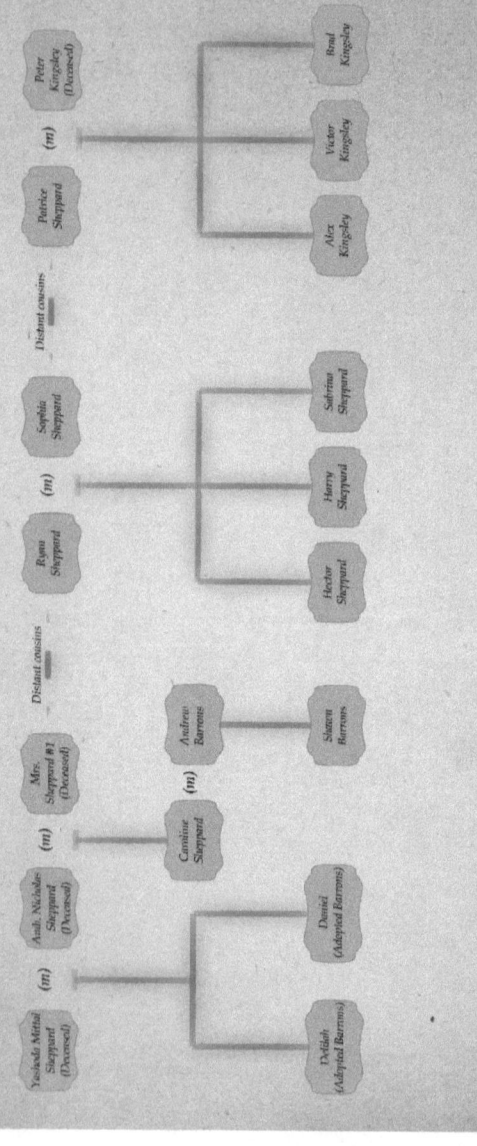

THE SHEPPARDS

Part I

Chapter 1

November 1988

New York, New York

Evening crowds thronged the brightly lit Times Square, gawking at the oversized billboards advertising *The Phantom of the Opera* and *Cats*. Outside the Marriot Marquis, commuters on their drive home honked, but ignoring the blaring horns and irate shouts, tourists still lingered on the pedestrian crossing.

In the vestibule at the entrance of the hotel, Temple let the warmth blasted by the heater soothe his stiff joints as he watched Noah Andersen, former attorney general, stride along the rain-slick sidewalk. Noah was only a few months behind Temple in celebrating his eighty-third birthday, but he still moved with the gait of a much younger man. Unfortunately for Temple, recent events brought the side effect of making him very much aware of the passage of time. He couldn't help but worry how many days he would have on earth to rectify his mistakes.

"Mr. Temple," called one of the secret service officers. There were usually four men in the security detail assigned to the former president. The doctor who was a part of the entourage was at the moment perusing a newspaper by the reception desk. Except for arthritis and a blood pressure problem, Temple was in reasonable health, so the medic generally had little to do. "It's safer to remain in the lobby," said the lead security official. "Besides, the *Vanity Fair* reporter is waiting to speak with you. He has the photographer with him."

"Apologize to the journalists for the delay, please," muttered Temple. "I know I promised them a couple of hours, and I will... I swear... something important came up." Before the magazine interview scheduled at the Marriott could begin, Noah called with the news he'd tricked Godwin and the rest of the Kingsleys into showing up at the same hotel.

Dressed in a black parka, the ridiculous jet-black dye job at odds with the age lines on his austere face, Noah skirted a vendor selling roasted almonds and pushed through the revolving doors to where Temple stood. After a quick nod at the secret service officers, Noah relayed the information he'd obtained. "Godwin's on his way, and so are Steven and Charles. They think one of their prospective clients is here to discuss a deal, but—"

"But nothing," snapped Temple. "My dear stepbrother is going to talk to me." The network of energy companies envisioned by the three men—Temple, Noah, and Godwin—was built on the backs of Lilah, her husband, and his brothers. Temple hadn't known Godwin was only waiting for the empire to be formed before usurping power. Thanks to the Kingsleys, Lilah and her husband—Godwin's adopted grandson—were arrested by the American military on false claims of treason. In the attempt to get her to the interrogation room, she was beaten by another of Godwin's grandsons and threatened with sexual assault. Lilah's legal expertise got her family off the hook then, but she, Brad, and his four brothers were now on the run, blackmailed into exile by the prospect of another prosecution for treachery against the nation. Everything—*everything*—was Temple's fault. His misplaced faith in Godwin caused it all. "I'm going to give Godwin one last chance to set things right," said Temple.

The former supreme court justice needed to explain how he could have done this to the young woman Temple thought of as a daughter. Lilah once dreamed of being a supreme court justice herself. *Temple* insisted she was born to answer a higher calling. Sacrificing her personal aspirations, she claimed the mantle of leadership over the energy sector. The same woman was now considered a traitor to the nation. Large sections of the press believed what was put out by the military and bayed for Lilah's blood.

Noah recently accused Temple of being a hypocrite for worrying about Lilah's physical safety when he himself manipulated her to build the empire. Temple didn't give a damn what he was called. It *was* personal now... not only because of the assault on Lilah. His position as president of the nation was misused by the Kingsleys in their pursuit of absolute power.

Oh, yes. Godwin was going to explain. Then, he was going to do exactly what Temple ordered. Lilah and her family would be back in the States, the rest of the Kingsleys offering abject apologies.

"When Godwin sees you here," said Noah, grim look in his bright-green eyes, "there's going to be another excuse why he can't meet you today."

Temple tucked his hands into his coat pockets. "Godwin needs an incentive, so we'll give him one." Turning to the officer next to him, Temple said, "Noah and I will be waiting in the restaurant. When Justice Kingsley gets here, let him know I've finally decided to speak to the media about the fiasco in Cuba but would prefer to do a joint interview with him. Inform my stepbrother the men from *Vanity Fair* are with me. Let's see if Godwin refuses to talk to me with the press watching." The Kingsley patriarch wouldn't want it known Temple was displeased with the family.

"I have the premier suite reserved," Noah interjected. "No need to wait in the restaurant, but don't you think it's better to avoid a direct confrontation? If Godwin can do what he did to his own flesh and blood..."

"What? He's going to have *me* arrested by the military?"

"Obviously, he can't pull the same trick on a former president, but I *am* concerned about your safety. After all, it was your note—" Noah stopped, a speculative look in his eyes.

It hadn't been only Lilah's arguments which put an end to Godwin Kingsley's antics in the military court. There was the little matter of the note Temple sent. Godwin didn't know until then Temple was aware of the darkest chapter in Kingsley family history. Even Noah wasn't advised of the contents of the note, understanding only that it was powerful enough to disarm a man like Godwin. Too bad it didn't stop the rest of the Kingsleys from threatening Lilah and the five brothers into running.

"Temple, you need to be careful," insisted Noah. "Whatever the info was, you're the only one who's in the know. It makes you vulnerable."

The former president nodded. "I get it. As I said, I'm going to give Godwin one chance. If he doesn't agree to do what I want... I'm certain he won't dare try anything with me, but you have my word both you and Harry will know all of it soon."

#

Ten minutes later

Outside the windows of the hotel suite, the sky turned black. The sounds of the city hardly filtered into the room. The living area was large by New York City standards and boasted of a comfortably elegant couch and matching chairs. There was a conference table to one side and a dining nook at the far end. The reporters were thrilled at the opportunity to interview the stepbrothers together. Noah, too. David and Aaron Kingsley, Godwin's adopted sons, were allowed to listen in on the interview but not the rest of the Kingsley entourage.

"Steven didn't know his cousins were going to run as soon as they signed over the business," Godwin lied to the press for his remaining heir, the sad smile on his face suggesting he wasn't sure if he believed it.

The gray eyes and the white ponytail added the impression of a benevolent elder to his unimpeachable reputation as a steel-willed arbitrator of justice. Lawyers, judges, and politicians alike cited rulings Godwin made when he was at the U.S. Supreme Court. Neither the government nor the media believed Godwin Kingsley had been anything but fair in the Cuba incident.

"Brad and his brothers claimed to Steven the transfer of power was so they could deal with the legal issues without destabilizing the network," continued Godwin. "Steven didn't realize they would leave the country right after. The stock remains in their name, so the idea must be to fight the charges from outside the country to avoid arrest, then return. But no one can deny Brad willingly walked into the Iran deal which led to said charges."

"It could be interpreted as Mr. Steven Kingsley having helped traitors escape," suggested one of the reporters.

Godwin huffed as though exhausted. "Yes, the feds expressed the same concern, but I reminded them Steven was part of the original investigation of the whole incident. Thank God they took my word for it, or *two* of my grandsons would've been in legal trouble. The rest of us—and Temple, of course—are doing our best to hold things together. What we want is peace... not only for the family... we want peace for the network, for the entire country. The chaos we have now will stifle growth all around. Employees will suffer, and so will partners. America... the other nations of the world... we're all interconnected and will be forced to go through significant financial pain if this issue isn't resolved quickly."

"The attack on Mrs. Kingsley?" asked the second reporter. "Sources say Major Richard Armor threatened her with sexual assault if she didn't cooperate. Isn't he a good friend of your grandson Steven? A couple of the reports claim she was dragged by her hair to the courtroom by Captain Charles Kingsley. Rumor has it she was, indeed, stripped of her clothes. Any comment, Mr. Temple?"

The politician managed to keep his grave expression in place. Played right, the more lurid version of events so gleefully spread by a salivating press corps could generate sympathy for Lilah in the right circles. "For the record, I do not believe Brad committed any crimes," Temple said. "Not on purpose. But the military is investigating it, so neither Godwin nor I can comment further. In the meantime, the Kingsleys and I will work through the unpleasantness in the family."

David and Aaron were at the conference table, their brown hair and Kingsley gray eyes proclaiming them as brothers. Both stayed mute. To the media, they would present a united front.

The moment the door closed behind the press, the air turned a lot colder. The secret service personnel were still outside the door, but David's sons, Steven and Charles, were finally allowed into the suite and asked to wait in the dining area. Steven's friend, Richard Armor, was with them as always.

Temple eyed the Kingsley men he'd known from their infancy, wondering how the two of them could look so similar to their father, David, yet be so different in behavior. The former president found David's fawning as repellant as Steven's arrogance and Charles's crudity. Temple was tempted to beat the young thug—the sex assaulter—to death with his own hands. What Charles did to Lilah would not be forgotten, much less forgiven. His superior officer, Richard Armor, had condoned... no, he *encouraged* the attack. Both men would pay for it. Fortunately for Godwin, the assault was the one thing which couldn't be blamed on him. Grinding his teeth, Temple stayed put on the couch and refocused his attention on Godwin.

"Let's not pretend you don't know why we wanted to see you," said Noah, sitting next to Temple.

"Who's pretending?" Godwin asked, drumming his fingers on the arm of the plush chair. "Steven never got along with Brad and his brothers. He admits it everywhere. So when the military approached him to set up a sting operation, he grabbed the opportunity. Unsavory... not illegal."

"Unsavory?" Temple asked. "Is it all you have to say? Just like Steven, Brad is your grandson. He was tricked into signing away a billion dollars for what he thought was an oil deal with Iran. He didn't know those men were nuclear traffickers."

"Brad's a grown man," Godwin said. "He *claims* he was tricked... as CEO of the network, shouldn't he have known better?"

"But you didn't just go after Brad, did you?" Temple asked, teeth clenched. "You had to get all of them out to control the network. Brad's brothers *and* his wife."

"*I* didn't go after anyone," Godwin insisted.

Noah laughed. "No, *Steven* did it. He involved your family business, Kingsley Corp, in a matter of national security without express permission from you, the man who runs it."

"I don't run anything, Andersen," Godwin said, his demeanor calm. "Steven's father is the CEO."

Irritation rising in waves, Temple snapped, "Cut the—" He took a deep breath. "David has an empty title as you well know. You and Aaron run the show."

After Godwin's father married Temple's mother, a contract was signed, giving their progeny exclusive rights to the company stock and the CEO position. The union produced one son, who eventually died of alcoholism. The second of the three children born to the drunk, Peter Kingsley, became CEO when he attained majority. After his departure, David got the job. He didn't have the faintest idea how to lead a business. Thankfully for the company, Godwin retained the position of president. Beyond a pained, reproachful look at Temple, David didn't object to the statement.

"Godwin," snarled the former American president. "You didn't inform me of what was going on, and you made sure Aaron knew nothing, or he'd have called me, and I would've put a stop to it."

Palms turned up in conciliation, Godwin explained, "I couldn't divulge anything. As Andersen said, it was a national security matter. Out of my hands."

Laughing scornfully once more, Noah commented, "Strange how well it worked out for you. You control the whole network now."

"Not me," Godwin corrected. "Steven's the acting CEO."

Temple flicked a glance at the dining table. Face stoic, Steven stared ahead, not bothering to respond to the implication this had all been his plan. His father, David, didn't speak up, either. Greed, of course. It made men admit to crimes they didn't have the brains to commit.

"At the very least, you watched Steven do it," Noah accused Godwin. "Not saying a word in court against the injustice. You knew there was no evidence to support Lilah's arrest, yet you let it happen. In fact, you actively argued against her. You would've let her be thrown into prison and suffer the consequences. Death penalty, even."

Godwin protested, "I might have argued against her, but it was only to make sure the law was followed. Afterward, I recommended that the court let them go. And Lilah didn't have to agree to Steven's terms and go on exile with Brad. Nor did Brad's brothers. As you said, there was no evidence left against them, only Brad. I didn't realize they would be foolish enough to risk their own safety for him."

Aaron finally spoke, "Father, I just can't imagine how you could let this happen to your own grandchildren. David, I wish you'd exercised a little more control over your son."

"Enough, Aaron," David ordered. "What Father did was for the benefit of the entire sector. I think my son is competent enough to be

CEO. Better than Brad, anyway. At least Steven wasn't foolish enough to gamble with national security. Besides, I'm hopeful the six of them won't come around again to bother us."

Aaron's eyes sharpened. The former president twisted sideways on the couch to stare holes into David. "What the hell do you mean?" asked Temple.

"They're still suspected traitors," David added hastily. "They can't return."

If the charge were lifted, Brad and his brothers *would* return, and the condition Lilah placed on the handover agreement meant Steven would be forced to cede control. Moreover, ownership of the stock remained with Brad and the rest, only voting rights on it going to Steven. The exiles would get stock dividends, no cash dividends. This way, the feds wouldn't have much reason to intervene in the transfer of power. All of it meant as long as the exiles remained alive, Steven's hold on the empire would not be secure.

"Out!" said Temple. "All of you except Godwin." Mild mutters rose, but no one dared disobey. Chairs scraped the carpet. One by one, everyone stood. "I apologize, Noah," Temple said. "I need to talk to Godwin alone."

When the room was empty, the stepbrothers faced each other in silence. Temple studied Godwin, sizing up possible outcomes of this conversation. Temple never expected to one day use the information in his possession as a weapon against the Kingsleys, but it needed to be done. Godwin brought them both to this moment.

"There's no one else here," said Temple. "Are you still going to claim you had nothing to do with what happened?"

"Steven—"

Temple shot a derisive look. "You made no effort to stop him, and you made sure no one who could have stopped the arrest was around while it was happening. Not me, not Noah. You told the court there was no reason to believe Lilah was innocent. Then, even after she managed to extricate Brad and his brothers from trouble, Steven went after them to force this exile."

"I wasn't even present when the last discussion happened."

"Are you telling me the former supreme court justice didn't recognize there was one piece of evidence remaining? Are you claiming you didn't see any way of dragging Steven and his friends out of the court before they caused more trouble?"

"You know how they are," Godwin tried again. "How Steven is."

"You simply went along? Incredible. The man who managed to bring the business back from ruin, the patriarch of the family, the man with enough clout to divide the company in two despite not holding a single share, was forced to go along? What was your reason? Did you take an oath to protect the self-centered princes of the Kingsley family or something?"

Gray eyes glinting with anger, Godwin maintained, "The law was with Steven, and as a former justice, I'm obligated to uphold it."

"Even if I buy all your excuses about the interrogation, what about the attack?" It was merely weeks before the arrest when Lilah escaped a murder attempt by an accused rapist. She might've been killed, along with Harry, the chairman of the network's board. Brad would've been left in sole control, and he would've been Godwin's puppet. The attack failed, and Godwin forged a new plan to get Lilah out—the arrest.

"Bringing in the rapist was *your* idea, Temple." Godwin stared back with no trace of anxiety. "Moreover, you never had a problem asking Andersen to start trouble between her and Brad."

"You know damned well what the plan was." Noah intervened in Brad and Lilah's marriage to make sure she carried no direct influence with her own husband. Then, the rapist was brought in to provoke Harry into an attack so he could be eliminated in what would be seen as self-defense. Once he was out of their way, Lilah would be sidelined for experienced elders to control Brad and the network... but only until she learned to operate in the world as it was, not what she wanted it to be. "What did you believe would happen after you asked the thug to kill her? Did you imagine after she and Harry were gone and the network was in your hands, I wouldn't say anything for fear of destabilizing things? Since she didn't die, you didn't want to take the chance I might change sides. Hence, the scheme with Steven."

Godwin's nostrils flared, conciliation morphing to faint menace. "Careful, Temple. Andersen also had contact with the rapist. It's a short line to draw between him and you. Try accusing me, and you're both going to find yourselves in trouble."

"All right," Temple said. "I won't. But neither will you say a word when I talk to the White House about a pardon for Brad."

"If I do?"

Presidential clemency was not expected to happen until the Cuba episode faded from public memory, which would take a while. Not only could the Kingsleys and their allies keep the story alive for longer, Godwin—as a former supreme court justice and the family patriarch—could potentially prevent the pardon from happening at all.

Lips twisting into an unpleasant smile, Temple said, "Remember the note I sent you while you were presiding over the travesty of an interrogation in Cuba. Harry has been asking me what was in it. So far, I've held him off, but what if he manages to wear me down? What if he decides to talk to the press about it?"

"Old story," Godwin dismissed, but his cheeks were flushed. His hands curled into fists at his side. "I didn't know you knew. It caught me by surprise in Cuba. Or I wouldn't have—"

"There's a politician in Louisiana you might enjoy talking to," Temple said. "Says the only way he could lose is if he got caught in bed with a dead girl or a live boy. True for supreme court justices, too."

Fleeting fear appeared in Godwin's eyes, followed by calculation. "We were both involved."

"Yes, we were," Temple admitted. "We threw Amber—a *child*—into our half-brother's path to create an alliance with Barrons O & G. *With* blessings from Andrew Barrons. Only, I wasn't aware our dear brother was not the one who caught her eye."

The red splotches on Godwin's face turned nearly purple. "The stupid little... it was years ago. No one's going to care."

Satisfaction thrummed through Temple's arteries. "There was something I didn't put in the note. Ambrosia Barrons left behind *living, breathing* proof against which even you will have no defense. You've always known it, you were afraid I knew it, and it's precisely why you retreated in the military court. Not merely because you were caught by surprise."

Silence. Panicked silence for a few moments. Then, like a cornered cat, Godwin snarled. "How did you find out?" he asked, chest heaving with rage.

"My mother." Dying from the lung cancer which spread through her body, the woman confessed it all. Temple still didn't know if it were the morphine talking or if she'd been trying to make sure he always possessed a weapon against the Kingsleys. "God help me," Temple whispered. "I didn't do anything at the time. Thought it was just a mistake. One foolish mistake." And it was far too late. Amber had already been dead for more than a year.

"Your mother—" Godwin started, voice thick with venom. "Who else knows? Andrew?" The veins on his forehead bulged. "And what are you planning to do?"

"Andrew knows nothing," Temple said. "He and the rest of the world will continue to believe the story you put out about the nonexistent ex-boyfriend... provided you cooperate with my efforts to bring Lilah and her family home. Also, make sure Steven and gang don't try to arrange untimely deaths for them."

"How do you imagine you're going to get Steven to agree? If you're expecting *me* to talk to him, don't bother. He's not going to care what happens to me as long as he gets to keep his empire."

Temple had a good mind to demand exactly what Godwin feared... to have him sweat when Steven inevitably refused to play along. To have Godwin worry if Temple would hand over the information in his possession to Harry. But Temple couldn't allow the need for petty revenge to overcome common sense. He needed to move fast and get the exiles back before anything happened to them, leaving the satisfaction of payback for another day. Plus, events needed to be arranged with minimum damage to all concerned, or the stock market would suffer, as would the nation.

The former president reminded Godwin, "Without you as his general, Steven has no hope of winning political support. You don't need to tell him anything. Simply refuse to endorse his activities. He might rant and rave, but he'll withdraw from the arena. Remember, I'll hold you responsible if Steven launches another attack."

"What happens after Brad and his brothers get home?"

"You'll return their property." Tone derisive, Temple corrected, "I meant to say *Steven* will return their property."

"All right," said Godwin, eyes glittering with calculation. "Let's say I do what you ask. It's not going to magically bring about peace. The conflict will continue, which means both sides will suffer. Markets around the world will suffer. The best way forward for everyone concerned might be for Brad and Lilah and the rest to return as you want and for Steven to keep the network. I'm sure Brad will agree to forgive and forget. He and his family will be free from legal problems and will have plenty of cash from the stocks they will continue to hold in the company. Kingsley Corp will be in charge of it all."

"Argumentum ad consequentiam," Temple scoffed. "Conflict will continue if Brad and his family demand you return their property. The clash will be bad for the world; therefore, true justice would mean Lilah shutting up about what happened. Godwin, you're not dense enough to miss the logical fallacy in what you spouted. Some justice when the victims are the ones asked to surrender! Some peace when the poor suckers are cowed into silence by the threat of consequences! Peddle your warped idea of peace to someone more likely to buy it. In any case, truce is possible only with those who want the same, and Steven certainly doesn't. You don't, either. So I'm not giving either of you a choice. You *will* welcome Brad and the others back with open arms. You *will* return the network to them. Or—"

"Or you'll tell the media what you know about the Kingsleys. So that's your plan. Blackmail me for the remainder of my life to keep Lilah—your chosen heir—in charge of the oil sector."

"Remainder of your life? Either of us could kick the bucket any moment, Godwin. We're both trying to control the future by installing our own candidate on the throne." When the alliance was first formed, they agreed it would be Lilah... under the Kingsley family umbrella. Unfortunately, it turned out not to be enough for Godwin. "If you left her alone... if you simply left Brad as your heir... I was happy to have him leading the network along with his wife." Until the Kingsley scion chose to gamble it all away. Until he decided to treat the business as his personal property and his employees—including his wife and brothers—as chattel. "You urged him into a bad decision because it was the only way to bring the sector under sole Kingsley rule. Well... it's not happening. You realize I could call the press right now? How much clout do you think you will have left once the public hears what you did? But I'm offering you a deal for old times' sake. My silence for your cooperation. You lose absolutely nothing except the network which wasn't yours in any case."

Lilah wouldn't be content with merely getting back the empire she built. From her angry words to him before she left, Temple had a fairly good idea of what she was planning to do. After all these years of scheming, all these wasted *decades*, Temple was forced to admit Lilah was right. Dismembering the network was the only option left. They needed to keep it to themselves for now, or it wouldn't be just Godwin and Steven they'd be fighting. It would be the might of the network's extensive membership. Perhaps even Brad Kingsley. Once people tasted near absolute power, it was difficult to get them to relinquish it.

"You're not going to the press," sneered Godwin. "You can't. It won't be only me losing clout. What if I, too, tell all, starting with your role? All of us will be hounded out of the sector, including Steven and Brad. This would mean Lilah is unlikely to return to power. You won't risk it."

"Try me," invited Temple. "I'd rather have all of us out than leave Steven in charge. Do as I say, Godwin. You will at least get to save your reputation... your family's, too."

Godwin's breathing was audibly angry. "How do I know you'll keep your word?" he asked after a couple of seconds. "I don't want you saying anything after you get what you want."

"You'll have to trust me not to," Temple said. "Exactly like I trusted you to not go after Lilah." Fury came surging back, bringing with it a need to physically strike at Godwin. Before he gave into temptation, Temple wheeled around and strode to the door as rapidly as his old joints would allow.

Neither Armor nor Noah was around, but the Kingsleys were seated in the lounge by the elevators.

"Godwin has something to tell you," Temple said to the group. Turning to the secret service men, he asked, "Noah?"

"Went ahead to the lobby."

Watching the Kingsleys return to the suite, Temple called, "Aaron, walk me out, will you?"

#

A few minutes later

The waning moon was obscured by clouds, and fog danced around neon displays, but the crowds in Times Square had only gotten bigger. The noise continued unabated, honks and police whistles and chatter swirling around the streets. As he waited on the sidewalk for the valet to bring the Cadillac, Temple drew gloves over his hands, clenching and unclenching his fingers.

"Enough already," Aaron muttered, shivering in the chilly November air. "I'm moving to Miami."

Aaron made the same threat every winter, but he never carried through. He'd never leave New York as long as Godwin remained alive. Aaron might not be happy with Godwin at the moment, but it would take a bigger catastrophe to erase his loyalty to the man who'd been his father in every way which counted.

Aaron never really knew the alcoholic who was his biological parent. Just like with his half-brothers, David and Peter, the involvement of Aaron's father in his life had been limited to the useless gifts he gave the boy on his occasional visits. On the other hand, Godwin always took care to let Aaron know there was a place for him in the Kingsley home. For a young boy growing up with a Jewish single mom in the nineteen-thirties, the patriarch's acceptance would have meant a great deal.

Temple knew Godwin loved his adopted sons. *How could he then do this to...*

He didn't realize he said it out loud until Noah responded, "In Godwin's mind, he's not doing anything wrong. He truly sees the sector as the Kingsley empire. Family is everything, and the loss of one grandson is preferable to losing the last opportunity to establish

Kingsley supremacy over the world. I'm sure he does love Brad as much as he loves Steven, but either is acceptable loss."

Temple wasn't quite certain it was all about power. Years ago, he'd dismissed his mother's doubts about Godwin as ramblings borne of her insecurities. Her reasons for marrying Old Man Kingsley—Godwin's father—went far beyond a fondness for riches as most assumed. Still, she suffered the self-doubt of an actress who'd never been accepted by the New York high society. Even when she whispered into her firstborn son's ears the secret she'd been compelled to keep for Godwin, Temple shoved it into a corner of his mind as a slipup on the part of an otherwise exceptional man. But now... Godwin had genuine reasons to detest Temple's mother, yet how far did the displaced Kingsley scion take the hatred? Did Godwin's loathing extend to her progeny?

Aaron glanced back into the hotel. "Sir, are you sure about Father arranging the interrogation? I wouldn't be surprised if Steven were the only one behind this. After all, he did try to kill Brad once."

Temple chose not to enlighten Aaron how the Kingsley patriarch had been well aware of the old plot when it was hatched. "Brad and his brothers were the poor cousins then," Temple said. "Conning the top executives of the world's biggest oil conglomerate required political support which could only have come from Godwin."

"But I simply don't understand why..." Aaron continued, misery in his tone.

Temple advised, "There's no point in wasting energy figuring out Godwin's motives. Let's see what we can do to undo the damage. I think my little talk with him was enough to make him see reason, but until we get our exiles back, someone needs to keep an eye on things. Not just on Godwin. David's not trustworthy, either. He's blinded by his ambition for his son. Aaron, I need you to report to me."

"I already made it very clear I don't approve of what happened," Aaron said tiredly. "Neither of them is going to share company secrets with me any time soon."

"Be that as it may," Temple said, "they have no choice but to keep you around. A senior executive in your position cannot be ousted without notifying the board. So either they have to risk you divulging what you already know to the board members, or they have to let you stay. Whatever you learn, I want you to let me know. Keep your eyes and ears open for any mention of Lilah or the brothers."

Aaron asked, "Do you think Steven will attack them again?"

"Oh, absolutely... but not just yet. Steven won't dare anything without accounting for Harry, and a second simultaneous attack on him and Lilah this close to the last one would not be dismissed as coincidence."

"*You* need to be careful, Temple," said Noah.

"I'll be all right," said Temple. It wouldn't be easy to attack a former president. The Secret Service would take care of anyone who dared try. "Besides, what I just said to Godwin... I think he'll rein in Steven."

Nosing through the traffic, a black Cadillac rolled to a halt in front. Aaron said his goodbyes and left while Noah climbed into the front passenger seat.

"Sir," said a secret service officer.

"Hey," shouted someone from the sidewalk. "That's... oh, my God, that's—"

A flash blinded Temple for a second, and he took a startled step to the rear. Behind him, the secret service men muttered in annoyance. Temple held a hand up, stopping his security detail from hustling him into the car. Smiling casually, he waved at the photographer—a short, stout man in a blue *Don't Mess with Texas* hat.

A small crowd gathered, eager for conversation with the former leader of the free world. The officers around Temple shifted nervously and kept alert eyes on the autograph-seekers. Holding a pen with his gloved fingers, Temple signed the first page of a coloring book for a freckled five-year-old and to the delight of the child and her parents, added a rough sketch of Lady Liberty with a smiley face.

At the edge of the gawking group stood a thin young man, impatiently jiggling the hand tucked into his jacket. He didn't appear to be waiting for a chance to chat. More probably, he was annoyed by the crowd blocking his way.

"We have to leave," insisted the secret service man. "It's not safe for you out in the open."

Temple nodded. "Sorry, folks, got to go," he announced. The doorman helped clear a path, and Temple bent to get into the vehicle.

A car backfired. Without warning, a heavy weight landed on Temple, shoving him headfirst into the Cadillac.

Pedestrians screamed, and somewhere to the left, bursts sounded in succession, setting off a ringing in Temple's ears. Dazedly, he wondered who would detonate fireworks in Times Square.

Running feet, shouts, and a burning pain across his scalp. "Get off," croaked Temple, feeling the interior of the automobile seesaw around him. Acute nausea welled. His vision blurred.

"The Poet is down," yelled the driver.

Poet? Temple's secret service code name?

"Blood," said Noah's familiar voice, tone urgent.

"NYU Medical Center," said the lead officer of the security detail. The car door slammed.

Temple's body jerked back into the seat as the vehicle took off, sirens blaring. He never knew they had a siren. Blinking hard, he tried to stay conscious. "I've been shot," he stated, touching the wet spot on his head.

"Yes, sir," said the security officer who pushed him in. "We're getting you to a hospital."

"Noah?" asked Temple, the haziness increasing.

"Right here," Noah said.

The officer growled. "Damn it, we left the doctor at the hotel."

"I'll be fine," Temple said. He tried to sit up.

"Stay still, Mr. Temple," ordered the officer. He pressed something above Temple's left ear.

When they got to the ambulance bay at the hospital, Temple refused the wheelchair shoved behind his knees and walked in, blood-soaked handkerchief held to his scalp. Doctors and nurses dressed in scrubs rushed toward them. A young man garbed in a long white lab coat cupped Temple's elbow, urging him onto a stretcher.

Without warning, something shifted inside his skull. A renewed gush of warm moisture soaked through his glove.

Temple opened his mouth to tell the young doctor of this new development, but only garbled sounds escaped. Confusion... a strange heat enveloped his body. His pulse pounded erratically. He stumbled around to face Noah. "Get Harry," Temple tried to say, his breath exploding in frantic gasps. "The note... Amber..." What he said... the words... he wasn't making any sense.

A blunder, his mind bellowed. The arrogant belief he had Godwin checkmated... Temple didn't see the Kingsley offensive coming this soon. He never put up any barricades.

His knees buckled. Noah's lean form blurred and split into two, the overlapping images looming over Temple. Shouts echoed, thundering through his brain, but everyone seemed to be speaking in some foreign language.

Darkness converged. The figures in his field of vision merged into the night. Was this death? *Lilah... oh, God... Lilah.* Did the Kingsleys already send their thugs after her? *Hide!* he screamed inside his head. *Hide where they can't find you.*

Chapter 2

Same night

City Island, New York City

There was a cold knot in Harry's chest—fear and rage in equal parts—as he faced his parents and brother. His sister, Sabrina, was also at the dining table with her five-year-old son, Michael, asleep in her old room. The food on her plate remained mostly untouched. A sudden gust from the Atlantic rattled the glass doors between the kitchen and the patio.

"No, Harry." Hector was firm. "We won't let you sell your stock. I cannot imagine how you thought we would agree. I never thought I'd say this but thank God for Will Luce's stupidity. It was because of him Gateway got all the stockholders to sign buy-sell agreements."

After Will Luce, Harry's soon to be former father-in-law, staked his shares on a card game, Harry thought it prudent to have contracts amended to require board approval on stock transfers beyond a certain amount.

"Thank God," echoed Ryan Sheppard, Harry's father. They closely resembled each other with the same dark-brown hair and eyes. Only, Ryan had always sported a beard, and now, their views on what Harry was about to do did not match. "Son, I agree with Hector. You cannot sell your stock... not at the scale you're planning. The same goes for Sabrina's. And Lilah's. I've already informed Grayson since he's her lawyer."

The lights flickered, fleetingly plunging the room into the same darkness of the sky outside. "I *need* the money," Harry pleaded, ready to agree to any damned condition his father and brother put forth. "The charges are treason." Temple refused to divulge what was in the note he sent to Godwin Kingsley, but the former president promised to make sure the Kingsleys stayed mum on the efforts to bring the exiles home. Funds were still needed... lawyers' fees, political contributions... the list of people to be satisfied before a pardon could be obtained was endless. The loose cash Harry had on hand was a pittance compared to what would be required.

"Yeah, the charges on Brad Kingsley include *treason*," mimicked Ryan Sheppard. "And you want to involve Gateway in the mess?"

"Involve?" Harry asked. "There would've been no Gateway without Lilah. You might not have been alive. Now, when *she* needs help, you're turning your back on her?"

Sabrina watched, green eyes nearly blank as her oldest brother and father vetoed Harry's plans. Sophia Sheppard, mother to the three Sheppard children, didn't say a word, but the stony look on her face loudly proclaimed her agreement with her husband's stance.

"You bring Lilah up time and again," said Ryan, tone unyielding. "What exactly was her sacrifice? Her adoption by the *über*-wealthy Andrew Barrons? Or her marriage to Brad Kingsley? Why didn't she refuse if it was such a big deal? You talked us into letting them invest in our companies. Now, you're trying to use Lilah and Sabrina's presence in the family to emotionally blackmail us. I see no reason for Gateway to continue giving blood money. Enough is enough."

"Trust me," Hector growled. "I'm not going to forget the fact my baby sister is married to the spineless idiot you call a friend."

Harry could barely see his brother's blond head and blue eyes through the fog of desperation. "If you won't let me sell outside the family, buy me out."

Ryan exclaimed, "Your personal assets are worth over two billion dollars; there are very few in the family who can afford to buy you out. Most of *our* assets aren't liquid, either. You're well aware of all this. Besides, I don't want you associated with them any longer. Which part of it can you not understand? You've managed to wreck your marriage, risk your life, and destroy your sister's future in your fondness for Lilah and the Kingsley brothers. We won't let you draw the rest of the Sheppards or Gateway into this obsession of yours."

Hector said, "Also, you're assuming Brad didn't know what was going on. What if you're wrong? What if he *did* know this was a three-way trade? Steven called me right after the fiasco in Cuba. He's upset Brad and the rest ran instead of staying to face the music. They left Steven in a very difficult position with the government. All in all, he's been the good guy in the mess, but you're making him out to be the villain. I have complete confidence he had nothing to do with the attack on you. Frankly, I hope Brad stays far away from the network. Steven needs to be the CEO. Harry, he's already told me he'll be happy to have you continue as chairman."

"Don't be a fool, Hector," Harry spat. "The first time I veto something Steven wants, he'll call the board together and have me kicked out."

"What makes you think the board will rubberstamp Steven's commands?" Ryan Sheppard asked.

"Because they all know I want Brad to return, dammit," Harry shouted. "They don't... they..."

"They don't want him returning," Hector completed, face twisted in satisfaction. "Because they don't want him getting the network and its member companies into any more idiotic deals. You see? No one wants him back except you. They trust Steven, and you should, too. You should continue as the chairman. We won't have the influence we did with Brad, but your presence will give Gateway enough of a say in things."

"And Sabrina?" Harry asked in furious disbelief. "Alex is her husband. Michael is your grandson... your *only* grandchild."

"So?" asked Hector, ignoring Sabrina's mewl of distress. Their mother didn't offer a word of solace.

Harry shook his head, unable to digest the heartlessness. "Let Steven know he can have all of Gateway, but he won't buy *me*. I promised Alex I'd get him home to his wife and son, and I plan to keep my word... even if I have to see my own father and brother and the rest of the Sheppards in court." He turned to his parents. "I never thought a time would come when I have to tell my family not to expect me back. My request for a leave of absence from Gateway will be delivered to the office in the morning. I don't imagine I'll be paid any form of salary, but if there are attempts to touch my stock dividends, the company lawyers will hear from my attorneys. If you feel you want me again in the clan, you know where to find me." Shoving his chair aside, he stood. "What about you, Runt?"

"Me?" Sabrina's normally clear tone was now dull. Gaze darting back to Hector and her father, she asked, "What about me? Alex is my son's father."

Hector answered her, his body rigid and expression pugnacious. "You want us to bring him back? For what? What if the next time he decides to sign something his idiot brother shoves under his nose, it's you who gets arrested? You're better off without him. Like Harry, even if you can't sell your stock, there will be enough money from dividends."

On a sharp intake of breath, she inquired, "You feel the same way, Father? Mother?"

"Sabrina," called her mother. "I understand your dilemma... but try to look at it from our point of view. You want your husband to return, but how can you possibly ask us to sacrifice Gateway for it? The livelihoods of so many people depend on the company. My advice to you is to be smart about this. Cool your temper and think with a clear head. If Harry can get a permanent agreement from Brad and Lilah to hand over control of the network to Steven, all problems will be solved. The two sides can call a ceasefire. Then, Alex and the rest can wait someplace safe until the public forgets about the unfortunate episode in Cuba. In a couple of years, they can request a pardon. The Kingsleys wouldn't oppose the plan at that point, and everyone can return home, secure and sound. I don't see why Lilah wouldn't agree. After everything that's happened, she should welcome the idea of truce. So should Brad."

"I don't know, Mother," Sabrina said. "Seems less like truce and more like surrender to the Kingsleys."

"Instead, you want us to surrender the Sheppard family business," stated Sophia. "I love you, but it's not going to happen."

Tossing the bright-blonde braid so like her mother's across her shoulder, Sabrina turned to Harry. "If you'll have us, Michael and I would like to stay with you."

Sabrina's belongings were being shipped from Panama, and she'd brought only a few things with her, so it wouldn't take her long to pack. Harry followed her up the stairs. Asking her not to wake Michael, Harry gathered the little boy into his arms. The rest of the Sheppards watched unmoved as the trio walked down, Michael's small head resting trustingly on Harry's shoulder.

"Both of you will return to your senses soon enough," said Ryan Sheppard. "Not a single person, not a single business involved in the network will support the Kingsley brothers after what Brad did. None of the politicians will cooperate... not without cash."

The phone rang. Sophia Sheppard pivoted and walked briskly to the wall set.

Harry kept his tone even, addressing both his brother and his father. "You can let Steven know I *am* going to stay on as chairman... but only to watch every move he makes. If he puts as much as a single step out of line, I'll use my veto. He'll need two-thirds majority from the board to overcome it. If... *when* he tries to retaliate by having me ousted, I will challenge it legally in every country where the network has members. I might not be able to control Steven, but I can and will paralyze him with lawsuits for as long as possible."

"Go ahead," ridiculed Hector. "Do your worst. You're determined to learn things the hard way."

Ryan nodded. "And until you do learn, the same people you claim to care for will suffer. Alex and his brothers might survive, but Lilah... a woman on the run, Harry! Try to imagine what she's going through now."

Harry laughed bitterly. "Very few people in the world would understand the reality of being on the run more than Lilah and me."

Ryan's eyelids suddenly flickered. The Sheppards had long buried their memories of the kidnapping of a teenaged Lilah along with Harry.

"Lilah *will* return," swore Harry. "And she will take back the network. Steven won't be able to do a single thing to stop her. You might cut off my cash flow, but Temple's still around. He will help her."

A sudden clatter interrupted the tension. "Ryan!" called Sophia, her voice shaking as she replaced the handset on the wall phone. Her blue eyes were filled with shock. "Mr. Temple's been shot."

Chapter 3

Two weeks ago, early November 1988

La Miel, Panama

The helicopter hurtled through purple clouds and vanished into the blood-red streaks at the horizon. Just like that, Harry was gone, leaving Lilah stranded in the clearing on the outskirts of the tiny village. Insects swarmed around her head, buzzing in anticipation. The rainforests of Darién Gap loomed on one side, its lengthening shadows crooking a finger at her in menacing invitation. Only the desperate ventured into the jungles straddling the border between Panama and Colombia, home to venomous snakes and lethal arachnids, jaguars and blood-sucking bats. And to outlaws like her.

"Let's go," muttered Alex. "Dangerous to stand around here after dark. We need to get to the village."

She jolted, fiercely trying to shut him out. She didn't want to see any of the Kingsleys... didn't want to hear their voices. The five men had betrayed her... Brad and his younger brothers. They dragged her into trouble with the American government to soothe the bruised ego of the eldest. Big brother needed reassurance *he* called the shots in the network, not his wife. Lilah Kingsley, CFO, was shut out of business discussions. Yet none of them would admit in court she didn't have anything to do with the deal—the *trap*—they stupidly walked into. Acknowledging it would've meant acknowledging Brad didn't have the authority to order her into it. In a blind show of family loyalty, the Kingsleys would've let her go to prison for a crime she didn't commit. The same devotion brought them all to this exile.

Lilah closed her eyes briefly, mocking herself. She *chose* to go on the run with the five brothers. Steven had offered her the option of switching sides. Grandiosely declaring commitment to her cause, she willingly tied her future to that of these cowards.

Yeah, right, jeered her mind. One arrogant woman had taken it on herself to save the world from the entire Kingsley clan, from the might of all the corrupt elites ruling the oil sector. She was going to save this infinite universe in which she was but a speck.

Gaze raised to the rapidly darkening sky, Lilah was attacked by a sudden longing to escape to the cliffs. In solitude, she could storm at the injustice of it all. Rage and resolve... doubt and purpose... the pressure in her chest increased until her rib cage threatened to shatter.

Yet she didn't utter a single word. In silence, she heaved the bulky backpack and strapped it on, neither asking for help nor offering any as the others did the same. Following Victor, she tramped along the dirt path lit only by the crescent moon hanging in the sky. Alex and Scott flanked her, Brad and Neil following.

As soon as it sank in they'd have to flee their home, Victor took charge, telling them he knew of a few places where fugitives from American justice could disappear. Since he used to be their company's troubleshooter, no one challenged him, but they didn't get much time to discuss details. Steven insisted on a deadline of forty-eight hours before he contacted the American government with a cooked-up story of Brad handing power to his cousin and running to avoid prosecution for treason. Nor could the exiles ask for Harry's help beyond flying them to this village. They couldn't afford to have him in legal jeopardy for aiding suspected traitors if they wanted him working for their return. He wasn't even informed of their chosen hiding spot. The fewer the people who knew where they were headed, the better.

Lilah stumbled and swatted away Alex's hand which suddenly appeared in her visual field.

"Are you okay?" Neil asked from behind. "I have some pills."

Both Alex and Lilah halted and turned to stare.

Neil stuttered, "Er... pain pills... if you want."

Pain pills... her period. After their arrest, she was so out of her mind from the agonizing cramps that she begged their captors for help. The blood staining her clothes was visible to every soldier in the military prison, to all the men with her now. Angry heat rushing into her cheeks, Lilah pivoted without a word and continued the march.

Catching up, Alex said, "Lilah, if you're in pain—"

Her hands clenched into fists, itching to take a swing at something... somebody. "Go away," she said, voice taut.

He begged, "Please, Lil—"

"There's a military base here," Victor snapped. "Better be quiet. *And keep moving.*"

Lilah straightened her shoulders. Her body might have been injured, but it would heal. Her pride was assaulted, but it survived. The enemy failed in their attempt to crush her. No matter what other obstacles the future chose to throw her way, she would not break. She *would* do what she set out to do and never, ever forget the Kingsley family's crimes. She could never forget the impotence of the five brothers. Contempt was all she felt for them.

She tugged the brim of her cap lower on her forehead. Her blue-black hair was already tied in a messy bun and tucked inside the crown. The bruise on her cheek could draw attention, and any observer might put together her hazel eyes and features to ID her as Lilah Kingsley, so she kept her head down.

They trudged through narrow, unlit lanes bordered by shadowed trees and single-story houses. Three male silhouettes argued in Spanish while a bent form sat on a stoop, only the loud mutterings giving it away as human. A cat darted across the dark path. None of the locals paid any mind to people they surely dismissed as tourists who frequented the village despite it being one of the world's hotspots. Somewhere in the distance, a dog barked. In the few minutes it took the fugitives to cross the village and reach the sea, sweat soaked Lilah's long sleeves and plastered her shirt to her torso. Under the cargo pants, her thighs itched from the heat. The glasses she normally used only for reading were now part of her disguise, but they kept fogging. The mild ocean breeze tickling her nape provided only slight relief.

The dull roar of the Caribbean Sea masked the sounds of the people plodding across the grassy, uneven shore. They walked past a cement cross overlooking the ocean. A wire ran from the power lines in the village to a light bulb at the bottom of the cross. In the faint glow, Lilah saw a palm tree with a "Wanted" sign affixed to it. A mustachioed guerilla glared at them from the picture. From what Lilah remembered of recent news reports, the rundown village was also a transit site for both revolutionaries and narco traffickers. Human traffickers, too, were frequently spotted, smuggling desperate refugees to Panama, from where they would make their way to the United States.

A flashlight glinted not too far in front. Alex stiffened.

"Keep moving," Victor repeated in an urgent whisper. "We're tourists, hoping to cross the border into Colombia. Nothing more. If it's a cop, be prepared to show the passports." The real ones, since there was no time to get fake papers made. They would try not to leave a trail if at all possible, but there was no choice in some situations, and this was one such. Steven did promise them a head start, so the police wouldn't know they were looking at a group of people on the run until much later.

The light bobbed closer. A couple of soldiers dressed in camouflage stopped by the Americans. "*¿Buscando el cruce?*" one of them asked, his cheerful tone ringing with the certainty that the group was, indeed, looking for the border crossing.

"*Sí, Señor,*" Alex said. He was the only one of them who spoke fluent Spanish.

The soldier pointed the flashlight behind him and rattled off something at high speed.

Alex translated, "He's saying we can cross, but we'd be better off staying in the village and waiting for the morning ferry instead of walking through the jungle at night. Something about man-eating cats and swamps." Nodding vaguely, he spoke in soothing tones and herded the rest of them in the direction of the border.

Chatting about *"yanquis locos,"* the soldiers disappeared down the path to the village.

Once their voices died down, Alex said, "They're right. Even if we somehow avoid the animals, the swamps can kill us."

Neil asked, "But *can* we afford to wait for the morning? If we get caught..."

"Jungle's out of the question," Victor said. "I know someone on the other side who can give us a midnight boat ride."

Loud snores greeted them in the hut where traffic between the two countries was supposed to be recorded. The immigration official—or whoever he was—slumped in his chair with eyes closed, slapping at his neck where mosquitos gorged on blood. With each grunt, his belly expanded, threatening to pop off his shirt buttons.

The only other occupant of the hut was a guard, and his gaunt face beamed in response to the hundred dollars Alex handed him. The guard waved them through, not even bothering to look at their passports. Paved stairs on the other side of the hill led to the Colombian town of Sapzurro. No one saw them clamber down. As the soldiers on the Panamanian side said, only the foolish or the drunk or the desperate attempted the crossing after sundown.

At the bottom of the steps, Victor halted to issue a terse reminder. "Don't wander off." He gestured toward a shadowed grove. "Tourists hang around the beach, so we'll have to go through the woods without getting deep into the jungle."

A frown evident in his voice, Scott asked, "How will we get to the boat you mentioned if we avoid the beach—"

Without warning, salsa music blasted out. Scott jumped.

"Tourists," Victor repeated, voice barely audible over the thundering music. "Just follow me."

He led them into the grove with Alex and Scott still flanking Lilah and Brad. Neil brought up the rear. Moonlight dissipated. The music from the village suddenly became a great deal quieter, the chirping of insects rising in decibel level. Palm trees bordering the narrow, unpaved path swayed gently, setting up an ominous rustling.

"No matter what you see or hear," Victor muttered, "don't stop."

Seconds, minutes... harsh breathing, wet leaves squishing under their shoes... the smell of fear, the stench of sweat... darkness, unrelenting darkness... the men around Lilah were reduced to moving shadows. Something glinted in front. A flash of white to the left. Almost involuntarily, her eyes went to it. Round shape, holes in the middl— *A skull?*

A sharp scream erupted from her mouth before she bit down hard on her lip. The shadows around halted. Her entire body shaking, she pointed toward the *thing*. It was probably mounted on a stick, but to Lilah, the skull seemed to be hovering in midair.

"Keep *moving,*" came a mumble in Victor's voice.

"Narcos," Alex muttered an explanation. "Or someone else." The victim's head was left there as warning to anyone who might think of crossing the criminals who ruled the jungles.

Heart thundering painfully within her rib cage, Lilah resumed her trek. The salsa music completely died out. Even the leaves seemed to have stopped rustling, leaving only the rhythmic chirping of whatever insects inhabited the rainforests of Central America. Sweaty fingers wrapped around the straps of her backpack, she counted each footstep and tried to push everything else from her mind but safety.

They needed to get to a secure place, somewhere they could hide while Temple and Harry worked on getting a pardon for Brad. It might take a few months—maybe even a couple of years—but they *would* return. This nightmare would end at some point.

Light glimmered above. The crescent moon reappeared with the gentle roar of the sea. When they exited the grove, it was into an isolated cove. There was a pier with two boats—canoes, both—tied to a post. A small building stood mere feet from the sandy beach. From the size of it, there couldn't have been more than a couple of rooms inside. A single bulb hung by the front door, emitting dull light. The walls were painted a garish green. No, blue. The yellow light only made it look green.

Mosquitos buzzed around as Victor knocked on the door. When it opened, there was a loud exclamation and a rapid discussion in broken English.

"Ten dollars," Victor said finally.

"Done," said the voice from inside the house. A man stepped out, clad only in khaki shorts and flip-flops. Following him was an orange-brown dog, its tail furiously wagging. Except for muted whimpers, the animal did not make any noise.

Victor's contact led them to the pier and gestured them into one of the boats. The wooden bars stretching across the width of the canoe acted as seats. They settled themselves in the same pattern they'd assumed since climbing off the helicopter—Lilah in the middle, surrounded by the five men. Victor's contact was at the rear end, and his canine companion at the bow, its tail still wagging away. Water lapped gently against the sides of the boat. Motor rumbled into life. A breeze blew against Lilah's face, drying the sweat on her skin. They pulled away from the shore.

It was a midnight boat ride as Victor promised. There was no food, no drink to make it the fun adventure it might have been mere days ago. There was zero conversation.

A soft bark came from the bow. "*Silencio,* Magnus," said the boatman, asking his dog to be quiet. "I hear something."

"Military boats," Victor explained. "Remember, we're tourists. Out for a night of—I hear it, too."

The rumble grew louder by the second. Lilah tensed. Alex's breathing was calm, measured. Too measured... as though he were readying himself for battle.

"Not the police," muttered the boatman. "Migrants."

The second boat, packed with silhouettes in human forms, chugged by, sending lukewarm water spraying all over the passengers in the first one.

Wiping the droplets from her face, Lilah stared at the craft going in the direction of Panama. Like her and her companions, the people in the other vessel were desperate. They were scared for their lives and betting everything on getting into the United States.

"Keep moving," Victor urged the boatman.

The migrant boat continued toward America and the promise of freedom. Lilah turned away as the exiles resumed their journey, going deeper and deeper into the shadowy waters. *Safety,* she mumbled in her mind. They would conceal themselves in the ominous darkness and wait for backup. Help would arrive—soon.

Part II

Chapter 4

Back in November 1988, the night of the assassination attempt

New York, New York

The crowd outside the medical center building was a few feet deep, some puffing on cigarettes, some jogging in place to keep warm. Ignoring the flashing cameras and shouted questions, Harry pushed through and showed his ID to the stern-faced cop posted at the entrance. Other officers also dressed in NYPD blue swarmed the lobby. "Mr. Andersen left word," said the fellow at the door.

Calling on patience he didn't feel, Harry waited as he was patted down, the contents of his pockets examined. He didn't bother asking the cops how the injured president was. No one would have answered.

The elevator deposited Harry and the officers flanking him in the ICU. The nurses' station had only uniforms, save for the clerk manning the telephone. The glass doors set around were wide open, showing empty rooms. Not a single patient or family member was to be seen. All of them promptly moved of course. Security for Temple aside, the possibility of a second attack would always be considered, which meant civilians needed to be evacuated.

There *was* one room where curtains were drawn, its VIP occupant shielded from prying eyes. Armed men stood outside.

The curtain twitched. "Harry," called a familiar voice.

The mischief-maker. Noah Andersen might look like a monk, but for Harry, the former attorney general would forever be the one who instigated the problems in Lilah's marriage. Noah confessed as much on their trip back from Cuba. Harry wasn't yet ready to forgive, but this... this attempt to murder Temple... they'd have to thrash out old grudges later. Jogging to Noah, Harry asked, "How is he?"

"The bullet's stuck in the skull. It didn't get to the brain, but there's swelling inside." Noah's face was drawn and starkly pale. "The surgeon said something about fractures."

Insistently, Harry asked, "He's going to be all right, though?"

With trembling fingers, Noah smoothed back his hair. "They say vital signs are good. But the rest of it... body functions, his mind... we don't know yet. Harry, I think Temple said your name before he fainted. Maybe he wanted to talk to you before being taken to surgery, but we couldn't afford to wait."

"Can I see him now?"

Inside the room, artificial light flooded the bed. There were a number of doctors and nurses moving around the patient, shielding him from Harry's view. One of the secret service agents stood at the head of the bed. A ventilator puffed air. Machines beeped. On a monitor, green squiggles sped by, showing the beating of a heart.

Seeing Noah with Harry, the staff drifted aside. Harry reared in shock. He hadn't expected this for some reason. The aged frame of the president nearly sank into the middle of the ivory-white bedding, the tube coming out of his mouth connecting him to the ventilator. The salt-and-pepper hair seemed to have turned entirely gray overnight. The bright-blue eyes which usually glinted with intelligence were closed. The towering personality who dominated American politics for the better part of a decade now lay helpless at the mercy of machines.

With unsteady steps, Harry moved closer and took the hand which lay on the sheet. Cold. Frail. The fingers within his hand twitched. "Is he in pain?" Harry asked one of the doctors.

"We don't think so," the medic offered. Pausing, he added, "We're about to put in an arterial line. If you don't mind..."

Leaving the staff to their jobs, Harry and Noah padded out. Noah groaned. "An assassination attempt. I warned Temple, but it never occurred to him to worry about his own safety."

Was no life off limits for the enemy? Not even the life of a former president, an eighty-three-year-old man? The root of this evil was the network. Lilah was right... the empire was now a monstrous creature, devouring all morals and all sense of humanity, power its only objective. "The shooter?" Harry asked out loud.

"I haven't had a chance to check with the cops. There was a crowd... could have been any one of them. Could have been from one of the buildings, even. But someone must've seen something. There were hundreds of people just at the intersection."

"If he hasn't been caught already, he's not going to be," Harry said grimly. "At least not in any shape where he could lead us back to the Kingsleys."

"I agree. Godwin might be a criminal, but he's not stupid."

"Godwin Kingsley is an extremely clever man," acknowledged Harry. "*His* hands are going to remain lily white even if the assassin does get caught."

"Yeah, just like Steven ended up taking the blame for the mess in Cuba, there will be some fool ready to claim credit for this, too. Even if Temple dies!"

If the former president died, the information in the note which stopped Godwin would be lost forever. Hoping against hope, Harry asked, "Did Mr. Temple say anything to you about what he had on the Kingsleys?"

"No, not a word. I warned Temple it was dangerous to have one man keep the secret, but—"

"Might he have written it down somewhere? As a kind of insurance policy against Godwin..."

Noah shook his head. "Temple would've told me if it were something he dared put in writing. The fact I didn't know means he believed the information was too sensitive to record. Such things were stored in memory. It's been his habit for decades. Plus, it was about Godwin... Temple really believed the best of Godwin. So did I as you know. Neither of us imagined we'd need any sort of insurance. After what happened in Cuba... Temple was going to tell you and me what was going on if the Kingsleys refused to cooperate, but he never really believed *he* might be in any danger. He is a former president... all the security. And Godwin knows his stepbrother would've given him one last chance before revealing anything. Perhaps when they were alone, they even discussed continuing to keep things quiet. Then... the assassination attempt." Turning to peer into the room, Noah continued, "I'll go through whatever papers Temple has at home. Given the circumstances, I doubt he'd mind. Still, chances are low we'll find anything."

Following the gaze of the former attorney general, Harry eyed the hospital staff crowded around the bed. The monitor beeped with reassuring steadiness. Who else besides Temple would know the dirty secrets of the Kingsley family? Someone... was there no one else in DC who'd heard gossip on the former supreme court justice?

\#

Later the same night

Elsewhere in the city

"No money and no political support," Harry whispered, fingers clenched around the arm of the chair. The sky outside the apartment windows brightened, dawn bringing the grimy concrete buildings of lower Manhattan into view. Not having had the time to shower in the last couple of days, he smelled as rank as the garbage piled on the street.

Lilah's brothers, Daniel and Shawn, were sprawled on the couch, having rushed to Harry's apartment as soon as they heard about the shooting. Dante—Harry's boss in Gateway—was also there, thinning gray hair disheveled and dark face pale. Tucking Michael back in for the umpteenth time, Sabrina rejoined them in the living room. "What about Barrons O & G?" she asked, throwing a questioning glance at Lilah's brothers. "Will Andrew..."

They both shook their heads, the same desperation in their demeanors.

Harry pinched the bridge of his nose. "Barrons O & G always had buy-sell agreements. The board of directors won't let Dan sell his stock."

"I was never given any to begin with," Shawn said, blond stubble now on his face to match his hair. He'd been disinherited years ago for his refusal to conceal his sexuality. "Andrew himself wants no association with the Kingsley brothers at this time."

Harry had already instructed Dan not to try any threats to quit with Andrew. The mess made by the Kingsley brothers was simply too large, and Barrons O & G wouldn't be able to handle the political fallout if they decided to support Brad. Andrew was first and foremost a businessman. Even his adoptive son would come second to his company. Harry could walk out of Gateway and keep his stock at least on paper, but not Dan where Barrons was concerned. If Andrew told Dan to go ahead and quit, the faint hope of future support from a major stakeholder in the network would collapse.

"But Lilah..." Sabrina said, mouth opening in shock. "Stock in all three companies, but she can't touch any of it even to save herself?" Lilah's shares in the Peter Kingsley Company would be of no use, either. Steven might have been forced to let the exiles keep the shares to prevent potential government interference, but they signed away voting rights as part of the deal with him. They would get no cash dividends... only stock dividends.

Bitterness surged in Daniel's eyes. He possessed the same dark hair and irises as Caroline—his and Lilah's half-sister, the woman married to Andrew Barrons. Daniel had begged for her support, but his plea was rejected. "Apparently, it was perfectly fine for all of them to use Lilah for their own purposes, but now, there's no one willing to stand by her."

Harry also used her, no matter how lofty he told himself his motives were. Lilah's twin should've been beating him black and blue, but Dan's primary concern at the moment was his sister's safety. Shawn's, too. The two men were ready to sacrifice everything to bring her back home, including their rage at all the people responsible for her predicament.

Shawn was in the process of selling his tech investments, and the funds would be transferred into Lilah's Swiss bank account. Those financial institutions were close-lipped as hell, so nosy governments trying to track the exiles via cash movements were destined to fail. The money would be enough to take care of expenses but not to buy a pardon. Her connections across the globe, the assets in various countries... a couple of Lilah's old schoolmates had called, frantic with worry when they heard what happened to her. Saeed al-Obeidi, Harry's old friend from Libya, was ready to help any way he could. They were all told to stay under the radar.

The intrusive fingers of American authorities reached almost every corner of the world. Unlike the Swiss firms, individual sympathizers who aided the exiles could come off worse in a tussle with Uncle Sam. Plus, Steven... who knew what he'd do to anyone who helped his enemies? No one whose efforts weren't absolutely needed would be allowed to risk themselves.

Fingers on the amber beads circling his neck, Shawn exclaimed, "I simply can't wrap my mind around any of this. Steven's condition... Brad... his brothers blindly following him into exile... Lilah, too."

Steven insisted on all of Brad's brothers agreeing to the exile, or he'd be arrested right there. Lilah was given only two choices—switch sides or leave with her husband. Joining Steven would've meant letting the Kingsleys win, which was out of the question. If she refused both options and decided to keep her executive position, it may have still led to Brad's arrest. Alex and the rest would never cooperate with Lilah in anything she wanted to do with the network. She'd end up fighting both sides with only one-sixth of the stock. Lilah's conscience prevented her from simply walking away from it all. She was forced to stick with Brad and get him pardoned. It was the only way she saw of regaining control over the network.

With the pardon done, the agreement between Steven and Brad meant the latter was entitled to get his own business—the Peter Kingsley Company—back but not to resume leadership of the wider network. The company CEO was also supposed to be the network's CEO, but the charter already had provisions for potential wrongdoing on the part of the senior executives and their ouster.

The chairman of the board would need to agree to reinstate Brad Kingsley as CEO. For that to happen, Brad would be forced to sign a contract with Harry to dismantle the network. Only the board could override the chairman's decision. The members were unlikely to favor disbanding, and if Brad exposed the plans instead of merely talking about the executive position, the board might oust Harry. But without Harry, Brad didn't have a prayer of being reinstated or even being pardoned. Oh, yeah, Brad Kingsley would have only one option left: agree to the terms dismantling the structure.

Before she left, Lilah made it clear to Harry she didn't want anyone else to know the entirety of her plans. Definitely not Brad until he faced the reality of exile, and the end was in sight. She needed him desperate enough to agree to any condition.

Dante said, "Whatever her reasoning, she's in danger because of her decision. Especially after what happened to Mr. Temple."

"She's already created enough problems for the Kingsleys," agreed Harry. "They're going to want to kill her before the feds get around to arresting anyone." Temple was the only one with clout enough to slow them down while the pardon was in the works. His presence promised both shield and weapon for the exiles. With a single shot, Godwin Kingsley destroyed—

Harry's muscles bunched from the need to put a bullet between Godwin's eyes, but he couldn't. Armor, Charles, Steven... the hands which reached for Lilah's clothes, the tongue which ordered the assault... the culprits still sat in the comfort of their own homes. Anything happening to them would be blamed on the exiles, unlike the attack on Temple which left the public perplexed about possible motives. The idea of the widely respected former supreme court justice condoning an assassination attempt was not something the press might buy. It wasn't the same for the six people accused of treason. Even if the passing of the Kingsley patriarch were camouflaged to appear natural, media speculation about the potential involvement of Brad and the others was sure to happen. The manipulative old man would be hailed as a martyr, his heir—Steven—acquiring the sheen of morality and respectability he didn't have at the moment. The chances of Brad ever getting a pardon would plummet.

Dante continued, "What about you, Harry? Do you think the Kingsleys will leave *you* alone?"

"You just told Hector you'll sue Steven if he tries to oust you as chairman," Sabrina whispered. "Oh, God."

"Quitting's not an option, Runt," Harry said. Besides the fact he needed the power of the position to get Brad to do as ordered, Harry's absence could make it easier for the Kingsleys to restructure the network to make sure the ousted CEO could not be reinstated. "No matter what Hector thinks, Steven and gang see me as a critical target. But they're going to give it a few months. If I turn up dead too soon, even the Sheppards would have to admit it looks suspiciously convenient after Cuba and what happened to Temple. With that, Gateway might withdraw support and create political problems. The media... the U.S. government... too much attention, too many questions. No, Steven won't risk it for *now*. He won't dare try anything with Lilah and the rest while I'm still alive. But at some point, they will."

"The Kingsleys hold all the cards," Shawn echoed everyone's worries, fear in his brown eyes. "What are we going to do?"

If only Temple left some clue somewhere about the note he sent to Godwin. It was surely related to the Amber Barrons incident. Harry spent the last few years fruitlessly chasing the story. Lilah even asked Shawn about it. They found nothing. Harry had been damned convinced they would... the suicide of a girl over a failed romance with Kingsley drunk was obviously bad for the family's reputation but bad enough for Godwin to buy off her parents? There was nothing else in his history which could be remotely labeled as suspect. Someone else surely knew about it besides the former president. People saw and heard things they weren't supposed to all the time... they blabbed... office assistants, household help, wives, mistresses.

Harry once even considered asking an old fling of Alex's—the notorious madam called Lupe Valdez—for help. From what Harry discovered, the lady started the first of her strip clubs with financial assistance from a Kingsley relative, a fact Alex seemed unaware of. There were rumors aplenty in DC about the madam and said relative. Perhaps she'd heard something of the Kingsley family history. Eventually, Harry had decided against approaching her. Lupe Valdez was an innocent bystander, and he didn't want to repeat old mistakes by placing her in harm's way.

Besides, the pre-nup in the Brad-Lilah marriage... Harry never imagined there was any risk to her. If he did, he'd have begged the Valdez woman for assistance and promised the entirety of his wealth if she could give him the answer to the Amber Barrons puzzle.

Harry groaned. There were times he felt so close to an answer he thought he could reach out and grab it.

"The hospital said Temple's going to live, right?" Shawn asked. "Once he wakes up, it becomes simply a matter of raising money."

Remembering what Noah Andersen reported, Harry said, "The doctors don't know the extent of brain damage yet. Something about pressures inside the skull."

"So he might *never* wake up?" Sabrina asked, voice rising in panic.

"No one knows for sure, Runt," Harry admitted. "We have to operate on the presumption he might not."

Grimly, Shawn said, "In the meantime, Godwin Kingsley will continue to play the part of the impartial justice. He will block our every attempt to bring Lilah home. There's no politician who won't take his word over ours."

"Godwin's reputation is spotless," Harry acknowledged. "He's a master politician hi—" Thoughts screeched to a halt, backed up, took off in a different direction.

"What?" asked Dante.

"Reputation... it's the key," Harry whispered, sitting forward. His mind went over possible scenarios. "We all have them. Politicians, judges, businessmen... you, me, Lilah, Alex, Godwin... and Steven."

"Huh?" asked Shawn. "What does any of it have to do with our problem?"

Harry leaped from his chair, barely hearing the others' confused exclamations. He strode to his room and returned with his SIG. "The Kingsleys took our best card," Harry explained, automatically checking to make sure his tactical knife was in its usual spot on his body. It was discomfiting to find the Ari B'Lilah missing—the blade was still with authorities as evidence in the Parker killing. "So we'll have to use one of theirs against them."

No matter how long it took, no matter what tricks Harry needed to pull, the exiles *would* come home.

Chapter 5

Two weeks ago, November 1988

Colombia

The sky stayed dark when the Panamanian boatman pulled his vessel ashore at Capurganá. The cove was small... and empty of people. Yelping softly, his mutt darted among the rocks as money exchanged hands. The splashes of the returning boat were still audible when Victor led the group through a palm grove to a tiny hotel he'd stayed in before. Only he entered.

The rest waited, listening to every stray sound and eyes darting toward every fluttering leaf. An extradition treaty was in place between Colombia and the U.S., and each acquaintance they encountered was a leak risk. Victor deemed Ecuador a reasonable hideout though the country also had such a pact with the Americans. But the Ecuadorian government frequently flipped the bird at Uncle Sam, citing the low likelihood of a fair trial to certain fugitives. Unfortunately, Lilah and the Kingsley brothers would have to live in fear of Steven's assassins in either place... but only if the exiles went through the official entry point into the nation and lived under their own names. Assumed identities would be critical to their safety.

Five minutes later, Victor emerged from the hotel, his face pale and eyes worried. The contact he was depending on was off someplace else, visiting relatives. Alex cursed long and hard. Without said contact, their only other option was to approach the narcos to arrange the trip.

"No," Lilah said immediately. There was no disagreement. Being indebted to the drug cartels was not something any of them wanted.

The cash-only, no-ID purchase of a second-hand van in a nearby town put a serious dent in Victor's funds, but they simply couldn't leave any more tracks for Steven to follow. The rest kept more dollar notes stuffed about their bags, into their clothes, shoes, wherever else they could possibly imagine. They'd need it until Lilah could access her Swiss bank account. Money and weapons... the two critical things each packed before leaving Panama. Each carried a pistol. Alex's beloved sniper rifle and a folding submachine gun were tucked safely into his backpack.

They reached the border town of Ipiales without being bothered by the police, but armed cops swarmed the place. *Seven miles,* Lilah thought, her eyes on the magnificent church built over a ravine. Only that short distance separated the Basilica of Our Lady of Las Lajas from Ecuador. It might as well have been an entire ocean. *Please,* she begged the mother of God.

The exiles took residence in a cheap motel an hour away in Pasto, Alex telling the owners they were a family bringing their sister to the shrine in the hope of a miracle cure from some mysterious ailment. Victor called his contact several times each day, hanging up without giving his name. Only when he returned to update the rest would Lilah venture out of the room she barricaded herself in. She didn't talk to any of the brothers unless absolutely necessary.

Two weeks after their arrival, Victor ran in with a newspaper. The pictures... Temple, a blurry image of Times Square... "God," Neil whispered. "Now what?"

Perhaps it was the divine lady indeed helping Lilah, but Victor's missing contact finally answered his phone the next evening.

Their van roared out of the motel the same night. Brad took the first turn at the wheel, driving to another border town, San Miguel. At one of their bathroom breaks, they bought waterproof boots as instructed.

Lilah fidgeted in the back seat, unable to sleep as she planned. Her insides rattled each time their van bounced into the potholes riddling the asphalt. Working in the oil sector, she'd gotten used to the smell of diesel fumes, but now, it added to her queasiness. Rigs dotted the landscape, and parts of the greenery were covered in black grime. Sections of the road were closed off for cleanup of debris from explosions. The drilling outfits and pipelines were frequent targets of malcontents.

There were many checkpoints along the way, but none of the vehicles were stopped. "FARC," Victor explained, naming the guerilla organization operating in the country. "The cops are too scared to stop anyone." Indeed, there were sandbags in front of the police stations they saw.

At least they were on the move. Through the window of the vehicle, Lilah peered up at the sky. They'd been on the road for more than twelve hours, and it was almost noon the next day. Her unusual carsickness was nearly at an end, but the journey was only beginning.

In a few minutes, Scott brought the van to a halt on the side of an unpaved road. A few feet in front was the San Miguel River. The official border crossing was miles away. On either side of the dirt path, mountains loomed, their green cover broken by the occasional clearings and pastel-painted wooden huts. And oil wells. Across the water was the Ecuadorian town of Lago Agrio, where the Peter Kingsley Company owned rigs.

Victor gestured toward the forest. "The six of us going together will draw attention, but I can't go alone. I need backup."

"Either you or I will have to stay with the rest," Alex said immediately. They were the ones who could best protect the others in case of an attack. It was a necessary precaution until they were in Ecuador, living somewhat safely under new identities.

Victor nodded. "Neil? Scott?" Leaving the rest in the van under the protection of Alex and his weapons, Victor jogged off with Neil. Disappearing into the jungle, Victor called out, "We'll be back by dark."

Lilah stared at their departing backs and muted the small voice in her head. Victor wasn't unaware of the risks around. He would take care.

The group waited in silence. At times, one of the men got out and walked around, eyes restlessly scanning the perimeter. Not a single other vehicle drove by. When Lilah opened the door, Alex was standing with a hand on the roof of the van. He turned to her, a question on his face.

"Bathroom," she said, looking around for a decent spot.

His eyelids flickered.

Without waiting to see what anyone else had to say about it, she strode toward a bush. There were footsteps behind, but she didn't check to see who was following. If they'd been this concerned about her safety, if they believed her warning about their criminal grandfather, she'd be in the privacy of her own room.

When Lilah finished, she walked next to where Alex was standing guard. Instead of continuing to the van, she rubbed her glasses clean on her shirt and turned a three-sixty to study their surroundings.

Trees packed both banks of the muddy river, extending all the way to the foothills of the Andes. Wisps of mist rose from the green canopy. In the water, a head bobbed up. A boy waded to the rocky beach and darted into the jungle. A loud grating echoed from the woods, subsiding as quickly as it erupted. Lilah jumped. Screeching birds flew up from the trees, escaping into the afternoon sky.

"Let's wait inside," Alex said, his worried eyes fixed on the spot where his brothers had disappeared into the forest. "If we're forced to make a run for it..."

She didn't need to be told twice. What *had* been the noise? It sounded almost... metallic. Like steel scraping against rough rock. Only, amplified a thousand times. From inside the van, she peered intently at the jungle but saw nothing to give her a clue.

Minutes stretched into an hour. Hours into a tense eternity. There were no more noises outside the van or within it. The horizon soon turned the bright yellow of impending sunset.

"What's keeping them?" Brad exclaimed.

"Victor did say it would be dark by the time they returned," Scott muttered, stretching his legs in the seat next to Lilah's.

She wiped perspiration from her lip. Yes, but the area was rumored to be where a major portion of the world's cocaine was produced. As the CFO of their company, she hadn't even wanted to risk venturing into oil production in the region, but Victor insisted he could handle it. He did. At the time, he had money and the backing of the American government. Now...

It couldn't have been another hour before they heard his familiar tone calling Alex's name. Lilah sat up and squinted through the window. Three shadows came out of the jungle, silhouetted by the bright rays of the dying sun. Victor's giant form gave him away, and the shadow with the runway strut was surely Neil.

"Darwin," Victor introduced the guide, opening one of the doors.

"Really?" Alex asked, curiosity in his eyes in spite of their dire circumstances. He moved over to make space.

"It's a common name around here," Victor explained. "Because of Galapagos Islands." The naturalist's excursion to the islands changed the world's beliefs.

Sliding into one of the seats, the young man grinned. When his eyes caught on Lilah, he took off his baseball cap and bobbed his head.

The engine vroomed into life. The van bumped over grassy land, heading straight toward the trees. Lilah couldn't see any paths, but Victor swerved left, revealing an opening just wide enough to fit the vehicle.

Immediately, her ears were assaulted by a cacophony of screeches and laughter. Startled, Lilah looked up. Monkeys, their fur a dirty brown, slept on branches, cackled at the car, or swung from tree to tree. Unseen birds joined chirping insects. There was little light filtering through the leafy canopy. Jolting and bouncing, they drove over the dirt path, spraying mud onto thick trunks and gnarly branches and bristly bushes.

Within minutes, Darwin said, "Right here." Tucked between the trees was a thatched hut. Part of the roof was missing. The rusted door hung partially loose. There didn't seem to be anyone around. Victor parked the van behind the hut. When Lilah climbed out, she could hear the gurgling of the San Miguel River over the noises of the jungle.

"Do you live here?" Scott asked Darwin.

"No, *señor*," said the young man. "Nobody live here no more."

"Let's go," said Victor.

Abandoning the van, they followed him, squeezing between tree trunks, slapping aside the branches blocking their path, and ignoring the tears left on their clothes by thorny bushes. The gurgling of water got louder with each step. Lilah scratched at an itchy spot on her neck, just below her left ear. It wasn't as though she packed bug repellant for this trip. At least all the traveling she did meant she'd been given every imaginable vaccine.

Something leaped from a rock on their right, disappearing into one of the bushes. A frog, its head and neck a bright red. "Careful," said Victor, coming to a halt by a tree. "They're poisonous." He nodded at Darwin. "You first."

"Okey-doke," said the young man, his tone a perfect mimicry of the farm boy accent from American movies. Darwin squeezed sideways between two trees and... disappeared. Lilah crowded around with the rest, peering over Neil's shoulder to see where the guide had gone.

They were at the edge of a rock-strewn slope. Endless bushes, grass. There was a mud track going downhill. More like a *muck* track, with Darwin sliding down on his behind, toward the river at the bottom of the slope where a long, narrow canoe waited. There was another young man standing inside the canoe, a push pole in his hands.

One by one, they followed Darwin, Victor bringing up the rear. With her right hand gripping the strap of the backpack, Lilah tried to control her descent with the left, but the muck wouldn't let her. She slipped and slid, her fingers futilely reaching for the bushes on the side. In the few seconds it took to get to the river, they were all caked with dirt. Mud clung to their clothes, their boots, their hair, their faces. Every backpack dripped with sludge. Her cap was gone. Except for Neil, all of them seemed to have lost their headgear.

"We'll have to wait until it gets darker before getting into the pirogue," said Victor, wiping dirt off his brow with the back of his hand and nodding toward the canoe.

When the sky turned the purple of twilight, Darwin and his friend took them across, using push poles to keep their journey silent. A couple of times, the boat threatened to get stuck in shallow water, and Victor got out to push them along. By the time they got to the bank on the Ecuadorian side, it was completely dark, the moon in hiding somewhere.

With Darwin keeping an eye out for onlookers, they scrambled up the bank. Mud sucked at their boots in the twenty-minute trek through the trees. There was nothing Lilah could see except the bob of Victor's flashlight in the pitch-black darkness. The sounds continued unabated. *Mosquitoes, too*, she thought, scratching the back of her grimy hand.

When they broke out of the jungle, another car waited by the roadside, its headlights turned off. "Too bad we can't go there," Brad said, staring in the direction of the oil rigs where a few lights were still on. The Peter Kingsley rigs.

A part of Lilah's mind, detaching itself from the rest, noted she felt only extreme annoyance at hearing her husband speaking. And contempt.

"One of the first places they'd check," Victor agreed.

Waving his hands about, Darwin said, "Boss, I'm a little afraid. Too many people saw you when you were coming here."

Preempting "Boss" Victor, Alex asked, "Are *you* going to get into trouble?"

"Not if he keeps his mouth shut," said Victor. "You'd better."

"'Course I will," said Darwin.

"Your friend?" asked Victor.

"Sí señor," agreed the second lad, his eyes glinting.

Victor stared hard for a few seconds. "Tell your buddy," he said to Darwin, "I'm not joking. Not a word about this. Not to his friends, not to the chick he's seeing, not even to his mother. Got it?"

"No, no," Darwin said. "We're best friends. He's not gonna say anything. But the narcos, the guerrillas... they always watch for strangers. They might find out where you are. Be careful."

After the two young men left, Victor hustled everyone into the car.

Scott asked, "What does the cocaine ring have to do with us? Or the terrorists? It's not like they're going to get enough money out of us to make it worth their while."

"But Steven could," Neil said. "If the local criminals somehow let Steven know we're here..."

Alex opened the driver's side door. "Let's get to Quito. We need to call someone... see if there's been any progress in Mr. Temple's condition."

Only the whining sound of the engine filled the long silence which followed. All of them were wondering the same thing. What would happen to the pardon now?

The exiles' route to Ecuador - part 1 (markings later made by the CIA)

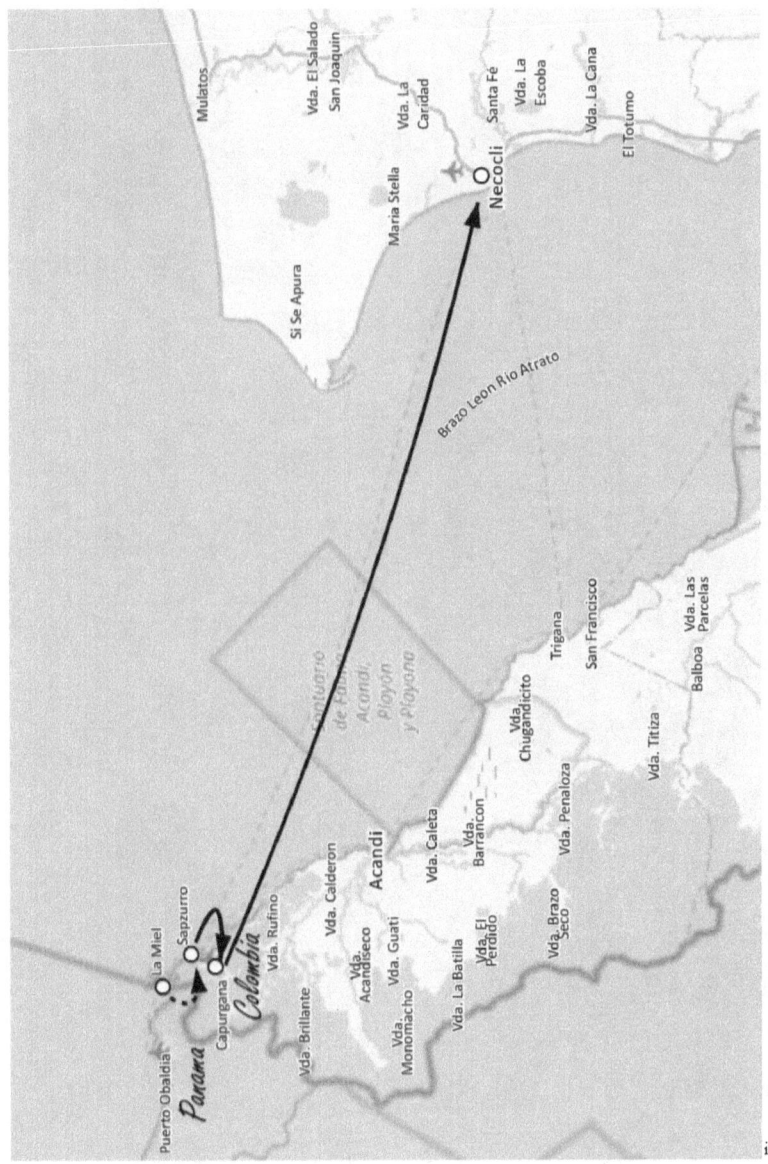

The exiles' route to Ecuador - part 2 (markings later made by the CIA)

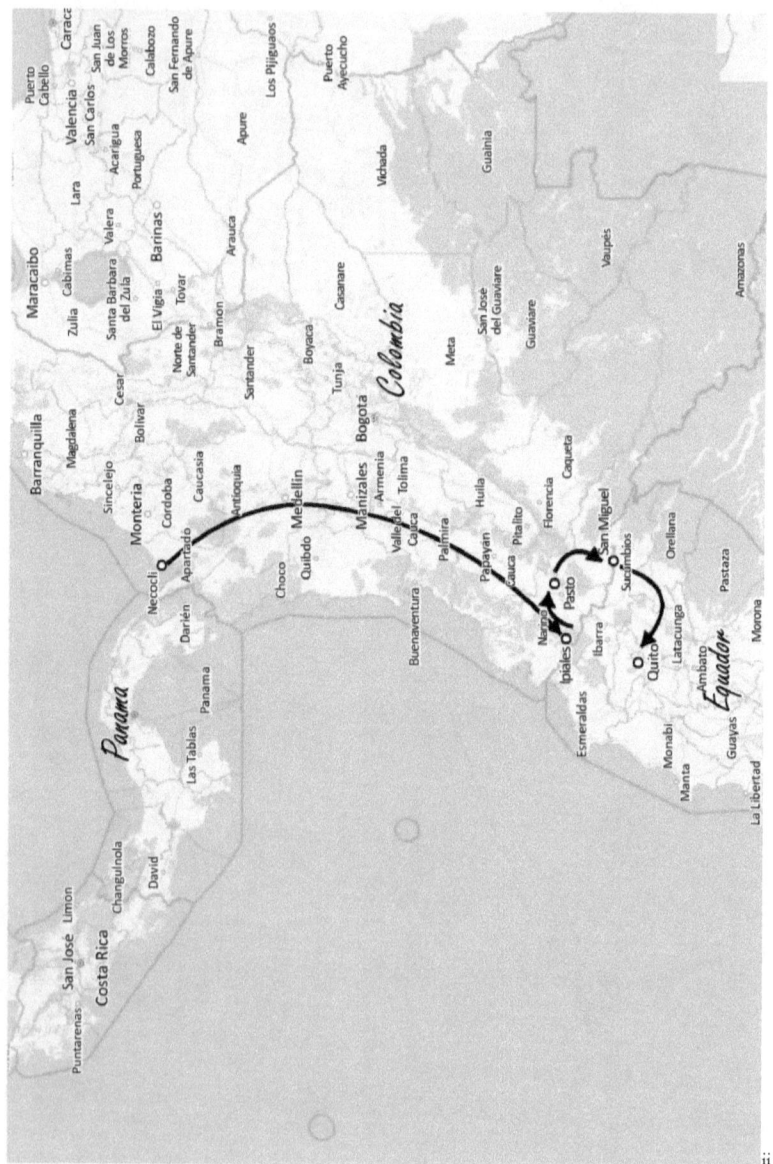

Part III

Chapter 6

Back in November 1988, three days after the assassination attempt

Washington, DC

Harry was grateful his brother-in-law even agreed to talk. Liam surely knew the reason his sister walked out on her marriage to Harry. Verity had begged him to tell her there was nothing between him and Lilah. His silence drove her away. In spite of it, Liam went along with Dante when Harry called for help. For the good deed, Liam ended up taking a knife in his shoulder. His wound needed extensive surgery, followed by exercises to help him regain his strength. He was in the middle of a physical therapy session in his DC apartment when Harry called. Liam didn't sound happy, but he didn't refuse admission to Harry. Of course it was because Liam knew what happened to the Kingsley brothers. Dante updated him after the six exiles left their home. Liam would be anxious about his old friend, Alex.

The apartment was a typical bachelor pad with comfortable furniture arranged around a television. No flowery scents, just the aroma of takeout Chinese. The radio played Bobby McFerrin's "Don't Worry, Be Happy."

Harry leaned back on the couch, wishing he could relax into the pillows, but sleep was a luxury he couldn't yet afford. He desperately needed something to drink, though. His throat was parched.

Standing in the middle of the floor mat, Liam grimaced as the physical therapist—a young Filipino woman—hardheartedly urged him to keep pumping the four-pound dumbbells. Injured muscles could make even that low a weight seem like a heavy load. Sweat plastered his blond hair—very much like his sister's—to his scalp. "So whaddya wanna talk to *me* for?" he grunted out to Harry.

"I need a favor."

Liam's gray eyes—again, similar to his sister's—widened. "From *me?*"

"I need you to introduce me to someone you know," Harry said, flicking a glance at the therapist. He couldn't bring it up until she was gone. "As a matter of fact, a mutual acquaintance of yours and Alex's."

"Huh?"

Willing Liam to catch on, Harry added, "There's a place you... uhh... visit frequently? You took Alex there a few years ago. Right before his engagement to Sabrina."

Frowning, Liam repeated, "Huh?"

"You told me you consider her a personal friend."

"Who... oh!" Liam dropped the weight to the floor. "I've had enough for today," he said to the therapist. The young lady tut-tutted. Smiling, Liam added, "I'll catch up later. I swear." Harry waited as Liam hustled the therapist out and closed the door behind her. Clicking the lock, Liam asked, tone ominous, "Lupe? You want me to take you to meet Lupe?"

Harry tried to explain, "Yes, I nee—"

"Get up," ordered Liam, his eyes slitted in fury.

Harry stood, but he was *not* going to leave the apartment until he had his say. "Hear me out, plea—" A punch landed on his jaw, weaker than he deserved. The arm attached to the fist was recovering from a knife wound. Harry staggered but didn't fall, didn't hit back.

Liam faced Harry, his hands still balled at his side. Teeth clenched, he asked, "You want *me* to take you to a strip club?"

Rubbing his jaw, Harry said, "Yes, but not *any* strip—"

"What the hell is wrong with you, man?" Liam shouted. "You just broke up with my sister! Did you already forget her?"

Harry sighed. "This isn't about—"

"I don't give a damn!"

"Do you give a damn about Alex?" Harry asked. "You two were friends long before Verity and I got married." Liam grunted, his eyes still narrowed in anger. "I think Ms. Valdez can help Alex. She's not going to agree if a random stranger like me pops in with..." With a sigh, Harry came clean. "I left a few messages at the club, but she hasn't called back. I doubt she will. She knows you and—"

"You have balls," Liam spat. "Help *Alex?* You mean, help the woman who destroyed my sister's marriage."

"Liam, I never crossed the line with Lilah. Not even once—it doesn't matter. Fact is I was a pathetic husband. Verity is better off without me."

With an angry laugh, Liam said, "I agree with you there. She should've never married you."

"I understand your feelings... and Verity's. But remember, I have a sister, too. Sabrina is married to Alex. Don't you think getting *him* back home is important to me?" Nostrils flaring and mouth twisting in a snarl, Liam continued staring hard at Harry. "Please... I need your help." When no answer was forthcoming, Harry added, "I get why you don't feel any sympathy toward Lilah but try to put aside your anger for a moment and remember Alex. He's one of the good guys.

You've known him a lot longer than me. He would've damn well helped you if the positions were reversed."

Liam's eyelids flickered.

"And remember the thugs who were trying to get me," continued Harry. "No question they were working with the Kingsleys. The interrogation in Cuba was a setup... all of it... the attempt to kill me, the arrest of the five brothers, what happened to Mr. Temple."

Jerking back, Liam asked, "Temple, too? Shit!"

"Yeah." Harry nodded. "There's no proof, of course. Chances are there will never be any proof unless someone supporting the exiles looks for it."

"My God," marveled Liam. "This is... man, it's hard to believe! If the Kingsleys went that far... Alex... poor bastard." Tone turning gruff, Liam added, "Dante already told me most of it. He doesn't lie... Major Armor got Charles to attack Lilah. The sons of bitches... assaulting women!" Walking to his equipment, Liam picked up a towel from the floor and wiped off his face and neck. "What makes you think Lupe can help?"

Harry disclosed no specifics, stating simply none of his allies around the world could openly offer assistance and risk angering the U.S. government. His connections in the military and intelligence agencies would not aid him when suspected traitors were involved. Nor could he use said connections to visit the exiles. He couldn't even know where they were at any point as it would get *him* into legal trouble, something they couldn't afford. Someone needed to be willing and able to give Harry the lowdown on certain people who could help arrange a pardon.

Liam's friend—the madam—was acquainted with some very powerful men. A fact Liam most certainly was aware of. The concern on his face revealed quite clearly he suspected Harry was planning something dirty.

"We have to move fast," Harry said. "The longer they remain in exile—"

"The greater the chances Steven will have them killed," Liam finished. Contemplating a spot on the carpet, he stayed silent for a few seconds. "You and Alex saved my father from his own stupidity," he finally muttered.

Liam and Verity's father—Will Luce—had also been a major shareholder in Gateway before he was foolish enough to lose all his stock to Harry in a card game. The shares were held in trust for his kids by Gateway's board. Both Harry's consent and a majority vote by the board would be required to release the stock back to Luce, a move Liam fervently agreed with. Harry never considered it a life debt, but if the episode served to convince Liam...

"All right," Liam said. "I'll see if Lupe will agree to talk to you. Ain't gonna happen overnight, so you might as well return to New York for now. And... umm... make sure you shower before you meet her."

#

After Harry left, Liam turned off the radio and called, "You can come out now."

Verity scurried from the bedroom where she'd sought harbor. "Of all the things! Whatever prompted you to hit him? I hope you didn't damage your poor shoulder." She kept scolding in her lilting voice as she guided him to the couch.

His knuckles hurt more than his shoulder, and his ego took a beating when Harry barely stumbled from the lame excuse for a punch. Not as if Liam intended to admit it. In a pitiful voice, he said, "I think I need a nap."

The words and tone earned him a sharp look. "You simply want me to shut up."

Liam grimaced and snapped, "Verity, I'm fine. Stop nagging." He could have bitten his tongue off when saw her eyes fill with tears.

"Papa didn't want to talk about my divorce, either," she wailed.

"Dammit, sis," Liam said gruffly. "You know what Dad's like."

"No, I don't," she sobbed. "Papa's always been nice to *me.*"

True enough. With his son, Will Luce, Sr. had been absently pleasant and nothing more, but he spoiled his daughter rotten. Liam frowned, wondering what happened to make their father ignore Verity right when she needed the support of her family.

Copious tears ran down Verity's face, her nose just as red as it used to turn when they were children squabbling over toys. Liam's heart wrenched. All she had were a disinterested father, an annoyed brother, and a husband who never even asked how she was doing.

"Tissue?" she asked, delicately holding a hand to her face.

Liam heaved himself up and grabbed a clean towel off the pile next to the exercise mat. Handing it to his sister, he collapsed back onto the couch. "Looks like it really is over between you and Harry, huh?" When Verity nodded, Liam said, "Can't say I'm surprised."

Above the terry towel, her eyes widened in shock. "You didn't think we would last?"

"I hoped you would but wasn't counting on it." Liam remembered his initial amusement at Verity's adulation of Harry, surprise at her excited announcement they were dating. The concern grew when Harry asked her to marry him. Liam didn't like her hero worship of her then-fiancé and didn't think for a moment Harry would provide the pampering Verity was used to.

"Why?"

"Verity, you're my sister." Liam remembered the mounting certainty she would be an ornament on her husband's arm, nothing more. True to his fears, she shared Harry's apartment and his bank account while he shared his life with Alex and Lilah. "I wanted someone who'd appreciate you for what you are. Harry didn't see you as your own person with your own outlook on the world. I don't know if you understood his."

"What are you saying?" she asked, voice trembling in bewilderment and hurt. She tossed the towel to the coffee table. "That I didn't do my part?"

"I'm sure you did, but Harry's needs and yours were—are—very different. He's not someone for happy domesticity, Verity. He thrives on all the... his passion for what he does borders on obsession. His true love is his mission."

"Lilah," Verity corrected bitterly.

Or maybe the two were inseparably intertwined. Thinking back to the India trip, Liam muttered, "Whatever." His main concern right now was emotionally extricating Verity from the mess. "I don't think you would've said yes to Harry if you knew what he's really like. It takes a different kind of personality to absorb all the shocks and thrive along with him."

"If you knew all this, why didn't you stop me?" Verity cried.

Because whenever he saw her look at Harry, there were stars in her eyes. Liam wanted his sister to have everything she wished for. He shrugged. "I hoped I would be proved wrong."

Anger returned in waves when he remembered how she tracked him down on his business trip to New York. There was the hysterical phone call telling him she'd left Harry. When she arrived at Liam's hotel room, she sobbed out her husband refused her the one thing she demanded: for him to categorically declare he was not in love with Lilah. Liam's fists itched with the need to thrash Harry. Between her sniffles, Verity muttered something about Harry's boss, Dante, so Liam called him, only to be commandeered into helping Harry escape criminals. Liam hadn't understood one word of Dante's terrified ramblings, but he went along. For his concern, Liam was rewarded with a knife to his shoulder by the assassins hunting Harry.

Gently, Liam said, "You fell in love with a mirage, Verity. The handsome hero and successful businessman. The charmer who flirted with the pretty girls at the family picnic. You were so proud of being the one he chose. But it's only the façade he puts up. Inside, it's a different story... while my baby sister is all about pinks and sparkles and sunshiney smiles. A princess."

"And Lilah?" Verity asked, her eyes once again glittering with tears. "The tabloids sometimes call *her* a princess, too." Yeah, but not since she ascended to the imperial throne of the oil sector. No matter how the press referred to the network—a corporate authority, oil mafia, whatever—Lilah Kingsley was invariably called its empress.

"Does it matter what Lilah is? Just don't blame her for the breakup of your marriage. Blame Harry. Because the man you fell in love with never existed, and he knew it."

Dolefully, Verity asked, "Why are you defending that woman, Liam? You're making me feel worse."

He squeezed her shoulder. "I'm only trying to make sure... don't condemn the wrong person, sis. I don't want you upset about me helping Alex and the rest, which would include Lilah. They need me... not too many people around who're willing to take their side on this."

"Heh? Why? They can return if the charges are removed, can't they?"

"How easy you make it sound. I hope everything works out just so."

"It will," Verity said, confidence in her tone. "You won't let anyone do that to Alex." Obviously struggling to bring a brave smile to her face, she added, "Harry won't, either."

"So you won't mind if I work with Harry? I mean, we owe him and Alex. Without them, we'd have lost all the stock. But it won't be only Alex returning, you know. Lilah will also be back."

"I know," Verity muttered. "All I wanted was for her to stay away from Harry. I never wanted anything *bad* to happen."

A rush of affection coming over him, Liam hugged her to his side. It struck him how accurate his words were. Verity was all sunshine and sparkly colors, extending her generosity to even her rivals. She was a butterfly princess who tried to soar with an eagle.

"Why are you laughing?" she asked.

Hurriedly stopping, Liam said, "Uhh... something I remembered."

The phone rang.

"Tell me," she demanded.

"You wouldn't understand." He leaped up from the couch. "Someone's calling."

"You sit right here, Liam," she said, eyes narrowed. "Or I'm going to scream. *While* you're talking to whoever it is."

God save him from sisters. "Verity, I get calls from work."

"I don't care. Were you laughing at me?"

"No, why would I?" The ringing continued. "I need to take the call. Don't you say a word."

She jumped off the couch and raced to the phone to block his access to it. "I'm not letting you talk to anyone until you tell me."

Liam flung his hands heavenward. "I just remembered something stupid Alex and I did together. *Now* will you let me pick up the call? Please don't get me fired!"

The way her face was scrunched up made it clear she didn't completely believe him. Nevertheless, she moved aside. The ringing stopped.

"Great," he said.

"Call them back," she suggested, tone now guilty.

"Let me see who it was." They waited for the answering machine to turn on.

"Liam," said their father's voice. "Call me, will ya? I need you to talk to Harry about getting the stock back. I don't see why he has to keep it with Gateway's board. Not when he's divorcing our Verity."

"*I'm* divorcing *him*," Verity muttered.

"I need the money," continued Will Luce. "The salary from Gateway just ain't cutting it."

"Don't call back, Liam. Papa's going to lose it all again."

"Not going to," Liam assured her. They were both well aware of their parent's weakness for cards.

Chapter 7

A week later

New York, New York

"I'm not going anywhere," Sabrina insisted, gripping the armrests of the chair tightly. She had to force herself not to leap out and strangle the visitor on Harry's living room couch. Noah Andersen, former attorney general, was there for a private conversation with Harry, but Sabrina didn't trust the old fellow in the least after the role he played in destroying Lilah's marriage.

"I suppose it doesn't matter if you hear," Andersen said. "In fact, it might be better..." He huffed, the gaunt cheeks puffing briefly. Twisting to face Harry at the other end of the couch, Andersen said, "We have very few avenues left to bring the exiles home, and there simply cannot be any dissension between us. I want to lay out all the info I have about the whole saga... the good, the bad, the ugly. I can't take the chance of you learning of it from someone else, perhaps someone who will put the worst possible spin on it."

The first attempt to form a Kingsley-Barrons-Sheppard alliance... two planned marriages... Patrice Sheppard with Peter Kingsley and Amber Barrons with Peter's father. One union soon fell apart, and the second didn't even get to the altar before the girl killed herself. The only thing the three families achieved was to trigger anger from Jared Sanders, the criminal ruler of the oil sector.

Everyone knew Sanders was merely waiting for the right moment to strike back. Then, Lilah flew to Libya to visit Harry one fateful Thanksgiving weekend. The adults involved were aware of the risks, but all of them mutely watched her walk into danger. The cash-strapped Sheppards were in fact persuaded by Andrew Barrons's bribe into issuing the invitation to the girl to get her out of his way. The Barronses wanted time alone with Lilah's twin to prep him for his entry into society as their heir.

"Oh, God," murmured Sabrina, her heart breaking. "Our parents, Harry... they brought it on her."

Harry didn't respond... not with a word, not with a look.

"Temple didn't know..." Andersen continued. The then-senator became aware of the girl's presence in Libya only after the fact. Following the rescue of the two abducted teens, Temple deduced what happened during their encounter with the rapist, Colonel Parker. "We figured out Parker was in Sanders's pay. And by 'we,' I mean Temple, myself... and your parents."

Sabrina gasped in shock, but Harry still didn't make a sound. He stared straight through the window, staying still. Very, very still.

The Sheppards requested yet another favor from Temple—his silence about Parker's whereabouts. In return, Ryan Sheppard added a sum of money to the bank accounts of Lilah and her twin, under the pretext of some savings scheme their deceased parents had been part of which the couple's lawyer wasn't aware of until then. Harry's family could scarcely afford the deal, but they were willing to fork out any amount to keep him from putting himself in further danger by going after Sanders's thug.

"Temple agreed," Andersen said, his voice low. "He'd seen the potential in Lilah by then." Temple chose to keep everyone's dirty secrets, forcing them to cooperate with yet another scheme to build the grand alliance.

"What about justice for Lilah?" Sabrina demanded. "Did anyone think about what *she* wanted? None of you thought it was important at all?"

"Of course it was," Andersen acknowledged. "But law and morality don't exist in a vacuum." Sanders was still out there, threatening more businesses, more families. The alliance was badly needed.

"What was my parents' excuse?" Sabrina asked bitterly. "Pretty sure they were not in it to save the world."

Tone gentling, Andersen advised, "Sabrina... it's easy to judge, but the human mind bets on things working out all right. Ryan and Sophie were desperate for cash, and Lilah was going to stay only a couple of days. I imagine your parents thought she'd be safe enough. Afterward, they simply prioritized their own child—Harry."

"Did they have questions after the board meeting?" asked Harry, speaking for the first time since Andersen started his narration. Ryan Sheppard surely recognized the name when Parker announced himself.

"No," said Andersen. "Neither you nor Lilah ever told them there was friction between you and Temple. Perhaps they thought the rapist joining the network was simply coincidence... nothing to do with Temple. Perhaps they were too scared to say a word. Perhaps Ryan wanted to do his own investigation before saying anything. Since Parker died, they probably assumed you were no longer in danger. Lilah's emotional state didn't matter to them. They didn't actively mean her any harm, but for your parents, you came first. A lot of families would take the same approach."

After the former attorney general left, Harry and Sabrina stayed put in their places for a while, each wrapped in miserable silence.

Abruptly, Harry said, "I should call Dan. He deserves to know what Andrew did... what our family did."

"Be careful what you say to him," Sabrina said. Lilah's twin wasn't aware of the sexual assault she survived. "And more importantly, ask him about Amber." Sabrina didn't explain how *she* became aware of the story. "Who knows? Maybe he overheard something from the Barronses." Before the events in Cuba, Harry had refused to involve Lilah's brother because of worry over how he'd react if he realized how many people were targeting the network. Now, if there was a one-in-a-million chance Dan knew something, Harry needed to take it. "Lilah already brought it up with Shawn, but—"

Lilah hadn't wanted to suggest to her adopted brother that his father might have covered up a suspicious death. It was one thing for him to help her in the face of Andrew's indifference, but accusing the man of an actual crime... familial feelings might have prompted at least a discussion. There was no telling how the oil tycoon would have reacted. Lilah had still brought up Amber's name casually in Shawn's company, and he seemed to know no more than everyone else.

Sabrina talked about how she and Lilah also went digging for gossip in other quarters. Neither Patrice nor Alex had ever heard about Amber. "It's incredible how..." Sabrina sighed. "I mean it would've been a big deal when it happened, but apparently, no one saw anything, heard anything."

"Money," Harry said grimly. "It's been making people blind, deaf, and dumb for a long time. No matter. This thing in DC with... uhh... a friend... I hope like hell we get something." He didn't elaborate on whatever the plan was, only stating he wanted to try and keep her out of it.

#

Hours later, Sabrina was in another chair, this time in the second bedroom of the apartment. Michael was asleep on the bed. The shadows around deepened when she closed the portable computer on the side table. It was no use... she simply couldn't focus. What was she hoping to achieve, anyhow? She no longer possessed access to the sophisticated systems owned by the Peter Kingsley Company to investigate anything related to the Kingsleys or anyone else. Nor was there any way to contact the exiles over cyberspace. None of them knew enough about computers to connect digitally.

Trying to relieve the crick in her neck, Sabrina looked out through the bedroom window. The streetlights were on, but the sky was dark. Not much of a moon and no stars. Somehow, she imagined Alex's baritone voice, his mouth tickling her ear as he whispered his intention not to waste a single minute of their son's nap time.

Where are you now? Sabrina asked. Did he even have a bed to sleep in? Thanks to their father's desertion, the Kingsley brothers learned at an early age how to make do with very little, but still... Sabrina wished she were with her husband. *If not for Mikey...* God, she was scared. So, so scared. For Alex, for Michael, for herself, for Lilah, for Harry. For all of Alex's brothers.

The not-knowing was the worst. Grayson Sheppard, the company lawyer, was the only one who was told where the exiles were headed. His communications with them would be considered privileged. Anything Sabrina or Harry wanted to tell Alex would go through Grayson.

Alex... oh, God, what are we going to do? The first time in her life she was well and truly frightened was when Mikey was caught in the raid on the offices of the Peter Kingsley Company. She couldn't think of anything beyond her baby. She didn't even *see* the battered face of her husband until he was handcuffed. When she learned Harry was alive, the panic ebbed slightly. She knew he'd find a way to get them back home. She'd clung to that faith even when she learned about the exile.

Fear came surging back now. The entire world seemed to be conspiring against them. If her family hadn't invited Lilah to visit so many years ago... if only she said no to the alliance... but Harry had been so determined to build their empire. Maybe he was doing it again. Maybe he was using Lilah as pretext to regain control over the network. Was it why Hector tried to tempt Harry with continued chairmanship?

No, Sabrina refused to believe it. If so, returning to reclaim their lost property would only leave Lilah more broken than ever before. Harry would ask her to continue as Brad's wife. She might be better off staying away from all this madness, from all of Harry's scheming.

But if she did, the network would never return to Harry's hands. Then, why would he help Alex clear his name? Without Alex—

Stop, Sabrina ordered herself. She knew her brother. He'd never betray her faith. The last few weeks had cut the moorings from her, that was all. Sabrina was left not knowing where she belonged, whom to trust.

"Bad man," came a tinny voice from the bed. "No, *bad man.*" Sabrina started. In the dim glow of the nightlight, Michael was thrashing around on the mattress, blankets twisted around his legs. "No, don't hit Daddy. Mama... *Mama.*" He woke on a scream, eyes round and wild. His little chest heaved in panicked breaths.

Running frantically to the bed, she gathered her baby boy to her chest and pacified him with kisses on his temple. "Bad dream, Mikey. That's all it was. You're okay." Her own heart was pounding. *My God! What did he see?*

"Runt?" Harry's voice called softly from the door, the light from the living room streaming in through the crack. "What's going on?"

"Uncle Harry," Michael said, tears flowing down his cheek. "My daddy..."

In two quick strides, Harry was at his nephew's bedside, going down on one knee to face him. "We'll bring your daddy home, I promise," Harry said, holding a hand out. "Come here, bud."

Michael disentangled himself from his mother's embrace and scrambled out of bed. Sobs died into soft snivels as he burrowed into Harry's shoulder.

In a couple of minutes, Harry settled the little boy back against the pillows, waving Sabrina away. She returned to the chair. The duo in the bed fell quiet, each buried in his own thoughts. With their thick, dark hair, they looked so similar they could've been father and son.

Except Michael inherited Alex's cognac eyes while Harry's were coffee brown. Cappuccino as Lilah once called them... long before the Kingsleys came into her life. Lost as she was in dreams of her childhood sweetheart, Lilah never even heard the theatrical groan from Harry's thirteen-year-old sister.

"Uncle Harry?" Michael called again.

"Yes, buddy?"

"The bad men hit Daddy... and Lilah," the boy whispered tearfully. "I wanted to stop them, but my legs wouldn't work." Shifting, Michael looked into his uncle's face. "I tried. *I really did.*"

Sabrina didn't know she'd leaped from the chair to run to Michael. Horrific visions of what Charles Kingsley might have done to her baby ran through her mind. She would've snatched her son from Harry's side, but Michael's focus was one hundred percent on his uncle.

"I know you did, Mike," said Harry. "The best thing you could have done at the time was stay hidden, so it's good your legs didn't work."

It was clear Michael didn't believe him. "There was blood coming outta her mouth," the boy said. "And from Daddy's head."

Harry closed his eyes. On the mattress, his fingers clenched into a fist, giving the lie to the quietness of his tone. "Hmm. If you did run to them, the bad men might've hurt you, as well. Your daddy would've tried to stop them, and they would've hit him more. Lilah and your uncles could've gotten hurt more, too. You see, Mike?" While the boy was still digesting the idea, Harry spoke to his sister, "I'll take him tonight. You get some rest."

The dark circles around his eyes nearly matched the color of his irises. "You're tired," she objected.

"It's for me, too," he said. "There are times when men need each other's company."

Michael squared his shoulders and sat up, making Sabrina bite back a reluctant smile. She nodded.

She spent the rest of the night tossing and turning. *My poor Mikey, feeling he failed as a man! At the grand old age of five!* She wished she could call Alex to talk to his son. Simply hearing his daddy's voice would help him. Her, too. *What are we going to do? Mikey and I... what if Alex never comes back? What* is *Harry planning?*

#

It must have been a few hours later when sounds of life started in the street outside. Sanitation trucks collected garbage before the day began. The knock on Sabrina's door was a welcome break from the thoughts which kept going in circles.

Outside, Harry stood with two coffee mugs. "Mike's still sleeping in my room. I have to meet Noah again in a couple of hours. We need a good defensive strategy and not simply for me and the exiles. All of us need protection, including you."

Sabrina frowned. Why on earth did she—

"There's a press conference," Harry continued. "Once it's done, I'm hoping we'll have the luxury of time. Afterward, I'm flying back to DC. Liam's setting up a meeting with someone."

Liam? In Panama, Sabrina had been too distraught to ask what happened to Verity when assassins invaded Harry's apartment. Only when Sabrina and Michael got to New York did they learn Verity walked out mere minutes before assassins barged in, which probably saved her life.

When Sabrina heard Harry claim there was someone who could help, she assumed he meant some acquaintance from his military service or the oil sector. But Liam? Sabrina made a rueful grimace. Verity's brother was not likely to be terribly pleased with Harry at the moment.

"Yeah," said Harry. He glanced at the low table by the window where Sabrina had left her computer. "But he's agreed... Runt, there's something else..." Harry wanted to know if the fact he saved Lilah's life from the rapist created the same problem in her marriage as it did in his.

Sabrina took the proffered coffee and trudged to the living room with Harry. As they sat together on the couch, she blew gently on the froth topping the mug and narrated the storm which raged in the family home in Panama the last few weeks. Brad's paranoia about an affair between his wife and his brother... Alex's need to prove his loyalty to his family overcoming all reason... Lilah cut out of the loop in their workplace. The power of attorney which was intended to keep Harry safe was used to keep Lilah or anyone who might speak on her behalf away from him. She was isolated except for Sabrina.

"Thank you for helping her," Harry said.

"Heh? What do you mean?"

"Lilah talked to you about Amber, didn't she? There was at least one person for her to... then, the... uhh... virus which destroyed the info in her computer... it had to be your doing. I asked Shawn, but he told me it was surely you. No question the Kingsleys planted evidence in the device. No way they didn't. If you didn't do whatever it was..."

"Yeah, it was me," Sabrina confessed. "Lilah was worried Andrew was involved in the conspiracy, so she didn't want to involve Shawn. She knew I've been messing around with computers a long time."

"Messing around, huh?" Harry asked, smiling. "You held off some of the best technicians in the U.S. military. My sister, the secret genius. I'm surprised Alex never said anything. I would've expected him to brag."

Tone hard, she said, "He didn't know. Thank God. Or he might've somehow stopped me from doing that, too. All of them would've been in military prison."

Remembering the events leading up to the arrest, Sabrina's hands itched to pummel all five of the Kingsley brothers. Yeah, including her husband. When he first told her about the impending exile, she was too frantic to ask how he could've done this to her, to their son. Brad's life was important to his brothers, but didn't the lives of their wives and children count for anything at all?

"It's best if we continue to keep your part quiet," Harry said. "Shawn's already fielded a couple of inquiries from intelligence agencies."

Again she asked, "What do you mean?"

"They think it was him," Harry explained. "He's the logical choice—her adopted brother and an acknowledged computer expert. I asked him to keep dancing around the questions. Dan said he'll claim he asked Shawn to do it… if needed." Andrew Barrons would choose his business over his heir any day, but this thing with the feds posed no real risk to the company. What Dan supposedly did was well within the law before the arrest. Under the circumstances, Andrew would not let Dan land in trouble. "Because of Dan's claim, Shawn will also be safe."

"Why would anyone even bother to find out who planted the logic bomb? It was Lilah's device; she was entitled to do what she wanted with it."

"It won't matter. The government won't be the primary problem. Whoever did it thwarted Godwin Kingsley's plans. The culprit is going to be in his crosshairs. Regardless of legalities, he could insinuate you helped traitors escape justice and cause you no end of trouble... perhaps even with child protective services."

Fear—cold and metallic—froze Sabrina's mouth. Her eyes swung to the bedroom where her baby boy was sleeping.

"Yes," said Harry. "You have Michael to think about. There's another thing. Victor wasn't married to his son's mother, and I don't know the nuts and bolts of inheritance laws in such cases. But Michael is definitely heir to Alex. Depending on what Brad and his brothers have done with their wills, your son is perhaps the sole legal heir to the Peter Kingsley Company. Sabrina, if Steven and gang succeed in killing me and Alex and the rest, you'll be the only one standing between Michael and the Kingsleys."

Chapter 8

Same afternoon

Long Island, New York

It was Harry's first visit to Temple's home. The garden was big, giant trees with cinnamon-red bark lined up along the border, but the house itself was a modest gray stone structure, simply furnished. There were four bedrooms, two of which were used by the security detail, and there was a housekeeper who came by daily.

In the office which held only a desk and a chair and a few notepads with pens, Harry held the phone to his ear and confessed with shame his family's part in Lilah's trauma. The shocked silence from Dan was brief, followed by the furious declaration he would confront his adoptive father. Harry had to remind Dan again and again they'd eventually need support from Andrew Barrons.

"I couldn't avoid telling you," said Harry. "It's critical we all know who did what and who not to trust. But don't let it distract you from what's going on *now*. We need to bring Lilah home. Everything else must come after. Focus on Barrons O & G and tell me what you got so far."

"I swear I will—" Dan paused, his angry breathing audible over the line. "Right... bring her home first." It took him a few more moments to relate certain happenings at the Barrons place of business. "It's going to take time."

There were tasks for Lilah's twin to perform in their quest to get justice. Dan had taken on a mission certain to invite retaliation from the Kingsleys if they got to know. It wouldn't be easy even for Godwin to arrange electronic eavesdropping on the Barrons line, but the feds? Oh, yeah... both Harry and Dan were careful what they said in the conversation.

"None of the board members want to meet me one-on-one this soon after what happened," Dan muttered. "It's gonna take a lot of work to convince them."

"Expected," Harry agreed. They'd already discussed his plan to get help from Lupe Valdez. Once again, no details, but Dan couldn't fail to figure out what Ms. Valdez's involvement would entail. "Whatever you do at Barrons, stay under the radar, Dan. Lilah's not going to want you gambling with your safety. Also, if I end up in trouble somewhere down the line, you and Shawn and Sabrina will be pretty much the only people left on our team." Of course Dante would try to help, and so might Liam.

Dan didn't scoff at the suggestion having Harry on her side ever helped Lilah. No matter what role the Sheppards and Andrew Barrons played in the saga, Harry and Temple were the ones most responsible for the mess she found herself in. Dan knew it well. Someday, the recriminations would come. The day she was back home safe and sound, Dan would take the swing at Harry he so richly deserved.

I will make it up to her, Harry swore silently. Someone called his name, causing him to glance toward the door of the office.

From his position, Harry could see the room across the hallway— the one luxury in the residence, the large library they were using for today's press conference. Temperature was kept at a steady seventy-two, the air relatively dry. Books, old and new, lined the shelves on the wall. First editions and famous texts in their original languages were arranged in glass cases. Dante Alighieri and Rudyard Kipling competed for attention with Tom Clancy and Danielle Steel. A paperback lay spine up on the chair next to the window: *The Cardinal of the Kremlin.* There was a steel-doored locker hidden behind one of the shelves, the same one Noah spent futile hours looking through for any records on what might have been in Temple's note.

If Godwin didn't already know Temple never revealed the Kingsley secret to anyone else, it would've been made clear by Harry and Noah's silence on the matter even after the assassination attempt. Harry considered bluffing about it, hinting to the press he was in possession of info which could bring down the Kingsleys. It might have prompted Godwin to act rashly and discredit himself. Perhaps it might trigger a reopening of the case.

Or... as Noah warned, what happened to Temple could be repeated. The former president would've made sure evidence against his stepbrother was not stored anywhere it could be found, so neither the media nor law enforcement would be of any help. Godwin would know it or at least hope for it to be the case. However, the threat of exposure from Harry could cause the former justice to ignore any possible withdrawal of support from Gateway and launch an immediate attack to get rid of the only remaining obstacle in his way. Harry might believe he could fend off strikes, but what if his luck ran out at some point? The exiles would then be left without their two main allies. Harry couldn't take the chance.

"Gotta go," he said to Dan, keeping his tone steady. "The press conference is about to start."

As Harry walked into the meeting area, the hum of chatter from the journalists occupying the rented chairs peaked slightly. Nearly all news organizations in the U.S. had their top reporters attending the event. The recent attack on Temple meant interest in the former president skyrocketed, and Harry's phone calls to editors around the country claiming involvement by the Kingsley family in the back-to-back attacks ensured a packed room. It was a significant accusation to throw around, and Harry had already fielded questions from media well-wishers about the stupidity of the move.

They didn't know Noah Andersen decided on the press conference. The former attorney general's legal cunning was perhaps the only weapon left in Harry's arsenal unless and until Lupe Valdez came around.

Nodding at Noah, Harry took the second chair at the low table in front of the journalists. "Good to see you here, sir," he said to the veteran pressman in the front row. The gent was known for his low tolerance for fakery. Raising a hand, Harry greeted the bespectacled fellow seated toward the back. "How's it going, Ron?" They'd met at one of the events during the expansion, Harry and Alex making the novice's day by giving him an exclusive joint interview.

There were more familiar faces, but a minute or two of chitchat was all Harry did. The eagerness to get down to the topic of the hour—the impatience—was almost palpable.

"Temple's going to be on the ventilator until the swelling goes down," Noah explained to the press, voice gravelly from lack of sleep. Since the assassination attempt, he'd been busy. "Under sedation."

"Any updates on the shooter?" asked the reporter in glasses.

Noah shrugged. "You know as much as I do. All the relevant agencies are investigating, including the NYPD."

"You expect them to find a connection between the attack and Mr. Sheppard's allegations claiming the Kingsleys tried to kill him?" the fellow persisted. "Isn't it why you called this press conference?"

"Mr. Andersen," interrupted the journalist from ABC News. "Did Mr. Temple know about Mr. Sheppard's concern? What was his take on it?"

Sipping water from a glass, Harry stayed quiet and waited for the former attorney general to respond. Noah had grilled him on when to speak and what to say.

"Temple and I have known each other a long time," Noah said.

"I get how you've been friends for years," the ABC reporter interrupted again. "What America wants to know is what he thought of this situation between the Kingsleys and Mr. Sheppard. After all, the Kingsleys are Mr. Temple's family."

"Harry was... is his protégé," Noah supplied. "Also, in case you needed reminding, Petty Officer Harry Sheppard is a military hero. A Medal of Honor recipient. Temple was saddened by the conflict, of course, but he also wanted it thoroughly investigated. No one is above the law, not even the Kingsleys."

"Mr. Andersen, I have a question," said a woman, her eyes sharp in a face covered with wrinkles. "You seem to believe Mr. Sheppard's version of events. Can you confirm that?"

"I believe in justice," Noah answered, tone firm. "Plus, what would Harry get out of lying about something as serious as attempted murder?"

"Well, what do the Kingsleys get out of attempting murder?" she asked. "The former justice, Godwin Kingsley, made it very clear he wants peace between his grandsons."

Harry interjected, "May I answer? I have never kept it secret I consider Brad Kingsley and his family my friends. Some of you may also know we're related. Brad's brother, Alex, is married to my sister. Alex and Lilah are friends of mine. When they were arrested..." Pausing, Harry struggled with the temptation to name the main perp, but Noah had cautioned him against it for various legal reasons. "The night Steven Kingsley got them arrested, there was an attack on me. I believe Steven was trying to get *me* out of the picture at the same time. Trained assassins tracked me through New York City. The bomb on my—"

"Yes, we're aware of the bomb explosion on your boss's boat," the woman said, not bothering to mask her impatience. "We also know about your connection to Alex Kingsley. The people of this country hold the Kingsley brothers in contempt. Those five men were in a position most can only dream of and got carried away by all the power and the money. Lilah Kingsley helped them betray their fellow Americans. Our readers have no sympathy for arrogant women like her. Besides, those who marry for money do generally end up paying for it."

"Lilah *Barrons* married for money?" Noah asked, friendly amusement in his tone. "You're joking of course."

"For power then," retorted the journo. "The Cuba incident made that very clear. Even our female readers—*especially* our female readers—won't forgive her for what she did. Using her looks to get ahead betrayed everything the women's rights movement stands for."

A muscle hardened painfully in Harry's jaw, but anything he said to the media in Lilah's support carried the potential to further fan the flames of gossip. "C'mon," scoffed an unknown voice from elsewhere in the room. "Poor lady was just attacked. She's endured enough trauma through no fault of her own."

There were vigorous nods of agreement from the crowd, especially from the journos who knew Harry and the Kingsley brothers on a personal level, but no one actually disputed the substance of the criticism. Even to the section of the press which supported Lilah, her role in the network was reduced to a pawn who made the best of what she got. Nor did anyone object to the existence of the network itself. Lilah was right. Once such a vast power structure was built, there would be many whose interests were tied to it. They would fight to their last breaths to keep said power.

"So?" snapped the female reporter. "Ms. Kingsley's trauma is minor considering the charges involved. Mr. Sheppard, under the circumstances, you're not going to be able to help her or the Kingsley brothers, so why would Steven Kingsley worry about you being alive? What would the Kingsley family gain from having you killed?"

Harry countered, "Public opinion on Brad and Lilah is only *opinion*, not fact. I've worked with both of them for years. Is there anyone here who can claim to know them any better than me? I firmly believe—no, I *know*—they're innocent. Men trying to kill me the same night of their arrest was no coincidence. The NYPD has a duty to investigate."

"Aren't they?" asked the woman.

"Yes," Harry acknowledged.

Major Phillip Potts, son of General Potts and a Kingsley hanger-on, was part of the team of assassins. Harry never mentioned it to the cops or to the press. The Kingsleys surely had some excuse ready, and even if they didn't, Noah was of the opinion the Pottses would fall on the sword to save Steven. Harry would store away the info for now, waiting for the right moment to deploy it. So would Dan. The general was the one who got Belgian authorities to detain Lilah's brothers at the airport for suspected terrorism, thus preventing them helping her. It took Temple's clout to get the two men out. Daniel was not going to forget the Pottses' role in his sister's ordeal.

"Unfortunately, the explosion destroyed most of the evidence," Harry said to the reporter. There were the corpses of the would-be assassins, but vigorous support from Dante and his son as well as Liam—all three of who witnessed parts of the attack—made sure the cops couldn't pin the blame on Harry.

The woman laughed. "Come on now. No proof to offer, but somehow, you expect the media to buy your story. Mr. Sheppard, these are dangerous times. Not just your gun and knife attacks. Terrorism, bomb blasts... what happened to you was coincidence, that's all."

Glancing at the book on the couch, Harry said, "Ma'am, once or twice may be coincidence, but three times? Planned attacks, all of them."

"*Three* times?" called out another journalist.

Noah interjected, "Good to see you again, old friend. You're working for the new channel now, right?"

The veteran reporter smiled. "Yes, Mr. Andersen. For Fox. To get back to what Mr. Sheppard said... the first attack you're referring to must be the unfortunate episode involving Colonel Parker during the board meeting of the Peter Kingsley Network. The... er... attempted rape." Thankfully, the rapist colonel ended up dead. "The second one... the simultaneous events in Panama and New York where the Kingsley brothers were arrested while Mr. Sheppard was fighting off home invasion? Are you confirming for us you suspect the Kingsleys of arranging the attempted assassination? Was it the third attack?"

Noah leaned forward with his elbows on the table. "Dick, how many years have you been covering politics?"

The reporter grinned. "More than I care to count, Mr. Andersen."

"Then you don't need us to spell it out," Noah said. Mutters went around the room. Uneasily, the journalists eyed each other, all of them clearly wanting a scoop, but none willing to risk accusing the influential Kingsleys without solid evidence. Shaking his head, Noah added, "No, not coincidence."

"You have proof of *that* at least?" the woman reporter challenged.

"I have my thoughts on the matter," Noah said. "Proof is for the police to gather."

She nodded. "Meaning that there's none. Mr. Andersen, you can't fail to realize there are other things going on in the world. The communist bloc is battling itself. The West is waiting to see if this will be the end of the Cold War. In the middle of such historic events, you call this conference only to... what a waste of the media's time."

Chapter 9

The same night

Upper East Side, New York City

Steven Kingsley turned off the television, tossing the remote to the brocade pillows piled up at the other end of the couch. He'd been afraid Phillip Potts's name would pop up at the press conference. Instead... "I don't believe this! Sheppard just went on TV and announced he thinks we tried to kill a former president. Is he crazy? Or maybe he thinks *we* are."

Instead of answering, Godwin stood from the armchair and paced the Persian carpet. Like the rest of his apartment at the family mansion, the living room was also lavishly furnished with eighteenth-century pieces. Two velvet-covered chairs with a small oak table in between faced the television. On the remaining two sides of the carpet, matching couches completed the square. "So close," he mumbled, the gray eyes of the former justice telegraphing extreme annoyance. As always, his longish white hair was tied back with some sort of leather ribbon.

Sprawled with his legs draped over one arm of the second chair, Charles was belting out a ditty about inviting a girl to eat him alive. In between lines, he gulped down after-dinner sherry by the mouthfuls—the rich, nutty wine from the Kingsley cellar meant to be savored. Charles—like all Kingsley men—had dark-brown hair and shared gray eyes with Steven and Godwin Kingsley. With everything going for him—decent enough looks, money, clout, the education said money and clout bought him—Charles still acted like an idiot.

Trying to ignore him, Steven asked the family patriarch, "So close to what?"

From the other couch, Richard Armor raised his blond head, interrupting his murmured conference with Stanley Gander, Steven's uncle. "To victory," Richard said. "Your cousins should have been sitting in military prison as we speak."

"We didn't expect Lilah to save their fool necks," Steven admitted. "Charlie, keep it down, please! It's the least you could do after the mess you made in Cuba."

"Me?" Charles whined.

"Yeah, you. If I were Rich, I'd be throttling you right now. Do you know much trouble he's in because of you?" Because of Charles, Richard's handling of the Brad Kingsley case was under investigation.

"Rich hasn't said anything," Charles muttered.

"For *my* sake, you fool," Steven retorted. "You're my brother, or he'd have beat the stupidity out of you a long—" Noting the smirk on Godwin Kingsley's face, Steven stopped.

The patriarch had called Charles a "turkey" since the debacle in Cuba. Thanks to Richard's coaching, Charles managed to come across as normal while assisting in the courtroom... until Lilah brought up the assault which happened out of the judges' sight. She persuaded the court she was being victimized, physically *and* legally. Richard's quick thinking saved the day, allowing Steven to pressure Brad's brothers and his wife into fleeing the country with him or risk having him put to death for treason. Steven defended Charles tooth and nail, accusing Godwin of underestimating Lilah's legal skills, instead. Not that Steven harbored any doubts as to his brother's contribution to the fiasco of an interrogation. After all, Charles barely escaped time in military prison for what he did. It took intervention by General Potts for Charles to be permitted to leave the army with an other-than-honorable discharge. As Charles's superior officer, Richard was under investigation for allowing a sexual assault to happen in his presence. Also, for some of the remarks he made to Lilah. But admitting to the patriarch Charles was indeed a "turkey" would've been tantamount to admitting he needed to be removed from their team. Perhaps permanently.

Idiot he certainly was, but Charles was important to Steven. They were brothers. If Godwin needed Steven as frontman, he'd have to put up with Charles.

"No point in worrying about it now," Richard said, blue eyes steady and calm. "Let's figure out what to do about this new problem Petty Officer Sheppard created for us."

Next to Richard, Uncle Stanley—his figure slight with nondescript features—stayed silent, but the expression on his face conveyed encouragement.

Steven was grateful for their support, especially Richard's. Godwin had not been thrilled at the friendship between one of his grandsons and the chauffeur's son. He'd suspected Richard of maneuvering himself into the Kingsley social circle to advance his own cause and said as much. Steven didn't care what Richard's original intention was; he'd stood by Steven through thick and thin.

"How can anyone take what Sheppard said seriously?" Steven asked. "Forget how Mr. Temple is in fact family. He's a *former president!* Only a moron would—" As one, Steven and Richard turned to Charles. Uncle Stanley was also gaping at his younger nephew. "Charlie," Steven called, tone ominous. "Did you?"

Tilting the glass in his hands until the sherry hovered at the edge, Charles asked, "Did I what?" His voice was absent, his eyes still on the wine.

Uncle Stanley wiped sweat from his brow. Steven and Richard exchanged glances. *Phew.* "Never mind," said Steven. "What's Sheppard hoping to get with this stunt?"

Still pacing the carpet, Godwin said, "He's trying to stop us from getting what *we* want."

"We already got what we want," Steven objected. "Sort of. Brad and his brothers are out of the network; so is Lilah. All we need to do is make sure they stay out."

Richard muttered, "Which brings us back to what your grandfather said. 'So close.'"

"Every single time," Godwin agreed, tone frustrated. "Right when you think things are falling into place, something happens. I should've never trusted you imbeciles. Stupid, the whole lot of you. How in God's name did you fail to realize Harry Sheppard is not easily killed? Don't you know how many times *Jared Sanders* tried? We needed a foolproof plan, and you... it is because of *you* Harry is still around to cause problems. Steven, didn't you swear left and right your friend, Mr. Potts, would 'take care' of Harry?"

Steven refrained from pointing out Phillip Potts wasn't merely his friend. The major was the son of a trusted Kingsley loyalist, General Potts. Nevertheless, Phillip did fail to kill the former SEAL *and* got himself injured in the attempt. Deciding to find a hospital not too close to the scene of the crime, Major Potts left New York City. Unfortunately, the E.R. staff detained him while they contacted the police about the gunshot wound. He came up with some excuse about being mugged, but two days passed before the cops released him. He'd been unable to send a message to the Kingsleys, and they didn't realize Harry was still alive until they were well into the interrogation in Cuba. Godwin confirmed that the news of Harry's escape was what the note he got announced.

A big worry remained whether Harry or his father who'd been snatched in the same operation managed to identify Phillip. Neither father nor son mentioned Major Potts to the cops. Nor did Phillip's name come up at the media event, yet Godwin clearly wasn't mollified.

"Who employed Mr. Potts?" asked the Kingsley patriarch. "*You*, Mr. Armor. Perhaps it's my fault... for trusting the chauffeur's son with the job."

What? Steven shot a glance at his friend. Richard was still seated on the other couch, but his shoulders were suddenly stiff, his eyes now furious. With an angry growl, Steven stood, ready to have it out that very second. "Grandfather, I suggest you remember you need me as much as I need you. I might put up with what you say to me, but I *will not* let you insult my friends."

Face red, Richard said, "Your grandfather is upset about Sheppard's press conference. Else, he wouldn't have forgotten who saved the day in Cuba, would he? When his arguments lost, no less."

Godwin smiled, looking every inch the former justice. "Are you daring to claim you're better than me, Mr. Armor?"

Snarling, Richard stood to face Godwin. "Wouldn't dream of it, sir. Just pointing out this *chauffeur's son* was the one who won the battle for you. Yanked victory from the jaws of defeat, so to speak."

"P-p-pardon me, Justice Kingsley," Uncle Stanley stuttered in his refined southern accent. He stood, the papers on his lap sliding to the carpet. "As Steven said, you need him. He needs both you and Richard. If we start fighting among ourselves, we're never going to win this game. Steven, I suggest you apologize to your grandfather."

Steven snorted. He hated the sycophancy. Stanley didn't need to fawn over the mighty Kingsley family just because his sister, Grace—Steven's mother—married into it. Grace and Stanley Gander might not have been as wealthy as the Kingsleys, but their family was no less respectable.

"No one has to apologize to me," Godwin announced. "Steven has his priorities. He loves his little brother and his friends. His grandfather doesn't make the list, unfortunately." The former justice's eyes glinted when he looked toward the chair where Charles was still lovingly studying his wine.

A cold frisson of fear ran down Steven's spine.

"I won't ask you to pick between me and your family, Steven," Richard said, a warning in the words. "You'll always have my support regardless of Justice Kingsley's opinion of my efforts."

"There," Uncle Stanley said, fluttering his hands. "Problem solved. Right, Steven?"

Steven didn't take his eyes off Godwin. Didn't dare. "I didn't mean any disrespect, Grandfather."

Slowly, Godwin nodded. "I have to admit Mr. Armor did save the day in Cuba... eventually. All the money in the world and none of my grandsons have the intellectual capacity of the servant who grew up in the apartment over our garage."

Steven gritted his teeth.

"We have other things to worry about," Uncle Stanley said and settled himself back on the couch.

Resuming his pacing, Godwin said, "Temple, for instance. It could have worked out so well for us. If he wakes up... we must make some kind of arrangements. Claim he's incapacitated from the head injury. A court-appointed guardian is the only way to make sure he does not get a chance to say anything to anyone which could hurt us. All his communications need to be supervised."

Steven paused for a second before sitting back down. Lost... it's how he sometimes felt trying to follow his grandfather's train of thoughts. The night at the Marriot, Godwin informed the rest Mr. Temple announced his intention of pressuring the current president for a pardon. Steven was arguing furiously, wanting to finish Brad off before the pardon happened, when they heard the commotion outside. No one paid any mind; this was downtown Manhattan, and sirens were not an uncommon event. Then, the lobby called the hotel room, asking them to stay put until the cops arrived.

An attempted assassination. It was surreal. Confusion and fear aside, there was relief the biggest problem was gone from their paths.

But the calculation Steven now heard in Godwin's voice was bone-chilling. *No,* Steven assured himself. It was one thing to target a fool like Brad and another to orchestrate an attack on a former president. Godwin would have to be much further gone into his psychopathy to arrange it. The clarity in his grandfather's gray eyes said he was still in possession of the sharp intellect he was famed for as a supreme court justice.

Hell, even if Godwin had completely lost his marbles, the timing didn't add up. Minutes prior to the episode, he'd been in the hotel room in Temple's presence without the chance to even make a phone call. Of all the people who were out of the room, only Richard and Noah Andersen left the lounge while Mr. Temple and Godwin were talking. Richard was calling a client, not arranging an assassination. The Kingsleys couldn't possibly have anything to do with the incident.

"I can talk to Temple's son about placing him under legal guardianship with me." Godwin continued fuming, "But this media thing with Harry..."

"Sheppard," growled Charles, not bothering to change his awkward positioning in the armchair. "Grandfather, why don't you let *me* handle things? I can take care of whoever you want. Him and his stupid press conferences!"

"Steven," Godwin bit out. "Tell your brother if he has nothing of intelligence to contribute, it's best he stays silent."

Head ready to explode, Steven said, "Charlie, please."

"Don't worry, Grandfather," said Charles, finally sitting up and setting the glass of sherry on the side table. Red wine sloshed about, a drop of it spilling onto the carpet. "I do have a good idea. Can't we sue Sheppard? He can't go around saying such things about a supreme court justice!"

"Charlie, Harry never took Justice Kingsley's name," Richard pointed out. "Only Steven's."

Charles shrugged. "So?"

"Steven has a..." Richard hesitated. "...reputation. If he sues, the courts will allow a process called discovery. All the gossip from the past... the incident where the assassins shot at Brad and his brothers in California... Sheppard could get the authorities to poke their noses into it. He could try even now, but without going through official channels, he will likely fail. The board will not pay any mind, either, given how everyone knows he wants Brad to return. With the discovery process, Sheppard will have legal muscle behind him. He could find something problematic. The network's board will be forced to respond, perhaps even kick Steven out. Remember the reason we gave out for the transfer of power from Brad to the Kingsleys."

Steven nodded. If Brad could resign as CEO because of possible legal trouble, Steven could be asked to, as well.

"The only name Harry brought up was of someone he was sure could be damaged at least by innuendo if not by actual evidence unearthed in the process of discovery," agreed Godwin. "He never mentioned me. If he did, all credibility would've been lost unless he produced some kind of proof... which he clearly doesn't believe he will find, discovery or not. The cops would've laughed him out of the building. The board, too. The public would've completely discounted whatever he said about the shooting in Times Square."

Charles gulped, staring at the rest in turn. "Can't we do the same thing? I'll call the papers and say Sheppard did... uhh... whatever. He *must* have done something, somewhere. No way he didn't."

"Anything we bring up could cause collateral damage in places we wouldn't want," Godwin said brusquely. "There are people in the government and elsewhere who won't be happy if such information leaked. Harry knows all this."

Reluctant admiration in his tone, Richard said, "Good strategy."

Godwin snapped, "Noah Andersen is Harry's adviser. The young man is remarkably shrewd, but I doubt he understands the nuances of the law well enough to do what he did all on his own. Have you seen Andersen's record? Justice Department rarely lost cases under his leadership. He schemes but makes sure to stay just within the line. Now, he is helping Harry. Whereas *I'm* saddled with fools."

Ignoring the taunt, Steven asked, "But does it matter what he said about me as long as we don't try to sue? Maybe a couple of journalists will buy the story. Sadly for Sheppard, it's not as though he can do anything at this point with it. Not without money or political support. Even Gateway is openly against him now. Hector says other Sheppards with stock in the company have been grumbling about things a long time. This issue with Brad gave all of them a chance to get back at Harry."

"Petty Officer Sheppard just made sure *we* can't do anything about *him*, either," Richard said from the chair, his eyes peculiarly intense and fixed somewhere in the distance. "Anything happens... the media will remember what he said about you and the Kingsleys."

"Why would it matter?" Steven asked again. "Sheppard has no money, no influence, and no evidence against us. In any case, we couldn't have done much about him right now, with or without the press conference. Too soon after the Cuba incident."

Harry's claim of being chased by assailants all across Manhattan while his friends were under interrogation in Cuba was dismissed as happenstance. If he were to be killed while the episodes remained fresh in public memory, the narrative could change. The exiles needed to go, as well. There was a limit to the number of back-to-back attacks which could be passed as coincidences, especially if said attacks ended in deaths. Convenient disappearances would also look suspicious at the moment. Some politician in some country would see opportunity to kick up a fuss, and the whole plan could unravel. Even in the United States, where media opinion was currently against the treasonous six, there were journalists sympathetic to them who were lying low only for the time being. The owner of the tabloid, *The Big Apple Reporter*, was certainly one. The fellow played a big role in the takedown of Sanders and no doubt would start talk again, this time with the Kingsleys as target.

Besides, there were the Sheppards. They might be happy about the chance to bring Harry down a couple of notches, but he and Hector were still brothers. Ryan and Sophia Sheppard were still Harry's parents. If they believed for a moment Steven was actually trying to kill one of their own, there would be hell to pay. Also, Dan Barrons... his adoptive father wouldn't let him drag the business into trouble, but it didn't mean he completely lacked connections and clout of his own. Noah Andersen was another problem. Between the three groups, questions would surely be raised in friendly media. Once again, it was impossible to close the mouths of all political types. Some fellow would see advantage in siding with the dissenters.

The Kingsleys simply couldn't risk it when they were this close to a complete victory. They needed to plan their next steps with deliberation. "We will take care of Harry and Cousin Brad," Steven assured his grandfather. "At a time convenient to us. Also, once Brad's out of the picture, Harry might not even be a problem."

It wasn't like before when Cousin Brad was in charge of the network, and the Kingsleys were forced to plot the demises of all the three people standing in their way. Now, Steven was already in possession of documents awarding him all the powers of the CEO as well as the voting rights of the brothers and Lilah. None of it would be returned unless a pardon was granted, which was unlikely to happen after Brad's death. Control of the network would be secure with the Kingsleys once Brad was taken out of contention for good. Harry Sheppard was the chairman, but even if he were left alive, there would be little he could do on his own besides make a general pest of himself.

Richard looked back at the notepad on his lap. "We can't do anything to Brad *until* Sheppard's out of the way. Unfortunately, his media stunt significantly prolonged our wait time before we can afford to do anything to any of them."

"Explain," Steven demanded.

"Bottom line is you should be the one controlling the network," Richard said. "Permanently. For it to happen, Brad should never be able to return. Nor should anyone else fight you for it, right?"

"Right," said Steven, nodding.

"Consider the scenarios," continued Richard. "Possibility number one... we get Brad and only him as you said. Then, the rest won't have any reason to stay out of the country, especially his wife. He is, after all, the reason they agreed to run. The brothers... after what they did, no board member, no court will trust them with power over a structure like the network. But Mrs. Kingsley... she's the only wronged party in the whole Cuba fiasco since she was the only one who never agreed to Brad's little gamble. She also gave the military the sob story about Charlie attacking her. Sheppard will use his position as the network's chairman to hammer in both points with every board member. He could also talk one or more of Brad's brothers into supporting her. If the tactic fails to sway the board, they will approach the courts. The only consolation is Brad's death will happen outside the country, so many will dismiss it as coincidence... wrong place, wrong time... mugging... some excuse can be made so we don't get slammed with criminal charges. Regardless, with Mrs. Kingsley remaining blameless, end result will be a demand for us to return the rights on every last share. What if she talks the government into turning over administrative control as well to her? The CEO position doesn't need to depend on her share of the company stock. Your grandfather can confirm there's a chance she would win."

"Couldn't this happen even without the press conference?" asked Steven.

"Yes," Richard acknowledged. "But now, Sheppard can point out he warned everyone about the Kingsleys. We're talking about an assassination attempt on a former president, followed by the death of a once-powerful fellow connected to him. The authorities will certainly investigate further. The majority party... the minority... and we're not talking about the United States alone."

"Yeah." Steven nodded. Perhaps one or two desperate autocrats would've tried it if it were simply a matter of Harry dying too soon after the Cuba episode. Now... "Every dime-store dictator will see Brad's death as a damn good opening to put the squeeze on us."

"Exactly," said Richard. "Once again... remember the reason for the transfer of power." The same ethical concerns which supposedly forced Brad to resign could be applied to Steven. "There is also the problem of members smelling blood in the water. The probability of Sheppard winning a board vote or in court shoots up."

"Got it," said Steven. Politicians aside, it wasn't as though the member companies of the network were run by meek, unambitious leaders who would pass up a chance to make a power play. "All right... Sheppard is the strategist, so we focus on him first. There will be a little more delay than we anticipated, but we can make it happen."

"Every delay makes it more likely your cousin will get a pardon," Richard said. "Let's imagine the press conference didn't happen, and we target Sheppard an acceptable amount of time has passed. Let's also say we succeed. Mrs. Kingsley will immediately—and correctly—conclude Brad is unlikely to get a pardon in the foreseeable future with neither Mr. Temple nor Petty Officer Sheppard to help. She will return, with or without Brad and his brothers. Who knows? It might even push Alex into the same conclusions. He could also return and support her."

Steven objected, "But without Sheppard—"

"Without Sheppard and without the presser he did, Mrs. Kingsley *might* be able to create enough hue and cry to catch the government's attention," Richard elaborated. "With your grandfather on our side, what she says could be dismissed as the rantings of a woman who can't accept the fact she lost. Which is why the press conference is a problem. She will remind every man, woman, and child in the country about Sheppard's accusations. His family will also likely pay attention. Suspicion... investigations... same outcome as the hitjob on Brad."

"He wouldn't be able to return, but we'd lose to her," brooded Steven.

"You think it would stop with a loss?" mocked the family patriarch. "The Kingsleys will pay with blood for Harry's death. Lilah will make sure of it. Don't repeat the mistake of underestimating her, Steven. I let your friend take the lead in Cuba, and he seems to have imagined she would make an easy target... big miscalculation. She has the potential to be far more ruthless than any of you... than even Harry. She *cannot* be left to live after Harry's death."

The major was allowed to lead because the former justice wanted to maintain his clean reputation, but Richard didn't deny the accusation. "Mrs. Kingsley is cunning. Also, stubborn and ambitious. The combination is dangerous. She is Sheppard's preferred candidate. Even from the grave, he will make sure she remains in control. If he doesn't die, he will use every trick in the book to get Brad his pardon."

"A move worthy of a grandmaster," Godwin interjected. "Eliminate the black king, and the queen wins the game. Don't eliminate him, and he gets the time to work on a new approach."

"Possibility three," said Richard. "We get Mrs. Kingsley first."

"Harry will go from merely dangerous to absolutely lethal," Godwin said. "An enemy with nothing left to lose is the enemy we have the most to fear from. But there's uncertainty involved in waiting for an adversary to destroy himself... we found out in the Parker situation." The ploy was tried using the rapist, but the criminal got himself killed, instead.

Richard shook his head. "I would've advised against the strategy if I knew about it before. On one hand, you were counting on the enemy losing it to the extent of going on a suicide mission. On the other, you were hoping he retained enough sense not to risk collateral damage and try something like a... say, a bomb explosion... which you would've had little protection against. Too risky."

"Understand the psychology of your opponent better, Mr. Armor," Godwin said. "It's critical both in a courtroom and in the war room. Harry *would* have lost it if Lilah died at Parker's hands. What he would not have done is consciously opt for any plan which could cause civilian casualties." The former justice smiled almost to himself. "Lilah's ghost wouldn't have let him make the mistake. Unfortunately, Parker turned out to be a loose cannon. Regardless, it remained a potential path forward for us... until the press conference. Now, if Harry attacks..."

"Can't we ask for protection?" Steven queried. "Same as you planned before with Parker?"

"On what grounds?" asked Godwin. "It was different when Temple was with me. A former president can request enhanced security, and it's not likely anyone will balk. Before the media stunt, we could've at least tried claiming we need protection against Harry because he was blaming us for what happened in Cuba. Or we could've hired private security. No matter what we opted for, Harry would've attacked once something happened to Lilah and your cousin. Our men would've retaliated. We might have been able to pass Harry's death off as the tragic outcome of an act of violence by an unhinged man. Not any longer. The media will immediately decide we planned it."

"The incident count against Steven will go up to five," agreed Richard. "The problems in Cuba, the attack on Sheppard in New York, the attempt on Mr. Temple, Mrs. Kingsley's death, and finally, Petty Officer Sheppard."

"Even if Brad is left alive, he's not likely to get a pardon without anyone to help," Steven mused. "But the board won't want me to continue, either."

"Brad's brothers..." Richard shook his head. "Let's say they return, but the board won't let them take over. Most likely, control would pass to a surrogate they agree on. Dan Barrons is certainly a possibility... or his father. Perhaps a complete outsider. There could even be a succession war. None of which is a good outcome for us."

"The major is trying to explain why we're back to needing all three on the list to go," said the Kingsley patriarch. "Brad's brothers, too, to make sure there are no loose ends. There shouldn't be significant delay between any of the moves. It's the most complicated of all approaches but also the least likely to cause problems in the future provided we carry it out after an adequate amount of time passes. Steven, I hope you understand I'm talking about the situation prior to the press conference."

"Now," said Richard, "even if no one from their side remains, there's a good chance the board will act. Or the courts. Or both."

"The kids," mused Godwin. "Even their guardianship will be accounted for. We will not be allowed anywhere near the network or the boys."

"It's like the president's wife claiming her husband tried to kill the Democrats," Charles said, tone mournful. "Nobody would believe her now, but if she died tomorrow, the Congress and all those people will ask President Bush to resign."

Everyone in the room glanced at Charles, not quite certain how to respond to the succinct summary coming from the most unexpected of sources.

"So we can't do a damn thing about Brad or Harry or Lilah for a long, long time," Steven finally said, flopping back into the couch. "Shit."

"Not until the public forgets about Sheppard's accusations," Richard agreed. "Which could be a couple of years from now... maybe more. Unfortunately, if we let it go on too long, there's a good chance he *will* find a way to bring Brad back."

"Harry's working on something as we speak," Godwin interjected.

"You can bet on it," Richard agreed.

Tone dubious, Steven asked, "Without money?"

Godwin halted in his pacing and wheeled around to face Steven. "Weren't you listening the last few minutes? In a single day, Harry managed to put a stop to our... it's insurance against anything happening to anyone on their side, even their families."

"Defensive tactics," said Richard. "He's planning an offensive strike... we need to figure out where, when, and how."

"And what do we do with the info?" Steven muttered. "Sit on it?"

Richard smiled. "No. We get Sheppard and your cousins and Mrs. Kingsley as soon as we can."

"Huh?" Steven frowned. "But you just said—"

"The enemy changed his game plan, and we will change ours accordingly," Richard said, scribbling something on his notepad.

"Sheppard is anticipating our moves and accounting for them. So let's see if we can get someone else to do the job for us. Someone Sheppard would not see coming."

"Put even a grandmaster under enough pressure," Godwin said, "he becomes too focused on checkmating the king, and he blunders. He forgets there are other pieces—pawns—which can as easily take him out."

Richard nodded.

"Intelligence," Godwin remarked, looking approvingly toward his servant's son. "Blood always tells."

What the hell now? Steven glanced at Richard, but his wary eyes were fixed on the former justice.

"You look like your mother," Godwin continued. "Got her brains, too. And the strong will."

Steven always thought Richard's mother was sweet, but she never struck him as particularly sharp or strong-willed. But then, she'd raised a son like Richard. So perhaps Godwin was right.

Richard's face darkened. "I'm adopted as you well know."

With a small smile, Godwin said, "I do know. You do look like her."

Weird. Steven made a mental note to warn Richard about compliments from Godwin Kingsley. He'd complimented Brad and his brothers often enough. Look where it led.

Evidently, Richard harbored similar thoughts. "Thank you?" he said, an inflection at the end of his words.

"You said we need to get everyone together," muttered Charles. "But we don't know where Cousin Brad is."

"Hopefully, it won't be long before we do," said Richard. The feds were also looking, but they'd already refused to share any findings with the Kingsleys though Steven had been part of the original investigation. With all the accusations and counteraccusations floating around after Cuba, the government thought it prudent to keep the family out altogether. Didn't matter. In fact, it could even work out in the Kingsleys' favor how they were never officially told about the exiles' hideout... less chance of being accused of killing them. The trackers hired by Steven and Richard were anyway on the job. "Our plan for Sheppard needs to be ready to go at a moment's notice. Once we locate the exiles, we must take care of all of them at a single go."

"Too bad," Godwin muttered. When the rest of the room turned toward him, he added, "It's a shame Mr. Armor was not born a Kingsley. I might actually have to tell your mother as much."

First, derision, now, unstoppable affection. What was the Kingsley patriarch up to?

"I'm happy where I am," Richard said, mild mockery in his eyes. Major Richard Armor was no Brad Kingsley to be taken in by empty words.

"What do you recommend?" Steven asked. "For Harry, I mean."

Richard twirled his pen around. "Steven, you said something about the other Sheppards having knives out for Harry. We need to see—"

"Not the Sheppards," Godwin said thoughtfully. "There's someone who wants Harry gone even more than us. Armor, I want you to talk to this person. Also, keep an eye on Harry. Anything out of the ordinary, report to us. I'll call Temple's son tonight about the legal guardianship. We simply cannot afford to have him say anything... he can't be allowed to open his mouth to the media or the authorities or anyone at all about the Kingsleys. You, Steven, focus on locating the exiles and keep in touch with Hector. Make sure the Sheppards never have reason to suspect us."

"What about the Barronses?" asked Steven, speculating silently on who the former justice's pawn could be. "Lilah's brother could start trouble."

"I want the older one watched—Shawn," said Godwin. "The feds think it was he who helped Lilah put the virus into her computer. His support of her is unexpected... and worrisome."

"Maybe," said Steven. "Daniel's her twin, so I'd worry more about him. What if he talks Andrew into—"

"Not going to happen," dismissed Godwin. "I know Andrew. The brother who could create problems is Shawn, and the father figure we need to watch is Temple."

"Fine," said Steven. "My job's gonna be easy. Hector already trusts me, and Brad's little brothers have made enough enemies over the last few years. Lilah, too. People will line up to volunteer."

"The criminal class is not to be trusted," said the patriarch. "You should find someone within the FBI. Such informants rarely blab since they have almost as much to lose. In fact, I'd use someone else to contact the FBI. The trick is to create so many layers the name of the person who made the original request becomes impossible to trace."

"Easier to find a criminal within the criminal class." Steven grinned. "Much cheaper, too. All it takes is the hint of a reward for information leading to their capture."

Eyes narrowed, Godwin said, "I hope you're right. Make sure you don't do anything to damage the Kingsley reputation."

Steven laughed. "Grandfather, the family honor is already in tatters. I'm considered halfway to a criminal, and Cousin Brad betrayed the nation."

"Get to work," commanded Godwin Kingsley, extreme annoyance in the glance darting between his grandson and the son of his chauffeur. "Steven, wait here. We have things to discuss... the operations of the Peter Kingsley Company and the network."

Steven oversaw the workings of both entities in his capacity as CEO, but Godwin expected his commands to be carried out without question. After what happened to Lilah, Steven wasn't about to decline. Plus, Godwin Kingsley's sharp mind and the experience of his eighty-three years were not to be discounted. The old man was physically fit, too. The Kingsleys who didn't drink themselves to death or otherwise die of unnatural causes tended to live well into their nineties, mental faculties intact. Godwin most certainly expected to do the same and would pull every trick to control the family business even from the grave.

When the door shut behind the rest, Steven warily eyed the old fellow as he unlocked one of the cupboards and brought out the chessboard. All the Kingsley grandchildren were forced to learn to play, but none retained interest. There were Godwin's cronies at the club he could match wits with, and he sometimes played himself.

"Sit down, son," said the patriarch, setting up the board with its hand-carved pieces on the desk. Carefully, he placed the last figure—the white bishop—next to the king. "Know what this is?"

Incredulously, Steven stared. The old man wanted a game?

Without waiting for an answer, the former justice said, "The priest, Steven. Clergy always stand next to the royal family. Symbolic, don't you think?"

Was it? A hard churning started in Steven's belly. "I... ahh... priest?"

"Priest... bishop... same thing. It is my opinion they're the most challenging of all pieces to master. I told you before... for the king to have power, the priest needs to bless him. Sometimes, he turns out to be of little help. In such cases, you trade the weak priest."

Steven couldn't help the gulp which escaped his throat. He didn't want to hear any more. He simply wanted to be away... as far away as possible.

"You don't have a clue, do you?" Lips curling in disgust, the patriarch stared at the Kingsley scion for a few moments. With a short, violent swipe, Godwin swept the figures off the board. "Get out of here."

Not waiting another second, Steven ran. He didn't stop sweating until his car exited the gates of the Kingsley mansion.

Part IV

Chapter 10

Later in the year

New York, New York

A phone call to one of the downtown restaurants had taken care of the Thanksgiving meal, but except for Harry, Sabrina, and Michael, there was no one at the table. Reflected in the eyes of the other two, Harry saw his own worry over the people who were missing from their lives. Happy voices from the past echoed in his mind, the forced cheer in the apartment not fooling even the young boy.

Every now and then, the three of them would throw glances at the phone, but it stayed mute. There were no calls from the Sheppard residence, and neither Harry nor Sabrina felt compelled to forgive and forget.

Dante was in California with his son, but Lilah's brothers visited toward the evening. As always, Dan wanted updates on any potential pardon and reported on developments at Barrons O & G. A golf game in Florida with a board member where he was careful not to mention anything about his sister, hosting a dinner for a septuagenarian VIP and his fourth bride-to-be... unfortunately, the coalition he was building would be of no help until the exiles were absolved of their alleged crimes.

The only other people Sabrina talked to on the holiday were Alex's mother and Victor's son, Gabriel. Patrice declined the invitation to lunch, apparently preferring to spend the day with Aaron Kingsley. Both went to NYU Medical Center to visit Temple and dined on hospital-provided food with Noah Andersen. Temple had been taken off life support machines, but he appeared confused, his speech garbled. Nor could he write anything though motor functions seemed otherwise normal. Neurologists were still running tests.

December brought the horrific news of a bomb explosion on Pan Am Flight 103 over Lockerbie in Scotland, which killed all two-hundred-and-forty-three passengers and crew members. Libyan terrorists were suspected to be behind the attack. Apart from an odd mention or two of Harry's connection to the place, his name disappeared from the front pages. So did the former president's.

Temple continued to make no sense whatsoever. The rescue plan for the exiles was stalled. Unless of course Lupe Valdez consented to help. Harry would keep shuttling between New York and DC and petition her until she showed mercy or got him thrown in jail for stalking.

He got Sabrina a gun, and there was a security agency hired to keep an eye on the apartment. Also, in case she needed muscle when going out. Neither Noah nor Harry believed there would be an attack on Sabrina or Michael. The press conference put paid to the possibility at least for the time being. Still, they couldn't take the chance of her being alone and without help when Harry was out of town.

#

Cold wind whistled in behind Harry as he opened the door to his apartment building. He took the stairs two steps at a time, dreading facing Sabrina. There would be the same question she always asked after one of his trips to DC. Did Ms. Valdez agree to talk? Harry would have to give the same response. No, but she hadn't rejected the idea, either. At least, not according to Liam.

"Ghostbusters!" the screaming voices of children filtered out from under the door as the title song of the eponymous cartoon played on television.

When Harry entered, Michael was playing with his toy soldiers in one corner, not paying any mind to the Saturday show. The little boy looked up, his mouth curving in a hint of a grin, but he didn't move from his spot.

Sabrina was on the couch, face red with anger, eyes shooting flames at the magazine on her lap. She threw the periodical to the side. "Someone shoved this under the door." The latest edition of *People* carried a picture of the Peter Kingsley family in happier times on its cover. Taken at Michael's christening from the looks of it. "The article is all about how greed brought us down." Angry tears ran down her cheeks. "Alex... they say he... he... that he and Lilah... don't they realize he has a wife and child?" Wiping the wetness under her nose with the back of a hand, she added, "There's another one which says they're together somewhere, and I'm *here*. And it's true!"

There was nothing Harry could say in response. Sabrina had been a delightful young girl and grew up to be a lovable woman, but even she had limits to her tolerance.

"I'm sorry," Sabrina said. "I know... *I know* there's nothing between them. I handled it until now. Brad's idiotic fantasy, that's all. And gossip. Now... so many pitying articles." On a mirthless spurt of laughter, she added, "Poor Lilah. They make her sound like some idiot schoolgirl pining after her husband's brother. There's the same stupid rumor about Lilah romancing all the brothers, too. And guess what? Gossip is Lilah got you and Andersen to do the press conference because she wants revenge on the Kingsleys. Revenge! How about what *they* did to—" Breaking off, Sabrina huffed. "No one wants to hear the truth. They will all believe what they want to believe."

"Know what, Runt?" Harry asked.

"What?"

"You and Alex getting married is probably the only thing to go right for Lilah in the whole mess."

For a second or two, Sabrina simply stared. Then, she exploded into a high-pitched wail, followed by loud sobs.

Michael looked up in alarm. "Mama," he called, voice quavering.

Wildly waving a hand in the air, she called him to her. "I miss your daddy, that's all," she said, weeping into Michael's hair.

The boy cuddled close. "Me, too."

"I didn't mean to upset you more," Harry offered.

"You didn't," she said. "It really is because I miss Alex. I wish I could do something... *any*thing... instead of waiting around and letting you do the heavy lifting. Lilah... if there was something I could do to help... we were—are—*sisters*."

"Sisters forever," Michael recited. "Down with patriarchy!"

Harry blinked. "What?"

"Oh, Mikey!" Laughing through her tears, Sabrina dropped a kiss on her son's temple. "He's heard me say it. My boy knows how to make his mama happy."

Michael explained, "She's a femininist."

"Feminist," Harry corrected.

"That, too?" Michael asked.

Feeling off-balance, Harry said, "No, I mean—"

Wiping off her tears with the back of her hand, Sabrina interjected, "Harry, let me tell you before I forget. Verity's father called."

"What did *he* want?"

Sabrina shrugged. "I didn't pick up. Thought it might be the press. He left a message."

Harry walked to the console and pressed the playback button on the answering machine. Over the grainy sound of winding tape, Will Luce said, "Er... Harry, m'boy. It's Will. I... er... I was hoping we could talk. It's important." Harry frowned. Will rattled off a string of digits. Before he heard the whole message, Harry hit erase. It wasn't as though he didn't already know the phone number.

"What do you think he wants to talk about?" Sabrina asked.

"Nothing I'm going to like hearing, I'm sure," Harry said. "He'll have to wait his turn."

"What about Liam? Did you get to meet him?"

Harry tossed his jacket carelessly onto the coffee table and collapsed next to her on the couch. "Yes, I talked to *Liam*, but I'm waiting for... Runt, I was going to tell you later, but now's as good a time as any. You might hear stories about me which could be embarrassing."

"Involving Ms. Valdez?"

"Perhaps," Harry admitted. "No. I cannot tell you more. The fewer people in the know, the easier it will be for me to maintain my cover so to speak."

"Just stay safe, please," Sabrina said, a brooding look on her face. "Harry, I know it's probably more convenient if you're alone. I *am* looking for a place of our own for Mikey and me. Only, Patrice is staying with Aaron, and I don't want to move too far from her, so it may take time."

"You're not in the way. Stay here as long as you like."

"Yeah, but—"

"Believe me, it's better than coming home to an empty apartment. If you leave, I'll be alone with my thoughts."

There was relief in her smile. "It won't be for long, anyway. They'll be able to return, won't they?" she asked, desperate hope in her eyes. "Even if Ms. Valdez doesn't agree to help, the government will eventually have to admit Brad didn't actually do anything wrong. We can go to court or something to get the charges dismissed... right?"

"It's not what Brad did or didn't do at this point. He has become the symbol of corporate greed in the eyes of the public, and no politician fond of his career will dare express support. Without Temple in our corner, the Kingsley family has enough clout to make sure of it. Unless we find a way around it. As for going to the courts... Noah says trial in absentia would not work in this case, and even if it did, the outcome might not be to our liking. Right now, Brad has only been *accused* of treason. If the legal system agrees Brad betrayed the nation, no president would issue a pardon no matter how much time passes."

Another sob escaped Sabrina. "What if they can't... if they don't..." Screwing up her face, she tried to stop fresh tears. "Alex... and I can't do a single thing about any of it!"

Unless of course she chose to go on the run with him, making their young son a fugitive, as well.

Harry watched helplessly as his sister grieved, a fresh burst of rage engulfing him. For the millionth time since the exiles left, he wondered if it wouldn't be better to let Brad rot in military prison and get the rest to return. Not merely for Sabrina's sake. Dammit, Harry would've sold his soul to have the life Brad threw away. Hugging his sister to his side, Harry swore, "I will do everything in my power to bring your husband home."

"What exactly are you going to—"

"Uncle Harry," Michael called.

"Yes, buddy?"

"Can we get a tree so Santa can leave presents under it?"

#

The next day, Christmas Eve

Grayson Sheppard paid a visit in the afternoon.

"Everything okay, Uncle Gray?" Harry asked, both he and Michael studying the artificial pine delivered by the department store. Pre-decorated. Not ideal but better than nothing. Harry threw a glance over his shoulder. "I'm surprised my father didn't stop you from keeping in touch with us."

Settling himself next to Sabrina on the couch, Grayson smiled. "I'm the lawyer for our exiles. If helping them means working with you, Ryan cannot stop me." Also, before Grayson joined the Peter Kingsley Company, he was the chairman of the New York Stock Exchange. It wouldn't be easy even for the CEO of Gateway to tell him what to do. "Harry, I have to go to Lilah."

Pivoting, Harry asked, "Did something happen?"

"No," Grayson assured. "Her intern... the young Nepali lady..."

"Hema?" Sabrina asked. "Isn't she still with Patrice?" Shawn had offered Hema a job in his consulting company. Thinking she'd be more comfortable with people her own age, Sabrina suggested renting with some of her coworkers, but Hema adamantly refused, pleading with Patrice to be allowed to stay with her.

Grayson nodded. "She's been calling me every day and threatening to go look for Lilah herself."

"Uncle Gray!" Sabrina stood and paced the living room. "You can't possibly send Hema to her."

"I know," Grayson said, tone exasperated. "But I'm worried she's going to try something drastic. Run away or something."

Harry asked, "Won't the feds go after Hema once she meets Lilah? Hema might not even be able to return to the U.S."

"Exactly," Grayson said, nodding vigorously. "I'm just hoping Lilah can talk her into returning to India, at least. Better than having the young lady go hitchhiking across the planet. Anyway, it's not why I'm here. Lilah asked me to do a few things for her."

Harry left his nephew shaking the wrapped packages at the bottom of the tree and collapsed into one of the chairs. "What does she need?"

"Not only her. All of them changed their wills because no one expected this scenario. I'm going to file papers for them."

Breath caught in Harry's chest. The lawyer's words... the deaths of the exiles seemed a very real possibility all of a sudden. Sabrina whimpered. Harry stared at the elderly visitor, unable to respond.

Grayson considered the shocked siblings and gently added, "Sabrina, Lilah asked me to talk to you after she left. She specified I needed to do so privately. I went to your parents' home first. I didn't know you were going to be here."

Sabrina sniffed. "It's fine, Uncle Gray. She probably didn't want my parents or Hector to overhear. I don't think she'd mind Harry."

"Even before the whole Cuba mess, Lilah changed her will. Almost all of it goes to Michael, with you as executor. Harry and one of her Indian cousins—a General Mittal—will be trustees. If...er... for

114

some unfortunate reason, Michael cannot inherit, the entirety of it is supposed to go to an orphanage in India. Something else..." Grayson dug into his satchel, coming up with a carved box.

Harry got up and went to the window. Hands on the sill, he stood looking out at the street while fear swirled within. Lilah couldn't die. No matter what, he couldn't let it happen.

Grayson Sheppard's measured tones didn't make what he said any easier to bear. "It's her jewelry. Sabrina, I've been asked to tell you to let Victor's wife pick out a couple of pieces. You are to keep the rest."

Sabrina choked down a sob. "Couldn't *you* keep it, Uncle Gray? In your office or something? Lilah can take it from there when she returns."

"The entire box goes to Luisa if you decide you don't want it," Grayson said. "Also, these... Lilah did want you to put some pieces to the side to return to her when she's back home." He grunted. "Dammit... the bag's stuck in my pocket... got it."

"Her mom's jewelry?" Sabrina asked.

"Must be," Grayson said. "If she doesn't make it back, give them to Dan."

Harry gritted his teeth against the sudden squeeze in his left chest.

"This, too?" came Sabrina's voice. "This one can't be her mom's. It's only a trinket."

"Sentimental value, maybe?" Grayson offered.

Harry turned. Even before he looked, he knew what he'd find. In Sabrina's hands was a thin silver chain, dulled gray by time, with a small pendant in the shape of the Eiffel Tower.

#

The same night

For the first time in years, the lights were off in Harry's room. He lay across his bed, the hand holding the silver chain resting on his bare chest. His eyes were on the ceiling, but he saw nothing. Turning the pendant over and over between his fingers, he wandered the memories of the last few hours of their innocence.

Back in Paris, the spirit of his adult self leaned a hip against the backrest of a park bench. He rolled his eyes at the corny banter of a young couple in the throes of first love. Following them as they sprinted up the tower, he watched without shame as they kissed. When the boy promised his sweetheart a lifetime of laughter and friendship and kisses, Harry raged at the faithless sonuvabitch.

Outside the window of his room, an obscene curse was shouted in a loud voice. Harry snapped open his eyes, only then realizing they'd been closed. Voices were raised in argument... probably a couple of the drunks living in the Palace Hotel. The full moon cast a glow over the nearly empty streets.

The clock radio next to the bed said it was still many hours to dawn. Needing a glass of water, Harry left the room and started in surprise when he saw the child sitting cross-legged on the wood floor, partly hidden by the Christmas tree. "Waiting for Santa, buddy?" Harry asked.

Looking up with a jump, Michael shoved something behind him.

As Harry dropped to one knee next to Michael, the boy tapped a glittery red bauble with his finger, making it swing back and forth. Out of the corner of his eye, he peered at his uncle. Michael shook his head and grinned, displaying the newly acquired gap in his teeth. The little boy in Garfield pajamas and the bare-chested man looked at each other, both wearing identical expressions of speculation.

"I got a secret," Michael finally offered in barely suppressed excitement.

Resting his weight on one elbow, Harry stretched out his legs. "Wanna share?"

Michael glanced both ways before leaning forward. He said in a hushed whisper, "Daddy's gonna call. It's almost Christmas... Daddy won't forget. He always calls on special days."

#

An hour later

"The new cell phones," Sabrina said, tone miserable. "I bought them through a friend from college who works for Motorola. The model's not out on the market yet. Flip type... small and light. You can actually carry it with you most places. Plus, you'll get almost an hour's worth of talk time. Mikey must have taken one from my luggage."

The current devices used by the senior businessmen Harry knew—including himself—were not exactly portable. They needed to be plugged in nearly constantly. Unless he was next to a power outlet, a cell phone was not of much use.

"I gave Alex the numbers," Sabrina continued. "You know... to call me in case of emergencies, but he can't... not unless it's life or death. It's very easy to monitor these devices."

Harry pinched the bridge of his nose. "I hope Alex has the good sense *not* to call. You need to explain to Mike."

The child was now asleep on the couch. "He misses his family," his mother whispered, kneeling on the floor. Sabrina stroked her son's head lightly, but when she tried to gather him in her arms, he curled upon himself, murmuring in protest.

"Leave him here with me," Harry suggested. "There's some work to finish, so I'll be up." A lie, but Harry didn't want to return to bed.

117

The sun was barely coming up when Michael stirred. Looking up from the newspaper, Harry said, "'Morning, Mike. Merry Christmas."

"My presents!" Michael grinned and sat up, hurriedly kicking away the blanket twisted around his legs. A worried frown replaced the excitement on his face. "Am I in trouble?"

Harry laughed. "No. You simply wanted to talk to your daddy. It's hard to understand right now, but I don't think he'll be able to call. Not just yet anyway."

The boy's face fell. "But it's a special day," he whispered. "Daddy always calls on special days if he's not home."

"There are some people... some bad people... if your daddy calls, they might catch him."

"But I miss him," Michael whimpered. "And Lilah. And Uncle Victor. And everybody."

Harry studied the lad for a few moments. "Wanna know something, buddy?"

"What?"

"Your daddy and I are good friends. Before he left, he asked me to take care of you when he's not around. I assume it includes wishing you a great time on special days."

Michael's eyes rounded. "Are you and Daddy 'bros,' like Uncle Victor says?"

"Your mama is my sister," Harry answered gravely. "So yes, your daddy is my bro, and bros stick together."

"But Daddy's not here to stick to you. So who's your bro now?"

"I... uhh... guess I don't have one."

Michael offered, "*I* could be your bro if you like."

There was a strange warmth in Harry's chest. Tossing the newspaper to the coffee table, he gestured at Michael. "C'mon over here." The boy scrambled up, nearly tumbling over the blankets on his way to Harry. Steadying his nephew with an arm around his thin shoulders, Harry said, "I'd be honored to have you as my bro."

"Only 'til Daddy gets back," Michael warned. "Afterward, I'll find myself a new bro who's not so old."

Harry laughed. "All right. Now... go and open your presents." The phone on the side table rang, startling both uncle and nephew. Harry reached for the device. "Hello?" he said into the receiver. Club music played in the background.

"Liam here," the caller bellowed over the noise. "The lady you wanted to meet? She said yes."

Chapter 11

Christmas Day, 1988

Midtown, New York City

Outside the window of the Turtle Bay apartment, the sun was not yet up, and mild winter fog hovered over the East River. The UN building loomed not too far away. At the kitchenette, Richard poured coffee for himself and rubbed his fingertips over hair which was dyed black. No residue. The stubble which took a couple of days to grow had also been dyed last night. The brown contact lenses covering his blue irises were mildly irritating but manageable. Even his lashes were painted black. "You think I'll pass for an Irish mechanic?"

Steven sprawled in the chair in front of the television, watching a woman in elf costume trying to sell men's watches to the audience of the Home Shopping Channel. "Maybe slouch a little. Try not to look so... military." He groaned. "Rich, I'm sorry about Grandfather."

Godwin Kingsley had forbidden Steven from accompanying Richard, proclaiming how making deals with criminals in prison for attempted murder was a task meant for servants... not masters.

Richard took a sip of the brew. Black, no sugar. "Don't be," he said, meaning it.

From the time he rescued five-year-old Steven from a garden maze, the younger lad followed Richard everywhere. While he initially found it mildly irritating, the ingratiating smiles thrown his way by all the heiresses in the zip code whenever he was with the Kingsley boys soon changed his attitude for him. He saw how Steven continued to call him "friend," ignoring the taunts thrown his way by the other rich boys in their fancy Upper East neighborhood. So Richard gritted his teeth at Justice Kingsley's insulting words and reminded himself of the loyalty he owed Steven.

"He's right not to let you," Richard explained patiently. "But not for those reasons. If you go with me, and we get caught... you're the CEO of the network."

"I get it. Anything I do can be used against me. It could also be used against Kingsley Corp and Grandfather."

"More importantly, you're Justice Kingsley's only remaining heir." There was Charles, but he was worse than useless.

The former justice also refused to help arrange a private meeting between Richard and the criminal they had in mind, making it clear the servant was expected to take care of it on his own. The trail could not lead back to the Kingsleys. Richard wasn't worried. After multiple tours in Vietnam, he was no stranger to covert operations.

He needed to do this for Steven. The press conference performance by Harry Sheppard caused worse damage than perhaps even *he* anticipated. No one took the insinuation about the Kingsleys being involved in the assassination attempt seriously, but more than a few journalists scoffed at Steven's claim he didn't know Brad was going to sign over rights to what the media called the throne of the oil empire. Some magazines even suggested it might be a bloodless coup orchestrated by none other than Steven's uncle. The transcript of the interrogation in Cuba was not available to the public, but Lilah Kingsley's claim her husband was tricked by Stanley Gander somehow leaked to the press. Also, Noah Andersen was giving interview after interview, managing to plant *more* doubts in the collective mind of the nation about Steven.

The one bright spot was Temple's convenient incapacitation. *Very* convenient. What Richard could not figure out was how the former justice arranged it. There was nothing—*nothing*—to direct suspicion at the Kingsley patriarch. Even law enforcement wasn't looking for evidence pointing to the family no matter what Petty Officer Sheppard claimed. Not at this time and perhaps not unless one more propitious death forced attention onto the matter. Still... Richard didn't believe in coincidences.

Even if the killer failed, Temple remained unable to communicate. There was marked relief on Godwin's face on hearing the information. As had probably been on his own, Richard admitted. Pleasure at the timely impairment afflicting their enemy was not enough to suspect the Kingsley patriarch.

Richard would do what he said he would... he'd go to Rikers, the notorious prison. Correction: Rickie Brennan, car mechanic, would be going there. The fellow would claim to be a friend of one of the inmates.

Setting the coffee down, Richard gingerly picked up the grease-stained leather jacket from the bar stool next to the countertop. Even as a relatively poor lad growing up alongside the wealthy Kingsleys, he'd taken care to wear good clothes. Never second-hand like this jacket. If his parents harbored concerns about the money he spent keeping up with his rich friends, they never voiced it.

Frowning, he wondered how the senior Armors could prefer the tiny rooms over the Kingsley garage to this magnificent apartment he'd initially bought for them. From the fittings in the bathroom to the pieces of furniture carefully selected by the interior designer, the place was luxurious. Even the seven-foot Christmas tree next to the window was decorated with real crystal ornaments. By professionals, of course. Not that he could enjoy any of it the next few days.

"Steven, I'm going to the airport straight from Rikers," Richard said. "Problems in Corpus Christi." The drilling company he bought was located in the city. "It's the local FBI chief," he explained. "He wants to interview me tomorrow."

"Something wrong?"

Richard waved a hand. "Issues with some contract employees. No documentation."

"It's Texas. Workers walk back and forth across the border all the time."

"Tell it to the FBI chief."

"Will it cause problems for you?"

Richard waved a hand. "Nah. More of a nuisance than anything else. I'll be back in a couple of days." He grinned. "Can't miss your engagement party."

He still found it hard to believe. Oh, Steven liked women just as much as Richard did, but he always made it clear to the ladies who came through his life the title of Mrs. Steven Kingsley was not on the table. Apparently, the professional wrestler he met very recently at Hector Sheppard's gym changed his mind for him. Richard had been sure Godwin would object, but it didn't happen. All the former justice focused on these days was control of the empire. Also, Steven made it amply clear he wouldn't tolerate interference in his choice of friends, much less his freedom to decide whom he married. Godwin Kingsley surely knew it wasn't a fight worth picking when this much else was going on. Time enough for it once they took care of their enemies.

To Richard's amusement, Steven blushed. "Get going before traffic gets bad," he said.

"It's Christmas," Richard said and wrapped a scarf over the bottom half of his face. The hat was placed firmly on his head. Not only was his identity now hidden from any acquaintance he might pass, no one who lived in the upscale apartment building would see Rickie Brennan and remember the rough mechanic being there. "Not too many people will be out on the roads today."

The phone rang. Richard already had his hand on the wall-set next to the refrigerator when he realized it was Steven's cell phone.

Digging it out from his briefcase, Steven barked, "Hel—Charlie, what do you want?"

There were loud squawks from the bulky device, but the words weren't clear to Richard. The widening of Steven's eyes and the mild trembling of the fingers curled around the phone suggested the news was of some importance.

Stuffing the stained leather jacket into a duffel, Richard said, "Got to get to Rikers by seven."

Steven held up a hand. "Wait. We might have caught a break... and right on time." Smiling in satisfaction, he hung up. "A kid in Colombia got killed for helping a group of fugitives across the river to Ecuador. Apparently, the human-trafficking ring wasn't too happy about someone new encroaching on their territory. His girlfriend gave them the names of the people he smuggled out, and the ring contacted Charlie, hoping to get the reward."

"What?" Richard exclaimed, pulse thundering. "How... fugitives... were they..."

"Yup, you got it right." Steven nodded. "We've located Brad and Lilah." Precisely when they were about to put in place the arrangements for Petty Officer First Class Harry Sheppard.

Chapter 12

An hour later

Rikers Island, New York City

Contrary to Richard's expectations, traffic in New York did not let up even for the birth of the Son of God, but he didn't give a damn. Tapping fingers on the steering wheel, he snarled in satisfaction. Once the morning's meeting was done, Richard would be on his way to repaying the debt he owed Steven. A few old scores would also be settled—not simply with Alex and his brothers but with the woman in their lives, the cunning Mrs. Kingsley.

The clock on the dashboard read six-fifty when Richard pulled up next to the bus stop. Before getting out of the car, he exchanged the cashmere coat for the leather jacket and snapped a tiny diamond stud onto his right ear. Opening the small jar bought specifically for the purpose, he coated his fingers with a thin layer of grease.

Riding the bus, waiting in line at the registration building, being patted down for weapon... filling out forms, waiting again for the shuttle to the housing units... and waiting. The thirty or so people in line in the room were muttering in annoyance. An unkempt toddler wailed for her "joo-sy *now.*"

There was a sudden commotion at one end, accompanied by barking. The chatter in the room came to an abrupt halt.

"All right, everyone," shouted a guard. "Line up against the wall."

"This is unusual," the fortyish black woman next to Richard enunciated.

"Oh, yeah?" snapped the guard. "Write your congressman."

Richard stood very still as the police dog sniffed at him. The German Shepherd's square-cut muzzle got so damned close to his crotch he could feel the wetness in its breath. *Shiny coat, bright eyes,* Richard noted approvingly though he was at the receiving end of the canine officer's suspicions. He liked dogs.

Before Steven Kingsley decided the chauffeur's adopted son would be his best friend, Richard went friendless except for the massive dog once owned by the family patriarch. He sensed a kindred spirit in the intelligent animal—a German Shepherd like this one. They were both servants of the Kingsley family, endowed by God with spirit far outclassing their masters.

Finally convinced Richard was not smuggling contraband into the prison, the police dog's handler moved on to the visitor next in line. At an order from the corrections officer, Richard once again offered his ID—the fake one. Finally, they let him on to the shuttle taking visitors around the detention center. The vehicle looked more like a school bus than prison transport. At his destination, he was again patted down for weapons. Finally, he was allowed into the visiting room, carrying nothing but a white slip of paper with his name and the prisoner's name.

"McCoy," the guard at the inner door shouted for someone, looking back into the room behind.

McCoy—Gateway's former affiliate—once tried to murder Neil Kingsley. At the time, Neil had been staying at McCoy's home in Casablanca, trying to get his company to sign up to the network they were building. No one knew McCoy was embezzling from Gateway. Feeling pressured to open the books, he attempted to poison the young doctor, instead. Daniel Barrons, who accompanied Neil on the trip, was also poisoned. A confluence of fortunate events saved the men's lives. Unfortunately, Harry accused his brother, Hector, of orchestrating the murder attempt, and the friction between the brothers exploded into all-out enmity.

The prisoner walking in wearing the gray jumpsuit didn't look like a cold-blooded murderer. His short, lean build topped with dark, curly hair and blue eyes suggested someone you'd want to have a beer with. He scanned the room, face showing confusion.

"Jimmy," Richard shouted before the man told the officers he didn't see anyone he knew. He leaped out of the chair in blatantly feminine enthusiasm.

Guards rushed. Screams filled the waiting room. A heavy black officer landed on Richard. His spine was slammed against the wall, head hitting concrete. While pain was still radiating from his skull to his neck and shoulders, Richard was patted down a third time. He giggled. From the inside door, McCoy watched, puzzlement in his drawn brows.

Finding no weapons, the guards were convinced Richard was not a threat. They debated whether to let the visit continue.

"Officer, I swear," Richard said. "I was just *so* excited to see Jimmy. Me and him, we go way back. But he left New York and never came back."

Finally, Richard was allowed to return to the table and talk.

"Who are you?" muttered McCoy, sitting rigidly in his chair.

"Your old friend, Rickie Brennan from Hell's Kitchen. We grew up together." When McCoy opened his mouth to object, Richard reached across and caught the prisoner's hand in a tight grip—on top of the table as they were permitted to. Ignoring the looks of disgust from the cops, Richard continued, his face wreathed in an adoring smile, "Shut up and listen. You want to get out of here, right? And you want to make sure the man who put you here pays for what he did. There's someone who can help."

Eyes narrowed in suspicion, McCoy asked, "Who?"

"Will Luce, Harry Sheppard's father-in-law."

Part V

Chapter 13

Same time

Quito, Ecuador

Using payphones to call their lawyer—Grayson Sheppard—was Alex's idea. Before leaving Panama, they arranged for Gray to visit Temple's house daily, the one line they believed unlikely to be tapped. If anyone dared try—including the Kingsleys—the Secret Service would track down the culprit. Steven would be hauled off by federal agents for a long vacation at the expense of the American government.

So the first thing the exiles did after arriving in Quito was to locate a booth to ring Temple's number, leaving a vaguely worded message on the answering machine. Grayson decoded what was said in the message and answered a second call at the time mentioned. Afterward, he continued to talk to the exiles on agreed upon days. Of course they could leave messages at Temple's number in case of emergencies. Then, there was the hotel number which Grayson would use only in matters of life-or-death.

Lilah had not been fond of the plan, because the government itself could try a little snooping. All the feds understood was the former president didn't believe Brad Kingsley knowingly committed a crime. They didn't realize Temple was actively helping the exiles, and the Kingsleys would think twice before trying to claim the well-liked politician was colluding with accused traitors. It would end in Brad's arrest, leaving Lilah alive and possibly free. Not the outcome Godwin and Steven would want, *and* it could lead to closer scrutiny of their own activities. Still, there was a chance—albeit small—the authorities could decide on their own to spy on Temple.

So the exiles would call from random booths, leaving no discernible pattern. The messages left would be kept vague enough to make sure no one pinned anything on Temple. Grayson was supposed to be covered by attorney-client privilege, but there were loopholes the feds could use to force the location of the fugitives from him. If it happened, he promised to create enough ruckus in the media— using Mr. Temple if necessary—to alert the exiles.

Thank God I agreed, Lilah now thought. Or she'd have gone insane, not knowing what was happening back home. And thank God Temple was expected to live. The finest neurologists in the nation were working on the former president, but he was still unable to speak coherently. Neither did he appear to understand anyone. The politician—the most articulate man Lilah knew—was unable to communicate. He couldn't talk, and he couldn't write or read. Locked in his own mind... Temple might have preferred to die.

Tears sprouted in Lilah's eyes, blurring her vision as she strode down the sidewalk toward the payphone, Victor right behind. Impatiently tugging off her glasses, she brushed away the moisture. She didn't want to think of her parents' graves in Green-Wood, didn't want to imagine Temple being laid to rest. There was a time she saw her beloved papa in the politician.

When Lilah returned the glasses to her nose, she was at the intersection across which was the booth. Alex was already hovering right by it. Lines of anxiety marked his face. Victor would be just as worried. Temple was, after all, family to the Kingsley brothers.

The other three men in the group remained in the hotel room since going out all together could draw attention. The brown hair shared by the Kingsley brothers—except for Neil who was blond— did not especially make them stand out in Quito, but they'd grown beards, regardless. Clothes were picked to help the exiles blend in, especially where Lilah was concerned. Loose cotton hoodies pulled low over her forehead, drab jeans, sturdy sneakers, and the spectacles which were now a constant presence on her face helped keep her identity concealed. Unfortunately, Victor's large size could hardly be disguised. Also, unlike his brothers' blue eyes, Alex's were an oddly translucent brown. The only other thing they could do was limit their outings to the later hours of the day.

The sky was fast turning the deep red of twilight, and the shop across the street was pulling down shutters on the nativity scene at the display window. Lilah tugged her hoodie farther over her brow as she and Victor watched for a break in traffic. The neighborhood was unusually light on crowds, but cars were still hurtling down the cobbled street. The salsa music which blasted from shops during business hours had ceded sound space to the purring of engines and frequent honks.

Seizing a lull in the stream of vehicles, Lilah and Victor dashed across, dodging the few other pedestrians. Within seconds, more cars appeared on the road, skidding to a stop at the traffic light, their horns blaring. The payphone rang—probably somebody dialing the wrong number.

Even after the ringing stopped, Alex stayed put, not trying to make the call. Gray was not yet over his anger at what Brad and his brothers did. Lilah's father—the late ambassador—might only have been distantly related to the New York Sheppards, but she carried the same last name until her adoption by Andrew Barrons. As a young boy, Harry called the lawyer Uncle Gray. Therefore so did Lilah and her brother. Grayson Sheppard included the twins among those he considered family.

Gray had made it clear he preferred to converse with Lilah, which was just as well today of all days. The Kingsley brothers had read an interview given by their sainted grandfather, asking for peace. The hopeful looks in their eyes was enough to inform Lilah of the thoughts running through their brains. From the oldest to the youngest, all five believed Godwin's claim he was unaware of what Steven was planning. Once the military got involved, the family patriarch apparently didn't have choice except to play along. As a former supreme court justice, Godwin Kingsley was expected to put the nation's needs ahead of his clan's, and his arguments in Cuba were merely a matter of allowing the law to take its own course.

None of the five brothers would buy what Lilah had to say about Godwin, and she didn't need them wasting precious phone time asking about potential support from him. What she was waiting to hear was an update on Harry's progress and assurance on the safety of the people she left behind. Grayson was unlikely to have anything to say about any new developments in the attempted assassination of the former president. Godwin Kingsley was too smart a man to leave tracks which could lead to him or his cronies. Brad and his brothers remarked nastily on how convenient it was for the evil cousins, but not one of the five would believe Godwin was involved.

Skirting a street cart selling sausage slices and greasy fries, Lilah reached for the door of the booth. As if on cue, the phone resumed ringing.

Rough fingers gripped her elbow. She was jerked backward, and her feet slipped out from under her. The world tilted. Lilah screamed, her free hand flailing. The darkening sky seesawed. Her glasses slid off her nose, hanging from one ear. The back of her head hit something hard. Pain shot across her scalp.

Shouts sounded all around. There was a violent tug on her other arm, and suddenly, she was free. Pushing her glasses back into place, she scrambled up with Alex's hands assisting.

Victor was struggling with a large man next to a stopped car. A plump woman looked on, her mouth hanging open. Another man ran out from the store next to the phone booth. *"¡Llama a la policía!"* he yelled for the cops.

Black clouds moved across the sky, dimming whatever was left of the day. Thunder rumbled. A few drops spattered, then the deluge started. Lilah's hair and clothes were plastered to her body in a matter of seconds.

Victor got the assailant in a headlock. "Run," he bellowed.

Lilah didn't wait for specifics on where. She pivoted and sprinted, Alex at her side. Around them, the few men and women present on the street scurried about in confusion, seeking cover from the sudden squall. Through the downpour, Lilah could barely see two feet in front.

Alex turned to check, continuing to run, but backward. "Victor," he shouted.

"Right here," Victor gasped, appearing at Lilah's other side. He grabbed a large potted plant from outside a shuttered store and pitched it behind them. "Don't stop; the thug's got friends."

"How many?" asked Lilah, not breaking her run.

"Three, altogether," said Victor, urging her to the front.

"Got my gun," Alex grunted.

The last thing they wanted to do was attract the attention of the police by using guns. They would be extradited to the U.S. in a heartbeat. Lilah was about to snap at Alex when Victor said, "Not here." He seized a garbage can and heaved it behind him. Days-old food and plastic bags spilled across the wet road. There were yells, presumably from the thugs. Victor grabbed whatever he found on their way and flung it behind, but the footsteps following them didn't stop. "This way," Victor said, shoving her toward a side street.

Rain poured heavily, lashing across the empty road. They tried to avoid the pools of yellow light cast by streetlamps but still couldn't lose their pursuers. Lilah's lungs burned with the effort, but she managed to keep up with Victor and Alex. Or they were going slow to not let her fall behind.

"They're gaining on us," Victor shouted over the loud sounds of the downpour. As the thundering footsteps got closer, he yelled to Alex, "It's no use; we have to face them."

"Look for—" Lilah began.

Grabbing her arm, Victor pulled her into the nearest alley and thrust her toward the back. The two brothers covered the mouth of the lane, Alex's gun drawn and ready. Lilah took her pistol from the ankle holster and prepared herself. The three assailants came to a halt in front.

The smell of rotten garbage permeated the alley. Fat droplets of water made loud metallic sounds as they beat down on the dumpster. "What do you want?" Victor asked, voice harsh. "Is it money?"

One of the men gestured at Lilah. *"La tipa."*

"The chick?" Alex translated. "They want Lilah? What the hell for?"

The brothers moved shoulder to shoulder, completely blocking her from sight. On the left, Alex growled, then his weapon clicked. Immediately, there was a second click, this one from the criminals.

Victor held his right hand up. "Bro, ask them why they want her."

Without waiting for Alex to interpret, one of the trio spoke, "We get the broad. Those were the orders. Long live the revolution!"

"Revolution?" Alex parroted.

There was a loud hawking sound, then the ruffian on the left—barely visible over Alex's shoulder—spat to the side. "We are RC," he shouted. "You kill Rafael; we make you pay."

Rafael? Who was—Lilah's attention was on the man who was talking when there was a sudden movement at the periphery of her visual field. Victor caught the weapon arm of the criminal on the right. Violently twisting the man's limb, Victor jerked him forward. He kicked out with his left leg at the thug in the middle, hitting him in the crotch. With a high-pitched scream, the second man fell to his knees.

Yelling, the third criminal pointed his gun at Victor, but the shot never came. He crumpled to the ground with a surprised look, clutching his chest, blood gushing between his fingers. Alex turned his smoking weapon on the remaining two.

Victor used his other arm to bend his captive's head over his knee. Lilah couldn't quite see what he was doing, but she heard a sickening crunch. Body flaccid, the criminal fell. His mouth still worked, and his eyes were wide open in shock. The one who was already on the ground, nursing his groin, scrambled up and ran. His screams of fright faded away within seconds.

A man dead from a bullet to the chest, the second one badly injured from what looked like a broken neck. Lilah scanned the street. No witnesses except the thug who fled.

Alex tucked his gun back into his belt and pulled the shirt down over it. "It was them or us; we had no other option."

Lilah took off her glasses and wiped the water from her eyes. "What about the one who escaped?" she asked, the sounds produced by her smoke-damaged vocal cords raspier than usual. Her hands shook unexpectedly.

"Shit," said Victor. "He's gonna have friends."

"Let's get out of here before he decides to bring them to the scene of the crime," Alex said.

Keeping to the shadows, they hurried along the empty streets of Old Town. In this part of the city, residents withdrew to their homes after sundown. Plus, the budget hotel where they were staying was only a few blocks away, so they were likely to make it back before the corpses were discovered.

"Dude," said Alex. "The *hombres* back there said something about revenge for Rafael's death."

So they did, but Lilah was confused. Alex was talking as though he knew who this Rafael was.

Victor's steps faltered. "What?"

"Hilda's brother," snapped Alex. "Remember?"

It took Lilah a few seconds to recollect who Hilda was. Victor's girlfriend who'd died from flu, leaving behind their son. Lilah never got the chance to meet her.

"I do remember," Victor snapped back. "But it makes no sense. Hilda was from Mexico, not Ecuador."

Lilah didn't get it, either. Why were the three Ecuadorian men trying to get her as revenge for Hilda's brother's death? He was a random Mexican-American man they were unlikely to have heard of. Come to think of it, what had the Kingsley brothers done to invite the retaliation?

Voice hard, she asked Victor, "Did you kill this Rafael?"

"Long story," Alex said, squelching further questions.

Not that she asked many questions these days. Lilah had not spoken to any of the Kingsleys since their exile started, not unless absolutely necessary. She didn't even eat with them, preferring the solitude of her room. Right now, getting to safety was her priority, but as soon as they reached the hotel, she'd have to break her silence. She needed to know why she was being hunted for a murder committed years ago, in a city thousands of miles from where it occurred.

Gaze turned firmly away from Lilah, Victor echoed Alex's words from before. "There was no option but to kill him."

Victor always thought he had good reasons for everything he did. Even for his part in enabling Brad's bad behavior. But then, so did the rest. Perhaps the Kingsley brothers' past was catching up with them—and with her. Her lower lip trembled involuntarily.

Rain slowed to a drizzle by the time they reached the door of the hotel, but water still dripped from their clothes. Victor's boots squished when he walked up the narrow stairwell. Lilah was about to follow him when the stairs appeared to tilt sideways. Hand on the railing, she stopped on the first step and tried to blink away the fuzzy feeling in her head. She should have known. The shaking, the trembling, and now, the dizziness—her body's reminder it needed food even as her mind rebelled against the pleasure of eating. Her dinner of lentil soup and herbal tea the night before had been her last meal.

"Are you all right?" Alex asked.

Ignoring his question, she continued up to their rooms. Not hers... no one was allowed in there without express permission. A private chamber for her sandwiched between the accommodations shared by the brothers meant one of the men was always forced to stay up on watch. Assumed identities or not, what happened in Cuba guilted them enough to not take chances with Lilah's safety. Her insistence on privacy also meant they burned more cash every week. There was her Swiss bank account, the money in it to be accessed through checks deposited in a local account opened under a false name. While the Swiss could be relied upon to stay mum about where the money went, the banks in Ecuador were under no such obligation. Hence the false name—a felony. The only other option was to financially cut themselves off. Survival would mean taking on odd jobs, which wouldn't make them the kind of income they needed to keep running. Still, none of the brothers dared suggest she share space with her husband. Even Brad didn't say a word, accepting the living arrangements with a martyred glance.

"You're late," started Brad, opening his door. Taking in their bedraggled, blood-stained appearance, his eyes widened. The normally refined voice raised in alarm, he asked, "What happened?"

Hurrying in, Victor explained, "We didn't even get a chance to talk to Grayson. Someone tried to snatch Lilah. Said something about Rafael."

"Who's Rafael?" asked Scott.

"We need to leave Ecuador," Alex said, closing the door behind him. "Rafael was Hilda's brother, Scott. He... ahh... tried to attack Hilda and Victor when we were staying at his bar. Ended up getting killed."

Not such a long story, after all.

"It was years ago," Brad exclaimed. "What's going on?"

Going to the wall safe, Alex pulled out documents. "My money is on Steven tipping them off." He went to the next hiding place— under the mattress—and tossed more papers onto the side table.

"But how did they track us here?" Brad asked. "And what did they want with Lilah? It was Victor who—"

"Revenge, I guess," Alex said. "Who knows how they managed to locate us? We'll figure out the details later. Right now, we need to get going."

"How did you escape?" Brad asked.

Victor snapped, "How do you think? One bullet and one broken neck. The third one got away."

Alex sorted the passports—fake and real—on the side table. On day one of their arrival in Quito, they'd started preparations for a quick getaway. Victor's local contacts turned out to be quite talented in esoteric fields like counterfeiting.

"Dude, we need to leave. Pronto." Striding through the connecting door into the adjoining chamber which he shared with Victor, Alex continued, "Lemme get the rest of the stuff."

Copies of their legal records were stashed in every one of their rooms, along with forgeries they might have to use. The special luggage made by another of Victor's friends in the city could adequately conceal their weapons from airport security systems provided they didn't try to carry the bags with them. Despite all the terrorist attacks in the recent years, security personnel hardly ever examined checked-in paraphernalia. Alex didn't like the idea of being separated from his precious weapons, but it was the best way to make sure they were armed at least once they landed on solid ground.

"Yeah, we need to leave," said Brad. "If the cops learn you two killed locals, we're going to be deported, whatever the official policy. We should get out of here."

"And go where?" Neil asked.

Smoothing back hair, Brad said, "Someplace where the U.S. can't have us extradited. China, maybe."

"Macau," Scott corrected. "More Westerners there. We... umm... will fit in better."

"It's pretty far," Victor said.

As though the distance matters, Lilah thought in bitterness. A few feet away or a few thousand feet, not only did they have to stay out of reach of American law, they also needed to avoid the clutches of Steven Kingsley. They would be far out of sight of the people who loved them. But why would Steven have paid the criminals to attack her when Harry remained alive?

The woolly feeling in Lilah's head got thicker. She blinked rapidly, hoping it would dissipate.

"Doesn't matter how far we end up going," Brad said with finality in his tone. "For sure, we can't stay *here.*"

The twins left to pack, and Victor was already at the door, but Lilah somehow couldn't make her limbs move. It was as though her legs weighed a ton.

"Lilah?" Victor called, his voice coming from a distance. "Are you okay?"

Her knees buckled. She found herself caught from the back, Victor's voice screaming, "Neil!" close to her ear.

Lilah was only vaguely aware of Victor carrying her out to her room. With the rest of the brothers staying at a respectful distance, Neil gave her a brief examination. Eyes troubled, he announced he couldn't find anything overtly wrong but suggested they take her to the local E.R.

"No," said Lilah, her tongue thick. "My glasses, please." She needed them only for reading, but since their departure from Panama, they'd become part of her disguise. "Alex is right; we need to get going." She sat up, and the haziness immediately worsened.

Handing her the glasses, Neil said, "But—"

"But nothing," she snapped, trying to focus on his blond head. "We don't have time to waste. I'm sure it was because I skipped lunch. There's a candy bar in the desk that will hold me for now."

Victor said, "I'm going to get you something more solid. Some of that lentil soup, maybe. You seem to like it. A couple of slices of toast to go with it."

Lilah gritted her teeth. "Victor—"

"Let me bring you something," he implored. He'd been on a nonstop guilt trip since their arrival in Quito. *"Let me get that for you, Lilah,"* and *"Lilah, let me go with you."* Usually, she declined to respond, striding along the streets to the university library where English-language newspapers were available for free, letting him trudge doggedly behind. She was forced to admit his giant form was a deterrent to the miscreants hanging around this part of the city.

But now, she needed him—all of them—to go away. She needed to focus, to figure out before they left for China or wherever. The attack... she never thought the Kingsleys would dare try anything unless they had Harry accounted for. From what Grayson said before, Noah Andersen's tricks would have put a hold on any such plans. Something was going on, but what?

"We can't have you faint again," Victor said, his silver-blue eyes stubborn. "I'll bring up the food, and the rest of us will pack while you eat."

"Yes," urged Brad. "You were just attacked! Take a few minutes to get over the shock."

The shock was hearing him speak to her directly for the first time since the events in Cuba. His tone oozed concern.

As everyone else in the room turned to him almost at the same instant, Brad flushed. "It's because of me you... I'm sorry. You're used to a comfortable life, and I—"

"Thank you, Victor," Lilah said abruptly. "I'd appreciate some soup and toast. Can I get some privacy while you take care of it?"

There was silence for a couple of seconds. Then, Brad nodded. The brothers filed out, Victor in the lead.

"Alex?" she called. "I need a word."

All five men had turned when she spoke. Face set, Brad pivoted on his heel and strode to the door.

Closing the door behind the rest, Alex said ruefully, "He didn't like it."

"So?"

Alex shoved his fingers into his dark-brown hair. "Lilah, I get we don't have the time, but I... I was waiting for a chance to talk to you, and who knows when you'll again feel like... what happened in Cuba... I want to apologize." He spoke rapidly as though trying to cram all he'd been thinking of the past few weeks into a few seconds. "Brad made a mistake. We all did. But try to understand it was me who started this mess. As soon as I figured out you were Andrew Barrons's daughter, I should've stayed away. No, not completely true. I should've been clear with you Brad was the intended groom, and there would've been none of the drama in public. There would've been no stories in the media. Everything snowballed from there. Brad... my God, Lilah, can't you see he loves you? It would kill any man if he thought..."

Mistake? Not the word she would've used. Brad had refused to believe her when she declared over and over there was nothing between her and Alex. Any praise from any quarter about her work elicited sneers from her husband. In a fit of jealous rage, he locked her out of business discussions. Lilah begged the Kingsley brothers not to trust any deals mediated by their cousins even if brought with the blessings of the family patriarch, Godwin Kingsley. Thanks to their faith in Godwin and their need to prove loyalty to big brother, none of them heeded her warnings. Alex, her supposed friend and supporter, blocked off any and all ways she could contact Harry, the one person who could've stopped Brad's insane gamble. *Of course* the deal turned out to be a trap. The brothers were arrested on charges of treason, along with Lilah. She still could've accepted everything was a mistake until then, borne of human insecurities. Perhaps she could've put it all behind her.

But the events in Guantanamo Bay... menstrual blood was seeping down her legs when Charles Kingsley ripped her shirt, exposing her breasts. A gleeful Armor ordered Charles to drag her naked to court if needed. When her tired body wouldn't stay upright, she was yanked to her feet by her hair.

In a court full of men, a disheveled and blood-stained Lilah denied all awareness of whatever contract Brad signed. No, the five men did not intentionally get into any nuclear deals with Iran, but she wasn't at all involved in the discussions. Even knowing she could be put to death for treason she didn't commit, not one the Kingsleys would speak up in support of her. Even after seeing what Charles did to her, they wouldn't break ranks. They all were aware of the brutal violence waiting for her if she were to be locked up in a prison where the likes of Charles and Steven and Armor made the rules. She might have even begged for death at the end of it all.

Alex did say something toward the end, but his words were not what saved the day. It took a note from Temple to force Godwin to back down. The court released the prisoners, but there remained a picture of Brad with nuclear traffickers. He didn't know the history of the men he was shaking hands with, but the photograph was used by Armor and Steven in a nice bit of blackmail. Brad and his brothers were forced to flee, Lilah in tow.

And Alex thought his miserable excuses would soothe her anger? He was the only one among the five brothers who'd heard what Lilah had to say about Godwin, but he didn't believe her. If he trusted her... but he didn't. He still wouldn't... not about Godwin. Nor would most other people back home.

Some magazines had quoted Lilah's words from the interrogation to accuse Steven's uncle of arranging the events in Cuba, and the exiles gladly pounced on the excuse. The unholy quartet of Steven, Charles, Gander, and Armor took the blame for everything. Alex Kingsley refused to credit the people he loved with ill intentions. Brad... perhaps the fact she never acknowledged Alex all these weeks soothed her husband's ego enough for him to express remorse. But the moment Alex's name crossed her lips...

"I was only trying to make it up to my brother," Alex finished.

"You can go to hell and take him with you."

The conciliatory expression on Alex's face faltered. "Lilah, for God's—"

"No!" She held up a hand and scrambled out. "I don't want to hear it. I asked you to stay only because there's something we need to do. Call..." *Who? Sabrina? Harry?* No, they couldn't risk it. Not unless it was truly an emergency. Lilah's legs still felt wobbly, and she stumbled, only to be caught by the elbows. She shrugged loose from Alex's hold, willing her body to cooperate. "Call Uncle Gray. Can't be a coincidence those men found us, but it couldn't have been through the phone line." If anyone dared track the exiles' calls to Temple's home, it would be the American government. An arrest would've been the outcome in that case, not attempted murder.

Alex huffed out a breath. After a couple of seconds, he said, "It was Steven, obviously. He probably paid those thugs to keep an eye out for us."

Lilah mocked, "Really?"

"C'mon, Lilah. Please."

How many times had *she* pleaded with him? *"Please, Alex... listen to me, please... something's going on."* Ignoring the pain and reproach in his eyes, she said, "I think something's happened back home. To Harry." If it turned out to be the case, she'd have to... her plan B... Lilah's heart squeezed hard. Harry... how could she think of alternatives when they didn't know if he... the network, the Kingsleys... no trace of them would remain after Harry's death. She would make sure of it.

"Remember what Grayson told us," said Alex. "Steven won't dare touch Harry what with all the rumors going around about the attack on Mr. Temple."

"Yet they dared another attack on *us* with Harry still alive?" Asked Lilah. "No, not adding up."

"It's a genuine concern," Alex agreed. "But Harry Sheppard is not your average man. If they did try again to kill him, it would have been big news in the oil sector. Stock market problems... etcetera, etcetera. We would've heard about it even here in Quito. What's wrong, Lilah? You know we can trust him to take care of himself."

"What is wrong?" she asked disbelievingly. "You don't find *anything* wrong?" Without warning, rage exploded to the surface. Breath came in short, angry gasps. They were in this hellhole, hiding from everyone they knew, praying every night to be still alive when the sun came up. She hadn't seen the faces of those she loved, hadn't talked to them in weeks, hadn't felt the affectionate warmth of another human starting months before this exile. She didn't know if her best friend was still alive.

"I'm sorry. It came out the—"

"What is *wrong*?" she yelled. Lilah tried to limp to Alex, wanting to shake the life out of him. His face and form blurred, and she stumbled back onto the mattress.

She barely heard the door opening, was barely aware of Alex and Victor sitting on either side of her. Victor Kingsley's gruff voice echoed strangely around, asking Alex what happened. Alex mumbled something in response.

"This was a long time coming," Victor said.

The sympathy in the statement somehow got through the thick fog around her. She gritted her teeth, trying to steady her breathing and not give in to tears.

Alex got up to go to the side table and returned with the food tray.

Food... she needed to pack... "Thank you," she said, voice hoarse. "I'll be ready to leave in five minutes."

Ignoring her dismissal, Victor said, "Would you eat, please?"

Not wanting to prolong the argument, Lilah took the tray and put it on her lap. Breaking off some bread, she dipped it in the soup before stuffing the soggy piece into her mouth.

"Have we decided on Macau?" Alex asked.

"Yeah," said Victor. "As Scott said, it's our best bet." The Chinese-administrated region didn't have an extradition treaty with the United States.

Lilah choked down the bit of food in her mouth. "Which passports are we going to use?"

"Let's stay Americans for now," Victor said. He meant *fake* American documents, of course. "At least we won't have to explain the accent. Plus, with U.S. passports, we won't need visas for the first thirty days." Since their arrival in Quito, they'd all studied the travel requirements for various potential hideouts. They all knew Macau allowed American visitors to apply for visa extensions after the initial period was up. Or they could simply overstay.

Alex argued, "But see what happened in Ecuador. We were found in less than two months. If we get mixed up in something, and they figure out we already broke their laws with document forgery, they might not care about extradition treaties. Are we going to end up running from place to place?"

"It's not like we have a choice," Victor muttered.

Food tray in her hands, Lilah stood. "You go ahead and get things ready. I'll be downstairs in a few minutes. Also, the two of you need to get back on guard duty for all of us." Until they once again managed to hide themselves under different identities, the boxer and the sniper would need to provide protection for the entire group, not only Lilah. When the men were at the door, she said, "Thanks, Victor. For the food, I mean."

His mouth quirked. "Merry Christmas."

Lilah jerked back. She'd forgotten. From the way Alex was gaping, so had he.

"The cook was surprised you asked only for soup," Victor clarified. "She wanted to know if we didn't celebrate."

#

An hour later

They were forced to wait at the airport in Quito until dawn to take the first flight to Curaçao, the Dutch colony. From there, they would fly to Amsterdam, then to Hong Kong, only a ferry ride away from Macau. Every single one of them would be praying all the while to avoid discovery.

The desk at the Quito airport's departure lounge was currently unmanned, and the announcement system was silent. Other than the Kingsley men sprawled on plastic chairs, there were only a few passengers milling around, casting curious glances at Lilah who, in spite of the open paperback on her lap, was staring at the tall man by the payphone. When his hand went to the phone, she stood with alacrity.

Lilah strode to Alex, reaching him before he could dial. "No," she said.

He didn't hang up and didn't look at her. Shoulders shaking, he said, "We're leaving Ecuador. Even if they track us through this call, we'll be out before anyone gets here."

"It's not the point," Lilah said. "The second you call, the government will have reason to harass them."

"My wife," he begged. "My son."

Michael... his innocent, trusting face... the baby smell of him. His warmth as he cuddled against Lilah, demanding, *"One more story."*

The ache in her heart threatened to bring her down for the third time that day. "We can't," she whispered. "For *their* safety."

With his free hand, Alex punched the wall next to the phone. "How long is this going to go on? For how long am I supposed to not talk to my wife and child? My mother... she must be going crazy with worry."

"You should've thought about it before," Lilah snapped. Perhaps she should feel guilty at her sharp words. Patrice... the poor woman. Her sons were her whole world. She would be praying for their safety.

But Alex... for the life of her, Lilah couldn't bring herself to empathize.

With deliberate care, Alex replaced the receiver in its cradle. His eyes pinned on the device, he enunciated, "You are a cold, hard..." His throat worked.

Lilah glared, almost wanting him to utter the epithet.

"You hate your husband," Alex muttered viciously. "You hate me. Why did you decide to go on this exile with us? *I* didn't have much of an option if I wanted to keep my brother alive. But you... you could've stayed home. You could've divorced Brad for what he did. Hell, you could've agreed to work for Steven. So why are you here?"

Tone mocking, Lilah said, "As you said, Brad's my husband."

Out of the corner of her eye, she could see him watching the two of them. There was a hint of satisfaction on his face, as though... her complete disregard of his existence never bothered him, but her conversation with Alex in her room did. Now, watching them argue, Brad was once again happy. Yes, this mass of pettiness and insecurities was her husband. He'd stay her husband until she achieved what she wanted.

Alex sneered. "Right... you can't stand the sight of him, but you still... is the network so goddamned important to you? Is it what you're all about? Power?"

"Believe what you want," she said. "Instead of behaving like a three-year-old, why don't you call Mr. Temple's line? We do need to let Uncle Gray know where we're headed."

Alex puffed out a few breaths through pursed lips. "It was uncalled for, and I'm sorry. The network is too powerful to be left in Steven's hands. We all get it." Without waiting for a response, he dialed the former president's number and left a cryptic message on the answering machine about celebrating Chinese New Year in Monte Carlo. Hanging up, he slouched against the wall. "Hope Grayson figures it out."

"He will. Once he knows we left Ecuador, he'll try to put the message together with our possible destinations. Unfortunately, so will Steven."

"Only if he gets to Temple's phone," Alex reminded her. "How can he?"

"I don't know. How did he find us here? We believe it was not through Mr. Temple's line, but what other explanation is there?"

"I was thinking," Alex muttered. "It might not even be Steven. I mean, we've made enough enemies over the years. What if Hilda's brother had been a part of an international gang or something? If I remember correctly, he did have something to do with drug smuggling. Maybe his friends were independently keeping an eye out for us." His lips quirked. "The Ghost of Christmas Past just paid us a visit."

Except, this was no Victorian novella with a guaranteed happily-ever-after, and the criminals were no benevolent shades. "How many such ghosts can we expect?" she asked.

"Not as many as you're imagining," Alex answered, tone subdued. "There were times in our lives when survival was an issue. You know most of the stories already."

Ignoring the mild reproof, she asked, "So what's your theory on how they found us?"

"Think about it. Steven's probably spread the word about our likely hiding places. Remember, all those people in Panama and Colombia saw us on our way here. Some criminals probably heard

149

and put things together and decided to avenge their dead comrade while they had the chance. It would explain why they attacked us with Harry still alive."

"Lovely," she said, rubbing her brow with a fingertip. "So Steven doesn't know where we are—not yet—but we can still expect everyone with a grudge against us to come out of the woodwork."

Grimly, Alex said, "Yeah. We've got to be careful. You seem to have been designated easy target. I'll ask Victor to stick close. Looks like you've forgiven *him*. You even let him bring you food."

Lilah said nothing in response. As though forgiveness could be bought for the price of a bowl of soup! But then, Victor's crime was not on par with Alex's. She'd always known where Victor Kingsley's loyalties lay. The giant soldier-turned-chef never made any secret of the fact his brothers came first.

Voice low, Alex argued, "If you can forgive Victor, why not the rest of us? Why not me? I made a mistake, Lilah. The same mistake Victor did. We both saw our brother hurting. We thought he'd know what he was doing with the business. I know mine was the unkindest cut of all, but—"

Tone cold, Lilah corrected him, "You give yourself too much importance."

Before Alex could respond, a female voice mumbled over the announcement system, calling their flight.

Lilah sat alone in the plane, looking out at gray clouds through the small window. As Alex said, the thugs in Quito were probably acting on their own, not because Steven Kingsley orchestrated another simultaneous attack. Pushing enemies and disloyal friends from her mind, she whispered a prayer of gratitude for small mercies. Sabrina and Michael were safe in the warmth of their home. So were

Dan and Shawn. Mr. Temple might have been incapacitated, but he was alive.

And Harry... a shudder went through her. The thought of something happening to her best friend... Lilah didn't know how she'd survive after to put into place any alternative plans. *Stay safe,* she warned him for the millionth time. *Wherever you are. Don't do anything stupid and get yourself killed.*

Chapter 14

December 1988

The Carlton Hotel, Washington, DC

A cold, dry wind blew through the streets of the American capital. Men and women in thick winter clothing hurried along the sidewalks to their destinations. Though Christmas had come and gone, brightly lit shop windows were still dressed in elegant reds and greens. Silver bells still rang outside the department store entrance where a Salvation Army Santa Claus asked for donations. A few blocks down stood the newly renovated Carlton Hotel. Halfway between the retail outlet and the hotel, within walking distance of the White House, a discreet board announced the presence of a well-known gentlemen's club, Eden.

It was a night similar to this when Lupe Valdez met Alex Kingsley. Lupe still remembered every moment of the encounter. It had been warm for a North American winter, and inside the club, the temperature was as usual kept a pleasant seventy-two.

#

Six years ago, February 1982

Eden, Washington, DC

White light washed across the crystal dance floor, and a sheet of water cascaded over the rough gray stone wall which served as backdrop. Vines twined around columns of quartz. Frosted glass bowls filled with ripe apples and peaches were set near chaise lounges. Frolicking in this artificial paradise were Eden's Angels, their hair loose, their smooth bodies visible through thin, translucent robes. Blondes, brunettes, redheads. Long curls, pixies, and everything in between. Some slender, some pleasingly plump, some a perfect ten. All beautiful.

They twirled across the stage between potted plants. The angels fed each other ripe fruit, letting juice stain lips that were already bright red. When they stripped, it was to shower under the stream to the soft music of lyres. They let the water run down perfect breasts and thighs, laughing joyfully, ostensibly unaware of the lustful eyes in the darkness beyond looking their fill. The audience could only watch, not touch. They weren't allowed to even speak to the angels.

As the owner of the club, Lupe was decently covered... more or less. The neckline of her silvery gown plunged deep, and the side-slit on the skirt was thigh high, but what was revealed of her Amazonian figure served to entice rather than titillate. Her Gibson Girl hairstyle and the makeup she wore to enhance her dark eyes added to the aura of classy sensuality. Not that she was currently visible. Lupe kept herself concealed behind the back wall, out of sight of the patrons while keeping an eye on happenings just the same. Observing the hands extending from the darkness to drop notes into the discreetly placed tip jars, she sighed in satisfaction. The jars were emptied several times a night, but the hefty entry fee alone would've made the club profitable. The patrons were always delighted to pay. This was no ordinary strip club, after all, with poles and hardwood floors and garish lighting. This was Eden, where rich and fashionable men came to watch angels cavort.

Soundproofed walls separated Paradise from Oasis. Patrons went to Oasis for drinks and to sample the excellent cooking offered by the club's chef. For those with annual memberships, most of it was free of cost. There was also another dance floor, open to everyone. There, Eden's Angels transformed themselves into Lupe's girls and were free to mingle with whomever they pleased. If they chose to accompany someone home, they were required to leave an address and phone number with the security chief. Both Paradise and Oasis were patrolled by a team of former soldiers dressed to fit in with the clientele. Any proceeds the girls earned from such trips were theirs to keep. In fact, Lupe insisted on it. She didn't want to be accused of running a brothel.

There were some who called her a female version of Hugh Hefner. Lupe gritted her teeth whenever she heard the observation. Unlike the gentleman, she'd been alone in the world with no family to loan her money to start a business. Her lack of papers to prove citizenship meant banks invariably showed her the door. But she was determined to turn her dreams into reality, and she used her most valuable weapon: the information she collected over her years as a stripper. She approached JD, a congressman known for his sexual perversions—a *married* congressman with presidential ambitions. They agreed on a trade: the use of her body for a year in return for his help with financing for Eden. JD took care of everything... the money, licenses, bank accounts for the operation of her establishment.

On the day she opened the club, everyone else in the business told her she was doing it all wrong. Lupe was advised to keep the entry fee nominal and make up her losses on food and drinks. But she'd learned something about her adopted country, the U.S. The value a customer placed on something very often depended on the price tag attached to it. So she decided to charge the patrons—they were never to be called customers—exorbitantly for the mere pleasure of seeing the angels in all their God-given glory. The "formal wear only" dress code was strictly enforced.

The past few years showed Lupe she'd been right to trust her instincts. Eden grew from a mere strip club to the place to belong to if you wanted to be counted as somebody in DC. The club was now at the point where Lupe needed to introduce membership cards. Some asked for one; some she invited.

Most politicians came through here. So did businessmen of all stripes. Lupe made it a point to cultivate all of them, performing introductions when requested, fading into the glittering background while deals were done. She'd recently opened two more clubs—one in LA, the second in Las Vegas.

But no, she was no *Señor* Hefner, surrounded by lovers ready to cater to every fantasy. Lupe rolled her eyes. Forget about boy-toys—her sex life had been nonexistent the last couple of years. The rule she made for herself had a great deal to do with it: no hanky-panky with patrons. None with business associates, either. Unfortunately, that took care of most of her acquaintances, men and women.

Still, not bad for a thirty-year-old immigrant with no papers. America was truly the land of opportunity. Here, the sky was no limit for those willing to work hard. Lupe loved it.

She frowned, noting the two angels on the left side. They were giggling, handing an apple to someone in the audience, apparently tempting him into climbing onto the platform. The stage was supposed to be off-limits to the patrons of Eden. At a snap of Lupe's fingers, a tuxedoed waiter materialized by her side. "What's going on over there?"

"Mr. Luce," the waiter whispered.

Of course! Liam Luce was the young man she'd run into when she was working for her old boss. She doubted he'd been old enough to be let in, but the seedy establishment never cared about such details. Liam rescued her from being roughed up by a group of drunks that night. They'd been friends since then. He was probably the only true friend she'd had since she... the only true friend she'd ever had. She knew his family was rich, but she never asked him for help opening her club. Money usually tainted friendships. Liam knew about her entanglement with JD. After all, he'd been the one she called to take her to the E.R. after JD dropped her back home with a dislocated shoulder. Except for making her promise to ask if she needed something, Liam never prodded. For that, she was grateful. And neither ever mentioned sex, not even on a casual basis.

If Liam didn't ever try to push Lupe into physical intimacy, he harbored no qualms taking advantage of his closeness to her to sweet-talk her girls into bed. Unfortunately, a large percentage of the girls were *corto de luces*—dim bulbs—and could not be trusted not to make the mistake of falling in love with Liam. He was likely one of the handful of men to treat them as human beings. But they weren't permitted to indulge him while they were on stage. The illusion of undefiled innocence needed to be maintained along with that of ripe sexuality.

Lupe glided forward, maintaining the elegant posture she'd taught herself with difficulty. Skirting the plush chairs around the stage, she reached the blond man on the left. "What are you doing?" she asked through clenched teeth. "You know it's not allowed."

He twisted around, a bright smile lighting his gray eyes. Blowing a kiss to the angels—one of them with a nipple peeking out of her robe—Liam stood. "Lupe, darling! I need a favor." He grabbed her by the elbow and led her to the side, biting into the apple gifted by the angels as they walked.

Lupe's belly rumbled, reminding her it was past dinner time. Grabbing the apple out of Liam's hand, she took a bite. ¡Dios mío!

Sweet and crunchy. Juice dribbled down her chin. She took a second bite, trying to keep the chomping noises down. He reached for the fruit, but she swatted his hand away. "Mine," Lupe said, her voice indistinct around the chunks in her mouth. "You go eat at Oasis."

"I want you to go to Oasis. Or send someone."

"Huh?"

"A friend of mine is visiting. His name is Alex."

"Why didn't you bring him in here?"

Liam said, "I would've, but a couple of your girls caught me before I could. Can you send someone over? I didn't bring him just for the show. He'd appreciate the company. Female company, I mean."

"One of those, huh?" Lupe felt no sympathy. It was a jungle out there, and if a man couldn't bring himself to talk to a woman on his own, he didn't deserve to get laid. Survival of the fittest and all that. "You want one of my girls to mind your friend so you can have a good time. Sorry, we don't do daycare for virgins."

Liam's eyes widened, and he let out a crack of laughter. Heads turned toward them.

"Shh!" she ordered.

Shoulders shaking with suppressed mirth, Liam suggested, "Why don't you go and take a look at this... virgin?" Lupe arched an irritated eyebrow. Okay, so maybe Liam's buddy was not a virgin. But if he needed help dealing with women, he couldn't be a smooth talker, either. "Go on," Liam teased.

"You know what? I will. Someone needs to tell him to take... what d'you call it... baby steps... before coming to a place like Eden." Pursing her lips, Lupe pivoted and went in the direction of Oasis.

Her annoyance subsided on her way out. She didn't intend to be cruel to the poor man. The least she could do was buy him a drink before sending him on his way. He was Liam's friend, after all. Also, new patrons always needed to be warmly welcomed, sexually experienced or not. Or it wouldn't be long before the stellar reputation she built up went down the drain.

As soon as she stepped into Oasis, another waiter appeared at her elbow. "Find me Liam's friend," she instructed.

"Right there, Ms. Valdez." The waiter gestured with a tiny nod.

Where? She recognized most of the faces waiting for drinks, and those she didn't were already talking to the ones she did. Liam's friend was supposedly new in town and had difficulty striking up conversations.

On the dance floor were a few couples gyrating to salsa music, and beyond the space, chairs were set around low tables. A few men lounged on the plush seats, smoking and chatting. Some of her girls were wandering around, flirting with patrons, but their attention seemed to be centered on... what? Who? Lupe strained to see around the writhing bodies on the dance floor. Then, through a small gap in the crowd, she caught a glimpse of Liam's friend, Alex.

Heat... that was her first thought. Even from a distance of ten feet, she could feel the heat radiating from him. Muscular body, covered in a white dress shirt and black pants, relaxed into the velvet-covered chair. Long legs stretched out in front. He possessed a face God surely made for the female half of humanity to drool over. The dark hair was disheveled, whiskey eyes somber. *"Madre de Dios,"* Lupe whispered.

She watched as one of the girls pranced to him. A petite blonde with bouncy curls. Without waiting for his by-your-leave, the girl seated herself on his lap. There was a trace of a frown on his face

157

before it turned into a half-smile. Shaking his head, he said something to the girl. She pouted but took the rejection with good grace. His eyes followed her as she disappeared into the crowd, and the frown returned. Lupe took in the expression and sighed. The girl was twenty-two and liked to pretend she was sixteen. She looked it, too. Most of the patrons were titillated by it, but not so Alex, it seemed. Lupe needed to make things clear to him. She didn't want him reporting her establishment to the authorities for employing underage sex workers.

Shoulders back, chest out. Head held at an attractive angle. Donning the posture she used with great effect, Lupe glided forward. "Hello, I'm Lupe."

The divine-looking man looked up, his gaze sweeping over her form. Moving his blazer from the chair next to him to the glass table in front, she seated herself and leaned forward to place a light hand on his forearm. His eyes automatically went to her cleavage. Lupe hid a smile of satisfaction. The gold-tinged skin she inherited from her Spanish ancestors, the dark hair and eyes, the high cheekbones of her native forbearers... all blended together to form an exotic face. As for her body... well, people called her an Amazon. But she possessed the curves to go with her bones, and the silvery gown showed them off well.

"Alex," he replied, his eyes meeting hers.

It was then that she noticed the quiet desperation in his dark gaze. An acute pain. Lupe almost jerked back at the intensity of the emotion. Her heart trembled. "Ayy... I... Liam sent me." Hiding a wince, she chided herself for the unusual incoherence. "Let me get you something to drink." As soon as she raised a hand, a waiter was at their table. In the few minutes it took for the drinks to arrive, she said, "You met Nikki."

"Who? Oh, you mean the blonde kid who just tried to give me a lap dance?"

Perfect opening. Lupe smiled. "Nikki's twenty-two. Only, she's not quite so ready to leave her teens behind." He blinked, something like suspicion passing across his features. Another wave from Lupe brought the waiter back. "Ask Nikki to bring her ID over here. Our guest wants to take a look."

"Ms—" the waiter started, puzzlement in his eyes.

"We're good," Lupe clarified. "Alex just wants to be sure Nikki isn't actually sixteen."

Face flushed, Nikki reached them the same time as the drinks. "Here," she said, thrusting the ID under Alex's nose.

Lupe hid a frown. Barring threatening situations, the girls were expected to be pleasant to patrons. She'd have to schedule a chat with Nikki once the evening was done.

"Why are you working here?" Alex asked the girl.

"Because it pays well," Nikki retorted. "A lot more than what the diner did. *And* I get health insurance." She grabbed the card out of Alex's hands and flounced off, the waiter following.

Eyes on her departing back, Alex remarked, "I thought she'd make up some kind of excuse."

"She might have," Lupe said. "Only, you made her angry."

Shadows returning to his face, he muttered, "I seem to have a knack for angering women."

Lupe wondered who she was, the one who hurt him. Only a bitch would've broken this lovely man's heart. "Here," Lupe said, handing him his drink.

Sipping Absolut Cranberry, he asked, "What's *your* story? Putting yourself through college or single mom?"

Interesting! He had no idea who she was, and here she thought she was gaining notoriety with each passing day. Also, was that a sneer she heard in his voice? Instead of the annoyance she'd have expected, Lupe was overwhelmed by an inexplicable need to tease him out of his melancholy. She laughed. "Neither. I own the place." His eyebrows rose. "Surprised?"

"No... yes... I guess someone has to own it."

"But you expected... a mafia kingpin in a striped suit, maybe? I could change if you like."

"Into a suit?"

"Or nothing at all." Lupe blinked. Where did that come from? She had her rule: no sex with patrons.

His pupils wide, he stared. He didn't say no, but he didn't say yes, either.

He was turning her down? Turning *Lupe Valdez* down? "You're not tempted?" she asked.

"Oh, I am," he said. "A lot. In fact, when I first saw you, I thought... but I don't..." He groaned, shoving fingers through his hair. The hopeless pain was back in his eyes. "There's... was... someone, but she decided she didn't want me."

"Really?" Lupe asked, finding it hard to believe. No flesh-and-blood woman could possibly refuse so gorgeous a specimen of manhood.

"Yeah, but there were circumstances—"

"Excuses, you mean," Lupe scoffed. "You're going to do what? Remain celibate all your life for her sake?"

"No," he admitted.

"So... is that a yes?" she asked playfully.

"Huh?"

"To my earlier question. Would you like me to change my clothes?" Into nothing at all as she'd promised.

Silence. As though he didn't know what to say.

Lupe never pleaded with a man before. Never had to. Holding her hands up to flaming cheeks, she mumbled, "I wish I never said that. I'm so embarrassed right now I could die."

"Don't be," he said quickly. "I was only thinking... I'm leaving for Texas tomorrow."

"I'm not talking about a lifetime commitment, Mr. Alex Whoever-You-Are. Haven't you had a one-night stand before?"

"No."

Taken aback, she asked again, "Really?"

He shrugged. "Never saw the point."

"Well then, let me be the one to show you the joys of unconditional love."

"Unconditional love?" He laughed. "You mean, sex without expectations."

"'A rose by any other name...'"

"Shakespeare? *Romeo and Juliet?* You're full of surprises."

Lupe didn't disillusion him. DC was an unforgiving town to anyone deemed less worthy. The veneer of sophistication she cultivated demanded the illusion of a classical education, and she'd memorized a few elegant-sounding quotes, using them to great effect with her VIP patrons.

Within minutes, they were in her private rooms on the upper floor. *"La Paloma,"* her favorite song, played in the background. To her surprise, he didn't object when she demanded to tie him up. But then, everyone in Oasis had seen them leaving together, including the security guards. Liam would hear about it. Alex surely knew he was not likely to come to any harm at her hands.

With a sudden pang, Lupe wondered if *she* would escape this night unscathed. If her heart would escape unbruised. Shaking off the gloom, she proceeded to put everything she knew into the performance, starting with tying his wrists to the headboard. Watching her sinuous movements, he growled, and frank arousal replaced the shadows in his eyes.

Then, she crawled on top and unbuttoned his shirt, placing little kisses all across his pectorals. When she dipped the tip of her tongue into his navel, he surged up, his hardened groin connecting with her breasts. She laughed and straddled him, peeling off his pants. His breath came in short gasps.

She wasn't done teasing him. Oh, no. Lupe intended to drive him so, so mad. She stood, swaying to the music, and drew the pins from her hair, letting it fall heavily on her shoulders. Her hands went to the thin straps of her dress, the gown slithering to her feet in a silken pool. Caressing her body, she invited his eyes to linger on her cleavage, her belly, her thighs. Finally, when her limbs felt too heavy with desire to continue dancing, she climbed on top and let them both soar.

In the morning, she watched, silk sheets bunched around her hips as he dressed. "Stay," she demanded.

He glanced up, buttoning his cuffs. "We both agreed this would be a one-night deal."

Anger surged. "I don't usually sleep with patrons."

"I didn't mean to imply..." He sighed. "I'm not in a good place... not a good time to start things. I'm leaving for Texas tonight."

She contemplated him, a pain of her own mingling with the humiliation of his rejection. And empathy. The shadows were back in his eyes. This woman—this fool—had wounded him bad. "Her loss," Lupe said. At his questioning look, she added, "Whoever's got you running."

"The loss is all mine." He closed the door behind him.

As soon as he left, she leaped off the bed and called Liam, wanting to know more about Alex.

"I heard you left with him," Liam muttered. "Lupe, I wish you hadn't—"

"I don't need your sympathy," she snapped. "Just tell me who he is, and I'll make sure we meet again."

"You can't," said Liam. "Not Alex."

"Why not?" she demanded. "You don't think I'm good enough?"

"The thought never crossed my mind. Lupe, he is Alex *Kingsley*. I wish I told you before you went to him instead of trying to tease."

"Whoever he is... Kin—Kingsley?"

"Yes. He's Helen Drummond's cousin."

Helen Drummond, born Kingsley. She was the woman married to Rep. Jack Drummond, a.k.a. JD, the man whose plaything Lupe had been for a year. She'd made it a point to find out all she could about the wife and her immediate family which included her brothers. Steven never showed up at Eden in DC, but he'd visited the club in California a time or two with his friend, a Richard Armor. Lupe didn't encounter either man in any of her trips to inspect the Los Angeles establishment. Charles... he'd been an enthusiastic participant in many of JD's sick games. Yeah, Lupe knew the names of Helen Drummond's close relatives but never bothered to check into the woman's cousins. Lupe had never heard of Alex Kingsley. Not until today.

"Madre de Dios," she muttered weakly. Lupe would have been the first to admit she didn't have many scruples when it came to consensual relationships. But even she had her limits.

Liam didn't bring up the topic of Alex Kingsley in his later visits to Eden, and she was thankful. She eventually convinced herself it hadn't been love at first sight. Such a thing didn't exist! But anytime there was something in the tabloids about the Kingsleys, Lupe made sure to read it. She broke open a bottle of champagne when news of Alex's wedding reached her, proceeding to get herself smashed. When she saw the birth announcement of his son, she hurried to her parish—the Immaculate Conception Church—to light a candle, severely resenting the sympathetic smile she imagined on the face of Virgin Mary. Saying a prayer for a baby was a normal thing to do! The mother of God had no business laughing at Lupe.

The news about the mess in Cuba disturbed her quite a lot. She told herself it was a good thing Alex never returned to Eden. Meeting him again would have brought her only trouble, and the label of traitor he now carried proved it.

Chapter 15

Back in December 1988

The Carlton Hotel, Washington, DC

Snapping fingers almost caught Lupe's nose. "What?" she asked, feeling cross when she missed a step. Even after all these years, she had to consciously remember to walk like the upper-class women whose men she served.

"Are you with me?" Liam asked.

Rolling her eyes, Lupe stopped to turn a three-sixty in the hotel lobby. Crystal chandeliers hung from the ornately coffered ceiling, the multitude of lights reflecting on the gleaming floor. Guests lounged in lushly upholstered armchairs and chatted in muted tones, seemingly oblivious to the charms of Gilded Age architecture. Palladian windows looked out into the open-air restaurant where chairs sat empty in the cold night, but Christmas bulbs still glowed on trees and bushes. When she completed her turn and came face-to-face with Liam, Lupe said in mock surprise, "Oh! You're still here. So I guess I *am* with you."

He laughed. "I mean, where did you drift off to for the last couple of minutes?"

She shrugged a shoulder. "Memories. Of... of *you*."

"Good ones, I hope."

"*I* hope they'll still be good after today. I'm worried you're going to get me mixed up in trouble. This Harry Sheppard is your friend Alex's brother-in-law, right?"

Liam grinned, not answering. He was well aware she already knew who Harry Sheppard was. The first time she noticed *Señor* Sheppard was when his sister married Alex. Their relationship was the only reason she never extended the commodities broker an invitation to apply for membership at Eden. But she'd studied him as she studied every powerful man—and woman—who had reason to come to her town. Information was not just the key to success, it was essential to survival. Thinking of the Green Card locked up in her room, Lupe smiled in relief. The amnesty announced by the U.S. government made survival a little easier. In a few years, she'd be fully American.

With Liam ambling alongside, Lupe continued her practiced glide, her heels making sharp little clicks on the tiles, the shimmery bronze skirts of her strapless gown swishing around her legs. She hadn't bothered to change when she left the club with Liam. *He* was wearing an off-the-rack suit and tie as usual. Liam didn't seem to care where he shopped. But then, when you were known to be rich, buying clothes from department stores made you eccentric, not cheap.

She wondered for the thousandth time since agreeing to his request if she'd lost her marbles... or why would she consent to meet Harry Sheppard? He'd left messages at the club, asking for a one-to-one on a business matter, but she ignored those. Lupe wasn't born yesterday. The commodities broker never made any attempt to contact her or ask to be a patron until his friends got into trouble with the government. Oh, yeah... she could see the plea for help coming from a mile away. Then, Liam called. It had been at the tip of her tongue to tell him what he could do with his petition when the image of Alex Kingsley's whiskey eyes swam into her mind. Lupe managed to resist temptation only for a few days. She wanted to see what was going on with Alex, and his brother-in-law was sure to know. So here she was, walking down the lobby of the Carlton Hotel.

Lupe frowned, reminding herself she was a pragmatic businesswoman. *Not romantic at all!* "Treason," she muttered. "Alex Kingsley is on the run from the government, and you want me to talk to his brother-in-law. What about?"

"Harry will tell you," Liam said. "There he is."

At the farthest end of the room, a man—also dressed in a dark suit—stood and turned in their direction.

Dark hair, cut short. Lupe couldn't see his eyes from this distance, but she knew from pictures that they were a lovely coffee color. He was tall, but his height didn't awe her; at seventy-one inches in her stockinged feet, she was no shrimp. What she hadn't been prepared for was the aura of power radiating from the broker. *Something about the stance,* she thought dazedly. He reminded her of a black jaguar she once spotted in her native Argentina. Nervous all of a sudden, she hummed a familiar tune under her breath.

"We're not at the club, Lupe," Liam said, his voice amused.

"*Idiota,*" she said. "*Ave Maris Stella*" is not a club song."

Liam's laughter sounded loud amid the muted voices of the hotel guests. "You need a prayer before meeting Harry?"

Feeling foolish, she mumbled, *"Tú es un retard jodido."*

Being called an effing retard simply made Liam laugh harder. "Oh, Lupe, such sweet words from you I never hoped to hear."

She gathered her poise again. The people she encountered expected to see sophistication, not vulgarity. Somehow, this meeting made her anxious enough to revert to the behavior of her adolescence.

The ease with which Liam greeted the broker surprised her. They were brothers-in-law, but not for much longer if the gossip she picked up was correct.

Harry Sheppard smiled into her eyes. "Thank you for agreeing to this meeting, Ms. Valdez. Liam tells me you had trouble finding someone to cover hostess duties for the evening."

The warmth in his gaze dazzled Lupe for a moment, but she was no ordinary gal to be taken in by a handsome face and a charming grin. She'd learned the hard way not to trust, starting with the lowlife boyfriend who'd taken her virginity and the money she scraped up to get them both to the United States. He disappeared after a week, but she still managed to cross the Rio Grande.

There was the same rakish appeal in Harry Sheppard's smile. Only, amplified a million times. She'd thought him powerful, and up close and personal, the power seemed magnetic, compelling her to stay when she'd have rather left.

Shoulders thrown back, eyes wide. A flirtatious hand on his forearm. Leaning forward ever so slightly to suggest intimacy. If Harry Sheppard had his stance, Lupe had hers. "Playing hooky to meet a good-looking, young broker is never any trouble, I assure you. Only pleasure."

To her surprise, his gaze didn't drift down to her boobs. In her adult life, Lupe had come across only a handful of men she didn't *want to* manipulate. Alex Kingsley was one of them. There was Liam. Seldom did she encounter someone she *couldn't* manipulate. The bastard, JD, was one such. *No, éste es peligroso. Éste Harry Sheppard.* Harry Sheppard was dangerous.

He gestured toward the seating. Something rustled around the broker's left wrist... a dull-looking silver chain with a tiny pendant dangling from it. "Please sit," he requested.

With a professional eye, Lupe noted the elegant way the furniture was arranged. The settee was covered in rich red velvet as were the armchairs, and silk pillows were thrown about, inviting visitors to relax into luxury.

Liam occupied one of the chairs while the broker seated himself next to Lupe on the settee. A server appeared, asking if they'd like to order something. *Eighteen seconds,* she counted, mentally sighing in satisfaction. It took the server eighteen seconds from the time of their sitting down to show up. The average for Eden was fifteen.

"Coffee, double espresso," Lupe said. It meant sleep would be a long time coming, but she wanted to be hyperaware for this meeting. Liam asked for Coke, and his brother-in-law stuck to water.

"You're a fan of specialty coffee?" asked Harry Sheppard.

"I love it," answered Lupe. "There's a coffee chain—Starbucks— out in Seattle. Their espresso is to die for."

"Never heard of them," Liam said.

Lupe smiled. "You like the coffee at the club, don't you? We get it through their mail order service." She turned to the broker. "But we're not here to talk of the magic beans. What do you want?"

His eyes widened at the bluntness of her tone. "All right, we'll get down to business. Will you consider taking me on as a partner?"

What? It took a couple of seconds to register. "What?"

"What?" Liam echoed.

"In your clubs," the broker specified as though the idea hadn't been clear. "You have ten if I'm not mistaken. Due to open the eleventh soon."

"In Macau," she said, smiling in pleasure. It was the first city she traveled to after she got her Green Card. When she arrived in the U.S. as a teenager, her only aim had been to make a life for herself in the country. But with success came a desire to see the rest of the planet. Places like Las Vegas, Macau, Monte Carlo, London... the rich and famous went there to lose their cash on wine, women, and cards. Oh, yes, it was a good business decision. "But it's going to be a few months before Macau Eden opens. You want to be my partner? Why?" He should've been talking about Alex and asking for her assistance.

"Why does anyone invest in a successful business, Ms. Valdez?" the broker asked. "For profit, obviously. I assume you'd prefer a private backer to finance your expansion. Banks charge hefty interest."

"I hope you know what you're doing," Liam muttered, a look of uncomfortable surprise on his face.

Ignoring him and the bait of interest-free loans, Lupe said, "The money you'd make will be a pittance compared to what you already have."

"Call it a vanity purchase," the broker offered.

Lupe laughed. "No, not that. There's a... what d'you call it... personality type who makes vanity purchases. You're not it." Leaning back, she studied him. No sweating, no flushing. No trembling fingers. No shifty gaze. "I have a feeling you're telling me the truth," she announced. "You *are* looking for profit."

It didn't make sense. Eden and its sister clubs made money but hardly enough to entice a billionaire like Harry Sheppard. For a man like him to buy shares in the clubs either meant vanity purchase as he'd said, or he was looking at it as the means to greater rewards. But what rewards could he hope to make from a strip club even if it were one with Eden's reputation of patronage from the country's political eli—

Lupe hissed. "Information. That's what you're after. You want access to the club's books." Forget simply asking for help... if she even dreamed of giving him what he asked, the business she built would be no more.

"I assure you I'll cover any losses," said the broker.

Punching the settee hard, she said, "Losses? How can anyone begin to cover—I worked my butt off to build the clubs, Harry Sheppard. You're trying to destroy everything!"

"Shh," Liam said.

Lupe shook a finger at him. "You... you brought me here to listen to this *insulto?*"

"Ms. Valdez," said the broker. There was tension in the set of his shoulders. "I never meant to insult you... okay, what if I buy the clubs outright? I'll pay you more than market price."

She bared her teeth. "It might not be a billion-dollar enterprise like yours, *Señor, pero mi negocio es mi bebé.* My business is my baby. I'm not going to let you sacrifice my *child* for whatever you have in mind!"

The waiter was hurrying toward them with their order. Normally, Lupe would have taken care to wait until all unrelated parties left before making her displeasure known. Not tonight. She was too incensed by the offer. Too hurt by Liam's betrayal. Didn't he know Eden was all Lupe had? Her eyes teared. She stood.

"Lupe," Liam said. "Hear him out."

"Please... don't leave yet," said the broker. "You know you won't get a better deal from any of the banks, but if you don't want it, I'll take back whatever I just said."

"Yeah, you will," Lupe said, tone bitter. "I know your type. You'll take it all back, and as soon as I leave, you'll call the bank and ask them to withdraw."

"Sir?" called the waiter, his eyes skittering between the three guests.

Standing in one quick move, Harry Sheppard took the tray from the surprised waiter, quickly placing it on the side table. "Thanks."

Looking dazed, the waiter asked, "Will it be all for tonight?"

"For now, anyway," said Liam.

As soon as the young man left, Lupe said, "Enjoy your drinks. I'm off."

Harry Sheppard said, his voice soft, "Ten minutes, Ms. Valdez? At the end of the time, you can walk away if you want."

"If I don't give you the ten minutes, you'll talk to the bank?"

The broker didn't deny the accusation, confining himself to saying, "I hope you'll stay... for Liam's sake, at least."

Liam's sake? Lupe had thought he was here only as an intermediary. Head jerking toward him, she asked, "Are you in some sort of trouble?"

"Not me," Liam muttered. "Er... a friend of mine. Alex Kingsley. You know—"

"I remember him," Lupe said, shooting a warning look at Liam. "He's been to the club. Married Mr. Sheppard's sister if I'm not mistaken."

"Well, you know what happened to Alex," Liam continued. "The papers are still talking about him and his brothers being fugitives. Harry's trying to bring them back home, and we need your help."

"The truth, Liam," she demanded. "Are you in trouble? If not, why are you getting yourself mixed up in this? Is Alex Kingsley so important to you?"

"We're friends," Liam exclaimed. "It's good enough reason. Also, Alex and Harry helped my family out of a tough spot a few years ago. With our stock... long story. I'd like to return the favor. Lupe, please help. Alex needs you."

Thoughts and emotions bombarded her from every direction. The joy of hearing his name uttered out loud, the urge to run to his rescue if not into his arms. Concern about Liam's safety. Fear over what Harry Sheppard would do.

"Ms. Valdez," the broker interjected. "I'd like another chance to explain things." Once they were all back in their places, he said, "First, let me apologize."

"For what?" she snapped, regaining some of her composure. "For the deal you first offered or for underestimating me?"

There was a glimmer of... something in the broker's dark eyes. "For both, actually. I didn't realize you would so easily figure out my plan."

"The bimbo stripper. High school dropout. Easy to fool. I know how your kind thinks."

"No, the businesswoman who needs financing. I assumed you'd jump at my offer."

"I am thirty-six years old, *señor*. Maybe I don't have a college degree, but I've been around the block a time or two. Not that easily fooled."

"I understand it now. And for the record, I only have a GED."

"Huh?"

"High school, Ms. Valdez. I never went to college, either."

It was as though he threw a switch, interrupting her train of angry thoughts. The broker was only thirty-two. For him to have achieved this level of success... she'd taken it for granted... some magazine once reported that he was fluent in almost ten languages.

Harry Sheppard continued, "I wasn't lying, by the way. I would've reimbursed you for any losses you might've suffered if you took my offer of partnership, and a buyout would've left you considerably richer."

"You also assumed one or both of your plans would've worked. You'd have failed, Mr. Sheppard."

"Oh?"

"For one, the books don't have any information in them except the patrons' names and relevant data which is already public. I'm not stupid enough to write down anything sensitive. Nor do I ever try to memorize what I hear in enough detail to get me into trouble." Only fools failed to realize certain bits of information were better forgotten.

"For another?" the broker asked.

"Taking over and collecting info going forward wouldn't have worked, either. If Lupe is Eden, Eden is Lupe. You may be The Harry Sheppard, but you could never replace *me*. Once you took over, the club would cease to exist in the minds of DC society. No one would bother to visit."

"What would *you* suggest?" the broker asked. "Assuming you're prepared to help."

"At the moment, I am not," she said. "But I am prepared to listen... for Liam's sake as you said. Let's hear the plan, starting at the top."

"All right," said the broker. "Cards on the table, then. My usual sources of information have been blocked off. I'm constantly watched."

"Not surprising. You're related to Al... to the Kingsleys."

"Do you believe Alex is guilty of treason, Ms. Valdez?"

Lupe's head snapped up. There was something in the broker's tone... *surely, Alex hasn't said anything about me... no, this man is his wife's brother. He couldn't have.* "I barely met him once. Don't know him well enough to reach a conclusion. It doesn't matter, anyway. The courts decide that sort of thing."

"*I* know him well. Alex is a man of honor, and he'd never betray the nation he swore to protect. He and his brothers were tricked, so I want to give them a fair chance at fighting this. When the issue is brought before our elected representatives, information about who's planning to do what will be the key to success. I no longer have access to the information, but you might be able to help us get around the hurdle."

She objected, "As I said, neither I nor the books will be of help. There's nothing in the club's records, and our patrons know it. They trust me to be blind, deaf, and dumb to what they do."

"You could have allowed me to think there was and let me find out after I spent money," the broker murmured.

Lupe shrugged. "I don't operate that way."

The broker blinked but didn't make any further comments on it. "Is there some other way? Your employees, perhaps?"

"My girls, you mean?" Lupe was astonished. Most of her girls were anywhere from late teens to their thirties, with few resources to help themselves let alone six people on the run from the U.S. government.

"Yes. The authorities might be able to block *me* from getting information from the right people, but no one can stop men from going in search of a good time."

Disappointment. This was his alternative? Who knew such a pretty face hid such an ugly mind? "I won't ask my girls to whore for you."

"Not what I meant at all," the broker said. "There are a few of them who already choose to meet your custom... your patrons outside the clubs. They have access to a few key people I'm interested in. I'm offering them a legitimate job."

"Trapping the men?" she asked bitterly.

"No, Ms. Valdez. Being informants. Steven Kingsley's brother-in-law, Rep. Jack Drummond, was instrumental in getting you the finances to start Eden. Because of his connection with you, a lot of the congressman's acquaintances frequent your club. In fact, rumors suggest the politicians supporting the Kingsley family use Eden as meeting place. I want intelligence on any communication they have with any of the Kingsleys—Steven and Godwin, especially. Evidence of anything remotely illegal. If the sexual shenanigans of politicians are part of the material, I'll make sure your girls don't get dragged into it."

"Lupe, look." Liam leaned forward, elbows on the arms of the chair. "Harry's working to get Alex and his family pardoned. Godwin Kingsley is working just as hard for Steven, lobbying the politicians. We need to know who to target and how. All your girls would have to do is tip off Harry if they see or hear something interesting. There's nothing for you or them to worry about."

"Nothing except trouble with the Kingsley family." Trouble with JD, the sadistic bastard who once pulled her arm out of socket for not obeying his orders fast enough. "I'll have to think about it."

When Lupe walked away, her mind was full of chaos. She trusted her own judgment... and the extensive study she did of Alex Kingsley over the years. She did not for a moment believe he would sell out his country. But to take this big risk for him... no way!

They were almost at the front doors of the hotel when Liam said, "I'm sorry, Lupe. I swear I wouldn't have let Harry anywhere near you if it weren't for Alex."

"It's all right," she said automatically.

"Dunno what Harry will do if you also refuse to help."

Waiting for her coat at the counter, she asked, "Also?"

"Yeah, the Sheppards refused to void Harry's buy-sell agreement. He can't sell his stock without Gateway's permission, and what he has on hand won't be enough to bribe everyone he needs."

Alex was married to one of their own. Families! Lupe shook her head, emphatically empathetic. Her own worthless tribe in Argentina kicked her out at fourteen, friendless and penniless. But Alex was not quite in the same position. Not with a brother-in-law willing to spend millions to buy into— "Wait a second," she said. "Gateway refused to let Harry Sheppard raise money?"

Handing over a dollar, Liam accepted the coats from the girl at the counter. "Yeah. Can you believe—"

She pivoted and marched back into the lobby, forgetting all her sophistication.

"Lupe!" Liam was again at her side. "What are you doing?"

"Going to tell that con man brother-in-law of yours what he can do with his effing idea." Men and women jumped out of her way, their curious gazes following her, but Lupe didn't care. Harry Sheppard had taken her for a fool, and he was going to learn everyone who tried it so far lived to regret it.

"What are you talking about?" Liam asked, jogging to keep up. "Harry's no con man. He told you the truth."

Halting, she wheeled around to face Liam. His puzzled gray eyes were searching hers, no trace of guile in them. "He fooled you, too," she ground out.

When she turned back, Harry Sheppard was on the settee where she left him, now looking toward her as though he'd been expecting this furious return. It took them less than ten seconds to reach him. Liam said to his brother-in-law, "I don't know why, but she's mad at you."

The broker stood, his coiled stance again reminding Lupe of a panther. But she was too angry to give a damn. "Ask him," she said to Liam, boiling blood galloping through her veins. "How he plans to invest in Eden when he has no money."

"He has money," Liam corrected her. "He's a billionaire."

"A billionaire whose company won't let him sell his stock," she spat.

"But that was only when he planned to use it to bring Alex back," Liam objected. "Right, Harry? Gateway would let you—"

"Let him what? Sell the stock to buy shares in a strip club? *Madre de Dios*, Liam! Do you actually believe the people in Gateway would've been too *estúpidos* to figure out it was also for Alex?"

"No," the broker admitted. "They wouldn't have let me."

Confusion on his face, Liam asked, "Harry?"

"I'll tell you what happened," Lupe said. "He tricked me into believing he wanted to buy into the club and threatened to block the bank loan if I didn't agree. But he knew I wouldn't agree and that I'd be looking for another way to save my business. Then, he added the sob story about Ale... his other brother-in-law's plight. Finally, he came up with this bright idea of having my girls spy for him. Which is what he wanted in the first place!"

"If I brought it up without the threat, would you have agreed?" the broker asked.

Hissing, she said, "You needed me too frantic to think. Or I'd have started to wonder why you—with all your connections—would trust a stranger like me with this. Why you couldn't make 'campaign contributions,' the same as every other con man who wants to stay out of jail."

"I already admitted my usual sources won't talk to me," said the broker. "Not the CIA, not the FBI. The politicians I donated to won't take my calls. You're one of the few options left. Also, prior investigation told me you're a straight shooter where business is concerned. No matter how frantic you were, you would've flatly refused and not strung me along for nefarious purposes. *You* wouldn't have conned me, and I never intended to con you of anything, either. I never had any intention of going to the banks about your loan. It was only a bluff."

"This is not a card game, Harry Sheppard. This is real life. *My* life. No, I wouldn't have agreed to even consider your idea if I weren't desperate." She didn't say no outright because of Alex, not the loan, but the broker didn't need to know the little detail. "I'm the woman who stands to lose everything in this dirty game of yours."

"I have *already* lost most of everything I held dear," the broker said.

"Really?" she scoffed. "I don't see your lifestyle suffering even if you don't have your billions to throw around."

Eyes flaring, the broker said, "I'm not talking about money. The things which made my life worthwhile were taken from me. The sacrifices, the tears... all turned out to be useless. What I have left is the hope of bringing them back someday. I want to bring Alex back to his wife and son."

"My club makes *my* life worthwhile, *señor*. I told you, my business is *my* child. What you're asking me to do is choose between my child and—."

"A five-year-old boy who's missing his father," the broker interjected.

Michael. She knew his name even if she'd never seen him, never wished to.

"The choice between action and inaction is always before every one of us," Harry Sheppard continued. "Every moment of our lives.

179

Some choices are terrifying, some not. But all are consequential. I apologize for trying to pressure you. Now, I'm *asking* you to make a choice. A free choice. Pick a side, Ms. Valdez."

"If I don't want to?"

The broker inclined his head. "Then, your indecision itself becomes your decision. Your choice will still be consequential, but you would have surrendered control to your fears."

"What do you mean?" Lupe demanded. "My clubs will continue to operate as before. Or are you trying to threaten me? *Again?*"

"No. What I meant to say is we're all..." The broker gestured with his hands, causing the trinket wrapped around his wrist to swing. "You, me, Liam... we all have the right to decide what to do. If you give it up, there will still be consequences... for Alex and the rest."

"Bottom line is," Lupe bit out, "you want me to consider consequences to me versus consequences for someone else."

The broker admitted, "We can take measures to mitigate risk, but there will never be zero risk."

Liam said, "Lupe, you know me, and you've met Alex. Jack Drummond—"

Lupe shot him a warning look.

Without missing a beat, Liam continued, "—has been visiting your club since you first opened. Steven Kingsley's brother-in-law. Remember what you know about all of us before you decide."

"As for any potential harm to you or your business..." said the broker. "I'll do everything in my power to keep it from happening."

"'Everything' covers a lot of room, Harry Sheppard. I'm no fool to trust such grand vows."

"What if I put it down on paper? I might not be able to sell my stock, but I can name you as my beneficiary in the event your business suffers from helping me. If I die, Gateway will either have to put up with you as a shareholder or buy you out."

"All your money?" Lupe scoffed. "For a brother-in-law? *No creo. I don't believe.*"

"Some time ago," said Harry, "I set myself a task. Blinded by my focus on it, I made a terrible mistake. It eventually caused a great deal of harm to several people, including Alex. He's not a traitor, Ms. Valdez, and I don't want him penalized for a crime he didn't commit. So yes, I am doing it for him."

#

A day later

Afternoons were when Lupe dealt with the piles of paperwork involved in running the clubs, but she found herself unable to concentrate. Sitting at her desk, Lupe scribbled on a notepad and weighed the pros and cons. Jerking the file drawer open, she took out the folder labeled "A.K."

The newspaper clippings she gathered over the years... a head-shrinker would probably recommend she toss her collection into the fireplace and focus on building an actual love life, but Lupe couldn't help herself. It wasn't simply about being a sucker for a pretty face with a sad story to tell although as far as weaknesses went, hers wasn't the most terrible. Not when she wasn't harming anyone. Collecting information was her habit, and in Alex's case, she liked to stare at his pictures in her maudlin moments and torture herself with what-might-have-beens.

Lupe flipped through the clippings. Wedding announcement, articles from business journals, tabloid items... but not a single photograph of his son. Well, nothing which showed his face. There were a couple from when Michael was a newborn, one with an article claiming he was the love child of Alex Kingsley and his beautiful sister-in-law.

Lupe frowned. She'd read articles on the woman—Lilah Barrons Kingsley. Some of the media resented her greatly, calling her snooty for looking through them and walking on, but not a single reporter wrote anything on her without mentioning what a stunner she was. Lupe often wondered if *she* were the one who broke Alex's heart. In fact, Lupe was almost certain it was the case. A run-of-the-mill failed romance shouldn't have brought the kind of pain to a man's face Lupe saw on Alex's so long ago. But having to endure the same fickle lover as his own brother's wife would bring anyone to his knees. Lupe once even sent a membership invitation to the woman's twin, Daniel Barrons. It took her less than five minutes after mailing it to regret the idea, but thankfully for her, the Barrons heir never responded.

If Lupe agreed to help the broker, it wouldn't be only Alex returning home. It would also be the woman who'd been cruel enough to inflict hurt on him. If gossip had it right, they'd resumed their affair. Actually, a few of the tabloids insisted Lilah Kingsley was married to all five brothers. Ridiculous, obviously, but Lupe wouldn't be surprised if the woman were *sleeping* with all of them. What better way to make sure she ruled the roost? Lupe might have considered it herself in a similar situation.

Why would Harry Sheppard consider bringing the woman back when it was his sister who suffered the most from the betrayal? Why would he want to bring Alex, the faithless husband, back? Then again, some of these upper-class women put up with outright abuse from the bastards they married only to maintain their lifestyle. Perhaps Sabrina Sheppard Kingsley was one such. Or perhaps the broker was also in the Lilah woman's thrall and wanted to bring *her* back. Actions... choices... consequences... what a lot of crap he was going on about, anyway! No, Lupe didn't want any part of it no matter how much money she was promised in the broker's will.

In the evening, she sat at her vanity, getting ready for the club. Painting her lips a soft pink color, she reprimanded herself. *Lupe Valdez, you have no reason to sacrifice yourself to save Alex Kingsley.* A one-night stand, for fuck's sake! That she spent the last few years mooning over the man was her private foolishness and nothing to base a decision of this magnitude on. *If innocent, he can return and face the courts. If guilty, well... his wife is better off without him. Too bad for the little boy.* The reflection in the mirror assured her there was nothing for her to feel guilty about.

She frowned when she saw Liam's familiar face in Oasis. Sashaying to the small crowd gathered around him, Lupe fixed him with a gimlet eye.

"Lupe," cried a blonde who looked as though she were sixteen. Nikki had looked that age for more than ten years now. "Have you seen a more adorable baby? His name is Michael."

"My friend's little boy," Liam explained, thrusting a picture under her nose. "You know him: Alex Kingsley."

Involuntarily, her gaze went to the small snapshot. A gap-toothed young child smiled happily into the camera. The kid looked like his Uncle Harry, except he had his papa's whiskey eyes. Lupe ground her teeth.

Later, she strode to the table where the *faux* sixteen-year-old was giggling into Liam's ear. After she sent the young lady flouncing off, Lupe said, tone irritable, "In my office... now."

Rocking lightly in the chair behind the desk, she listened to Liam as he told her the story of what happened to Alex and his brothers and the woman in their lives. A lot of it Lupe already learned from media reports. The rest... Liam wouldn't lie to her... his friends were tricked into a fake deal, arrested. The Kingsleys were plain effing brutes. Perhaps Lilah Kingsley was as haughty as some in the press claimed... perhaps she wasn't. Perhaps she slept with all five brothers... perhaps she didn't. But to beat up someone while her family watched, powerless to help! While her staff and her guards stared in horror! The authority of the American government was used to assault a defenseless woman. Clothes ripped off, her body exposed to lust-filled criminals like Charles Kingsley, a bleeding Lilah was forced to a courtroom. The business she built with her sweat and blood was stolen from her.

The poor lady... Lupe knew what it was like to battle the world of men. She knew firsthand how terrible the Kingsleys were. Once they lost their money and clout... once JD and Charles were rendered weak... oh, to see them finally pay for what they did to her! To watch while Harry Sheppard pounded them into dirt, every piece of their worthless bodies screaming for mercy...

"What's the punishment for treason?" Lupe asked abruptly. "Prison?"

Liam nodded. "Yes, and sometimes death."

Her heart jolted. Barely able to bring the sounds out, she asked, "Hanging?"

"Injection, I think."

A woman who was so brutally victimized would die at the hands of the perpetrators of the assault. A soldier would be killed by poison introduced into his body—a criminal's end to a man who lived as a hero. His little boy would grow up in shame. *Lupe's* child would survive, outwardly untouched by the ugliness. Inside, Eden would be where the enemies gathered to celebrate the demise of a good man. They would assault their victim once again, even in her death.

Lupe closed her eyes for a second, taking a deep breath. Voice clear, she said, "Let Harry Sheppard know he's invited to the New Year's Eve party at Eden. You, too. Black tie."

Part VI

Chapter 16

December 31, 1988

Macau

Discarding her backpack in the middle of the lumpy mattress, Lilah eyed the garish green walls and the sagging floors of her room. The air was stale, and she could clearly hear Victor's booming voice from the room to her left. Silently, she castigated herself for taking the clerk at the information kiosk in the ferry terminal at his word. He'd assured them the Lotus Hotel was a mom-and-pop store. Oh, there were the mom and the pop—George and Christine Wu. As an extra, guests got to see young Chinese girls dressed in sparkly tops and micromini skirts on the sidewalk outside, teetering on stilettos as they handed business cards to tourists.

But the exiles were all tired after the week-long journey taking them from Central America to Hong Kong, ending in the boat ride to Macau. No one voiced objections to the location right in the middle of the prostitution center. Plus, in this establishment tucked into one of the many alleyways, the exiles stood a better chance of escaping the notice of authorities. As in Ecuador, the money in Lilah's Swiss bank account needed to be accessed through checks deposited in a local account opened under a false name. Again, a felony.

A soft knock sounded. "Lilah?" called the subdued voice of Scott.

Both he and Brad were at her door. Lilah didn't immediately kick her husband out. It took less than a minute for her to regret the lapse.

"Let's go out for dinner," said Brad, pushing his glasses up his nose. At Lilah's astounded glance, he flushed. "It's New Year's Eve. And I meant all of us."

"What's there to celebrate?" she snapped.

"I get it," he said, tone soothing. "You're upset at..." Brad waved a hand, indicating the shabby room. "You're Andrew Barrons's daughter... used to luxury, not this rough life."

As though she were a spoiled rich girl, sulking at being deprived of silks and jewels! A nasty smile curled her lips. "So are you. Used to luxury, I mean. The papers called you the emperor of the oil sector. Butlers, maids, chauffeurs... the best of food and drinks, designer clothes... all gone. Victor—boxer, chef, corporate troubleshooter— now does manual labor, lifting and carrying things for us. Alex Kingsley, decorated veteran and ladies' man, stands guard. Neil and Scott... instead of in the operating room or the astrophysics lab, they're here. What tragedy! My heart breaks!"

Holding up both hands, Brad said, "All my fault. I should've known better than to trust Steven and his uncle, but we need to at least try to get past what happened. Forgiveness is important. Lilah, I admit I did something I shouldn't have. It was a mistake."

"A *mistake?*" Lilah widened her eyes. "Do you think what you did is the same as..." She shrugged a shoulder. "...forgetting a birthday? Or maybe you're talking about forgiving Steven. He never did anything to *me* until the interrogation in Cuba. Are you asking me to forgive *him?* What's a little battery and sexual assault between relatives, heh?"

At the door, Scott shifted from foot to foot, looking at any spot in the room but the arguing couple. Behind him, the rest of the Kingsley brothers appeared. In one sweeping glance, Victor took in what was going on and hustled his family in to close the door behind.

Why they didn't simply leave, Lilah couldn't understand. Perhaps they were afraid she'd do bodily harm to the precious eldest.

Brad inclined his head. "You're entitled to be angry with me and the Kingsley family—"

Glancing heavenward, Lilah said, "Oh, thank you."

Brad sighed. "What I mean to say is anger is counterproductive, and forgiveness is the key to getting past bad feelings. Grandfather said as much in the magazine interview. He wants us to set aside thoughts of revenge and work toward peace. Neither side can thrive when there's conflict."

"Revenge?" Lilah exclaimed. "Is that the new word the Supreme Court of the United States now uses instead of justice? Or is it only you and Godwin who don't understand the difference?"

Ignoring her objection, Brad continued, "Peace is important, including where Steven's concerned. He tried a lot of tricks before he finally got us in Cuba. I've forgiven him a lot in the past, and once we return, I'll put the latest unpleasantness also behind me. Afterward, Grandfather will help us get the business back. It's the only way to bring some kind of normalcy to all our lives."

"What you said makes it amply clear you understand neither peace nor forgiveness," she said. "First of all, peace is not simply about avoiding conflict. Secondly, forgiveness—not holding a grudge—is mainly a *personal* virtue. Even when it is practiced by those in authority, clemency has its time and place. A first offense, someone who really didn't know any better, someone who was coerced into a crime, someone who regrets what he did... which of these groups does Steven fall in to deserve pardon? I could still understand your inclination to forgive and forget if you believed we'd never get to return. You can't mount an attack from a weaker position, especially with public opinion against us. But you clearly expect to get everything back. You expect to be in charge again. When someone in a position of authority refuses to hold a repeat offender accountable for intentional acts which he clearly doesn't regret, it is called dereliction of duty, not peace or forgiveness, and it leads to more crime. Such a leader who refuses to carry out his sworn obligations to those under his protection should never be put back in charge."

"Lilah—" Alex interjected.

Keeping her stare on Brad, she held up a hand. "You knew what kind of a man Steven was, and you still jumped into a deal in which he and his uncle were involved. Negligence is the most charitable label for what you did. Instead of making sure Steven paid for his prior crimes, you—intentionally or not—aided and abetted him. You let things escalate. During the military interrogation—"

"I'm trying to move on," Brad said. "But you keep rehashing the past. What's the point of wallowing in toxic feelings?"

"Will you stop making it seem like I'm at fault for..." Lilah took a deep breath, trying to tamp down fury. "Instead of doing your duty, you're... know what I think? You're making sure Steven and gang end up with all the blame while you... you get to be the well-meaning leader who always wanted peace. Hey, even your stupid stunt which got us into this mess could've been to make peace with your cousins." She laughed bitterly. "If... when we return, you don't want anyone using what happened in Cuba against you. What if the network's board refuses to let you back into the executive suite? Can't have that, can we?"

"You're wrong," Brad said. "It's not about either of us. Trust me... I really do get your need for payback. *You* need to understand revenge is not always the correct answer. Or I would have put an end to Steven's tricks long ago. Kingsley Corp, Peter Kingsley Company, Gateway... these businesses have thousands of employees. Corporate wars don't end pretty. People will lose jobs. My God, survival might become an issue for some of them. It's what Grandfather was talking about in the interview, and I agree one hundred percent. I will not risk all those lives and livelihoods. Don't let anger and vindictiveness blind you to potential consequences."

"*You* will not risk their lives?" Lilah mocked. "Where did this wisdom go when you got us into trouble in the first place?" Slitting her eyes, she stared hard at Brad, then at each of his brothers. "He's expecting all of you to buy it... which you will... as always. At least ask yourselves this. I could've been killed because of what you did. Now, your brother wants me to forget the *injustice*... he wants me to forget what those animals did to me in... all in the name of peace! And if I agree? Will everyone sit together around the campfire and sing "Kumbaya"? We all know what's going to happen. Your cousins will continue doing exactly as they please. In fact, they will escalate since they know there's no punishment coming. More innocent people could be thrown in jail. They could be killed. Charles and his buddies will attack more women. At what point are you going to say enough is enough? When he gets to *ten* victims? A hundred? A thousand? I mean... what *is* the magic number? How many people will be forced to suffer so the Kingsleys can live happily ever after? And before we know it, many lives *will* be ruined... precisely what your brother claims he doesn't want. I agree revenge is not the right answer. Neither is his perverted idea of peace."

Teeth clenched, Brad said, "Right now, it's not about ten women or a hundred or a thousand. It's only about a single person—you. The wellbeing of regular people is what's important, not one woman's thirst for blood. We all need to put the Cuba incident behind us."

"Do you not hear yourself?" Lilah asked. "You're demanding that I—the person who was wronged—shut up, instead of making sure the criminal stops committing crimes. You're putting the responsibility for any consequences on *my* shoulders rather than on those of the criminals... or on your own shoulders for letting injustice happen on your watch."

Brad huffed. "You are a lawyer. Of course you know the right arguments to make, but it still doesn't make you right. Revenge will only lead to—"

"Enough!" She shook a finger in his face. "Don't misrepresent my demand for justice as some kind of vendetta. Don't you dare! My parents... my mother was a lawyer herself. My father was a diplomat. They taught me the difference between revenge and justice. Revenge is irrational... inflicting harm in response to harm... it perpetuates itself. There is no closure involved. Justice is utilitarian... well-thought-out punishment for past crime in order to prevent future harm. I want society to take a good, hard look at what happened and pass verdict on everyone involved. It's the only way to get closure... rational and impartial vindication! We all deserve it—the stockholders and the employees who trusted us, the families we left behind, even you and your brothers. And yes, I want justice for myself. You know why? Because it is my duty as one of the former executives of the network. It's *your* duty because you were the CEO and let things get that far. The people who trusted us with power need us to fulfill our obligations no matter what."

"If you actually believe what you say, you would be willing to do as I request," Brad said. "Put your personal needs aside and think of the network. Think of how we can get it back with minimum possible damage."

"Get the network back?" Lilah laughed once again, not bothering to filter her contempt. "You think Steven's going to hand it over because you ask nicely? You claim your grandfather will help you... he will do nothing to help you, you hear me?"

Heaving in a breath, Lilah massaged her brow with a fingertip. She didn't intend to bring up Godwin's duplicity. None of the five men would believe what she had to say about the family patriarch, *and* they would hold her words against her in any eventual war they fought against the Kingsley clan. As far as Brad and his brothers were concerned, the evil cousins were alone responsible for all the ills in their lives.

"If you want your own business back..." Lilah resumed, her tone steady. "...you'd better be prepared to battle Steven. You'd better be prepared to punish that thief for his crimes, or he'll never stop trying to steal what isn't his. Forget the fact *we* built the network. The structure is too powerful, too dangerous to be left in the hands of a criminal like your cousin. I will *not* let it happen."

"We should've taken care of Steven and Charlie years ago," Victor muttered.

Brad pivoted to face his brother. "I don't believe this. You're also against me now?"

"It's not about..." Victor huffed, annoyance clear in his grimace. "Bro, you gotta admit what she says makes sense."

"So what do you want us to do?" Brad asked. "Return to the States and kill Steven?"

"We're not doing *any*thing," snapped Victor. "Except wait around for Harry to save us. Our families must be going out of their minds! Mother... I cannot imagine what she's going through. And what about us? Are you telling me you're okay living like this? In this dump?"

"I worry every single day about Mother," said Brad. "She'd be the first one to remind you we weren't always rich."

"It's not the damn point," said Victor. "We have to be realistic about what's gonna happen after we return. I mean... we should be making plans. And what's our fallback if Harry fails? It's a possibility, don't you think? Look what happened to Mr. Temple!"

"Victor, please," begged Alex. "Brad, Lilah... you know Harry *is* working on getting us back. Until then, there's nothing we can do. Even the trip from Panama to Ecuador got us into trouble. Who knows if some other thug spotted us on the way to Macau? Anything we do, any move we make to get the business back will reach Steven. He *will* hear of it. Keeping our heads down is our only option at this time. Victor, I get what you're saying about accounting for all possibilities, but we all know Harry. The only way he would accept failure is if he died."

Yeah, simply lying low was turning out to be the hardest task for all of them, including Lilah. Passively waiting for someone else to mount a rescue... Lilah blinked. There was no choice. They needed to do this.

"No more arguments, all right?" Alex said. "At least for one night."

Neil stated, "We need to eat. Macau is a great city, and it's New Year's Eve. Once we get food and some rest, things will seem better."

"I'm not going," Brad announced.

"But—" started Neil.

Brad turned toward the door. "I heard enough from my wife and brothers this evening."

Victor growled. The rest exchanged glances. Scott sighed and said, "I saw a supermarket half a block down. Brad and I can get instant noodles. The rest of you go ahead. You should go, too, Lilah."

"The two of you should be safe enough on your own," agreed Alex. Unlike in Ecuador, no one knew the exiles were in Macau. Not yet, anyway. "Everyone else... hoodies, caps, sunglasses. We *cannot* take the risk of being recognized."

They could of course eat in their rooms. Lilah would be alone in the drab chamber, trying to shut out the sounds of the young prostitutes outside the window. She would be attacked by memories of her loved ones back home.

Dan... their birthday was coming up. He would be terrified, remembering the one other birthday he believed they couldn't celebrate together... their seventeenth, when she'd been on the run in Libya. Lilah told herself to ignore the ache which returned to her chest. There would be other birthdays.

#

An hour later, she was in Taipa, having walked there from the hotel. Crowds thronged the labyrinth of narrow, cobbled streets and alleyways, shopping, eating, or simply gawking at the red and gold lights set out to welcome 1989. A group of young people—teenagers, really—stood in an alleyway, passing cigarettes between them. From the glassy look in their eyes and the shrill laughter, nicotine wasn't the only substance being smoked.

Merely a block from the kids, Victor found the food stall he wanted. The line inside was many feet deep and the chatter several decibels louder than tolerable. By the time Victor and Neil returned from the counter with trays piled high with dishes, Lilah was beginning to wish she'd remained in the hotel. Alex was seated across from her, his mood having changed from conciliatory to morose. He made no attempt to speak. Not that she wanted him to, but silence was only bearable when it wasn't pregnant with guilt and regret.

Victor set a bowl in front of Lilah before seating himself. She stared at the duck stew over white rice, wishing she were tempted to take a bite. From the way the men were digging in, there was nothing wrong with the food, but she harbored absolutely no desire to even taste it. "Tangy," Victor mumbled, thick, brown sauce dripping from the corner of his mouth. The prospect of a decent meal appeared to have restored *his* good spirits. "Tomatoes and vinegar, with a splash of red wine."

"Doesn't taste like the Chinese back home," Neil said, talking gulps of cool soda between forkfuls of the spicy food.

Victor paused, throwing a glance at Lilah before using his thumb to wipe the sauce from his lip. "It's Portuguese-Chinese fusion. I'm going to get one of those pork-chop sandwiches. You want one, Lilah?"

Voice testy, Alex interjected, "Dude, does it look like she's hungry?"

"The stew's really good," Neil said. "Try it, Lilah. You'll see."

How considerate! Lilah mocked them all in silence. If only they'd been this thoughtful just a few months back.

"I have to talk to the chef," Victor said. "I want the recipe."

Neil snorted. "You think they have an actual chef? This is a fast-food joint."

"Anyone who can cook like this is an *artiste*," Victor said, tone emphatic. "They should give him a Michelin star."

"Or her," Neil commented.

Victor waved his fork, almost poking out Lilah's right eye. "Whoever. I need to talk to the *person.*"

"No," said Alex. "We can't afford to draw attention."

"But we're safe here, right?" Neil asked, voice lowered to a mutter. "No extradition treaty."

Leaning forward, Alex explained, "It only means they don't *have* to send us back, not that they can't. We shouldn't give them the chance. Remember, we've already broken their laws with our passports. So don't do anything which could get us noticed."

"Okay, I won't," Victor agreed. "But let's at least find something fun to do. Plenty of clubs around."

Before Lilah could object, Neil exclaimed, "Not just the regular kind of clubs. Guess what I saw on the way here?" At the expectant looks on the faces of the rest, he added, "Have you heard about the strip club chain back home? Eden? There was a billboard a couple of blocks down, announcing the opening of Macau Eden later this year."

Across the table, Alex made a strangled sound.

"Strip club?" Lilah asked, tone ominous. "Are you insane?"

Neil shrugged. "Like I said, it's not open yet, but we can go to one of the casinos."

"So they can separate us from our money?" Alex asked.

The casinos... Lilah hoped Brad wasn't stupid enough to go gambling under the circumstances. Until the events in Cuba, she'd comforted herself with the thought he risked only a small amount on any given day. She never imagined he'd be stupid enough to wager the entire business and the freedom of his wife and brothers on a—

"Look," said Neil. "We don't have to gamble. Still, it's New Year's Eve, and they must have something arranged. Some kind of celebration."

"We're not here on vacation," Lilah snapped.

Voice tired, Alex asked, "Dude, did you already forget what just happened in Ecuador? If those... revolutionaries or whoever knew we were hiding in Quito, I'm sure there are people in Macau who're waiting for a chance to get at us."

Neil exclaimed, "We just got here. Harry being safe doesn't mean Steven didn't pay those thugs. He may have been just stupid enough. Or Charlie could've done it. Since *they* don't know yet we're in the city, we should be fine."

Alex shook his head. "Steven may or may not have paid them, but we can't take the chance he didn't. Which would mean there are *independent* agents looking for us."

"I can understand why those men in Ecuador might have," Neil argued. "We weren't very far from home. But this is the other side of the world, and we've been here less than one day! Who's going to attack us?"

Anyone they'd ever rubbed the wrong way. Alex had been the one to cover Asia on their buying spree, and he'd made at least one powerful enemy Lilah knew of. Jùn Wángzǐ, the drug lord of Burma. There was also Sanders. He was bankrupt and in prison, but still... who knew?

"How will they find us?" Neil continued. Voice lowering to a whisper, he added, "We didn't use the Kingsley name to get here, and we have our disguises." Besides the clothes, Neil kept a bandana constantly wrapped around his blond head, and all of them now sported beards.

"Lilah still looks the same," Alex said.

As one, the three men turned to Lilah. Her hoodie and glasses provided some protection, but if someone thought to take a second glance, her disguise would fall apart. "I'll stay in my room."

"For how long?" Victor asked, voice incredulous.

"Until we figure out what's going on back home," she said.

"Lilah, you're human like the rest of us," objected Victor. "You can't simply cage yourself in the *dump* of a hotel! I won't let you."

Eyes snapping wide, she asked, "You won't *let* me?"

Flushing, Victor took the porcelain cup in his large hands and gulped tea. "Wrong choice of words. I know I have no right to say anything after what I did... but..." Lilah tuned him out. The same sorry excuses offered by Alex. Brad was their precious big brother. They didn't think twice about giving in to his demands because they loved him. Victor imagined—as did the rest—Brad would know what he was doing. "...but you can't just stay in your room," Victor insisted. "I know *I* can't. What happens if Mr. Temple doesn't get any better?"

"You need a better plan than shutting yourself up," Alex agreed. "Or you *will* go crazy. Harry's working on something, and we hope it won't take long... but we don't know how long." Turning to his brothers, he added, "Doesn't mean we can afford to act like tourists, either."

Victor's face brightened. "You know what we *can* do?" Scooting his chair back, he stood. "I'll be back in thirty, tops." Before any of them could ask, he marched out into the street.

"Where's he going?" Neil asked, blond eyebrows drawn together in alarm.

Alex took a sip of the tea, keeping his worried eyes on his brother's departing back. "Victor talks a lot, but he's not going to do anything stupid... I hope."

It took Victor twenty minutes to return with half a dozen bottles and a stack of plastic cups. "Sagres beer," he announced.

Alex shook his head. "Drinking is also out of the question."

"No, it ain't," Victor retorted. "I plan to get sloshed until the last three months get wiped from my memory. You're going to let me."

Great! All they needed was a drunk former boxer. "Victor," Lilah started.

"It's either this or watch *me* go crazy," Victor said.

Flinging her hands in the air, she said, "Fine. Just don't get so wasted you can't make it back to the hotel on your own."

"We'll return before it gets to that point," he promised.

Lilah asked, *"We?"*

"Yes," Victor said, setting glasses around the table and pouring clear, gold liquid into each. "We are all going to indulge. Because without indulgences, life's not worth living."

Raising his cup, Neil said, "Happy New Year."

The froth lasted a minute or two. The aroma was fruity and the aftertaste bitter. Lilah grimaced.

"Not exactly the concoction of gods," Alex muttered.

Almost involuntarily, her eyes went to him. They were both remembering the same thing—the monastery in the Himalayas, the brew called *bhang*. Harry and Alex, high on victory and the drink, danced in front of the scandalized monks.

She'd dragged the semi-conscious men to their rooms at the guest house with the help of the staff, Harry switching from Indian cabaret songs to Hollywood romance and crooning "Heart and Soul" into her ear. Lilah smiled at the memory.

Getting the idiots to somehow stumble into bed, returning to her room only to stay awake deep into the night... she stared out through the window at the mountains in the distance. The moon was full, bathing the peaks in a silvery glow. Rekha, the transgender woman who procured the bhang for the Americans, was in the second bed and snoring loudly. It was no use. Lilah wasn't going to get any sleep next to a faulty car engine. She trudged to where the men slept and curled in a chair with the quilt pulled up to her chin. The clock on the wall said it was almost midnight. Almost New Year's Day.

Eyes on the seconds hand of the clock, Lilah counted down.

"Ten, nine, eight..." chanted the diners in the food stall, startling Lilah back to the here and now.

Her fingers still went up as though she never left the room in the monastery and could stroke Harry's hair from across time.

"...six, five, four..." shouted the crowd.

Lilah set her hand down just as she did a year ago. She didn't have the right.

"...two, one..."

Happy New Year, she whispered in her mind.

Chapter 17

A few hours later, December 31, 1988

Eden, Washington, DC

"Ten, nine, eight..." chanted the crowd.

The New Year's Eve party was going on full swing. The gathered crowd watched Dick Clark on the large-screen television as the ball dropped in Times Square. Lupe's eyes scanned the room. There. At the back of the crowd. Next to Liam.

Lupe inclined her head ever-so-slightly at the tuxedoed waiter behind the two men.

"...six, five, four..."

In one smooth glide, she was standing in front of the broker, Harry Sheppard.

"...two, one, Happy New Year!" cheered the crowd.

Plucking the champagne flute from his hands, she set it on the sideboard. Lupe saw the amusement on Liam's face, the expectation on the broker's. She smirked.

Before Harry could complete his frown of suspicion, the waiter—a nicely muscled young artist called Ira—stood between Lupe and the guests. Ira slid his arm across the broker's shoulders and drew his head close in an open-mouthed kiss. The broker's hands automatically went to Ira's elbows. Liam's jaw dropped. Lupe let her smirk turn into a wide grin.

On the stage, the band of Eden's Angels broke into a rousing rendition of *"Auld Lang Syne."* Noisemakers and whistles welcomed 1989.

Ira broke off the clinch and stepped back.

The reaction would come any moment. Harry Sheppard would either decide his machismo was more important than his crusade on behalf of his brother-in-law, or he'd prove his commitment to the task. Even if he walked away, it would be with the lesson he'd failed to manipulate her. Lupe couldn't help a little sputter of triumph.

"Thank you." Harry Sheppard said to Ira. There was a smile in the broker's eyes.

"For the kiss?" Ira asked, chuckling.

"For making me feel less lonely."

A sudden sound escaped Ira as though his mirth broke off in his throat. He stared at the guest for a couple of seconds before pivoting to Lupe. "I'm outta here," he said before striding off into the crowd. "Mail me the paycheck."

"Not cool, Lupe," Liam said in a voice only loud enough for the three people left to hear.

She didn't respond. Lupe couldn't take her eyes off the broker. Something about the shadows in his face... sudden unwelcome tears sprang to her lashes.

Two steps, and the shimmery fabric of her copper-colored gown draped across the tops of Harry's dress shoes. She wound her arms around his neck and dug her fingers into his silky hair.

The broker smelled of sandalwood and soap. Lupe took his warm lips with hers, tasting fruity bubbly on his tongue. Muscles flexed in his shoulders. Withdrawing, she slid her hands down his torso, letting her breasts brush against his chest. His heart beat in a steady rhythm under her palm.

"Another one for the show?" Harry asked, casting a half-glance at the curious onlookers.

"Not this time," Lupe answered.

A tiny moment passed before the broker nodded. Pulling back from her embrace, he wished her a happy new year and turned to his brother-in-law with the same greeting uttered in the same casually friendly tone.

Fifteen minutes later, Harry Sheppard and Liam were in chairs in Lupe's basement office. Frowning inwardly, she donned the brisk, business-like manner she used with associates. No involving staff in personal escapades... she ignored one of her own rules and ended up losing a perfectly good employee. On top of it, her attempt to bring the broker to heel failed big time. He'd disarmed her with a sad smile. She wondered who put the pain there. *None of your beeswax, Guadalupe Valdez,* she scolded herself. The last time she pondered the torment in a man's eyes, she ended up pining over him for years. Plus, *this* one already made it clear he was uninterested, apparently content to live with his wounds.

Not that the broker seemed particularly melancholy right at the moment. He was looking around the room, open curiosity on his face.

It irked Lupe to no end how even the men she discussed taxes with were disappointed by the simple décor of her office. "What did you expect? Red satin?"

"And gold lamé pillows," came the prompt response from the broker. Liam snorted. The broker held his hands up. "Kidding. I was only wondering how you managed all your clubs from this small room. What about your staff?"

"They work next to the sections they manage. For each club, I hire locally."

"Decentralization," the broker said. "I know someone who'd approve."

As though Lupe ever needed anyone's approval. She shrugged. "This room's plenty big for only one person." Hardwood floors, cherry desk with the warm rug beneath, file cabinet against the wall on the left. The small globe on the desk was marked in red with all the cities she planned to visit. There was a couch next to the street-level window on the right side. Liam was the only one who ever used it, hauled there by Lupe whenever she deemed him too wasted to drive home. Behind Lupe's desk was a wall-mounted console with the carved wooden statue of Virgin Mary on it, votive candle in front lit as always.

The broker's eyes swept past the statue, then returned. Curling her fingers into tight little fists, Lupe waited for a mocking smile, a derisive crack... something. "Nice" was all he said.

She exhaled. "Let's talk about your plan, shall we? I need some insurance for myself and the club. Also, we need to thrash out some rules before you talk to my girls about this... spy business."

"I've already made arrangements with my lawyer for you to be named beneficiary," said the broker.

"I will also need official documentation," Lupe elaborated, "of your promise to cover any and all losses the clubs might face over the duration of our collaboration. And I don't care what the losses are from because there will really be no way to tell if some problem was caused by a domino effect which went unnoticed."

Harry Sheppard nodded. "I won't be able to sell the stock in Gateway to reimburse you while I'm still alive, but there are properties in a couple of cities which would fetch nice chunks of cash. You will remain my beneficiary regardless of how much money is spent on keeping the books balanced."

"We're not done," said Lupe. "At the end of our business together—assuming we do win—you can take my name off your will. But you will pay off my existing bank loans *and* finance the opening of three clubs in three different cities of my choosing. A gift... any taxes on it will also be paid by you. There will be no asking for any of it back."

Her decision to enter into this partnership was based on her strong need to see justice... Lupe gritted her teeth. She never lied to herself before and wasn't about to start now. The satisfaction of watching the beasts who tore up her body being ripped to bits by Harry Sheppard would be oh, so sweet. The only other soul in this world who'd understand was Lilah Kingsley. It didn't mean Lupe didn't deserve to be compensated for her efforts.

"You will have the cash regardless of whether we succeed," the broker swore.

Shrugging, Lupe said, "I would assume you will need funds to stay out of prison in case you fail. Now, let's talk about some limits on what you're allowed to ask my girls."

The broker nodded. "I'll be grateful for whatever help they're willing to give."

"You can only ask," she warned. "No pressure. And *tell them*, for God's sake, what you're doing. They need to know what they're getting into. Don't try to trick them like you did with me."

"I swear I won't."

Was it a trace of amusement she heard? Lupe didn't give a damn. She cared for her girls. Many of the women in the business declined to use the sense God gave them and fell prey to drug dealers and pimps, often ending up addicted or worse. Lupe made sure that didn't happen to the ladies who worked at Eden. If some of them slept with a patron or two, it was of their own choosing. But Lupe still kept track of what was going on in their lives and protected them tooth and nail. They were the only family she had. Family trumped any need for revenge.

"More than any financial agreements we might make," Lupe continued, "I want to be clear the safety of my employees comes first. Whatever information you get, their identities will not be revealed to anyone, including the authorities. If it happens—and I don't care if the leak doesn't come from you—our deal is done. You will of course still pay me the money I'm owed."

"Of course," agreed the broker. "Security will be a two-part arrangement. First, our cover story." He explained the public would only know Harry Sheppard showed up in Eden for the same reason as every other patron... to watch beautiful women frolic without clothes. "The Kingsleys... yeah, they're going to realize something's up. I have something in mind as to what you can tell them. Regardless, we need to take precautions. Which brings me to the second part."

There would be more guards in the club, home safety enhancements for the girls. Lupe was to arrange on-call coverage with her security firm for any member of the team who might feel the need for protection when going out alone or in the dark. The bill would be paid by Lupe, but cash would be channeled to one of her overseas accounts by the broker. In case of emergencies, she was to contact him. If he turned out to be unavailable, she'd call Liam. Utmost caution was to be exercised on what was said over phone lines. Discussing anything mission-critical would be limited to certain areas of the club where they could either control physical access—as in Lupe's office—or camouflage their conversation in the general tumult.

Harry continued, "If anyone asks you or one of your staff directly about me... remember, I'm here for personal pleasure. Speculate on my reasons with them... I'm in the process of getting a divorce... my friends are in trouble, and I'm estranged from my family... I might be depressed."

Lupe nodded. "What happens if you do find something, and that person accuses me and my girls of leaking?"

"Neither you nor your girls know anything at all. Say maybe I bugged their offices. Or bribed someone. I could have stolen documents. Claim you're angry at the possibility I could've used your club for my activities. My membership will of course be canceled immediately. Offer to put in a complaint with the cops about me. Whatever it takes to make sure you don't put yourself at risk."

Liam yawned. "I'll leave the two of you to iron out the rest of the details. Got to catch the red-eye to New York." He explained to Harry, "Dad's already left a dozen messages. He said he's been trying to call *you*, as well."

There was a tinge of apology in Harry's voice. "I'm afraid I haven't had the time. I'm taking the early morning flight, too. Maybe I can—"

"I wouldn't worry," Liam assured Harry. "It's about the stock. Dad wants it back. Do me a favor—if you do talk to him, don't even hint you might return it. The way he sounded... I wouldn't put it past him to start gambling again."

Lupe glanced between the two men. Liam seemed to have immense trust in Harry, more than in his own father.

"I won't even pick up the phone," the broker promised. "In fact, neither Sabrina nor I answer any calls these days."

"Journalists?" Liam asked, voice sympathetic. "Verity's doing the same thing. She's gotten some calls, too."

"Tell her to do what we do," the broker advised. "Let them leave messages, and she can respond to the ones she needs to talk to."

When the door closed behind Liam, Lupe said, "Let's discuss what *you* want."

"All right... I'll give you a list of the politicians the Kingsleys are likely to have in their pocket. You'll know which of your employees are familiar with them... and who among the angels you can trust. Anything they see, they report to you or me. Meetings with foreign diplomats, businessmen, other politicians... anything we can use to induce a change of heart. I promise... what happens in the bedroom won't be used without express permission from the lady concerned."

"Will that be enough?"

"It's all I have right now. And whatever cash I can raise without selling my stock."

The audacity of what he was attempting... the entire American government versus Harry Sheppard, with only Eden's Angels to help him. "You're going to get yourself into trouble. I'm warning you, *Señor* Sheppard—"

"I swear I won't let *you* get into trouble for helping me."

207

"What about your safety?" Lupe asked.

"I'll be fine."

"The whole world will be gunning for you. Aren't you afraid?"

"Doesn't matter. Everything started with *my* mistake. So *I* have to fix this."

"You said the same thing before. What mistake is worth so much sacrifice?"

His eyelids flickered. "A mistake's got the same worth as what it destroys. I had this idea that... turned out to be stupid. Things snowballed from there to the point of Alex's arrest. I need to make sure he returns."

"You must be the world's best brother-in-law," she marveled.

"It's not only for him," the broker admitted. "Lilah was assaulted in front of..." Breaking off, he struggled to take a deep breath. "The bruise on her face... I might as well have done it myself."

Lupe controlled her eyebrows from rising in question. Harry Sheppard's obvious affection for the empress of the oil sector was new information. There had never been any rumors about them as far as Lupe knew. She puffed out a breath. *Señora* Kingsley's romantic misadventures were not of any concern to Lupe.

For a good, long minute, the broker sat in silence. Then, he dug into the inner pocket of his blazer. "Ms. Valdez, I have my list of politicians. Before we start working on it... any information you already have on the Kingsleys would be helpful... on Godwin in particular."

Lupe blinked. "Justice Kingsley? He never came here."

"I'm sure he didn't. He would've thought it beneath him... bad for the family's reputation. What I want to know is if you ever heard anything about him from the Kingsley hangers-on who did visit."

"Uhh..." Lupe tried to think. "If anyone ever mentioned anything bad enough that would help you now, I would've remembered. I mean we're talking about Justice Godwin Kingsley. The man is supposed to be cleaner than bleach."

Tone almost desperate, the broker asked, "Nothing about the Kingsleys and a girl called Amber Barrons? It's an old family scandal. She was seeing Godwin's half-brother, and he refused to marry her. She later hanged herself."

"Oy." Lupe put a hand to her chest. "The bastard. All these rich families have men like him. Us girls so need to learn not to trust them. But it doesn't sound like the justice's fault. And no... this is the first I'm hearing of her."

"Are you sure?" The broker huffed. "Of course you're sure. It's just... it would've saved us a lot of trouble. Okay... we'll work with what we have. Could you get the employee roster and help me make some notes? We need to see which of your trusted people would also have access to the men on my list."

It was then it occurred to her he was putting a great deal of faith in her word... in what Liam might have said about her, in her reputation as a straightforward business partner. But then, the broker didn't have many other options before him. Just like her, he was taking a calculated risk.

Lupe swiveled her chair to the left, scooting forward toward the file cabinet. When she bent to pull out the drawer with staff records, the chair tilted at a precarious angle, but if she could dance the samba in six-inch stilettoes, she could manage an unruly piece of furniture.

The broker continued, "We need an excuse to give to the Kingsleys... for my being here, I mean. They're going to tell your patrons I'm here to steal secrets, so we need to put up an alternate explanation people will buy... something other than divorce and depression."

Rummaging through the employee folders, she rolled her eyes. "Spit it out, Harry Sheppard. I'm sure you already know what you want to do." Only fools needed more than one encounter to learn a lesson. Lupe was no fool. The broker would not be able to take her by surprise a second time.

"If you have no objection to the idea, will you marry me?"

The chair tipped, toppling Lupe to the carpet.

Part VII

Chapter 18

Same time

New York University Medical Center

Sitting on the side of the bed, Temple wished he'd somehow asked his old friends to stay. His former secretary, Wilma, left a little after midnight, her face red and blotchy from weeping. Ten minutes later, Noah also padded out of the room. Even if they *did* stay, how could Temple communicate when he was trapped in his own mind? He could move every body part, see everything, hear every sound. He could still touch and taste and feel. Yet when thoughts fought to escape his brain, his tongue wouldn't cooperate except to make meaningless noises. His eyes longed to read words once familiar, but his mind refused to show him anything more than a jumble of scratches. He'd tried to write, but the end result was indecipherable even to himself. There was probably some medical term for the damage caused by the bullet, but Temple didn't know what.

He stared hard at the clock on the wood-paneled wall of the VIP room and angrily willed the numbers on its face to make sense. He knew it was around twelve-thirty only because it was where the hands pointed. The digits could have been in some sort of alien script for all he understood them.

His own damned mistake... he arrogantly imagined himself safe from Godwin's games. Temple growled, hurling the porcelain cup from the side table in the direction of the clock. It hit the crystal vase on top of the television set. The vase toppled, and water and roses spilled down the screen, intensifying the floral scent permeating the room. The cup crashed to the gleaming hardwood floor, breaking into sharp, little shards.

The anchor droned on in a language Temple didn't know. Except, the skinny, young man with the Hitler mustache was someone Temple had watched on CNN Headline News often enough.

The night nurse appeared at the door. *"Everything okay?"* Only the inflection at the end told him she was asking a question.

"I don't understand you," he tried to say. He didn't understand the words spilling out of his own mouth. "God," he begged, eyes tearing. Was it simply the damage from the bullet? Or was he dead already? Was he in hell for eternity, punished for the sins he committed?

Warm sympathy in her eyes, the nurse clucked. She bustled up, urging him back onto the yellow and orange pillows.

"No," he barked. "Do you know who you're talking to, young lady?" He swatted off the hand on his shoulder. "I am Temple, former president of the United States." Not a senile old man.

Turning her head toward the door, she said something. Two of the officers from Temple's security detail hurried in, letting the nurse step out. In one sweeping glance, the men took in the mess on the floor and Temple's angry expression.

When the nurse reappeared with a syringe, he said, "No."

Her eyelids flickered. She'd understood what he said. The gist of it, anyway.

"No," he tried once more, fighting the gentle hands of the security officers.

"You need to get some rest, sir," the younger one crooned, pulling the cream-colored comforter over his charge. *"It's late."*

Temple glared. He didn't like the expression on the officer's face. Smug, patronizing. The first chance the former president got, the young man was getting replaced.

The room blurred. Temple's head felt heavy. He would fall asleep any minute now, but he needed to tell them... something... about someone... "I used to be pres... senator... I'm..."

As soon as he woke, he was going to demand they let him go. With a campaign to run, he couldn't afford to be sick. This would be his second one after winning the senate seat left vacant by the death of his father back in 1941. As though it wasn't enough, the Kingsleys were creating headaches, as usual.

"I wish," Temple murmured.

He wished his half-brother had been born with more sense in his thick head. All the young man wanted to do was drink and go through as many women as he possibly could. The forty-year-old father of three boys wasn't really young, but to Temple and Godwin, the half-brother they shared never seemed to cross the emotional maturity of fourteen. His youngest son, Aaron, actually was fourteen, but he was level-headed.

Damn, the family tree was complicated! Godwin's mother was Old Man Kingsley's first wife. The lady was packed off to a mental health asylum not long after Godwin was born. Temple's mother was never married to his father, the senator. She walked out on her live-in lover and their newborn son, soon meeting Godwin's father. Divorce was not common those days, but Old Man Kingsley had his first wife's illness as an excuse. In any case, she didn't live long afterward. The old man's son with the second wife was the one who turned out to be alcoholic.

Thanks to the manipulations of Temple's mother, her drunk son ended up with the entirety of the Kingsley family business and the CEO title, Godwin drawing a hefty salary as the president of the company. Good thing he took control of the operations, or the lush would've bankrupted the whole clan. Unfortunately, the shares and the CEO spot could only be inherited by the progeny of the drunkard as per the terms of the contract demanded by Temple's mother. Godwin didn't have children, so there were no concerns about power struggles within the family. His half-brother managed to exercise his only talent and fathered three boys—two on his wife and the third with his secretary. The alcoholic proved a dad merely in name, and Godwin became the paternal presence in the lives of the lads. One of the three would eventually run the company.

"David," Temple mused., fighting the chemicals pulling him into slumber.

The oldest of the sons was out of the question. The simpering little idiot... half blind on top of it with women unwilling to give him a second glance.

Too bad Godwin refused to consider the youngest, Aaron, for the CEO spot. Even in his mid-teens, Aaron was showing himself to be intelligent and level-headed. But he was still an ordinary secretary's son. The illegitimacy wasn't Godwin's major concern. Unless Aaron's mother could somehow prove she descended from King David himself, Aaron would never be head of the family.

Peter, the middle son, it would be. He was a fine young man, but headstrong. Temple wasn't sure Peter would agree to what they had in mind, but there was the luxury of time in his case. Peter was only eighteen.

Where Peter's father, Temple and Godwin's half-brother, was concerned, his wife had initiated divorce proceedings. Once the situation sorted itself out, the drunk could finally be of some use to the family. Godwin and Temple would get the damned idiot hitched to the young lady of their choice. Unfortunately, he was proving difficult, unwilling to tie himself down a second time. No matter. Godwin would make it happen.

Two marriages, one with Peter as the groom, and the other with his alcoholic father as one. Two brides, one a Barrons, the other a Sheppard. An alliance... three families would unite to defeat their common enemy, the man who threatened the order of things in the world: Jared Sanders.

Chapter 19

Forty-one years ago, May 1947

New York, New York

"Amber," started Temple, unsure whether to be worried or amused. He'd been glad when Andrew Barrons proved all too willing to form an alliance against Sanders. The distant cousin Andrew suggested for the purpose was a spirited little thing, far too good for the intended groom. Temple never expected the seventeen-year-old to be this gung-ho about marrying a man more than twice her age. "I like your ambition, but—"

She wagged a finger in his face. "Stop right there. No 'buts.' Everything sounds much, much better without that ugly word."

Temple tried again. "Listen—"

Amber pouted. "There's another word I don't like. Will you stop being mean to me if I admit I'm ambitious? I want to have it all, Senator. A fantastic career, a handsome and successful husband..."

Hoo, boy. The half-brother he shared with Godwin was certainly not ugly, but he was a complete failure at managing the family business. Still rich, though. So perhaps Amber would consider him successful. He also much preferred to seek feminine warmth without offering the benefit of matrimony. Temple didn't want Amber inviting trouble. "We have to be careful. He's a little... skittish about marriage."

Her mouth curved into a delightful smile. "Isn't that why Andrew got me this position?" Internship with Godwin Kingsley, the junior-most justice on the United States Supreme Court. "So I can meet your little brother and sneak into his broken heart?"

Temple laughed.

Thanks to his drinking and philandering, the Kingsley scion's first marriage was over and done with, leaving both the parties involved wary of commitment. But if anyone could convince the playboy to take another stab at monogamy, it would be Ambrosia "Amber" Barrons. The bouncy, blonde curls framing her oval face, the lively, brown eyes, and the neat figure made for an attractive package in the fashionably cut green, mid-calf suit. Her devil-may-care attitude was the icing on the cake. As the singular female presence in Justice Kingsley's New York office, she drew the eye of every bespectacled young lawyer going over briefs, every middle-aged secretary banging away on a typewriter, and the elderly janitor currently making a pretense of changing the flickering light bulb.

"Let's get some privacy," Temple said.

Her fingers went to the amber beads she wore around her neck. "Why, Senator... I didn't know you felt that way."

"Huh? No!"

"Shame on you! A married man with a son. How old is he now?"

"Ten... I think." Frantically, he said, "Amber, I only meant we cannot discuss our plans in—"

She laughed, the sound pleasantly tinkling over his eardrums. "Senator, I was joking."

It took a few seconds for Temple to start breathing normally. "God, you nearly killed me there."

Laughing even harder, she said, "For a minute, you did look like a choking cow."

"Of course he did," came Godwin's voice. "He's a politician. Can't afford to have his name linked with young ladies, however charming. Also, try to remember this is an office. Not a place for you to practice flirting with random men."

Amber straightened, her cheeks flushing. "I'm sorry, Judge. I didn't intend..."

Temple rolled his eyes. At almost forty-three, Godwin was still considered a handsome fellow, but even as a teenager, he'd shown only glacial civility toward the female of the species. The *New York Daily Mirror*'s gossip columnist frequently speculated on the reasons behind his lack of appreciation for the fairer sex. Godwin countered how he already had two wives—Kingsley Corp and the law—with no time or inclination for romance. Every woman he ran into was invariably given the same deep-freeze stare.

"Are you done with the work I gave you, Ambrosia?" Godwin asked.

Tilting her chin, she peeped at him through her lashes. There was mischief in the way she bit her lower lip.

Temple made a mental note to warn Amber. Adopting a coquettish manner would only serve to annoy Godwin even more than he already was. She'd need his support in the family.

"I'll have it ready for you in an hour at the most," she said.

As she walked away, Temple chided his stepbrother. "You didn't have to send her off. She *was* only joking."

"I know." Godwin nodded, his eyes on her trim back as she disappeared into the little cubicle she called her own. "But women need a firm hand and she more than most. Or they start thinking they own you."

"Please don't change your mind about her. Where will we find another Barrons girl who's willing to marry an alcoholic womanizer? I'm still not sure why. I know she's ambitious, but there are plenty of men in New York—"

Godwin sighed. "She wants to be a lawyer. Law schools don't easily accept women, and I told her I will help."

Eyebrows raised, Temple said, "Remarkable."

"What about the Sheppard girl?" Godwin asked.

"Patrice? Not very ambitious. But intelligent, most certainly." Temple smiled. "The head of the school tells me she's soaking up classical Greek and Latin."

Godwin huffed. "I meant how are you going to get her to agree?" While the Barrons side of their plan was Godwin's responsibility, the Sheppards were Temple's.

"I don't think we'll have to do much. She's... lonely, I think. Happy to do what you ask in return for a little bit of affection."

Shaking his head, Godwin said, "Too much empathy will get you into trouble, brother."

"Too little will turn us into monsters like Sanders," Temple retorted. "The whole point of this enterprise is to create a system where criminal businessmen don't get the chance to take over crucial sectors. Why are we even attempting it if we cannot bring ourselves to feel compassion for others?"

Godwin's eyelids flickered. "Just make sure the girl cooperates. We have to act fast before the upstart, Jared Sanders, manages to destroy us all."

"We have to take our time; she's very young, and so's Peter. Besides, she needs some grooming. The Sheppards may be a well-respected family, but Patrice is strictly working class, financially speaking. She will need to learn how to be a Kingsley."

"I agree," Godwin said. "We cannot give Peter any reasons to refuse. His father's trouble enough."

"What's our brother's latest objection to Amber?" Temple asked.

"Nothing at all," Godwin said. "He simply refuses to show up at the office to meet her."

"Invite her home," Temple suggested.

"I have a better idea," Godwin murmured. "I'm going to have her join us on the yacht. If it doesn't do the trick, nothing will. Ambrosia might be a handful, but she's a delicious handful. The sight of her in a bathing suit should be enough to bring him to his knees."

Cheerfully, Temple agreed, "Our brother will soon find himself the proud husband of our delightful girl."

Godwin brooded, "Too bad. She needs someone who can set down rules, not a—"

Something crashed. "Sorry, Judge," said the janitor, climbing down from the stepladder to sweep up the pieces of the broken light bulb from the floor.

#

Back in the present

Early morning, New Year's Day, 1989

New York University Medical Center

"It's all he says?" Harry asked Noah, looking down at the former president thrashing around in the sweat-soaked sheets. "'See you' and 'sorry'?"

"I should've seen it," Temple murmured, whatever he was saying making no sense to the men listening. *"Amber, I'm so sorry... Shawn, forgive me. Lilah... oh, God, help her..."*

Noah shrugged. "And 'how are you?' Sometimes, he simply blabbers."

"He's never said anything about Amber?"

Noah said. "Not even in his sleep. After we last talked, I made a few inquiries with people I knew in law enforcement back then, but there isn't much more info than what we already have. So unless Temple recovers, the particular lead is going nowhere."

"Even if he recovers, we don't know how much of his memory he has retained," Harry said.

"The neurologists say evaluating mental function is difficult when the patient has global aphasia... he just can't communicate."

"How does he act? I mean... emotionally?"

"Angry, frustrated. I tried a few things to take his mind off. Chess... but he doesn't want to play... or he doesn't remember... I don't know. The only thing which seems to calm him are his Sinatra records. Sometimes, he looks at you like he's begging for mercy. I remember a German Shepherd the Kingsleys owned a long time back. When the dog got old and sick, he used to stare at anyone who passed by with the same expression... pleading to be put out of his misery. Finally, Temple took him to the vet and got him put to sleep."

Harry muttered, "I think I understand."

"I'm afraid Temple's going to start thinking the same," Noah whispered, cheeks pale and drawn.

"He has you looking out for him," Harry consoled.

"I wish I could get his son to visit more," Noah said. "Then again, they've never been close. After the initial flurry of calls, it's been you, Sabrina and her boy, Patrice, and Aaron. Oh... and some of the young men who interned with Temple when he was a senator—four of them to be precise." Noah paused for a moment or two before adding, "Temple held Patrice's hand and apologized to her a few times. By which I mean he said sorry over and over, but who knows what he actually intended to say?"

Harry frowned. "Could it have something to do with the note he sent to Godwin?" Patrice Kingsley certainly kept secrets. Her rejection of her own kin, the Sheppards, the peculiar relationship she shared with the husband who walked out on her... perhaps there was something about Alex's mother which Temple used to force surrender from Godwin Kingsley. Still, it was difficult to imagine Patrice keeping mum about a weapon which could help her sons.

"No," Noah said instantly. "It's impossible." At Harry's questioning eyebrow, Noah elaborated, "Whatever Temple knows about Patrice's life story, I know as well. Nothing about it would've been enough to stop Godwin. It was either about Amber or something completely unrelated although I can't imagine what else." The former attorney general paused as though searching for words. "I need to talk to Patrice. What she's doing right now is not safe... living in the Kingsley mansion... but..."

"She's surrounded by her sons' enemies," agreed Harry, noting the speed with which all expression vanished from the lawyer's face.

In a second, Noah sighed. "Everyone has secrets. If I thought it would help, I would've told you."

Harry nodded. So there *was* something about Alex's mother. Still, Noah not wanting to speak of it meant it wasn't anything useful in bringing the exiles home. Also, she would've surely done something with any weapon in her possession. Patrice Kingsley loved her sons.

Part VIII

Chapter 20

A few hours ago, December 31, 1988

Upper East Side, New York City

Leaving Richard at the gates of the Kingsley mansion, the cab honked once and took off without warning. He leaped back to avoid getting his feet run over and made a note of the license plate on the vehicle disappearing into the nighttime traffic. Chilly wind whistled between buildings and blew against his face, nearly freeze-drying his skin. His eyes watered. Giving up the idea of retaliation against the rude cab driver, Richard pivoted and strode along the path to the garage. On the way, he pulled his cashmere coat tighter around his torso and tugged the edge of the matching scarf up to his nostrils. Not much snow to show for such a cold winter, so his dress shoes still gleamed.

Decorated with white holiday lights, the pines circling the mansion glittered against the black sky, adding to the golden glow from the windows of the building. While the Kingsley garden was considered a luxury even in the affluent Upper East Side neighborhood, it was not the only mark of the family's wealth. When Central Park was built, Godwin Kingsley's father installed an indoor putting green on the third floor of the building from where he could enjoy the scenery without having to mingle with the riff-raff. The live-in staff did appreciate having actual trees around, especially during the holidays, but for the adopted son of the chauffeur, the green turf which mattered the most was the one within the mansion.

The side door to the garage swung open before Richard could knock. In the light spilling out stood a short, plump woman, sporting cheekbones inherited from her Apache grandmother. She smelled of warm chocolate and roasted nuts and was currently breathing twenty-five times a minute. Behind her, the Beatles sang "Please, Please Me" on the CD player. It was the one gift Richard's parents consented to accept from their adopted son. This particular song was playing meant Armor, Sr. was hard at work.

"Ma," Richard said, smiling in pleasure. "What are you doing down here? Were you baking cakes?"

"I saw you from the apartment."

"So you ran down the stairs? Be careful, please? We don't want another accident like last winter's."

"That was on ice," she said pertly. "Not on the stairs. You're not calling me old, are you?"

He held his hands up. "I swear I wasn't." But the gray in her dark hair and the wrinkles surrounding her warm, brown eyes gave testimony to the fact she was in her seventies. "Ma, why can't you and Pa move in with me?"

Grabbing him by his ear, she tugged, and Richard pretended to topple in as he'd done since outshooting her height at the age of ten. "Not again, Richie," she said, shutting the door. "We're happy where we are."

Lit as the interior was with bright-yellow bulbs, Richard could easily see every tool neatly stored in the cubbies, every rag, every container. Just as it had been in his childhood. There were four cars, a Ford used by the mansion's staff to run errands and two others belonging to David and Aaron Kingsley.

A slender man of average height, his once-blond hair now reduced to a few gray strands at his nape, was whistling along to the music. Armor, Sr. was hand-waxing the fourth car, the Mercedes-Benz 770 owned by the Kingsley patriarch. Richard had heard Hitler used the same model.

"You take care of the problems in Texas?" Armor, Sr. asked.

"Almost," Richard said.

The contractor working for his drilling company had connections with human traffickers, and the workers he sent were a mere step up from indentured servants, paying off the expenses involved in transport to the United States. There were also the women and children put to work, providing "relief" to the men. The local FBI chief arrested the contractor and wanted to know how deeply Richard was involved.

He'd denied all knowledge of it, obviously. But he'd known. The contractor came cheap, enabling Richard to drastically cut expenses. It wasn't difficult to figure out how such discounts were possible. To the FBI man, Richard expressed shock, keeping his annoyance under check. The migrants damned well had the option of going to the cops but didn't. It was an arrangement beneficial to all parties until the FBI decided to poke its nose in. Fortunately for Richard, there was no actual evidence of his awareness of the situation. He'd have to pay a fine, perhaps. But a light monetary slap would be it. He didn't want his elderly parents losing sleep over something as trivial.

Out loud, Richard said, "It's New Year's Eve, Pa. Can't you do the waxing another time?"

His father responded, "The judge needs the car tomorrow. You've heard the news. Mister Steven's gotten engaged, and they're having a party at the young lady's place."

The usual mix of exasperation and fondness came over Richard. Not only did he hear, he was the first one to do so. He was also going to be the best man at the wedding. Unfortunately, it never occurred to his parents their son was now almost equal to the Kingsleys and privy to the details of their lives.

Ma and Pa loved him, Richard harbored no doubt, but they never understood the boy they called son. Armor, Sr. was content to live and die as the Kingsley chauffeur. Richard, on the other hand, had always been hungry for more. He wanted to be someone, to do something. The life of looking in through the window was not for him. He wanted to be the one who owned the mansion. He was there... almost.

Richard was no longer merely the chauffeur's son or even simply an army major. He'd gotten his law degree and worked for a top-notch firm for a while. Eight years ago, he agreed to Steven's request to manage a Kingsley Corp subsidiary, but it didn't take Richard long to buy his own oil drilling business. He now possessed enough money to fund an expansion. There were moments when it occurred to him he might, one day, challenge Steven for the spot of top dog in the oil sector, but Richard always dismissed the idea. While he admitted he was ambitious, if there was one quality he valued more, it was loyalty. Steven was loyal to Richard, and he'd return the favor even if it meant he remained a Kingsley vassal all his life. But it was a good life, master of himself, servant to none... almost none.

This was the world Mrs. Brad Kingsley once threatened to rip apart. She'd vowed to sign over the percentage held by the Peter Kingsley Network to the worst possible investor she could find, one who'd bleed him dry. Lilah Kingsley refused to acknowledge his rank in the military, demoting him to a mere "mister" like the rest of the men who slobbered at her feet.

Richard snarled in satisfaction. Mrs. Kingsley went too far with him, but her fall came only when she laughed at Steven for something as silly as falling into a pool. A woman like her might have believed she'd get away with mocking a chauffeur's son, but she made the mistake of attacking a man with enough wealth and clout to tear her arrogance to shreds... the beginning of the end for her. She paid for the insults she heaped on them. Steven's brother—Charles—might be an idiot, but he beat the pride out of her. He threatened to haul her naked to the courtroom, her limbs visibly stained with menstrual blood. Oh, they were all in trouble for it. Perhaps someday, Richard would come to regret the episode. But he'd always savor the moment the rich, condescending bitch was stripped of her conceit.

Tonight, there was other business to think about. Godwin Kingsley had called him in—summoned them all—wanting updates on their plans for Lilah Kingsley and her male harem. Richard glanced at the wall clock.

"Meeting with the judge again?" asked his father.

"Yes, sir," Richard responded. "I've been invited to dinner."

"I'm so glad the judge is taking such an interest in you," his mother said, voice proud.

Richard gritted his teeth, trying not to bellow Godwin was not doing him an honor. The patriarch *needed* Richard because the Kingsley grandsons were a worthless lot, with the exception of Steven. And Alex, Richard admitted grudgingly. Victor, too. "Don't know if we'll be done before midnight. Thought I'd wish you two a happy new year before going on to the house."

"You don't have to return to your apartment tonight, do you?" his mother asked, eyes hopeful. "Your old room's still here."

He couldn't bear to be reminded of the time in his life when he'd been a mere servant, but a rush of affection coming over him, Richard hugged his mother. "I *am* going back to my apartment but not without sampling your cake. Why are you baking one, anyway? It's not like you knew I was going to be here, and neither of you is allowed to eat sweets... your health."

She laughed. "It's not for us. *You're* not going to get a piece, either. I'm sending it to the little boy."

"Little boy?"

"Mister Alex's son, Michael. He's here, visiting his grandma."

"What?"

His mother rocked back on her heels. "Don't you raise your voice at me!"

Shoving fingers through his hair, Richard said, "I'm sorry, Ma, but Alex's kid is here? At dinner?" What kind of a sick game was Godwin Kingsley playing? He knew the boy witnessed the arrest. Richard had mentioned as much.

When he spotted the lad during the raid in Panama, he was surprised at finding a toddler in the office building. Then, he figured the boy was Alex's. His unexpected audience didn't stop him from doing what he needed to, though. Besides, it was better for the child if he understood the realities of life early. After all, Richard was forced to. The powerful won every battle... it was the universal truth.

Mrs. Armor snorted. "Dinner with y'all? After what you and Mister Steven did to his family? I don't think so!"

"I was only the lawyer, Ma."

"Richie," she said, her Okie accent getting more pronounced by the second. "I love you, but I can still tell right from wrong. Mister Steven trapped his cousins, and you helped."

Even to the two people who'd been with Justice Kingsley long enough to know better, the old judge remained blameless. Steven Kingsley was now elevated to the status of main villain. Somehow, everyone seemed to have forgotten how Godwin's word had always been law in Kingsley Corp. How Godwin even managed to split the family business in two over Steven's objections. Yet the powerful old man was now cast in the role of helpless patriarch.

Wiping his hands on a rag, Armor, Sr. interjected, "Miss Patrice invited the boy and his mother to join her at Mister Aaron's apartment. I went to pick them up. They're not dining with the judge."

"Good. I mean, the woman would've been bad enough, but add the kid to the mix..."

Armor, Sr.'s gray eyes glinted. "You shouldn't be talking about Miss Patrice in such a tone, son."

"Why are you always so—" Richard never understood his father's support of Patrice Kingsley. There was a time when he even suspected an affair between the servant and the lady of the manor.

His mother soothed, "Miss Patrice has always been very fond of you, Richie. Don't you remember?"

He wished he could forget. As a child, he thought it fun to have Patrice Kingsley as a fairy godmother of a kind, handing out little treats when no one was looking. In his adolescence, he resented it, seeing it as yet another sign of the difference between her own children and him. *Class guilt,* he'd thought. But much as he hated being her pet project, the money she forked out helped with the extras so essential to fitting in with his upper-class schoolmates.

"I don't understand you," his mother complained. "With all that Miss Patrice has done for you, why couldn't you be friends with *her* boys, instead? What *is* the problem you have with them?"

Problem? As in one single issue? The preexisting friendship between Steven and Richard upon the reentry of Patrice Kingsley and her sons into the family fold had only been the first obvious roadblock. There were the casual insults Victor and Alex threw in Richard's direction. As though "son of a chauffeur" was going to be his identity the rest of his life! The greater the affection Patrice Kingsley showed him, the more intense the loathing he felt for her sons. He even took advantage of it where their boyhood fights were concerned, easily convincing her he had nothing to do with the dirty tricks.

Richard's parents hoped going away to college would give him a different perspective on the situation, but his antipathy increased. Exponentially. God only knew he had reason to resent the existence of Alex Kingsley. Since Richard's graduation, he'd made sure Patrice never got the chance to progress beyond basic civilities whenever they met. Unfortunately, his brusque dismissals on their rare encounters failed to deter her, and she continued to send him gifts at every milestone.

He didn't get Patrice Kingsley. Actually, Richard didn't get his own parents and their loyalty to the Kingsley clan. There was even a point in time the chauffeur invested all their spare cash in some shipping company associated with the Kingsleys. Godwin had been going on about the importance of such businesses in the modern economy, and his naïve servants believed him. From gossip Richard heard via other employees, this particular enterprise was driven under by Peter Kingsley, Patrice's late husband... on purpose over some disagreement with the company's owners no one knew about! It was soon after Richard's adoption, and with a baby in tow, the Armors couldn't afford to leave the position in an angry huff. Now... Richard begged his parents to leave the place. They could live in luxury but no... both preferred their life of servitude, castigating *him* for what he did to the sons of the same man who caused them to lose their life's savings.

Patrice couldn't have failed to understand Richard's role in the latest treachery. He was the one who talked her into supporting Brad and his idiotic schemes, making her an unwitting accessory to the crime. There was no excuse Richard could make up for this one.

"Never mind," he said. "I'd better get to the house before they start."

Chapter 21

Later the same evening

The Kingsley mansion

Upper East Side, New York City

Dinner with Godwin Kingsley was never a simple affair. The air of effortless elegance was maintained at all times. The staff glided in and out of the room, collecting empty bowls and carrying in the next course.

Steven and Charles didn't seem impressed, but they were used to the grandeur. Richard certainly wasn't. He was not the only outsider who'd been asked to dinner. General Potts, the former dean of West Point, was present.

Bitterness welled in Richard as he eyed his former teacher. Alex Kingsley's former teacher. Richard supposed he should be grateful for having graduated before Alex sauntered into the hallowed grounds of the military academy. Richard wasn't sure what he'd have done if he were forced to listen to the accolades heaped on the golden boy of the Kingsleys.

Richard had been the best marksman to go through the general's tutelage, but never did the dean treat him as anything more than another student. The faculty never sang his praises.

From the general's son, Philip, who was Richard's friend, he got to know of Alex's conquest of West Point. General Potts made sure the highest levels of army leadership got to know of Alex and his skill with firearms. Alex was the one chosen to represent the academy's student body to visiting politicians and other VIP guests. He was introduced to the men who mapped out the country's military strategy.

Talk of the gifted officer reached even Richard's unit in Vietnam. The colonel in charge tossed a question or two Richard's way, curious about the young man who'd grown up with him. Everyone wanted to get to know Alex, jockeyed to be on his good side.

Attracted by the wealth and fame, women flocked to Alex. Richard never lacked for attention from the fairer sex, either. Far from it, in fact, but he'd seen enough of upper-class mating games to know the choicest picks went to the more successful men. Not very different from the whores plying their trade in Times Square. Only, less honest.

Alex Kingsley was groomed for big things, while he, Richard, was expected to be happy with the small crumbs thrown his way.

#

Thirteen years ago, March 1975

United States Military Academy

West Point, New York

Outside the building holding the dean's office, a bugle sounded "Retreat," signaling the end of the day. Captain Richard Armor and General Potts pushed their chairs back from the conference table and came to attention, facing the direction of the music. They stayed in the same spot through the firing of the cannon to the end of "To the Colors." It wasn't as if there was anyone else in the room to express disapproval if they didn't, but the military academy was steeped in tradition, and few of its graduates ever forgot what they were taught.

Sweat trickled down Richard's neck. It was a cold spring in New York, but he was plenty warm from the anger sizzling across his nerves. He supposed he should've been thankful to be given the honor of this meeting though it was only on account of his friendship with Captain Philip Potts. But the general chose to hold the discussion in the conference room rather than his private office, thus clearly signaling his lack of interest.

When they sat back down, Richard resumed his objections to the general's blatant bias. Only he couldn't quite label it as such. "No, sir, I don't understand why you advised against my appointment to the South-Central Asian region," he said, keeping his gaze fixed on the picture on the wall across him. Good eyesight was a prerequisite for sniper training, and Richard still retained it. He could still see the general well in the periphery of his visual field. Gray hair, brown eyes, average height. Although nondescript in appearance, the general's posture would have given him away as a soldier as he sat at the head of the table, making notes in the folder in front.

"Because, Captain, your experience is in Vietnam, and neither Pakistan nor Afghanistan is similar terrain. Why would the army send you out of Southeast Asia?"

"Combat troops were withdrawn from Vietnam months ago. I'm no longer needed there as you well know." Since then, Richard had been in Japan. Twiddling his thumbs, mostly.

The general looked up, his expression thoughtful. "The nation cannot be in a perpetual state of war."

"Sir, but the nation has gone to the trouble of training me, equipping me. Why shouldn't it utilize my skills elsewhere?"

The general leaned back, hooking his ankle around a knee. He twirled a pen with his fingers. "How many years were you in Vietnam, Captain?"

As though he didn't know! "Twenty-seven months by the time troops were pulled out."

"Have you been back in New York afterward? Before today, I mean."

Richard hesitated. "This is my third visit."

The general smiled. "Your parents are still alive, aren't they?"

"Yes, sir."

"Brothers, sisters? Girlfriend?"

"None of the above, sir."

The general sighed. "Captain Armor, there is a certain type of soldier who finds it difficult in peacetime—"

"Permission to speak freely, sir?"

General Potts nodded.

"My request has nothing to do with war and peace. The army is my one chance to make something of myself. My skill with my weapon is my way out, and I'm not going to get very far if you stick me in a place like Japan."

"Ambition," the general remarked.

"I don't deny it," said Richard. "But the benefit would be mutual. I'm an excellent officer. I know how, when, and where to send my scouts and snipers to maximize advantage for our side. You could certainly use my skills as a commander in Afghanistan."

"And arrogance," the general added.

Richard inclined his head. "Call it what you will, but facts are facts. Name one who's better than me."

A wide smile lit the general's face. "Alex Kingsley."

Almost involuntarily, Richard's lips twisted into a smirk. "How did I know you were going to come up with his name?"

"Careful, Captain," the general warned. "You get only so many indulgences on account of your friendship with my son. I assume Philip is the one who told you I recommended against your appointment?"

It took a great deal of self-control for Richard not to snarl. "Philip talked to me because he believed my appointment—and the promotion to major which would have accompanied it—was sabotaged because it would have made me the executive officer of the battalion Alex Kingsley is headed for."

Face set in stone, the general said, "The fact it even occurred to you that you'd be in a position of authority over your rival should tell you something, Captain. Your weapon skills and your understanding of strategy have never been under question. What makes you less than Alex are your other qualities. You're conceited, dangerously competitive with your own colleagues, and prone to fits of temper. It's not only me. Haven't you wondered why you didn't get to command a company even as a captain?"

"Because I was needed in—"

The general continued as though he hadn't been interrupted, "Why the question of promotion to major did not come up until now in spite of your track record? The army considers you unfit for unit command, Armor."

Only the awareness this man was his superior officer held Richard back. He'd assumed he was simply being deployed where his skills could be utilized to the fullest. That he remained captain because of the congressional threats against grade creep in the armed forces. Joining the U.S. troops in Pakistan conducting covert operations against the Soviet-aligned Afghan government was supposed to have been a way around the problem.

A painful pulse pounding behind his eye, Richard said, "I'm not the first arrogant man to graduate from this academy. If I had a family with clout behind me, I'd have been in Pakistan today as Major Richard Armor. Alex Kingsley wouldn't have had to ask. You'd have recommended him for the position before he even thought of it."

"You're done here, Captain," the general said, his eyes flashing. "Also, since we're speaking frankly, understand this: the only reason you're walking out of here today without facing consequences is not that you're my *son's* friend. Steven Kingsley considers you one, and I cannot afford to offend him. Without the backing of the Kingsley name, you might have even been facing an other-than-honorable discharge for this insubordination. So show a little gratitude to the family. As far as Alex is concerned, I do plan on recommending him for promotion. You see, superior skill and good judgment aside, he has other qualities you don't have. The willingness to risk his life for a cause than for naked ambition. The ability to inspire and lead. All of which make him a hero and you an also-ran. Now, get the hell out."

Face burning, Richard stood. As he marched away, one thing was very clear in his mind. He wasn't going to get anywhere in the army hierarchy as long as General Potts had anything to do with it. Richard would never be acknowledged as long as the golden boy of the Kingsley family was around. But Richard possessed something Alex Kingsley didn't. Intelligence. In spades.

Richard returned to Japan only to ask for extended leave which would take him to the end of the mandatory five years of active duty. Back in Manhattan, he rented himself an apartment in Hell's Kitchen and over the next few months, got Steven to wrangle him invitations to every Kingsley event featuring senior military officers. Richard indulged in small talk, storing away gossip. Finally, he located someone with reason to loathe the Kingsleys, someone powerful enough to go toe-to-toe with their hired help, General Potts. Brigadier General Axeman was the commander of the Judge Advocate General's School.

There were rumors about Godwin Kingsley's involvement in the death of the general's brother, a reverend. The entire story was strange. Some girl, Ambrosia Barrons, had killed herself over Godwin's brother, and Rev. Axeman, her spiritual advisor, accused the Kingsleys of hounding her to her death. Very soon after, the reverend was transferred to some hellhole in South America where he got himself killed without delay. While it might have been the never-ending civil war in the region which took the priest's life, General Axeman blamed Godwin Kingsley, accusing him of arranging the transfer.

Richard had never before entertained the thought of practicing law, but with the general's help, he enrolled in the University of Virginia's Law School. Then, it was on to the master's course in military law. If the dean of West Point or the Kingsleys ever contacted General Axeman to advise him against accepting Richard, he never heard about it. If they had, the general might have even found a way to promote Richard while he was still in training.

Around the same time Alex Kingsley returned from Pakistan with captain's bars pinned to his uniform, Major Richard Armor became a reservist in the JAG Corps. The rank mattered more to Richard than his new job at the prestigious New York law firm.

Chapter 22

Back in the night of December 31, 1988

Upper East Side, New York City

Richard bit back a grim smile. The same General Potts was now the head of army intelligence and had been instrumental in getting the military to consent to the interrogation of Brad Kingsley and his family.

"I still don't understand it," Steven muttered, hiding the movements of his lips with the wine glass. The dining table was vast enough to require a certain decibel level for conversation to happen, but it was still prudent to whisper truths not meant to be overheard—especially since Charles was on Steven's other side and already swaying in his seat from the effects of alcohol.

Steven's eyes were on his plate, not on either of the men sitting on the other side of the table—Godwin Kingsley and Gen. Potts—but Richard knew what Steven was talking about. They'd discussed it *ad nauseum*, worried whether the general could be trusted.

But General Potts's loyalty turned out to be to the Kingsley patriarch rather than any of the grandsons. Richard took a sip of wine, thinking he should've understood the fact a long time ago. Justice Godwin Kingsley had been generous in his support whenever the general needed financial help, and his gratitude morphed into an affection for Alex. Richard should've seen it as soon as the general made the comment about not wanting to offend Steven.

"Money talks," Richard muttered back. "Your grandfather thinks the same of me, I'm sure."

"You've been my friend through all my ups *and* downs." Steven shifted in his chair. "Grandfather appreciates only one thing: the Kingsley family and its noble heritage."

The old fellow was in a good mood tonight, though. And why not? The takeover of the Peter Kingsley Company and the network was complete. Steven and his staff ran the show from Kingsley Corp offices—with Godwin pulling strings behind the scenes. Then there were their plans for Harry Sheppard. Thanks to Richard's visit to Rikers, the petty officer would soon cease to be a problem. Afterward, Lilah Kingsley's days were numbered. And Brad's.

"You did well, Mr. Armor," Godwin Kingsley said on cue.

Mouthing a spoonful of light mushroom soup, Richard inclined his head.

"I agree, Major," the general said. "It was an exceptionally fine job. Sheppard is not going to know what hit him."

How easily the rank tripped off the general's forked tongue. The justice himself always relegated Richard to "Mister." But then, considering what Godwin did to his own grandsons, Richard was lucky to be the ignored outsider. The situation changed after the episode in Cuba.

The hairs on the back of Richard's neck stood at the thought. The Kingsley patriarch's old, deliberate disregard of his servant's son was far preferable to the new friendliness. There was something... disturbing about the old man's recent pleasantness toward Richard.

Charles hiccupped, the rude noise earning nothing more than a mildly reproachful glance from his grandfather. "Steven," called the former justice. "Gateway's board asked no questions about Harry's performance at the press conference?"

Steven gulped his wine. "They're not exactly a loyal lot... but Hector believes me, and he can manage the rest. If *he* accuses us of orchestrating things, we may have something to worry about, but he hates Aunt Patrice, so we're good."

Patrice Kingsley again! Richard wished people would stop bringing up her name. He almost wished she'd say something about the arrest of her sons, ask him why. If she did, then this annoying niggle in his brain might stop.

"What's Hector's problem with Mrs. Patrice Kingsley?" asked General Potts, dabbing his mouth with a snowy-white napkin. "What did she do?"

"It's what she didn't do," Steven explained. "When the Sheppards started having their problems with Sanders, he got them arrested."

The general nodded. "I remember. It's when Harry was kidnapped."

"Yeah," said Steven. "Hector had called Aunt Patrice for help with the arrest. She was a Sheppard before marriage, so he thought she might get Grandfather to pull some strings."

"She refused?" the general asked.

Steven shook his head. "She wouldn't even take Hector's call. I was the one who talked to him. But by then, Andrew Barrons was involved, and they didn't need our help."

"Strange," remarked the general.

"Not really," Steven said, shrugging. "They're not the first family to have problems. I mean, look at the Kingsleys. It's like Brad's son calling *me* for help."

"Be careful of her," the general warned. "She's staying with Aaron, isn't she? If she persuades him to publicly denounce the Kingsleys, we'll be in trouble."

"Uncle Aaron will never go public against Grandfather," Steven said, waving a hand. "He says what he wants to within the family, but he'd never—"

Richard interjected, "You can't be sure of what's going on in your uncle's mind, Steven. General Potts is right; we need to keep an eye on both of them."

Godwin Kingsley took a sip from his glass, a small smile playing on his face. "Forget Aaron. *Patrice* will do nothing without my say-so."

"Forgive me, sir," Richard said. "I think you underestimate her." The woman brought up three boys on her own with barely enough income to put food on the table. It wouldn't have been an easy task for someone used to the Kingsley wealth. Not as if the poverty did anything to build character in her sons. On their return, they were just as disdainful of the chauffeur's family as could be expected from rich brats.

Godwin waited while the maid placed the next course in front of him. Lobsters cooked in their shells, topped with creamy wine sauce and chopped cilantro. "Patrice walked out of this house once. I'd thought about... but Peter would've stopped me if I used... I'd have completely lost Peter. Then, after his death, she returned without any pressure. Trust me, since Peter's not around to back her up, I can handle Patrice."

Suddenly, Richard was annoyed. "She seems like a woman with a sense of self-worth. I think you're mistaken."

The justice laughed. "Patrice does have a stubborn streak. It takes skill to get her to do what you want."

Steven snorted. "What skill? Her life revolves around her sons. All you need to do is threaten one of them."

A peculiar glitter in his eyes, Godwin smiled at Richard. "True."

Richard could point out several instances when she didn't take the threats to her sons seriously. Her peculiar affection for the boy growing up in the apartment over the garage had overwhelmed her interest in her family's safety. She was here in the mansion tonight, with Richard's own mother baking cakes for the woman to feed her grandchild—Alex's son. Richard huffed, hoping like hell he could get out without running into either Patrice or the kid. Why *was* she staying here, anyway? Was she keeping an eye on them through Aaron Kingsley? Or was it simply out of disdain toward the Sheppards as Steven believed? Nothing about Patrice Kingsley's behavior after the events in Cuba made any sense just as it didn't when Richard was a mere lad.

"—er Armor? Armor!"

"Rich," shouted Steven.

Richard's mind jerked back to the conversation at the dinner table, his eyes going to the grandfather clock. Not yet midnight. He could have sworn he'd spent hours with this group.

"Did you fall asleep?" asked Steven, tone amused.

"Must have," Richard mumbled.

"Justice Kingsley was saying we have almost everything ready," explained General Potts.

"The Barronses are constantly watched," said Godwin. "I don't expect Andrew to let Daniel try anything, and Harry would want Lilah's twin to continue on Andrew's good side. It will be important if she does manage to return. The other one... Shawn... he could be a problem."

"Unlikely," offered the general. "Shawn Barrons was all right as a student at West Point. Perhaps slightly above average in marksmanship... not really the hero type."

"The feds believe he's the one who fixed Lilah's computer in Cuba," reminded Steven.

The old soldier nodded. "I'm aware of it. Still..." Frowning, Potts added, "The only time I saw some gumption from him was when I asked him to remove his necklace... some yellow-brown thing. He said the necklace belonged to his mother, and he would continue to keep it no matter what the army had to say." Potts huffed out a breath. "He was in a military institution. There was protocol to maintain... respect for hierarchy. I did what I needed to do." Shawn Barrons was kicked out for insubordination.

"Amber," corrected Richard, remembering Shawn who'd been at West Point the same time as him.

Godwin Kingsley's head jerked up, his eyes fixed piercingly on Richard. "What did you say?" the former justice bit out.

Slightly puzzled by the reaction, Richard repeated, "Amber... Shawn's beads... what General Potts called the yellow-brown necklace. When he mentioned the thing, it popped into my head I'd also seen it at the time. Shawn called them amber beads."

A couple of moments passed before Godwin said, "Whatever jewelry he chooses to wear has nothing to do with our plans. What we should be concerned about is his willingness to help Lilah. He did it once with the computer. I also heard he sold his tech stock for her."

"He did," Richard admitted. "Shawn made a lot of money with his tech business, sir. It was all his own. We didn't have any way of stopping him from selling. He also sold Mrs. Kingsley's stock in Sun Microsystems and transferred most of the money to some 'unidentified' Swiss bank account. But we have nothing to worry about. The cash is not going to be enough to buy a pardon."

"Nevertheless," continued Godwin, "it shows he does consider her family and will help. The situation has the potential to be a problem. All the Barronses are being watched... but keep an eye on him, especially. Temple's son is working on paperwork to give me legal guardianship over his father."

"The good professor didn't have any objections to the idea," added Potts. The former president was not exactly on chummy terms with his son. They weren't estranged... not exactly. Professor Temple simply was as indifferent toward his father as Mr. Temple had been when his only child was growing up. "The justice is Mr. Temple's stepbrother, after all. And everyone knows they were... *are* close. Given the fact Mr. Temple's still not making any sense, it should be easy enough to get him certified incapacitated. Justice Kingsley can take over care."

Even while Temple was on the respirator, Godwin expressed his concern over and over to the press, fretting openly about the physical and mental challenges facing the former president if... *when* he woke. Whatever claims Temple made would've roused deep sympathies in government quarters and among the public, but they would've hesitated to take what he said seriously. Now... damned stroke of luck for the Kingsleys how he couldn't say anything at all. With the legal guardianship, even if Temple did regain capacity, anything he communicated to anyone would need to go through Godwin Kingsley. Temple would be a prisoner, essentially. *Poor man,* Richard murmured in his mind.

Potts continued, "Steven has things sorted out as far as Hector Sheppard is concerned. You, Major Armor, have the plan in place for Harry."

"Which brings us to the exiles," Godwin said. "Steven, what's the status on them? The trafficking ring told you they made it to Ecuador. But which town?"

Steven's eyes flew to Richard. The news they got earlier would ruin the patriarch's happy mood.

"Quito," Steven said. "Someone tried to kidnap Lilah a couple of days ago."

Godwin's fork arrested halfway to his mouth. "Better not be one of you. I told you we cannot touch her until Harry is safely taken care of."

Steven eyed his brother, Charles. "I checked. It wasn't one of us."

Charles seemed unaware of all the attention suddenly focused on him. He was scraping all the meat from the lobster shell onto his plate.

General Potts asked, "So who *was* it?"

"An old enemy of theirs," Steven explained. "Someone called in a kidnapping attempt, and the description of the woman involved somewhat matched that of Lilah. The Ecuadorian police found the corpse of one of the thugs."

Godwin asked, "How did he die?"

"Bullet. There was a second one with a broken neck," Steven said. "He was alive when the cops found him, but after one night in the rain not being able to move, they couldn't make any sense out of him. He died only a couple of hours after being found."

"Alex," said Gen. Potts. "And Victor."

"How did *you* come to hear of it?" Godwin asked.

"I told you already," Steven said testily. "Charlie and I contacted all the lowlifes our cousins ever ran into. Whoever gets them for us is supposed to get a reward. Unfortunately, these particular idiots in

Quito thought they'd get us to fork out more money by kidnapping Lilah. There was a third man who escaped. He called us to see if he could still get the reward."

"All of which means they're no longer in Ecuador," said Godwin, eyes glittering.

"I'm sorry, Grandfather," Steven said. "But there are some things beyond our control."

Godwin cleared his throat, his gray gaze pinning his grandson. "Unfortunately, those things always seem to happen only to you."

Steven flushed.

Godwin asked, "Why is this so difficult to grasp? Harry's fate is waiting to meet him, but unless we know exactly where the exiles are, our plan won't work."

"If I may?" Richard asked. "After I heard what happened, I spent a few hours going over alternatives. There are only a few countries Brad and the rest can hide out in without worrying about being extradited. Steven's idea of using anyone with reason to dislike Victor and Alex is a damn good one. Such criminals are most likely to have intel on illegal movements across the border. Among them, there's only one man with the resources and extensive enough connections across the globe to locate the exiles wherever they are."

"Who?" asked Godwin Kingsley.

"I'm sure you remember the drug lord from Burma," said Richard. "The one called 'Prince'? Alex got the Indian government and the CIA to break up his drug-smuggling ring. Men like Prince usually want revenge. He would likely be happy to help us. In fact, even before tonight, I heard rumors he's asked his connections in South America to keep an eye out for the exiles. We could talk to him about teaming up."

"Don't be a fool," Godwin said. "What if he ends up being a sell-out?"

"Prince seems a more cerebral type," Richard said. "I'm sure he'll understand the advantages of keeping the Kingsley family happy."

Godwin asked, "Who's going to make him understand? I told Steven it wasn't a good idea to contact the criminal kind for help, but he thought he knew better. A drug lord will be even worse. No, I can't let the Kingsley name be associated with that of this... Prince."

"You have no problems working with McCoy," Steven pointed out. "He's a criminal." The man had attempted to kill Neil Kingsley and Daniel Barrons. Thanks to Richard's efforts, McCoy's post-conviction bail was in the works.

"He doesn't know we're involved, does he?" Godwin asked. "Also, McCoy is a criminal with his own reasons to want Harry dead, and he was offered a solid enough bribe—freedom. Which makes McCoy more than hired help. He'll spend the rest of his life in prison if he doesn't cooperate. With Prince, revenge would be the only motive. As you just said, he has resources. From what I remember, he might not be able to travel, but he's living a good life in Burma. If Steven meets Prince, and the conversation doesn't go well—"

"The major could go to Prince," suggested Potts. "With an assumed identity, I mean. The terrain there is similar to what Major Armor is familiar with from his time in Vietnam."

At long last, the former dean had deemed Richard's experience worthy of acknowledgment. Richard silently counted to three and once again reminded himself of the friendship Steven showed him. "I could."

"It might work," Godwin allowed.

"No, Rich," Steven said. "As you said, Prince is no ordinary thug. You're not going to fool him with a disguise like you did in Rikers. Also, at Rikers, you were going to claim to be McCoy's lawyer if you did get caught. What if the feds catch you with Prince? What excuse can you give? Especially after we used Prince's drug deals to arrest Brad and his brothers. I'm not prepared to let you get into trouble only to keep me in power."

The former justice asked, "Are you prepared to lose the network?"

"I *will* talk to Prince.," Steven said, eyes angry. "I won't let you sacrifice Rich for it. There's a limit to what even I'm ready to do."

Godwin hissed.

"Steven," Richard said. "Calm down. Everything has a solution."

"What solution?" snapped Steven. "I know you want to help me, friend. But no. This is my job."

"Think clearly," Richard said. "You're engaged to be married. What if you and I and—" He eyed Charles. "—your brother take a trip to Bangkok? A bachelor party."

Arrested look in his eyes, Steven asked, "How do we contact Prince?"

"Put word out we're going to be there," Richard said. "Prince will come to us. Bangkok's close enough to Burma."

Godwin flung his napkin to the side. "Steven, if you get into trouble on this one, I will not help you. Do you get me?"

"Loud and clear," Steven said. "But I won't need your help. No one can blame the Kingsleys if Prince approaches us instead of the other way around."

Richard nodded in Godwin's direction. "Steven's right. The feds can't do anything to him because a drug lord wanted a conversation."

Steven asked, "Is there anything we can offer Prince other than revenge?"

"I believe you should listen to your grandfather," the general said. "Still... if you're determined to do this... China has Prince's son. If he doesn't cooperate, we can get the Chinese to make sure things don't look good for Junior."

"There you go," said Richard, forking lobster into his mouth.

Steven muttered, "All this is moot if Prince isn't willing to kill them in the first place."

"What do you mean?" Richard asked. "He has enough reasons to hate them."

Steven leaned forward, elbows on the table. "Victor and Alex tag-teamed the criminals who tried to kidnap Lilah. Two of them are dead. Why would Prince take the chance of the same thing happening to his men?"

"Prince's people are likely to be more competent," Richard pointed out. "Plus, it would be a problem even if we did the deed ourselves. If Victor and Alex are guarding Mrs. Kingsley, we'll have to get rid of them first."

Godwin Kingsley stared, the strange glint back in his eyes. "Who's going to do the honors, Mr. Armor? You? Don't forget Victor is a trained boxer, and Alex is one of the best marksmen to have gone through training with General Potts. Not too many capable of outshooting him."

The general nodded concurrence, tucking into the food.

Bitter memories contaminated the moist flesh of the lobster in Richard's mouth. "I have no doubt your grandson is good, sir, but

I'm better. I'm the one who can outshoot Alex Kingsley. I *am* capable of killing him."

For a second, Richard thought he saw a gleam of satisfaction in the eyes of the former justice. Glee, almost. Before he could consider it further, the old man blinked, and the moment was gone.

#

Later the same night

Upper East Side, New York City

Richard had thought the dinner would go on past midnight, but the Kingsley patriarch, unhappy about Steven's plans to travel to Bangkok, dismissed them all following a tame toast with champagne. Gravel crunched under Richard's shoes as he walked back down the path to the garage. Feminine voices floated to him from behind the tall hedges. He recognized the smooth, cultured tones of Patrice Kingsley.

Cursing under his breath, he waited for her to come around the corner and see him. Richard recognized the uncomfortable tightness in his belly as trepidation. Damn it, all he did was tell her Brad's deal would work out well for everyone concerned. More fool her if she actually believed it included her precious sons. Irritated at himself, Richard tugged the scarf from his nose. *I'm going to look her in the eye.* Patrice might have believed him out of affection, but Brad should have known better. *The CEO of a multi-billion-dollar enterprise, for God's sake.* But then, Brad had always been an idiot, groveling at Godwin's feet for approval. His mother and his brothers should never have handed control to him. The fact they did was their mistake, not Richard's.

Patrice's guest spotted him first. Sabrina Kingsley, Alex's wife. The sunny smile faded from her face, replaced by unadulterated hostility. There was a man behind her—a guard, from the looks of him.

Clearly startled by the sudden stiffness on her daughter-in-law's face, Patrice followed her gaze. "Richard," she greeted him, a wary note in her tone, yet somehow sounding hopeful and eager as well.

What is wrong *with this woman? Doesn't she know I'm the enemy?*

From the incredulous look Sabrina Kingsley shot her mother-in-law, it was clear the younger woman was thinking the exact same thing.

"We were on our way to the garage," said Patrice. "Your father offered to drop Sabrina and Mikey back home."

A small sound from Sabrina Kingsley's side drew Richard's attention. *Great, they've got the kid out in this weather. Couldn't they have simply* called *the chauffeur to have the car brought around?*

He didn't waste time on niceties with Alex's wife. Wishing *Miss* Patrice a good night, he was about to skirt them to leave the grounds altogether instead of returning to his parents' apartment, but the child's solemn stare drew his attention. *Looks sort of like his uncle,* Richard decided. The eyes were from Alex. Richard reached out to ruffle the silky, dark hair.

"Bad man," the boy said.

Humiliated, Richard pulled his hand back.

A distressed gasp escaped Patrice. Trembling fingers to her lips, she said, "Mikey! I'm so sorry, Richard."

"No, Patrice," came the firm voice of Sabrina Kingsley. "I don't believe Mikey did anything wrong." Kissing her mother-in-law's cheek, she said goodbye. "I'll call, but I do wish you'd consider moving in with us. We could use the company."

Throughout the short exchange, the child continued his unblinking contemplation of Richard. The soldier wondered what was going through the boy's mind.

Sabrina ignored Richard and tugged at her son's hand. Before walking toward the garage with his mother, young Michael Kingsley made Richard a promise. "My daddy will kill you."

"Oh, God," Patrice said. "Mikey, please..."

Richard could've told her not to bother being embarrassed. It wasn't the first time his death at Alex's hands was predicted—or the other way around.

#

Richard ended up wandering the city for a few hours. He couldn't face the thought of bringing in New Year alone, and here on the streets, there was plenty of company. The noisy crowds, the stink of cheap booze... he was even rewarded with a kiss by a very drunk brunette in Times Square.

It was after two when he finally got to his apartment. The phone was ringing. Not waiting to turn on the lights, he picked up the receiver and cradled it on his shoulder. "Hello?" he barked.

"Rich," said Steven, his voice excited. "I'm right outside with JD. Let us in."

Richard grimaced but did as he was bid.

JD—a.k.a. Rep. Jack Drummond—was the man who'd married Steven's sister, Helen. Richard couldn't think of another person he wanted less to see.

When Helen accepted JD's offer of his grandmother's antique diamond engagement ring, Richard's father tried to let the Kingsleys know what he heard through the servants' network in New York City. The women who tangled with JD were invariably seen sporting broken bones and black eyes. Only Aaron showed concern at the news, but he was told to zip it by the bride's own father, David. Such worries were trivial when compared with having his daughter married to a White House prospect.

Thankfully, JD seemed to know better than to mess with Helen. She was a Kingsley, after all. Not a single hair on her head could be harmed without inviting retribution. Instead, JD developed the habit of inviting Charles along on what he called exotic vacations. Richard and Steven knew what was going on, but both men were at loss on how to stop it without locking Charles up somewhere. The only consolation was Steven kept track of JD's trips. Any attempt at blackmail over Charles would result in JD's own downfall. Not that there had been any hint of extortive activity yet.

Then came Hector Sheppard's visits to the Kingsley mansion on Godwin's invitation. The elder Sheppard son used to teach boxing to Steven. For the sake of his protégé, Hector went along when he could with JD and Charles, keeping the Kingsley idiot out of trouble. Steven reported Hector used the occasions to imbibe as much as he wanted, but being in Charles and JD's company for days... yeah, Richard would also be drowning himself in drink. State of inebriation notwithstanding, few ever dared disobey the orders of the boxer.

Unfortunately, Hector's protectiveness didn't extend to the woman his brother was trying to rescue. Lilah was also a Kingsley but only by marriage, and the family name was not enough to save her. The patriarch himself declared Lilah Kingsley fair game. JD almost licked his chops each time she was mentioned.

Suddenly irritated with himself, Richard muttered, "A bitch and a whore."

It's what Lilah Kingsley was, and in her line of business, she needed to expect some bruises and dents. The only difference between her and the ones selling their flesh on Broadway was the price tag. The dollar amount Brad paid for the enjoyment of her body was high, but he wouldn't have had a penny to his name if it weren't for her connections to the Barronses and the Sheppards. What the hell did it make the beautiful and cunning Mrs. Kingsley?

"Doesn't make any difference to me," Richard snarled at himself. It was her own damned fault for acting as though she were better than everyone else.

He grabbed a bottle of Scotch from the rack on the wall, intending to start the new year by getting wasted. Even if he were forced to tolerate JD's unholy presence, there would be Steven to make up for it.

A couple of minutes later, Steven crossed Richard's threshold, followed by JD.

The abusive son of a bitch was in a suit, as usual. His light-brown hair was cut in some sort of boyish style. Add to the mix light-blue eyes and a lean physique, JD looked the perfect politician. Sick *and* slick.

"We may have a problem," Steven announced. "Or not. I'm not sure."

"What?" Richard asked.

"Harry Sheppard was in Eden tonight. You know, the strip club in DC? JD's contact notified him."

Petty Officer First Class Sheppard had just launched his offensive strike.

Part IX

Chapter 23

February 1989

Eden, Washington, DC

"Anyone interesting out there?" asked a voice, somewhere above Lupe's left shoulder.

She nearly jumped out of her skin. A hand held to her pounding heart, she scooted back two feet from the gray stone wall forming the backdrop of the stage. Lighting in the wings was kept deliberately dim so as not to spill over to the front and ruin the ambiance, yet Harry Sheppard's amusement was clearly visible.

"Shh," she said. The music would mask the contents of their conversation, but she didn't want the noises backstage messing up the show. "You should already know who's out there. I saw you talking to the girls."

His tone bland, the broker said, "Yes, I talked to them. Unfortunately, you already made it clear there's no compulsion to cooperate."

"There isn't," she said. "If they don't want to, I won't force them."

He asked, "What were you expecting me to do? Blackmail them into it?"

"Or ask them to *marry* you."

"Okay, the joke went a bit too far, I admit. I told you, I only meant for you to pretend I'm trying to get into your bed."

Lupe huffed. "Don't try it with anyone else here. Some of them are fool enough to believe... look, don't break their hearts when they're already risking quite a lot for you."

"I'm not going to. And believe me... I'm grateful... can't tell you how much I appreciate them for doing this. Thanks to the angels of Eden, I do have a few leads."

"Really?" Lupe asked, tone high.

Eyes glinting in amusement, he said, "Shh!"

She made a face. "What leads? And who?"

With a look of incredulity passing over his face, the broker said, "A few years ago, a dozen or so of the congressmen were more or less openly operating a club named—if you can believe it—Scoundrel Society."

Lupe shook her head. "Doesn't surprise me at all. Some of them think taxpayer money is part of their pay package." The women, too. Some bastards assumed every female within sight was literally up for grabs. And when under the influence or in bed, those men tended to divulge what they shouldn't.

"Apparently, some members of the old group now—"

"Harry," crooned a collective of feminine voices, interrupting the conversation.

A group of Lupe's girls approached from the dressing rooms, giggling as though they'd never left middle school. Led by who else but Nikki, the queen of overgrown adolescents everywhere. She was clad only in a cropped white tee and lacey underwear, her costume held between a thumb and forefinger. Lupe frowned. The perpetual sixteen-year-old's ploys to get Harry's attention stopped being funny after the first hour or so.

And these were the angels Lupe told Harry he could trust. He was relying on them to help him battle the Kingsleys. Lupe almost groaned. What had she been *thinking?*

Nikki carried something else in her free hand. A large pink cloth bag with a giant red heart on it. "It's a Valentine's Day gift. From all of us."

Lupe rolled her eyes. Harry wasn't the first rich and handsome man they encountered, but he was the only one who ever asked them to play James Bond's sexy sidekicks. Some of them were plain scared to do it, and some were tickled, but every single one tittered and blushed when his shadow crossed the club's threshold.

The corner of his mouth quirking up, Harry took the bag and drew out some kind of musical instrument. His smile faded.

"A bugle?" Lupe asked.

Nikki laughed. "No, it's a *saxophone. People* magazine said he plays."

"Not in a long time," Harry objected, yet his eyes were wide open as though mesmerized, his fingers running lovingly over the shiny instrument.

"Don't you have to go on stage in like..." Lupe glanced at her wristwatch. "...five minutes?"

With a kittenish smirk, Nikki said, "I have my things right here."

Then, without apology, she shrugged out of the tee and the panties, making a production of putting on the translucent robe. Unfortunately for her, Harry's gaze seemed glued to the saxophone.

When Lupe got her power of speech back, she exclaimed, "Nikki!"

The silly girl pouted. "What? It's not like you haven't seen it all before."

"Get to work," Lupe snapped.

Twirling away, Nikki said, "You're getting old, Lupe. No idea how to have fun anymore."

"Thank you, ladies," Harry said, looking up. "This is a very thoughtful gift. I... ahh... I didn't get anything..."

Nikki called over her shoulder, "You can play it for us as a gift."

"Will have to be another day," he said. "I'm returning to New York tonight."

Back in the office with Harry, Lupe pulled out her chair and sat, muttering, "I know how to have fun."

"What?" His winter coat was on the couch, but he made no move to put it on, his eyes still on the instrument. The gift bag was on the floor, next to his gleaming black shoes.

"I'm only thirty-six. Not old." To Lupe's horror, tears sprouted along her lashes.

With a mildly impatient glance, the broker said, "Don't be ridiculous. You're more beautiful than all of them put together."

Hands on the desk, Lupe rose from her chair, not quite decided whether to be annoyed by the tone or complimented by the words.

Harry dug into the gift bag and came up with a small box. "Good. The store didn't forget." Taking a wooden stick thingie from the box, he put it into his mouth.

A tongue depressor? The last place Lupe saw something like it was at her doctor's office. "What are you doing?" she asked.

Other than holding up a hand to request silence, Harry didn't explain. For the full minute that he sucked on the stick, Lupe wondered if the broker had gone around the bend. "Wetting the reed," he finally said, taking the stick out of his mouth and somehow maneuvering it into the brass instrument.

He played a quick snippet. Notes reverberated around the small office. When the broker moved the saxophone from his lips, he winced slightly. As though he couldn't help himself, he returned the sax to his mouth. A strange song, changing in tempo often, going from innocent promise to tragedy and heartbreak. The longing in his eyes... he was lost in the music. Was he laughing in joy or weeping blood? She couldn't tell.

Lupe dropped back into her seat, shaken by the feeling in the sounds.

When he stopped, he continued staring at the saxophone, his fingers tracing its curves as though it were a lover.

"What is it called?" Lupe asked. "The song, I mean."

"Stairway To Heaven." It's by Led Zeppelin."

"Play the rest."

He was silent for so long she thought he hadn't heard her demand. "Not this one," Harry eventually said. He played another tune, also plaintive. As beautiful as the first, but somehow, it didn't carry the same poignant quality.

"Which song is *this*?" Lupe asked.

Breaking off in the middle of a note, Harry said, "*L'Italiano.*" This one is by Toto Cutugno." The broker sang a couple of lines. If Lupe didn't know better, she could've sworn he was a native of Italy. Some of the reports on him did say he was a linguistic prodigy. Except for Spanish... somehow, Harry couldn't speak the language without a thick accent. "Always thought this piece would sound good on sax," he mused. "I can read music and play by the ear."

The last claim was made with a touch of boyish smugness, but Lupe didn't have the faintest clue what it meant. "Please continue playing."

He did. Sometimes hesitating, sometimes stopping altogether, he got to the end.

When the music died down, she clapped. "Lovely."

Beyond inclining his head, Harry didn't respond. He picked up the pink cloth bag from the floor and placed the saxophone in it before shrugging the worsted wool coat on. "I need to follow the lead I mentioned. There are also a couple of senators involved in uranium sales... it's amazing what the public lets them get away with. I'm going to contact Dan. I wasn't expecting to find anything here which could help him... I suppose I should've... we'll see...." Straightening his cuffs, Harry added, "Lupe, our security arrangements are satisfactory? Or do we need more guards?"

"No..." Shaking off the daze, she continued, "I believe we have an appropriate number." Any more, and the ambiance of the club would change. All male employees were provided evening clothes to blend in, but there was simply no camouflaging a certain type of man. Her girls did appreciate the enhanced safety measures at their homes and the availability of guards on call for any concerns. And Harry drilled them over and over on being careful when using phones. "You sound... did something new happen?"

"It's now common knowledge I've been spending a lot of time here. You've seen the tabloids. We can tell the rest of the world I'm your wannabe lover, but the Kingsleys are not going to buy it."

Lupe bit back a grimace. Not only the Kingsleys... news that Harry Sheppard was seen kissing a man at the New Year's Eve party in the club had spread. Thank God the yellow press couldn't locate the waiter involved—Ira. He'd simply vanished. Perhaps the young fellow decided he had enough of Eden and its inhabitants and returned to the hometown he once described as heaven. Gossip columnists of course knew Harry still visited the club, but they continued to speculate he swung both ways. His friendship with Alex was parsed for evidence of romance. Harry didn't seem to give a damn. The Kingsleys wouldn't give a damn, either, concerned only about the secrets their enemy might manage to ferret out from the club's staff and its owner.

Hands in his pockets, Harry went on, "I'll be in New York for the next couple of weeks, at least. Not sure how long it's going to take to chase down the lead. I wish..." Harry groaned. "If I knew what was in the note Temple sent, I wouldn't have involved you or your girls."

Lupe shrugged. "I understand what the world is like, *señor*. And I was already fully aware what the likes of the Kingsleys could do when I promised to help. You don't need to worry... I've been taking care of myself a long time."

"Don't make the mistake of underestimating the enemy," warned the broker. "Mr. Temple did. The cops say they don't have any leads on the assassin. Could be true... Secret Service admits there was a lot of confusion when it happened. The officers were busy trying to get Temple out, and the shooter ran before the civilians around caught on to what the hell was going on. The eyewitnesses are not even sure the same fellow everyone's talking about fired the gun. Still, the sketch has been on TV for weeks... hard to believe nobody, not a single person in Times Square saw him afterward. Unless, of course, there was a getaway vehicle waiting. Which would mean it was a pre-planned hit, perhaps with help from someone in charge."

"A hit on a former president," muttered Lupe. Talk in the press was the crime was committed by a random person, driven by drugs or his own diseased mind, who simply happened to see Temple on the street. Police updates also seemed to be pushing the same idea. Or why would the perpetrators not claim credit for their handiwork as was common in attempts on political figures? Why was there no triumphant declaration of punishment meted out for some imagined sin? But what Harry said... the likelihood of a heavily drugged or mentally ill person disappearing this completely...

"Temple wasn't the only victim who thought he'd be safe from the Kingsleys," said Harry. "What d'you wanna bet Amber didn't think she wasn't in any danger, either? She died—"

"—from suicide," completed Lupe. She'd researched the Amber Barrons story after their first conversation about it. Lupe saw what Harry had seen. Something about the tragic death of the girl simply didn't ring true.

"Lilah... she'd have been dead, too, if the Kingsley plan worked," said Harry. "It would've been three dead bodies, at least two of them in an effort to hide something Godwin doesn't want to come out."

"You think the Kingsleys got this Amber girl killed." An unexpected quiver went through Lupe's insides. She swiveled her chair to face the statue of Virgin Mary and sketched the sign of the cross. The votive candle glowed red, reflecting on the icon, throwing Her face into mysterious shadows. Spinning the chair back, Lupe said, "Like you said... if anyone from the family asks, I don't know anything about what else you might be looking for besides trying to get laid. Will they... I mean, they won't believe it's all *you* want, but what if they don't buy *my* excuse, either? I expect them to make life difficult, but attacking me or the girls... you think it's possible?"

"So you *didn't* completely understand the extent of—" Harry pinched the bridge of his nose and stared for a few seconds. "Do you want to back out?" he eventually asked.

"*¡Dios mío!*" Lupe muttered weakly. It took her a moment, but she straightened her spine. "I keep my word... bad for business if I don't."

With a slow nod, the broker said, "As far as my plan is concerned... reiterate to your girls they should only do what is possible without risking their safety. Under no circumstances are they to confront the enemy. Trust nothing you might hear from the Kingsleys and their hangers-on. They can promise you everything and the kitchen sink, but don't believe any of it. Alex and his family—including his mother—learned the lesson the hard way."

Chapter 24

A day later

New York, New York

On the couch in the living room, Sabrina tapped away at the keyboard of the portable computer, but she couldn't stop fretting about Harry's warnings. She would've anyway seen to arrangements assigning custody of Michael to people she trusted. Harry insisted the guardianship matter be dealt with as soon as humanly possible, going to the extent of hauling Noah and Grayson into the apartment to help her. The two lawyers were also talking to the couple who fostered Victor's son, Gabriel. So much legal jargon... family guardian and guardian of person and guardian of estate and whatnot... it was only then it occurred to Sabrina that there weren't many she'd trust her baby boy with.

Ryan and Sophia... their callousness about Alex... their past behavior toward Lilah... no way. There was Patrice...

Sabrina bit back a groan. How on earth could Alex's mother prefer to live with the Kingsleys after what happened? If she ever assumed charge of Michael, he'd be in precisely the same situation

Sabrina wanted to avoid—under Godwin Kingsley's control. There was also the strange matter of Patrice's behavior with Richard Armor. Sabrina didn't give a damn what lay behind the affection. She couldn't let her son be forced to watch his granny fawning over the same man who destroyed their family.

Sabrina glanced at the spot right below the window where Harry and Michael sat cross-legged, their attention on the two saxophones. Discarded on the floor not too far from them lay a magazine. "At least the Kingsleys have been completely off the tabloids for a few weeks," she said out loud.

Harry looked up. "Thanks to Donald Trump and his problems." *Time Magazine's* January edition showed the real estate mogul on its cover. *Saturday Night Live* even did a spoof on him and his girlfriend.

"He doesn't seem to mind all the gossip," Sabrina remarked. Shrugging, she added, "It's not like he's ever going to run for office."

She returned her focus to the digital weapon Shawn requested her to design. If only she could do the work in San Jose where his company, Game Changer Consulting, was located. She didn't dare for the same reason Shawn couldn't construct the weapon himself or ask any of his employees. He was now on the fed's watchlist, and the minute Sabrina outed herself, she would also come under scrutiny. For Michael's sake, she needed to stay under the radar.

Her little boy was currently engrossed with the shiny new saxophone, turning it over in his hands. On the television, the cartoons were on again, but Michael didn't look up. Harry had even brought his old sax out, surprising Sabrina. *I haven't heard Harry play in... oh, God, not since we left Libya, I think.* Michael picked up the new instrument and blew hard. Sabrina jumped. If the chicken in the oven suddenly started screeching, it wouldn't sound as bad. Michael simply snickered and asked his uncle to show him how to play.

Yeah, Michael's mama would make do with whatever little activity she got if it would keep him smiling. Harry didn't tell her exactly what was going on. From the nervous behavior of Dan and Shawn when they came to talk to her and from the specs Shawn provided for the virus, it was clear they were planning to sneak into the records of financial institutions. Apology and concern were writ large on the faces of the three men—Harry, Dan, and Shawn. No one would know she was the brain behind it, swore Shawn. As soon as she gave the A-OK, he'd deploy the weapon from some undisclosed location.

Sabrina blinked hard, wanting a distraction to dispel the worry. On cue, her tummy rumbled. Grimacing, she forced herself to close the portable computer and stand. Harry had some kind of arrangement with nearby restaurants to deliver food, but one more such meal, and she'd scream like a mad woman. Besides, Michael needed to eat healthy. Today was her very first attempt at cooking.

A minute later, she glowered at the charred chicken in the pan, wondering if she could pass off the blackened bird as a new recipe. Harry wouldn't dare say a word, but Michael wasn't gonna be kind.

"Uncle Harry," called the boy. "Play a song."

Heaving himself from the hardwood floor, Harry said, "Okay, buddy." A tiny replica of Eiffel Tower dangled from the thin, silver chain wrapped around his wrist. He'd taken it from Lilah's jewelry box without offering explanations, and Sabrina didn't ask for any.

"Listen to this," Harry said to Michael. Shuffling in place to the tune, Harry played the theme song from *Ghostbusters*.

Michael flung his limbs about and sang along. He and Harry proceeded to leap around the room in a weird war dance. Hearing the sound of childish laughter for the second time in one day, Sabrina smiled in relief.

The scene at the Kingsley mansion on New Year's Eve had scared her. Her baby was so serious and solemn. She'd taken him to a child psychiatrist within a week and intended to keep up with the visits, but how could a doctor's kind words erase all the horrific memories from his mind?

How was she going to erase the bitterness from *her* mind? Anger toward Alex for putting his brother above her, toward Harry and Temple whose grand ideas started it all... God, there were even times Sabrina caught herself feeling resentful of Lilah simply for being able to talk to Alex whenever she wanted.

Sabrina gritted her teeth, trying to keep in mind Alex's attachment to his family was a big part of the man she loved. The same bonds were used against him and his brothers. And *her* brother... Harry was trying his damnedest to make up for his role in the mess. Perhaps she needed to take her cue from her son. Michael made it clear whom he blamed—Armor and the Kingsley family.

Patrice had mentioned something about Steven and his engagement party. The Kingsleys were happy in their home, celebrating a new beginning while Alex was...

Your son misses you, Sabrina whispered in her mind. *Your wife, too.* She made a mental note to check on Victor's son. She'd been thinking of having him over for a visit. The company of someone closer to his age would do Michael good. Gabriel needed the reassurance of family, too. Patrice was his only living grandparent.

Alex's mother... what in the world was the deal with her? Any soft spot she harbored for Richard Armor should've been destroyed by what he and his bosom buddy did to Patrice's sons. Perhaps Noah Andersen would be successful in ferreting out Patrice Kingsley's secrets. Sabrina had casually mentioned to him how she ran into Major Armor on her visit to the Kingsley mansion to see her mother-in-law. Living amid their enemies wasn't the best idea, Sabrina worried out loud to Noah. The former attorney general nodded agreement and said he was planning to talk to Patrice.

Chapter 25

A month later, March 1989

Upper East Side, New York City

Aaron Kingsley's apartment at the family mansion was roomy enough for him and Patrice not to run into each other if they so chose. Since his lady friend was a widow who refused to leave her home a couple of blocks away, Patrice pretty much had the place all to herself. Except for Hema, Lilah's former intern. But now, Hema was making noises about leaving the U.S.

The domestic staff already gave Patrice enough strange looks about the living arrangements. She and Aaron were both fifty-five, but he was her brother-in-law. There was surely gossip in the Kingsley social circle about the unseemliness of it all. When Hema left... Patrice had survived society's mockery before. When someone was impertinent enough to ask why she couldn't rent her own place, Patrice simply said she preferred not being alone with her thoughts.

A lie... she didn't care one way or the other if anyone else was around. Nor was she panicking yet. Mr. Temple survived the assassination attempt, but he couldn't talk or do anything to help her sons. There was still Harry, and Daniel Barrons would want his sister home. The two men would move heaven and earth to get the exiles back. Patrice reminded herself of it every day. All five of Peter's boys would soon return.

Only once they did would Patrice leave the Kingsley mansion. They would all be back in Panama, living in the magnificent residence they built in Cerro Azul. Until then, she'd stay with Aaron in the Kingsley mansion. It was the one place Richard visited frequently.

Between the slats of the blinds covering the living room window, she watched him. Arms resting on top of his new Porsche, Richard was talking to his parents. Patrice smiled to herself, noting him running a loving hand over the hood of his vehicle, apparently showing off his latest acquisition. The sun was on its way down, its last red-gold rays bathing him in their glow. She couldn't make out his words, but he was animated, voice raised in excitement over the costly toy. Richard turned, and with a small gasp, she slipped to the side, heart thundering.

Patrice told herself to stop being a fool. He couldn't have spotted her behind the blinds of the fifth-floor window.

"You're going to give yourselves away one of these days," a voice said from behind.

With a yelp, she pivoted. "Mr. Andersen!"

At the door to the living room stood the former attorney general. He laughed.

Patrice stared, unsure what to do.

"How are you, m'dear?" Andersen asked.

He'd been every bit as friendly the day he threatened to reveal her secret. *No*, she corrected herself. He never actually threatened her. As a lawyer, he'd been too clever to try blatant blackmail. He merely reminded her of her shameful story right in front of Brad. Noah Andersen shut her mouth as surely as he would have if he held a gun to her head. From fear of what he'd do, Patrice failed to warn Brad. She allowed disaster to happen.

She'd met Andersen many times since then at the hospital, but that was in Aaron's company. Now, there was no one else around.

Andersen's smile seemed sinister, his laughter signaling only impending doom. She wanted to run out of the apartment... tell him to get out... something!

Voice quavering, Patrice called, "Aaron."

"I'm sure you know Aaron is with Godwin and David. They're going over plans for Steven's wedding."

She ran to the phone on the side table. "I'm calling security."

"Patrice!" Andersen steepled his fingers as though praying for patience. "I understand your... fear, but please hear me out. I'm not your enemy."

"Could have fooled me," she said, tone bitter.

"It was a mistake on my part," he said. "Plus, you're staying here, right in hostile territory! With Godwin and David living on either side of you. Can't *I* at least get a hearing?"

She said nothing, staring at him, not daring to blink in case he did something worse in that infinitesimal interval of time.

"I'm trying to help your sons," Andersen said. *"All* your sons."

Patrice picked up the phone.

"Please?" he begged, hands held out in supplication.

Biting her lip, Patrice debated herself. Andersen was in good part responsible for what happened between Brad and Lilah. But then, all of them contributed to the tragedy. Patrice, too. Even after she realized how Richard used her affection to set her sons on the road to ruin, she hadn't been able to utter a bitter word. While Andersen... the press conference he did with Harry... unlike her, the former attorney general was genuinely trying to make amends.

She pointed to the chair farthest from her. "Sit down there. I'm putting 9-1-1 on speed dial. At the first sign of trouble, I'm pressing send. Got it?"

A smile lit his wrinkled eyes. "I'll do as you say, but I'm an old man. Even as small as you are, you could easily beat me to death with your bare hands. And really! I never physically threatened you."

But he'd frightened her so badly that he'd taken on the aura of an executioner in her mind. "Sit," she said. "And start talking."

He did as he was bid. "Patrice, I think you should—"

"No."

"You haven't even heard—"

"I already know what you're going to ask. You want me to tell Richard... no, I can't!"

"No, Patrice. It's not what I want."

"Then, you want me to move out of here. Let me tell you. My living arrangements are none of your business."

His eyelids flickered. "Patrice, listen to me before jumping to conclusions. I came here to warn you *not* to make the mistake of talking to Richard about things. I came here to ask you not to move out of this place. Because Richard's history is not limited to what you know about him or what the people who brought him up know. What he did in Cuba—"

"What do you mean 'not limited'?"

"Richard's already run into trouble with the FBI. The fed chief in Corpus Christi is an acquaintance of mine. He called me because he knew of Richard's connection to the Kingsleys. His company is involved in some shady dealings."

"Businesses do shady deals all the time," Patrice said.

"But this is diff—trust me, it will add to the perception of him as a criminal."

"He is not a criminal."

"Really? You believe it even after what happened to Brad and the rest? My dear, there's maternal fondness, and then there's... believe it or not, I've always admired the way you brought up Brad, Victor, and Alex. You taught all five of Peter's sons to have each other's backs. Patrice, you're an incredibly strong woman... except when it comes to Richard. I've heard stories from Temple, and I heard what happened when Sabrina and Michael visited. Your daughter-in-law was confused by your behavior, and I couldn't think of a way to explain it to her. Frankly, I don't understand it myself. It's one thing to dismiss the dirty tricks back when they were all boys. After the incident in Cuba—"

"Peter's children didn't get along with Richard only because of his friendship with Steven." Patrice gritted her teeth. "You know it, Godwin knows it, and everyone in the world knows it! I don't blame any of my boys, including Richard, for the circumstances."

"So you're going to automatically take his side no matter what?"

"No!" exploded Patrice. "I don't take sides between my children. But Peter's sons grew up knowing... they got advantages Richard didn't have. Even now, they have many people helping them. The five of them will be home soon. Lilah, too."

"Let's hope you're right," said Andersen. "But what if—"

"I *am* right," said Patrice. "Lilah's brother is Andrew Barrons's son! He's not going to stand by and watch... Harry's sister is married to Alex. Who does Richard have except Steven? And we're both aware what *he's* like. Someone needs to... Richard will have my support whenever he needs it."

"To the point you're willing to ignore criminal activity?" asked Andersen. "You're going to ignore what he did to Brad and Lilah and the others?"

"Stop calling him a—" Patrice took a deep breath. "I'm not ignoring anything. Steven tricked my sons, and Richard helped, but it was a government-approved sting operation. Not ethical but not illegal, either."

"Are you kidding me?" Andersen hissed. "Brad could've been put to death for treason. And it wasn't the first time Richard tried to kill your sons, was it? What about the time in California? You were there when the hitman opened fire. Patrice, I came here to ask you to keep an eye on Richard. Anything you see or hear, you need to let us—"

"Stop," warned Patrice, her voice shaking but now from anger. "Don't you dare blame him for things he didn't do! Steven was the one who arranged the hit job, not Richard. He had no part in it. I will not sit here and let you scapegoat him."

"Steven!" Andersen closed his eyes briefly. "I'm beginning to feel sorry for the fellow. He gets all the blame for... Patrice, everything Steven did, each trick he pulled was done with full support from Richard. Better pray one or more of your boys don't end up dead before you admit what's obvious to the rest of us."

Patrice stood. "This conversation is over. You may leave now."

Heaving himself up from the chair, Andersen said, "Sticking your fingers in your ears and refusing to hear me will not change facts."

"What facts?" asked Patrice. "Richard is not stupid. He and Steven are friends... but helping in a murder attempt?! No way! Richard doesn't have any reason to want Brad dead."

Chapter 26

Nine years ago, September 1980

Hell's Kitchen, New York City

"What the hell does Cousin Brad have that I don't?" Steven paced up and down the linoleum floor, skirting the cheap suede couch and the teak dining table where Richard was working.

It would've been more accurate to say he was *trying* to work. Apart from Steven's narration of the latest episode of the Kingsley soap opera, there were the young boys—working-class Irish, most of them—throwing a football around on the street in front of the tenement building, shouting and shoving at each other. The kids, the vehicles honking at them, the drunks weaving about... the cacophony was relentless.

The view from his window matched the sounds. Buildings were covered in graffiti, some mere scribbles, but mostly obscenities and exaggerated sketches of the female anatomy. There was the video rental at the end of the block which specialized in erotica. The partially burned car in front of the porn store was the handiwork of Hell's Celts, the gang controlling the neighborhood. The smell of charred rubber had permeated the air for a week after the event.

The fire escape clattered. The football, obviously.

Steven wheeled toward the door. "This is enough. I'm going to go down there and tell those hooligans to stop."

"Don't," said Richard, not bothering to look up from the papers. "At least one of them has a dad with mob connections. The Kingsleys might be aristocracy, but here on the Westside, the mafia makes the rules."

"What the devil are the cops doing?"

Richard shook his head. "They can do nothing. They know who the boss is married to." He named the daughter of a prominent politician from one of New York's oldest families.

Steven hissed. "I met a state senator with the same name at one of Grandfather's parties."

"He's the man. Criminals and politicians together control most of the union jobs in this area."

"Isn't it racketeering?!"

Richard often despaired of his friend's naïveté. "And gambling. And loansharking. And snatch rackets."

"Snatch rackets?"

"Kidnapping for ransom."

"Why in God's name did you return *here* after law school?" Steven asked. "I know you didn't have much money when you left active service, but doesn't the law firm pay you well?"

They did. While living in a middle-class rental would be a step up from this place, it wasn't enough for Richard. "Just a year or two here," he said. "Once I save enough cash, I'm getting myself a home in Turtle Bay." He chuckled. "There's a house for sale on Katharine Hepburn's block."

"Wrong actress," Steven said, grabbing a chair and straddling it.

True. For as long as Richard had been able to appreciate feminine charms, Elizabeth Taylor was the benchmark. She was... perfection. Not for Steven, though. He needed his women even more stacked and preferred them blonde.

"You still have the same *Playboy*?" Richard asked, grinning.

A blissful look coming over his face, Steven said, "Hell, yeah." The edition carrying Jayne Mansfield's nudes had been one of his prized possessions since teenage years. "I'm gonna be buried with it... are you planning to buy the house? The one next to Katharine Hepburn?"

"No," Richard said. "I have my eye on a couple of the new high rises." Which brought them back to the reason for his current choice of homes—saving a healthy chunk of his paycheck.

But now, temptation had come his way, luring him toward a more powerful but less lucrative position. Unfortunately, if he decided to pursue it, he'd have to swallow some pride. "Steven, there's a job with the U.S. Attorney's office I might like."

Steven grabbed a handful of peanuts from the dish and popped them into his mouth. "Oh, yeah?"

"I'm going to ask my boss for a recommendation. Also, I'm hoping you can get your grandfather to put in a good word."

Steven raised an eyebrow, but he surely knew how it worked. Richard's Kingsley connection was now common knowledge in military and legal circles, and consequently, it was almost essential for Godwin to speak well of his servant's son. Even silence would prove damning. There could only be so many employers with grudges against the Kingsleys. So far, General Axeman had been it, and he'd died in his sleep the month before.

"Rich, you already know what Grandfather's like." Steven drummed his fingers on the tabletop. "Tell you what... I'll talk to Mr. Temple."

Incredulous, Richard asked, "The president? What have you been smoking?"

"Why not?" Steven asked. "He's my uncle."

"Great uncle," Richard corrected. "He's your grandfather's stepbrother. But why would he recommend me? The man doesn't know I exist."

Steven laughed. "He does. I've heard him ask Aunt Patrice how you were doing."

Frowning, Richard questioned, "Really? Why would he expect her to know?"

"He's probably aware of her soft corner for you, the poor little orphan," Steven teased.

"I have parents," Richard said, his voice tight.

Steven lobbed a peanut at Richard. "It was a joke, friend."

"I got it," Richard allowed. "But why did Mr. Temple want to know about me, anyway?"

"He's a politician," said Steven. "They collect information. Grandfather calls it the key to success in any endeavor."

Richard was forced to concede the point. Still, what could the most powerful man in the world hope to gain from information regarding a chauffeur's adopted son?

Steven asked, "What's your boss's name? Your future one?"

"Rudolph Giuliani. I heard him talk about the mafia groups in New York. Says it's high time someone cleaned up the city."

His hand stopping with a peanut held inches from his teeth, Steven said, "Wow. You plan to do the honors?"

"I'd be part of a team."

"I wish you'd be part of Kingsley Corp," Steven groused. "According to Grandfather, Brad's the best thing to happen to the company, and now, he's got Victor and Alex helping him. If I don't get enough backing from the board, Brad's going to end up as CEO. I need your support, Rich."

"What can I do? And you're not alone. Don't you already have your father on your side? Also, Charlie can join you, can't he?"

Steven snorted. "You know Charlie's hopeless. I prefer to keep him away from the business. Father's worse."

"Really?"

"You don't understand how bad things are for me," Steven said. "The Texas division of Kingsley Corp? It originally belonged to my mother's family. Before Grandfather Gander—my mother's father— died, he agreed to make the business part of Kingsley Corp."

Richard did know the business his friend was talking about—the Gander family's drilling outfit in Texas. Some time before Steven was born, the company was negotiating with the shipping corporation the Armor parents invested in—the one driven to bankruptcy by Peter Kingsley—for transport of oil to Europe. The Ganders were in dire financial straits at the time and desperately needed new customers, their old ones having been taken by the oilman, Jared Sanders. With the demise of the shipping business, Grandpa Gander didn't get the chance to arrange alternatives before banks came knocking. Since his daughter was married to David Kingsley—Steven's father—Godwin agreed to bail them out. The business would be annexed by Kingsley Corp after Gander, Sr's death, the shares to be held exclusively by his grandchildren. The Kingsleys were in oil services, not drilling, but the old judge was determined to extract a price for his help.

Steven knew all of it, knew what Peter Kingsley's weird vendetta against the shipping company did to his mother's family's livelihood. Hell, Stanley Gander, Steven's uncle, ended up working for the Kingsleys in some low-level office job. Still, Steven's loyalties were tilted more toward the Kingsleys than his mother's side. His main beef was with Brad.

Tone morose, Steven continued, "I wish Grandfather Gander straight up deeded the shares to Charlie and me. As things stand, control of the stock is with my father. Well, fifty-fifty between him and me after I turned twenty-five And what does my father do? Ask me! C'mon, ask me!"

Swallowing a chuckle, Richard asked, "What?"

"Nothing. Anytime I have a suggestion, Grandfather has him veto it."

"Stalemate."

"Yeah, and then, Grandfather gets to make the decisions. Guess who he put in charge of the office?"

Richard got a bad feeling he already knew.

"Brad!" Steven flopped back in his chair. "Cousin Brad is now running *my* company. Grandfather says he's more deserving than me."

"Hell," Richard spat out. "Couldn't you talk to your Uncle Aaron? Better yet, go to the board?" He'd always found Aaron Kingsley to be fair-minded, though unnecessarily deferential to his adoptive father, Godwin.

"Are you kidding me? Uncle Aaron *luuurves* the poor orphan boys. And he adores Grandfather. Even if he thought it was unfair, he'd never do anything about it. With all of them ganging up against me, what chance do I have with the board? Now, do you see why I need you in Kingsley Corp, Rich? People respect heroes like you. They'll listen to you."

"Your grandfather won't even recommend me for a position none of his grandsons are angling to get. You think he'll actually let me work for his company where I'll be butting heads with them every day?"

Eyes glinting, Steven sat up. "I have a plan. Simply say yes, and I'll take care of the rest."

#

A month later, October 1980

Greenwich, Connecticut

"Wow," said Richard. Guests—Kingsley Corp business associates and their families—were milling about, but he paid no attention to them, busy as he was taking in the glorious sight.

Godwin Kingsley's estate was magnificent. The ancestral mansion in New York would be divided between the surviving Kingsleys after Godwin's time, as would the other family properties. But *this* piece of land in the neighboring state was bought by Godwin with his salary as president of the company, and he was free to do with it as he pleased. Richard heard all about it from Steven on their ride here.

"You ain't seen nothing yet," Steven said. "The whole forty acres was landscaped exactly as Grandfather wanted it. *The Architectural Digest* called the house Georgian, whatever it means."

Richard had no idea what it meant, either. All he could say was this small corner they'd driven up to was near perfection. Someday... someday soon, he wanted it all to be his. Not this particular house, but the overwhelming display of power and prestige, the world waiting to pay homage... all of it. He set his duffel bag down and drank everything in.

The grass was already turning brown, but it didn't matter. Red and yellow leaves carpeted the level ground, trees bordering the large meadow sporting the same stunning hues on their branches. A cool breeze blew, rustling the fallen leaves before sneaking under Richard's collar to caress his skin. At the far end of the plot was the shooting stand, its rustic wooden roof and walls offering protection from the elements. Logs burned in a stone fire pit next to the stand. Already, a few men were lined up to try their luck with revolvers and semiautomatics.

On the near side, a giant red barn stood a few feet from them, offering refreshments or simply a chance to sit at the harvest-themed tables to watch the shooters. Hollowed out pumpkins overflowing with berries served as centerpieces. Red and brown fleece blankets were draped over each chair. Twig-wrapped tin buckets were lined along a long table, holding bottles of fine wine.

A waiter walked to them. "*Hors d'oeuvres,* gentlemen?"

"What's this?" Steven asked, saving Richard the trouble.

"Spinach-and-artichoke galette," said the waiter. "And pigs-in-a-blanket."

Biting into the flaky crust and spicy sausage, Richard peered at the stage on the left. "A band?" he hazarded a guess.

"Yeah," said Steven, waving a hand at the chairs set up facing the stage. "There's Grandfather... and Cousin Brad."

The recently retired justice was in the front row, holding court. A long line of politicians and businessmen waited to talk to him. Brad and his mother were seated directly behind Godwin. Richard grimaced. He'd hoped the woman wouldn't be here.

The wind carried Godwin's voice to them. "...Harry Sheppard... medal of..."

The name was familiar. "Is he talking about Hector Sheppard's brother?" Richard asked. Steven boxed at Hector's gym. Nice place. Polite employees.

"Yeah," said Steven. "Got the Medal of Honor. Hector's been going on about the hero of the family."

"What does your grandfather have to do with the Sheppard hero?"

"Petty Officer Sheppard is a protégé of sorts to Mr. Temple." Steven took a few steps closer to the family patriarch, Richard following. The conversation between Godwin Kingsley and the rest got clearer.

Petty Officer? President Temple seemed to take an interest in the underdog: chauffeur's sons, lowly sailors... "Enlisted man," commented Richard, dismissing Harry Sheppard from his mind.

Apparently, so did Godwin Kingsley. He twisted around in his chair to address Brad. "The family I told you about? I want you to make a good impression."

Brad smiled.

"Are you matchmaking, Godwin?" Patrice asked, laughing. "If so, I want to meet the girl, too. What's her name?"

"*Is* he matchmaking?" Richard asked, tone low.

Steven chortled under his breath. "Probably. There's no other way Cousin Brad's going to find himself a wife. He's not like his little brothers."

At the back of the rows of chairs were Alex and Victor... surrounded, as usual, by a gaggle of giggling girls. There was a third man with them, a blond fellow who looked like he just stepped off the pages of *GQ*.

"Who's he?" Richard asked.

"Neil, one of the twins," explained Steven. "He's starting medical school in a couple of weeks. You've met him before."

So he had. Eons ago. "Good-looking doctor with family money. No wonder the ladies look impressed."

Charles joined Steven and Richard, taking a swig from the bottle of beer in his hand. "The dork's here, too."

Steven hissed. "Charlie, you idiot. 'The dork' is probably the most dangerous of the lot. Have you looked into his eyes?"

Guffawing, Charles said, "Nope. I ain't one of those types."

Paying no mind to Charles, Richard asked, "Who are you talking about?"

"Scott," Steven said. "He stares. It's like he's analyzing everyone he meets. Cataloging us in his mind. It's scary. Also, he already has a Ph.D. In astrophysics!"

Neither of the twins joined the military, so Richard hadn't paid much attention. But now, he noticed the kid next to Brad. Scott Kingsley had to be in his early twenties but looked like a seventeen-year-old. Only, with extraordinary intelligence. Richard laughed. "Poor Brad."

"Huh?" said Steven.

"Must have been bad enough growing up as Alex and Victor's big brother. Now, he has to deal with The Movie Star Doctor and The Brain."

"Brad's a pathetic piece of—" Steven broke off to smile at a matron walking by. "But Grandfather's going to make him CEO if we don't do something about it. I need you in Kingsley Corp."

Richard nodded. "Let's see... looks like the shooting contest is about to start."

The guests surged to the stand. Richard watched Alex sauntering ahead, confident smile on his face. The golden boy thought he had it in the bag.

"Yo, Alex," boomed Victor, jogging behind. Hand on Alex's shoulder, Victor muttered something.

Alex's head jerked toward Richard and Steven.

"Make him salute you," Charles suggested, giggling. "You're a major, and he's a captain."

Richard chose not to be exasperated, but he needed to try hard. Very hard. "Neither of us is in uniform."

With a bland expression, Alex inclined his head at them and joined the group waiting to sign up for the match.

At the stand, Aaron Kingsley held up a hand. "Ladies and gentlemen, this year we decided to do something different."

Richard tuned Aaron out. Steven had already coached Richard on what to expect: a three-gun combat match, modeled after the recent one organized in Missouri by *Soldier of Fortune* magazine.

When it was Richard's turn at the registration desk, he said, "I have my own." He drew his AR-15 from the duffel.

The man frowned. "Everyone else is going with the M-14s we provide."

"The rules didn't specify the type of gun," Richard said.

"Because the invitation clearly stated equipment will be provided," the man argued. "We weren't expecting guests to show up with their own."

"You didn't say we couldn't," Richard countered.

The man exclaimed, "AR-15 is a smaller caliber. It will give you an unfair advantage."

Richard sneered. "You call this a contest open to all guests and let Alex Kingsley participate? He's a sniper, trained by the army. Talk about an unfair advantage."

Mutters rose among the guests. "True," someone said.

"I'll withdraw," Alex said instantly. "Did you come here just to start trouble, Armor? Also, I don't remember seeing your name on the guest list."

"Right," said Richard. "You offer to withdraw as soon as you run into someone who can actually beat you."

Alex snarled. "Beat me? You're lucky we're never going to face off in battle. You'd be dead before you got your weapon ready."

Richard laughed. "Bragging? What are you? A ten-year-old? Real soldiers let their weapons do the talking. As for killing me... how would you pull the trigger with your brains already blown to bits?"

"Stop, Alex," came a frantic feminine voice. Pushing through the crowd, the slight figure of Patrice Kingsley appeared and went to her son. Victor and Brad joined her.

From the stand, Aaron said, "This is supposed to be a friendly contest at a garden party. Not a grudge match. Major Armor, Alex is right. The party is for executives and associates of Kingsley Corp and their families. I know you're Steven's friend, but you don't work for us or for any of the businesses we partner with. Why are you here?"

"Uncle Aaron," Steven bellowed, face red. "Rich is my guest. Insulting him is like insulting me."

Aaron stiffened, his warning gaze darting toward the gawking onlookers.

Steven continued, "I'm as much a Kingsley as the rest of you. I have the right to invite who I want. Or did you happen to decide I don't?"

The crowd watched, avidly interested in the family drama being played before their eyes.

"This is not your home," Aaron pointed out. "It's your grandfather's. He has always limited this event to associates of Kingsley Corp."

Richard stayed silent, maintaining an impassive expression.

"Oh, yeah?" said Steven. "In which case, let me tell you something else. I've asked Rich to take over our Texas office from Brad. Richard *is* a Kingsley Corp executive."

It took a couple of seconds for the announcement to register. Shocked exclamations went around the audience. Chatter peaked.

"Steven," shouted Aaron. He nearly stumbled from the stand. "You can't simply appoint anyone you please to run an office. Also, this is not the venue to discuss such matters."

"No, it's not," Steven agreed. "But you insulted the man I had in mind for the job, so I was forced to bring it up. Anyway, now it's been established Rich does work for us—me, specifically, since the Texas office is mine—he can compete, can't he?"

"David," exclaimed Aaron. "Do something."

David Kingsley, as usual, had not been noticed by anyone. The group around the stand twisted and turned, trying to locate him. From the edge of the gathering, his voice said, "Umm... I'm not sure... what do you want me to do?"

"You don't have to do anything, Father," Steven said. "You and I have authority over the Texas office. Not Uncle Aaron, not Grandfather."

The crowd parted as though it were Red Sea parting before Moses. Godwin Kingsley strode to the front.

Before he could speak, Steven said, "Right, Grandfather? It's the agreement you signed with my mother's father. As you always say, contracts are sacrosanct. If a man violates the spirit of the contract, he's a man who cannot be trusted in business or anything else."

Richard thought he heard a suppressed groan from Aaron.

Strangely, Justice Kingsley only smiled, his gray gaze flitting between Steven and Brad. "You're absolutely right, Steven. You get to appoint whomever you want to an office you control. Brad, I trust you can see Mr. Armor through the transition?"

Smoothing back his hair, Brad said, "Ahh... okay."

That was it? Richard couldn't believe Steven's insane plan actually worked.

"Huh?" said Steven. "Umm... good. So it's settled. Let's go, Rich."

"Wait," said Richard. "We haven't settled the little matter of the contest. Am I allowed to participate or not?"

Lips curling into a grimace, the fellow at the registration desk said, "Yes."

Under his breath, Steven muttered, "Can we please leave before Grandfather changes his mind?"

"He's not going to," Richard muttered back. "Not after all these people heard him. This is my chance to go one-to-one with the golden boy."

Steven huffed. "Fine. Just make sure he doesn't win."

They went through multiple stages, three guns. The rifle, the shotgun, the handgun. At each stage, Richard produced from his duffel a better weapon than the one provided by the Kingsley staff. His was lighter to carry, easier to reload, less recoil. In the end, his overall score was two-hundred-and-forty-seven to Alex's two-thirty-eight. Once Richard was officially declared winner, they shook hands.

The breeze was chilly, but the heat and the smoke from the fire pit kept their bodies warm. Most of the guests drifted away. Godwin Kingsley stayed, his sons—David and Aaron—flanking him. Alex's mother and his oldest brother were there.

"I won't forget what you did today," Alex promised. The clouds gathering in the twilight sky threw his face into gloom. "Someday, we'll meet again with matched weapons. Then, we'll see."

The setting sun bathed Richard and Steven in red rays. Richard said, "In battle, you don't have the luxury of demanding the enemy dumb himself down to your level. If you were half as good as they claim, you'd have been prepared."

"Alex, please," beseeched Patrice Kingsley, tugging at his elbow. "The silly match is done. Let's go."

"Your son will be fine, Patrice," Godwin soothed. "Brad, don't worry about your position in the company. I have bigger things in mind for you than just one division."

"Thank you, sir," Brad said, voice deferential. "I knew you'd find something else for me to do. Kingsley Corp is a big company."

"Steven," Godwin said. "I'll see you back in New York. We need to talk about this." The patriarch left, his sons accompanying him.

"Enjoy your win while you can, Armor," boomed Victor, approaching the group. "In a month or two, you'll be begging us for help. What do you know about running an oil company?"

"Not your problem," Steven said, voice cheerful.

Nodding in Richard's direction, Victor said, "True enough. Kingsley Corp will survive even if the Texas office goes under. Armor will be all right, too. I'm sure Grandfather will be generous enough to put him in charge of the garage. He's the chauffeur's son, after all."

In an instant, Richard was back in his childhood, back in the apartment over the garage. Back in the wealthy Upper East Side school where kids introduced themselves by their parents' names. Where he had no address to call his own. The smirks, the pity. The embarrassment, the fury, the impotence. His hands curled into fists. Keeping his eyes fixed on the fire crackling in the pit, he counted his heartbeats.

Steven growled, "You—"

"Victor," shouted Patrice. "How could you?"

As though she never heard him say it before. The first time Victor referred to Richard by his position in society had been when they met after the return of Peter Kingsley's newly bereaved family to the mansion. Even in his anger, Richard knew Victor had merely been using it as an identifier. But the damage was done. Richard loathed all of them for it, and his disproportional fury revealed the chink in his armor to his enemies.

With a wave of his hand, Victor dismissed her reprimand. "He threatened to blow Alex's brains out... and you're worried about me calling him 'chauffeur's son'?"

The words ricocheted within Richard's skull, becoming louder with each repetition. Chauffeur's son. Chauffeur's son! CHAUFFEUR'S SON! His education at the most elite of all military schools, his skill with weapons, his degree in law, none of it mattered. He was always going to be the chauffeur's son to some people. "Major," he said, his voice thick. "I'm Major Armor."

Alex laughed. "Yeah. Couldn't get yourself promoted as a soldier, so you went to law school. Bet you failed there, too, and now, you're trying your luck in the oil business. The only way you'll ever win is by cheating. Like you did today."

In the clarity of the one moment, Richard knew he wanted Alex Kingsley dead. Richard wanted to watch Alex bleed drop by agonizing drop. Alex was everything Richard could have been if not for his lack of clout. Instead of showing some humility about the underserved accolades, Alex was mocking Richard for having had to claw his way up in the world.

"Alex," said his mother, her hands covering the embarrassment on her face. "No..."

Inclining his head, Richard echoed Alex's prior vow. "We'll meet again."

"Sure," Alex agreed. "When you're done destroying the Texas division."

"I'm so sorry, Richard," said Patrice, her fingertips touching his arm for a fleeting moment. "And... and congratulations. I'm glad..."

"Mother!" said Victor, voice high.

Ignoring her good wishes, Richard pivoted and marched away. When Steven caught up, Richard said, "They're going to make sure we fail."

"I'm going to make sure we don't. You're a smart man. I figure it will take you six months to start running the business without my help. A year, tops. You might even be building your own outfit by then."

Richard halted. "Thanks for the vote of confidence, but I wasn't talking about one particular office. Alex and Victor are going to make sure we don't get another chance to do what we did today. Whatever I say to the board on your behalf, they're going to speak against."

"But you're a hero—"

"So are they. There will be a dozen generals ready to vouch for Alex. I know Victor was in West Germany, but he was instrumental in getting hundreds of refugees out of Iraq. It's going to be my word against theirs. Also, didn't you hear Godwin? He has bigger things in mind for Brad than just one division."

Steven took in a sharp breath. "The CEO spot?"

"I think so. We may have just won the battle and lost the war."

"What do you suggest?"

"You'll never get to be CEO as long as Brad is around."

"But how do we get him out? Everyone else in the family loves him."

"There's only one way to make certain a man never returns."

"Huh?" Steven jerked back. "No! I can't... can I?"

"Then, be prepared to work under him for the rest of your life." The object of their discussion was walking down a tarred path, his mother and brothers in tow. To the house, presumably. "Think of it as war," Richard advised. "If you don't get the enemy first, he'll get *you*. Or you'll have to surrender. Trust me, Steven. Your only other options will be to dumbly take whatever your cousins dish out or risk being gunned down. Do you somehow imagine Alex and Victor are above finishing you off to protect their brother? You need to get rid of Brad."

Breath coming in rapid, shallow puffs, Steven stared at the disappearing backs of Patrice Kingsley and her sons. "What about the rest?"

Richard shook his head. "I'm not worried about the twins. But Alex and Victor... they can't be left alive."

Within months, their plans were ready. Patrice and her sons were about to go for a brief sojourn in the Kingsley vacation cabin in California. They would never return.

#

Back in the present, March 1989

Upper East Side, New York City

Except the Kingsley brothers and their mother did return. Brad married Delilah Sheppard Barrons, creating the Sheppard-Barrons-Kingsley alliance.

Driving away from the mansion, Richard shook his head. Each time he visited his parents, old memories attacked. Perhaps once the network's control was secure in Steven's hands, his brain would stop reminding him of events he preferred to forget. The day was close... very, very close.

Part X

Chapter 27

Same time

Eden, Washington, DC

Lupe never knew jazz was so seductive. If Nikki heard Harry play, she would've laid herself bare on the desk, saying, "Take me; I'm yours." To be honest, Lupe had been highly tempted to do the same.

It gave Lupe the idea of introducing jazz to Eden. She ran a quick and clinical eye over the newly hired quartet playing in Oasis. The young men cleaned up well. They'd objected to being told to cut their hair and don tuxedos, somehow considering it a betrayal of their principles, but the amount mentioned on the contract soon took care of their protests. In the stunned silence following, Lupe explained to them Eden existed to provide pleasure, and its musicians could not be allowed to resemble escapees from drug rehab. Which, she was forced to admit, had a high chance of being true given the track marks she noticed on their arms. She'd warned them their jobs would last only as long as they stayed clean. Lupe couldn't afford to have any problem children employed in her establishment.

"Ms. Valdez?" When she turned to the voice, the server balanced his tray in one hand and leaned forward to mutter into her ear, "The congressman is here, asking for you."

Damn. She'd hoped for more time. Maybe JD was here for a random visit... to join his comrades for an off-the-record meeting at the club or simply to enjoy the skin show. But he'd asked to talk to

Lupe. Her contract with Rep. Jack Drummond ended years ago, but the rumors in DC about the precise nature of their connection meant he took care not to be seen with her too often in public. JD was here to discuss something important enough to risk his public image... something like Harry Sheppard.

Lupe turned to the door with a wide smile and walked in the direction with both hands stretched out in welcome. "It's been a while," she murmured to the guest.

As always, JD was in a suit, light-brown hair coiffured in the boyish style favored by some American politicians. Only someone who knew him intimately would've noticed the cruel glint in the blue eyes.

There was another man with JD, again someone Lupe was familiar with. Brown hair, gray irises, tall... Charles Kingsley should've been considered handsome, but vulgarity was evident even in the way he breathed. Lupe swallowed hard, struggling to keep from retching. JD was sick and violent, but he didn't let that side show to the world, and Lupe could get away with pretending all was well in their equation. Charles... the crudity... her standing in the community would go down the drain in a matter of moments if anyone found out what she allowed him—along with JD—to do to her body. Thank God, Charles never showed up in Eden without JD. The politician was the leader in the duo, and his caution about his career meant the Kingsley idiot was forced to behave himself when in public with Lupe. And Charles never dared demand sexual favors from her after the contract with JD was done.

Still, pretending she wasn't acquainted with Charles Kingsley wasn't an option when he was frequently around JD. Instead, Lupe tried to keep her demeanor formal with Charles whenever they encountered each other in public, suggesting to the world she barely knew the fellow.

"Work keeps me busy," JD said. "But I needed to see you tonight about something important."

She pouted. "Here I thought you missed me." They would both play their public roles, of course. She led JD by hand to a table in the corner. Charles followed. Lupe signaled one of the servers over before seating herself. "What can I do for you?"

JD started to answer. Then, a humidor was held open next to him, and he turned to inspect the contents. *"Cubanos,"* he said, sniffing approvingly.

The lighter and ashtray were handed to Lupe. She leaned forward along the side of the table, holding the flame to the cigar. His eyes lingered appreciatively on her ample cleavage as he sat back and took a puff. His brother-in-law was apparently struck dumb by the sight of female flesh.

"I heard you acquired a new patron," JD said conversationally.

She laughed, giving the appearance of being well satisfied with her world. "I hope to keep acquiring more. The new club in Macau will open in a few weeks."

"Bless your mercenary little heart," JD said, tone amused. He leaned toward her, elbows on the table, cigar between his fingers. "I'm talking about a specific man. The oil broker, Harry Sheppard."

Lupe noted the studied casualness in her guest's tone. "I know he's connected to your in-laws. The Kingsleys, right?"

"Why's he here?"

"Heh? For the same reason as everyone else, I suppose... to see the angels."

The server returned and placing crystal glasses in front of JD and Charles, poured two fingers each of the club's best Scotch into it. As usual, Lupe got coffee. Iced, this time.

JD smirked. "There's gossip you'd like to get to know Harry Sheppard up close and personal."

Lupe flushed, remembering the very public kiss she bestowed on Harry on New Year's Eve. *National Enquirer* devoted an entire column to the embrace. Also, to Ira, the artist/waiter who was seen Frenching the broker. Other tabloids soon followed up with breathless commentaries on the "relationship(s)."

"You know how it works," she said. "If you add a little bit of spice to the welcome, they're likely to spend more."

JD swirled the whiskey around before taking a healthy gulp. "Has he been spending a lot?"

"Some."

"Does he have a special liking for any of the... er... talent here?"

"Congressman, you know our patrons have an expectation of privacy when they visit Eden." Lupe took a deep breath. "If you must know, Harry asked me to marry him." The moment the words were out, she wished she could take them back. Why the hell did she—all Lupe really needed to say was that the latest member of the club wanted the same thing from her as most men.

"What?" JD laughed, snorting liquor in the process. Charles, too. The idiot apparently couldn't stop laughing. Glancing impatiently at him, JD turned back to Lupe. "Sheppard doesn't want to marry you."

"Why not?" she asked in as mild a tone as she could muster. "I'm not good enough?"

"Don't be a fool, Lupe," JD said. "You call yourself a businesswoman, but this is still a strip club. You're what people politely call a 'madam.' *He's* Harry Sheppard. Look at his history! He's had some of the sexiest pieces of ass in the country. The woman married to Brad for instance... my wife's cousin, Brad Kingsley."

"Lilah Kingsley?" Lupe asked, continuing to keep her demeanor relaxed. "I thought she and Harry are friends."

JD snickered a second time. "Friends," he muttered, shifting in his chair. Charles's laughter morphed into blissful giggles. "No way in hell," JD continued. "I got to see her a couple of times. Wish I had the chance... point I'm trying to make is Sheppard could have anyone he wanted. Why would he want *you*?"

Rage soared, startling Lupe. Under the table, she curled her fingers into tight little fists and maintained the pleasant expression on her face. "You tell me."

JD continued, "Information. Sheppard wants information about the Kingsley supporters in the Congress. He's trying to romance it out of you."

Charles's titters got loud again, and he slapped his thigh in vulgar merriment.

"Did you come here to warn me, JD? How sweet." Perhaps she should be more careful not to antagonize the bastard, but Lupe couldn't seem to make herself stop.

His grin slipped. "Careful, Lupe. Our contract may be done, but I'm still a congressman. When I first heard about Sheppard's visits here, I was hoping you'd send him on his way, and I wouldn't have to do this. But you've entertained his presence here for the last three months. You've left me no choice. Remember this well, Lupe. There are some of your patrons who are not pleased about this newfound friendship. You don't want to run into difficulties renewing your liquor license. Or perhaps when a guest or two turns out to be underage."

JD didn't wait three months for her to come to her senses. He had been collecting evidence against her. "Are you threatening me?" she asked.

"Not at all," he said, tone smooth. "These are unfortunate things which can happen to any business. If and when such events occur, it's always good to have friends you can rely on. We've been friends since I got you the loan to start this club, haven't we?"

Around them, the music continued to play. Charles's laughter finally petered into small snorts. The soft clinks of delicate crystal glasses and the hushed tones of the wait staff added another layer to the noise. Lupe looked around at all that she'd worked hard to build. JD could destroy it with a single phone call. She was expecting this attempt to intimidate, and there were backup plans in place. So why was her defiance shattering, replaced by the familiar panic of powerlessness? Why was there this painful knot in her belly?

She blinked once. Twice. Voice controlled, she asked, "What do you want?"

JD smiled in satisfaction. "Keep Sheppard from getting too close to anyone significant but let him continue to visit. This way, he'll be the one under surveillance. By you. Feel free to pass on snippets you hear from me."

"Feed him false information, you mean."

Tapping the cigar on the ashtray, JD continued, "The Kingsleys would prefer not to have to deal with him at all. Unfortunately, he's escaped every accident arranged for him. The press conference trick he pulled... Steven will get into trouble."

"So you can't attack Harry directly."

"No, we can't," JD brooded. "This move into Kingsley territory was unexpected. Fortunately, it's also given us an opportunity to keep an eye on *him.*"

Lupe noted how easily he talked to her about the criminal activities of his associates. JD presumed her person and her business to be Kingsley property, and she was expected to keep her mouth shut about it all. Taking a sip of the ice-cold coffee in front of her, she tried to ease the tightness inside. "What if I simply cancel his membership? I don't want to take sides." Her girls would continue to collect information, channeling it to Harry through Liam. Or through someone else. As far as the Kingsleys were concerned, all communication between her and the broker would cease tonight. JD and his associates would be left without a way to force Lupe into working for them, instead.

JD took a leisurely taste of the fine Scotch. "President Reagan signed the amnesty bill last year. I assume you took care of your situation."

Slightly puzzled, Lupe nodded. JD had known of her illegal status since the day they met. That was the root cause of their unholy deal, after all. But it was no matter now. Her green card was safely locked away in her office.

"Are you aware of the good moral character clause, Lupe? The United States, I am sure, would prefer not to admit a woman with your history."

For a second, she thought she didn't hear him right. "Wha—no, come on! It's only a strip club."

"Right... a *strip club*. Where politicians gather to discuss the nation's affairs, and staffers flash money around. The media would eat it up. How did a woman like Guadalupe Valdez get to be an American?"

The walls seemed to move, closing in around Lupe. If she lost her permanent resident status, everything she worked for would go with it. Her club, the life she built in this town. She'd be back to where she started: homeless, penniless. Terror, sheer terror. Opening her mouth to speak, she found not a single word would come out.

Seeing it, JD smiled. "We have been friends for so long, Lupe. Haven't we? I don't want to see anything happen to you."

"Me, neither," said Charles, his eyes back on her cleavage.

Chapter 28

Two days later

New York, New York

Bagpipers and drummers marched down the street, celebrating St. Paddy's Day as the spectators clapped and cheered. Holding hands with Michael, Sabrina swayed to the song.

"Cadets from West Point," she hollered.

Michael's eyes rounded, and he dropped her hands to peer closely. "Like Daddy?"

Sabrina laughed. "Yup." The city was awash in green—clothes, flags, leprechaun figures—and beer. Even nature cooperated with the warm seventy-degree weather. "Look, Mikey," she pointed. "Horsies!"

It was late when they returned home. *Normalcy,* Sabrina mentally repeated the child psychiatrist's advice. Michael needed structure and routine to help him cope with his memories of the terrifying arrest and his father's exile. Well... routine was relative when they needed a guard to accompany them to most places. The burly fellow assigned for the day escorted the mother-son duo to the apartment. Sabrina had her key out when the door was suddenly flung open.

Dressed in a trim skirt suit with ginormous shoulder pads on the belted black blazer, a woman stood at the entrance. No, not a mere woman. *Amazon Queen,* Sabrina thought dazedly. Guadalupe Valdez, whose name was plastered all over the tabloids in connection with Harry's, had come visiting.

"You must be the sister." Ms. Valdez looked Sabrina up and down before twirling around in an absurdly fluid movement. She clicketty-clacked her way across the polished wood floor to the couch where two men sat. Sabrina could almost *see* the clouds of cinnamon scent floating behind.

Harry stood from the couch. "Sabrina, this is—"

"Not now," Ms. Valdez said, her sibilant voice dangerous and seductive. From the coffee table, she picked up ivory-colored gloves that matched her skirt and stuffed them into a giant patent-leather purse. "First, you need to marry me."

#

Later in the evening

Lupe Valdez was still shut up with Harry and Liam in the closet-sized room which served as an office. Apparently, she'd called Liam before she left DC, asking him to join her in Harry's apartment. Muffled voices sounded through the door, Liam's occasionally rising in agitation.

Sabrina eyed the wood panels speculatively, wondering if she dared barge in. She hated being left out, even if the intention was to keep her away from legal trouble. Before she could put thought into action, the door opened.

"Your brother is certifiably insane," Liam exclaimed to her before stalking out.

The Amazon was right behind, looking worried. Only Harry seemed nonchalant. "He'll come around. Lupe, you can return to DC. I assure you we'll get it taken care of."

Get what *taken care of?* Sabrina wanted to ask. The marriage proposal? Harry needed to explain the whole damned mess before Sabrina went totally bonkers and screamed her head off. Not that she'd uttered a word since finding the electrifying woman in the apartment. Sabrina was not the only one. Michael was watching their guest, mouth agape, as she talked to Harry in whispers.

Harry must have managed to pacify the Amazon, for her lips curved into a satisfied smile. "Yes," she hissed.

With another of her sinuous turns, she made for the front door, only to stop by Sabrina and Michael. "Pocket-size," the Amazon remarked.

Sabrina was not amused. Five-foot-one was not short! At least, not when compared to normal people. She drew herself up to her full height, such as it was, and threw her head back to look down her nose at the woman.

Only the softness in Lupe's eyes when her gaze landed on Michael saved her from the scathing remarks Sabrina had been composing in her mind. Not that Sabrina could've actually said any of the words out loud. She had a feeling if she opened her mouth, she'd only be able to manage hysterical laughter.

Part XI

Chapter 29

April 1989

New York University Medical Center

At least the room was pretty, Patrice thought, looking around from the armchair. Mr. Temple was by the window, staring down at city streets where cars honked and tourists enjoyed springtime in Manhattan. Specially installed bulletproof glass kept him protected. Guards stood outside the door to the suite. The former president was a prisoner in this room as much as his mind was in itself.

"Well?" Noah Andersen asked from the second chair.

Patrice caught herself before she shook visibly from fear. "Well what?"

"Did you get what you came here for?" Andersen mocked. "Satisfaction? The man who revealed your secret to me is not capable of saying another word to anyone else."

"No!" Patrice sat up in shock. "I never... look... Mr. Temple was there for me." The politician was the only one who'd stood by the bewildered young woman and guided her through the nightmare she'd been thrust into. "He would've needed to tell a couple of people to make arrangements, I suppose."

Andersen contemplated her for a few moments. Then, his eyes softened. "Yes, I took care of the legal details, but it wasn't the only reason Temple involved me. Patrice, I want to be completely truthful here. I knew what was going on from the time the Sheppards and the Kingsleys hatched the plan to have you marry Peter."

"I don't understand. What did *you* have to do with the Kingsley-Sheppard alliance?"

"Temple and I had been friends for a long time. We trusted each other and often shared information."

"You used that information to hurt my family," she said bitterly.

His eyelids flickered. "Yes, the family you didn't remember to ask about the last time we talked. You simply assumed they'd be fine."

Patrice hissed.

Holding up his hands, Andersen said, "Cheap shot, I know. You were scared and not thinking clearly. And you're right. I did have a big role in what happened to Brad and Lilah and the others. I can apologize all you want, but it won't change the past. What I could possibly change is the future. Your sons' future. With your help."

"I came here to visit Mr. Temple and also to ask you about my children," said Patrice. "But we're *not* going to discuss Richard."

"Patrice, Richard is nearly forty. He's an army major now... a lawyer... a successful businessman... not the helpless infant adopted by a working-class couple. He knows exactly what he's doing and has both the money and the resources to get it done. He doesn't need you to run interference." Huffing out a breath, Andersen shook his head. "All right. Believe what you want about what Richard did. Hold his hand if you feel so inclined. There's something else you should know, though. I was trying to tell you before, but you wouldn't listen. Temple and I are not the only ones who know where the baby went."

"The baby—" Her mouth dried. "But no one else was even aware that I was..."

"What? Pregnant at sixteen? Ryan knew and so did your father."

Her head swam. "They wouldn't have told anyone, would they?" she whispered. "I was a Sheppard... part of the family."

"They didn't. Not to my knowledge, anyway. But Temple could never have placed the child in the Kingsley household without informing—"

"Godwin," Patrice completed, feeling faint. "Oh, God. He knows."

"I'm worried what he's going to do with the information," Andersen said. "He may put you in a position where you have to make choices you don't like. Remember what he was like with Peter. He tried to use your sons to manipulate their father."

"Cuba," Patrice whispered. The Kingsley patriarch had argued against Peter's sons at the military interrogation. The five brothers believed their grandfather had only been trying to uphold the law, but Patrice wasn't sure about the explanation. Now... if Godwin planned to use her secret against her to help Steven...

Andersen nodded. "Yes... Cuba. Of course they were all in it together. What if Godwin tries to manipulate *you* this time?"

Thoughts raced through her mind. "How?" she asked. "All he can do is threaten to tell Richard and the rest of my children."

Tone deliberate, Andersen said, "Or he could threaten to betray Richard to the feds."

Patrice gasped.

"No matter what you think of Richard's role in events, he is easily identified as the main villain if Godwin so chooses. From the nasty tricks in boyhood to the hit job in California. There's also the FBI investigation of Richard's business."

Richard could end up as the fall guy for Kingsley misdeeds. Words tumbling over each other, Patrice asked, "What if I tell Richard the truth right away?"

Andersen stayed silent.

"It wouldn't matter, would it?" Patrice asked, voice trembling. "Even if I get Richard to cut his ties with Steven, Godwin could still go to the feds and blame Richard for everything."

"As I said to you before, do *not* talk to Richard about it. Godwin is sitting on what he knows for now because he needs Richard on their side and because he thinks he can perhaps use your secret against Brad and the rest. If there's a hint the situation might change, Godwin will make sure Richard takes the rap for everything. The Kingsleys will find it difficult to win without him, but Godwin's going to make sure they don't lose, either. Richard will end up in jail for everyone's crimes."

"Oh, God."

"I want you to continue in Aaron's apartment," said Andersen. "Not because Godwin will find you no matter where, but because the one way you can support Richard is by your presence in the Kingsley mansion. It's the one and only way you can help Brad and the rest. Believe it or not, they do need you despite all the other people helping them."

Dazedly, Patrice looked around the room. Mr. Temple was still at the window, still staring down at the streets. "What can I do?"

"Keep your eyes and ears open. Anything you find out, you let me know. Doesn't matter how big or small. Patrice, you don't need me to explain our situation. Any info you could get might turn out to be useful. Temple's not going to be of help. The neurologists don't believe there's anything more they can do. Harry and I are taking Temple home tomorrow. His son... he showed up once to visit. There were some questions about guardianship. Beyond it, the professor doesn't seem to want much involvement."

Abruptly, Patrice asked, "Have you said anything to Harry? About Richard?"

"Not yet. But we need to—"

"No."

"With Temple out of commission, Harry is the one person who can—"

"He's a Sheppard," said Patrice. "They can't be trusted."

"I think you underestimate Harry."

"Yeah, and you also thought it was fine to blackmail me over my past. Your bad judgment and interference destroyed my son's marriage and caused all the problems in my family. So forgive me if I don't put much faith in what you say. If you really want to make up for what you did, you will not talk to Harry about Richard. Ever. If you do, count me out of any plans you might have."

"What if your sons' lives are at stake?"

"Then, you explain your reasoning to me, and *I'll* decide whether to talk to Harry. But I don't see it happening. Richard may have plotted with Steven to trick them, but he hasn't killed anyone. Richard is not a criminal."

"I pray you're right." The former attorney general sighed. "But chances are you're not. Remember what Harry said at the press conference. There have been too many coincidences, ending with the murder attempt on Temple."

"Mr. Andersen," Patrice started, "it's one thing to make your claims to the media to warn away the Kingsleys. Don't try the same trick with *me*. Richard didn't have anything to do with the assassination attempt!"

Green eyes flashing, Andersen said, "It sure turned out very convenient for Steven."

"So have Steven investigated. Leave Richard out."

"Oh, I'm investigating," Andersen said. "Steven, Richard, all of them. Not merely to get justice for Temple, but because whoever was behind the attack is not going to stop there. And Patrice? The doctors say they've done all they can for Temple. Time and rehab might help some, but no one sounds hopeful about his prospects. See if you can spare a few minutes from your hatred of Ryan Sheppard to pray for Temple. He stood by you when the people you trusted did not."

Chapter 30

Forty years ago, January 1949

Brooklyn, New York

Outside the Brooklyn Paramount Theater, cars dropped off families and dating couples. Skirting an elderly gentleman, Patrice followed Ryan Sheppard into the lobby. Good thing weather wasn't bad for a January. It was just warm enough so Patrice could show off the clothes she'd bought the week before without freezing to death.

Her winter coat folded over her forearm, she adjusted the belt accentuating her small waist. The short-sleeved lilac sweater complemented the full skirt in deep purple, and the patterned neckerchief completed the picture of casual chic. She was told the colors suited her dark hair and eyes.

In his gray tweed suit, her "date" for the evening wasn't looking so shabby, either. Ryan's mature demeanor frequently had people thinking he was one of the war veterans, but he'd never been drafted. *Thank God*, Patrice thought.

For the millionth time, she expressed gratitude to the Almighty for bringing this brother into her life. Unlike the other Sheppards, Patrice and her widowed father were working class, almost poor. When Ryan's father contacted them a couple of years back, Patrice was surprised. She hadn't realized the rich branch of the Sheppard family even knew she existed. Their connection to Patrice and her parents was very remote... six or seven generations ago. Ryan once claimed Sheppards called everyone with even a drop of the same ancestral blood a cousin.

Patrice vaguely remembered some discussions about shares in the company or some such thing but hardly paid any attention, excited as she was by what Sheppard, Sr. promised her—a chance at something beyond the dreary future awaiting most of the girls in her neighborhood. In the months since, Ryan's father made sure Patrice was accepted to Miss Baker's School in Hartford, Connecticut. She also became a part of the family's life, this outing being an example.

Patrice hopped from foot to foot, impatient to be seated in the large hall, watching Calamity Jane in action.

Ryan smiled. "You're still such a child."

Patrice pouted. "You know I'm sixteen, but I've been waiting forever to watch *The Paleface*. Thank you for taking me."

"It's your birthday," he said, tone indulgent.

"I didn't think the school would let you take me out."

Classes started back after winter break, but since it was Patrice's special day, Ryan cajoled the Head into letting her return to Brooklyn to celebrate it with Ryan's family. He teased, "Bet you're happy to get out of the place."

"Oh, no," she said. "I love it there."

At first, it was merely an escape from her indifferent parent and humdrum existence, but at the school, she'd discovered a love of mythology and history. Patrice devoured the available books, learning all she could about the Greek and Roman pantheons. The principal was impressed and said something about Radcliffe, but Patrice already knew college was an impossible dream. She couldn't continue sponging off Ryan and his father once she was able to make her own living. She'd taken a few secretarial courses with the aim of getting herself a job in one of the big offices in Manhattan. Then, she'd find herself a nice young man to marry. A clerk or something. No one too ambitious, or he wouldn't have time for her.

"You don't have to lie to me," Ryan said, eyes twinkling. "Who likes school?"

Patrice exclaimed, "I do! I like everything about it." Well, almost everything. If she felt forced into something at the elite boarding school, it was sports. But Patrice didn't mind. Running around with a lacrosse stick was small price to pay for being given an opportunity she could have never even dreamed of on her father's income. She continued, "But watching movies with you is really nice, too."

Especially after the two weeks she'd already spent with them over Christmas. When Ryan Sheppard realized returning home for holidays was miserable for the young girl, he'd made sure she received a standing invitation to his parents' house. There were times she pretended to herself she actually was Ryan's little sister, loved and indulged by all of them. After all, she'd even been a bridesmaid at his wedding. He and Sophia were preparing to move to the Middle East to take over the running of the family's oil wells.

"How's Sophie doing?" Patrice asked. Ryan's wife was pregnant with their first child and having a difficult time of it, which was the reason she was not with them at the movies.

"Better. She'll be at the party tomorrow."

"Party?" Patrice asked, frowning. Then, she flushed. It wasn't as though the Sheppards needed to inform her of every small detail of their lives.

"Did I forget to tell you? Patrice, have you heard of the Kingsleys?"

She shrugged, indicating ignorance.

"They're one of New York's oldest families. Very rich. We—I mean you as well as Sophia and I—have an invitation to David Kingsley's engagement party."

Patrice gawked. "Me? Why?"

Ryan laughed. "Most girls would be thrilled to go to one of those parties."

"Oh, I am," she said with an emphatic nod. "But why would they invite someone they don't know?"

"You know Senator Temple. He's Godwin Kingsley's stepbrother."

Senator Temple was the nice man who occasionally accompanied Ryan on his visits to the school. Patrice liked the politician. He had twinkly eyes as though he found the world amusing. But there was always kindness in the blue gaze when it landed on Patrice.

"Mr. Temple thinks you have potential," Ryan said.

"Potential for what?" she asked, confused.

Smiling, Ryan said, "There's a young man he wants you to meet. His nephew, Peter Kingsley."

Her jaw dropped.

His eyes crinkling in mirth, Ryan said, "As you just reminded me, you are sixteen. I'm sure a thought or two of romance has entered your mind."

"Yes, but I was thinking... a clerk or a teacher or something like that."

"You don't want a prince?" Ryan teased.

Which girl didn't? Unfortunately, no prince was likely to want an ordinary girl from Brooklyn with average looks and no money. "I'm only Patrice. They're the Kingsleys. Actually, *who* are the Kingsleys?"

"The family owns one of the biggest oil services companies in the U.S. So rich your lack of money won't matter."

"But—"

"No buts," Ryan said firmly. "You're going to like Peter."

It almost sounded like a command. What a ridiculous thing to think! With a shrug, Patrice dismissed the idea. They weren't living in the eighteen-hundreds. Ryan wasn't very good with words; that was all.

#

The next evening

Upper East Side, New York City

Patrice was bored, and so was Peter Kingsley. The fitted bodice and full skirts of her dark-green gown set off her small, slim figure well, but he barely glanced at it. They discussed the weather. Twice. He wasn't interested in the movies, and she didn't care for baseball. When she talked about the Apollo Belvedere reproduction she'd just seen in the art gallery in his own home, Peter nearly fell asleep on his feet. What followed was an awkward silence. Nope. He harbored no interest in Patrice. None, whatsoever. Nor she in him.

She wished she could find a way to extricate herself from this excruciating boredom, but Ryan and Sophia were busy on the other side of the ballroom, talking to another couple. The duo whose engagement they were celebrating—David Kingsley and Grace Gander—was greeting well-wishers. The youngest Kingsley son—a sixteen-year-old boy called Aaron—had taken off as soon as the formalities were finished, ostensibly to escort his ailing grandmother back to her room. A pity, since Patrice would have loved to talk to the grandmother, having recognized the still-beautiful face from the silent movies she'd recently started watching. Sylvia Fontaine had portrayed a couple of the mythical women from the Greek classics.

Surreptitiously, Patrice eyed the clock on the wall. Another couple of hours. *Oh, God!* She was going to die of boredom by the end of the evening.

Senator Temple was only a few feet away. He at least seemed to find her interesting. Biting her lip, Patrice debated whether she dared interrupt his conversation with... the man shifted. *Darn!* It was the host, Justice Godwin Kingsley. The dark expression on Justice Kingsley's face made it clear an intrusion would not be opportune.

Slicing the air with a hand, Justice Kingsley said, "Impossible. She cannot be part of this family."

Patrice frowned, hoping they weren't talking about her. She was here only on Senator Temple's invitation and did not have any plans to inflict her being on the indifferent Kingsley heir.

"But what did Amber do?" Temple asked. "More to the point, where is she? Except for half a dozen hysterical phone calls with her ranting against you, I haven't seen or talked to her in months! Where is our brother?"

Amber? Patrice breathed a sigh of relief. Nothing to do with her, then.

"It's finished, Temple," said Justice Kingsley. "I have no way of forcing him."

Frustration evident on his face, Temple looked around the room, ruffling the hair on the back of his head with a hand. His eyes caught hers, and he smiled reassuringly. Patrice was struck again by how kind he seemed.

At her side, Peter shifted. "Maddie," he whispered.

"What?" When Patrice looked up, the change in his manner made her take half a step back. There was a light in his bright-blue eyes, suppressed excitement in his giant form.

She followed his gaze to the arched doorway. There—dressed in a dark-rose gown and long, white gloves—stood the reason for the change. The blonde was searching the crowd with her eyes. When she located Peter, she bulleted across the room, exposing an incredible amount of tanned leg as she ran into his arms.

His gaze caught Patrice's smile over the blonde's shoulder. With obvious reluctance, he set "Maddie" aside. "Madeleine Wheeler, Patrice Sheppard," he introduced the young women. "I guess both your families do business with Kingsley Corp."

Madeleine gave Patrice a quick once-over, her left brow rising ever so slightly.

Quickly, Patrice said, "My father has nothing to do with the Kingsleys. He works at the City Clerk's office."

The watchful wariness in the blonde's gray eyes was replaced by warmth. "Call me Maddie," she said. "My brother is one of Peter's accountants. Some of the ladies here can be... difficult, so Peter makes it seem like I'm an heiress or something."

Patrice couldn't help it. She treated Peter to a wide smile, thinking how lucky Maddie was to have him in her life.

Some of the caution returning to her voice, Maddie asked, "So if your family has nothing to do with the Kingsleys, who are you here with?"

"My broth—a cousin, really... but we're very close." Then, lowering her lashes, Patrice inclined her head once, letting Maddie know her territory was safe.

Satisfied, the gladiators called off combat. The prize, unaware of their silent conversation, looked fondly on.

The three of them chatted for a few minutes, with Maddie doing most of the heavy lifting. "Where's Aaron?" she asked Peter. "Patrice needs company."

Subtle. Real subtle. Patrice suppressed the urge to laugh. "You go ahead with... whatever. I'll be all right on my own."

"Thank you," said Maddie. "I don't mean to be rude. It's just that Peter and I don't get to see each other much since he went away to college. I swear I'll find Aaron and send him to you."

"No, please—"

But the couple had already taken off, hardly aware of anyone but each other. Patrice was still trying to decide which corner to hide in when a voice said next to her ear, "Boo."

She turned with a startled squeak. Her mouth dropped open.

Two feet from her stood the most beautiful man she ever saw. His lean body was covered by a tux, golden locks fell across his forehead, and a dazzling grin lit up ice-blue eyes.

"Apollo," Patrice breathed. The Sun God, come to life.

Chapter 31

Back in the present, mid April 1989

Upper East Side. New York City

Of course the Kingsleys couldn't avoid inviting Patrice to Steven's engagement party, not when the family elders were pretending the quarrel had only been between the clan's younger members. She still couldn't believe it. Amid all the conspiracies to commit murder and defraud his cousins, Steven Kingsley found time to fall in love—with a girl he met at Hector Sheppard's gym, a professional wrestler. Even more shocking was the fact that Godwin didn't object to the idea, but the family patriarch had his hands full with work these days. Plus, Steven surely carried some clout in the conspiracy, and Godwin would be careful in picking his fights.

Patrice paused at the arched doorway, wanting to run back to the quiet of Aaron's apartment. She couldn't. Andersen said she needed to keep an eye on the goings-on, and do it she must if she wanted to save her sons' lives. Here, all her enemies were gathered. Here, she had the best chance of overhearing something useful. The itch of guilt would then perhaps stop. She was doing her best by *all* her sons.

The ballroom glittered with thousands of tiny light bulbs. The crystal chandeliers were part of the original structure as were the gleaming tiles of Chinese design. Guests milled about, sipping fine wines and indulging in excited chatter. In the far corner, the band struck up a tune that sounded like a cross between European music and Latin American.

Patrice couldn't see Steven through the crowd. The criminal little brother, Charles, was not too far from her, laughing uproariously with a group of equally inebriated men, one of whom was Hector Sheppard. Patrice grimaced. Andersen might claim Harry was an exception amid the Sheppard males, but his brother clearly wasn't. The very fact that Hector considered the likes of Steven and Charles his friends was telling.

Another blond head glinted under the lights. A tall, straight-backed man spun a girl across the dance floor, both flowing to the drumbeat of the *carimbó*. Patrice started, trembling slightly. Richard—she would know him anywhere, from any angle.

More than a few people were staring at the couple and not simply because the miniskirt worn by the girl left very little to the imagination. The hip-to-hip, thigh-to-thigh movements of the Brazilian folk steps would have been considered scandalous in Patrice's day, but the ease with which Richard managed the wavelike motions made it seem beautiful. Patrice smiled. Unlike the Kingsley boys, he didn't have the benefit of being tutored in formal dancing, but just like Alex and Victor, Richard inherited her sense of rhythm.

"Patrice," called a weighty voice. Godwin strode forward with arms extended in welcome. "I was hoping you would decide to join us, my dear. No point in holding grudges. I tried my best, but what can we old people do to stop the young 'uns when they're bent on starting trouble?"

A muscle twitched near the corner of Patrice's mouth. Greeting the former justice with a kiss on the check, she said, "My sons and I owe you a lot, Godwin."

She heard the hiss, saw the flaring of his nostrils, but the smile on his face grew more expansive. Offering her his arm, Godwin led her to the newly engaged couple. She would, no doubt, pay for the sarcasm someday.

Standing near the bar, Steven was talking to his mother, Grace. Her back to Patrice, a big-haired woman waited next to Steven. The long, sequined dress with shoulder pads shimmered as she tucked a hand into the crook of his arm. The fiancée?

Patrice wondered what kind of girl would find Steven Kingsley attractive. He looked pleasing enough as did all Kingsleys, but the personality surely could not be attractive to young ladies. There was the Kingsley money, obviously.

"Steven," called Godwin.

Gritting her teeth against the intense desire to wallop Steven across his face for what he did, Patrice waited for him to turn. The young thug had the temerity to flush as he saw her. The woman with him also turned, and Patrice came face-to-face, or rather, face-to-magnificent bosom with Steven's intended bride. Patrice's lips parted in amazement at all the creamy bounty confronting her. She gawked for a second or two before tearing her eyes away to fix them on the bottles lined up along the bar.

"Would you like a drink, ma'am?" asked the young bartender.

"No... I mean, yes!" She *needed* one.

While her wine was being poured, Patrice muttered congratulations to the engaged couple.

"Excuse me," someone said.

Without turning around, Patrice smiled and moved aside. She'd know his voice anywhere, too. From the cry of the newborn to the slightly impatient baritone of the army major, every note was etched in her mind for all eternity.

Richard greeted his friend's fiancé with a kiss on the cheek, manfully keeping his gaze on her face. Patrice bit her lip to stop laughter from erupting at the fixed expression on him.

Accepting the glass of claret from the bartender, Patrice found a spot next to a rounded column and tapped a foot in time to the new song from the band.

Chapter 32

Forty years ago, January 1949

Upper east Side, New York City

"Kyriakos Phoebus Sabazios," said the divine being, twirling Patrice to his side so their hips brushed. They rocked together before he swung her out, and they faced each other again. "There are a few other names, too... from both sides of the family... but I stick to two or three when in America."

"Kyriakos," Patrice echoed, trying the syllables on her tongue. "Can I simply call you Apollo? When I saw you, I thought... er... I like reading mythology, and you look like how I imagine the Sun God."

Kyriakos/Apollo laughed. "Call me whatever you want... as long as you call me."

Patrice blushed. *Step, step, rock step.* She was back in Apollo's arms. She'd taken lessons at school and stopped needing to count a long time ago, but old habits died hard.

"Hey," he chided. "I like my girls to pay attention when I compliment them."

"Sorry," Patrice said, her smile wide. "And thank you. I love to dance. But the East Coast Swing is easy."

A blond eyebrow rose. "Is it so? Shall we have a contest?"

Patrice smirked. She was considered best among her schoolmates. Unless Apollo was a professional, he wasn't going to outperform her. "Do your worst."

Apollo looked around. "You think the Kingsleys will let us do the Balboa?"

"The... the Balboa? But that..." Involved touching. Lots of it. No, the Kingsleys wouldn't approve. Nor would Ryan.

"What's the matter?" Apollo asked. "Chickening out?"

"My brother and sister-in-law are here. They won't like it."

Sophia Sheppard was in one of the chairs, looking mildly sweaty. She'd told Patrice all the women in her family found the first three months of pregnancy difficult. Patrice hoped that would be it. Sophia and Ryan were preparing to go to some God-forsaken country in the Middle East to take over the running of the family business, and who knew what kind of medical care they'd find? This being their first baby, Sophia wouldn't even have the benefit of experience.

Ryan was by his wife's side, but his eyes were on Patrice. He was frowning. She responded with a smile. She'd have to tell him about Peter Kingsley and his preoccupation with the charming Madeleine Wheeler. A match between Peter and Patrice was not going to happen.

Apollo brought their dance to an abrupt stop. Hand cupping her elbow, he guided her to the doorway. "Let's go to the art gallery. You can still hear the music from there... excuse me, sir."

Justice Kingsley nodded, letting them pass.

A few minutes later

The music which seemed loud in the ballroom was a mere echo in the brightly lit art gallery one floor above. Busts and bronzes and paintings looked down on the only occupants of the room, the couple dancing on the patterned, red carpet in the center. Swinging her around, Apollo moved Patrice close to the small door in the back. Her spine collided with one of the rounded columns lining the gallery.

Breath whooshing out, she said, "It's impossible to dance in here. Too many things."

Whispering, "I know," he moved closer.

So close Patrice thought she might lose her balance. So close her breasts were crushed against his chest. The hand at her waist slipped down, squeezing her hip.

Suddenly uneasy, she said, "Apollo, I don't—"

"Shh." His lips caressed the spot where her neck met her shoulder.

"Miss Sheppard," a voice echoed. "Are you in there?"

Within milliseconds, Apollo let her go and scooted back a few feet. She was still trying to get her breath when Peter and Maddie hurried in, worry on their faces.

Peter's eyes darted from Patrice to Apollo. "Your brother and sister-in-law saw you leave with him and got a little concerned. I told them you might have come up here to take another look at the art." Nodding at Apollo, Peter said, "Didn't realize you two knew each other."

Patrice never realized Apollo was acquainted with Peter.

"We just met," Apollo said, a hand in his pocket. "And you're right. She did want another look." Eyes glinting with mischief, he added, "At Apollo Belvedere."

Patrice laughed, then swallowed her mirth, causing a very peculiar gurgle to erupt from her throat.

"This is the United States," said Peter. "I don't know how things work in Athens, but here we consider it good manners to let the lady's family know where she might be."

Patrice straightened, intending to tell Peter Kingsley off.

Preempting her, Apollo raised both hands. "My mistake, Kingsley. Won't happen again."

Peter nodded. "You should leave now. It's late, and you and I are supposed to go over contracts tomorrow morning."

Apollo's face darkened, but he didn't object to the diktat. Patrice glared at Peter, wondering how she could have been so wrong in her assessment of him. She'd thought him a gentleman, and here he was, being terribly rude to an underling.

Gaze steady, Peter continued, "I suggest you stay away from Miss Sheppard. Her brother's not too happy with you." Under his breath, he added, "Neither am I."

Patrice seethed. What business did an arrogant aristocrat like Peter have deciding her life for her? Threatening Apollo the way he did! But what could her Greek god do against such blatant intimidation by a man who could cost him his job? Still, Apollo didn't seem upset. There was a peculiar glint in his eyes, a smirk on his lips.

She accompanied Apollo to the door. "I'll write you," he promised, waiting for his car to be brought around.

"I don't want to get you into trouble with your boss," she whispered.

Apollo laughed. "Who? Kingsley? He's not my boss."

Apparently, Apollo was sent to New York to work in the American division of his family's shipping company, and Kingsley Corp was an important customer. Peter still had college to complete, but since the Kingsleys wanted the heir to learn the business from ground up, he was expected to work with Apollo in his spare time.

A prince, Patrice thought happily. Apollo was a prince. Not the one Ryan wanted for her, but still, a prince.

She refused to give up on her annoyance with Peter Kingsley. Equal or subordinate, it was no way to treat a guest in his home.

"Don't worry about him," Apollo soothed. "For all his money, Kingsley has the heart of a *migás*. You know... vulgar."

Patrice frowned. Her education included enough grounding in Latin and Greek to read even the classics in their original languages. What Apollo said didn't mean vulgar. It meant mongrel.

Before she could comment, the butler glided up, letting Apollo know his vehicle was ready.

Chapter 33

Back in April 1989

Upper East Side. New York City

"Miss Patrice, they're taking family pictures." Arthritic as his joints had gotten over the years, the octogenarian butler was no longer able to glide.

"I think I'll pass," Patrice said. "Looks like they're almost done." Grace Kingsley, Steven's mother, was headed their way. Patrice really didn't want to talk to the woman. Grace was present at the fiasco in Cuba. *How* could *you?* Patrice asked silently. *You didn't say a word while your sons were busy attacking my children. Not one word!* But Grace might divulge info Patrice could use to her sons' advantage. Once the old servant creaked off, the women smiled awkwardly at each other.

"Your daughter-in-law is lovely," Patrice blurted more for a lack of anything else to say.

"Thank you," Grace said. "I'm glad you didn't ask how she avoids toppling over."

"Wha—I'd never... someone *actually* said it?"

Grace nodded. "To me, thank God. Not to her. You know how it can get at some of these events."

Patrice knew very well. But she never realized Grace, too, had faced jibes. In the four decades since Grace's engagement party in the same ballroom, they never really got to know each other. If Grace removed the thick glasses she habitually wore, Patrice doubted she'd recognize her sister-in-law.

Abruptly, Patrice asked, "What color are your eyes?"

"Excuse me?"

"I've never seen you without those glasses. Even at your engagement party, you were wearing them."

Grace laughed. "Bright light triggers my migraine, so I don't take them off except at night. It's tough, what with David needing all the light he can get."

"He does?" Patrice already knew about Grace's headaches and David's inability to see well, but she never imagined it was as bad as what his wife just described. Truth be told, Patrice noticed very little about Steven's parents. The drama in her own life left her indifferent to other people's problems. "I know he has some trouble... but he seems to get around okay."

"If he's familiar with the place, yes. Or the room has to be well lit. When he reads, he has to hold the paper at certain angles."

"Some childhood infection, right?"

322

"Measles," Grace said. "That's how we met."

"What do you mean?"

"At the New York Eye and Ear Infirmary," Grace clarified. "My parents brought me here from Texas, hoping for some miracle cure. They thought for sure I wouldn't be able to find a husband with such ugly glasses on my face."

Despite her anger at Steven's doting mother, Patrice sputtered. "And you ended up with a Kingsley. What a lovely story."

"I just wish... it's been hard on David. Right from his first day at Kingsley Corp, people decided he was weak. But how could he make quick decisions when he couldn't see well? I told him a hundred times oil services was not the right business for him, but he never wanted to do anything else. He kept on trying to please—"

"Godwin," Patrice completed.

Voice low, Grace muttered, "David kept hoping... *he* was the eldest, not Peter. I begged David to stop trying. Nothing he did would've changed Godwin's mind."

"But David did eventually get to be CEO."

"After Peter's death," Grace said, her mouth drooping. "And only because the deal drawn up by Godwin's father specified the CEO spot and the stock would go to his second wife's children and grandchildren."

"Godwin could've chosen Aaron," Patrice soothed.

"Are you kidding? Godwin's nice to Aaron, but he'd never allow a secretary's son... David was the only choice. It's an empty title, anyway. Godwin and Aaron never let him have a say. There's also all the mockery about David and I being blind to Steven's faults."

Somehow managing to keep her tone gentle, Patrice pointed out, "Isn't there some truth to it? Don't tell me you and David didn't know what Steven was up to, Grace. You two were as much a part of the setup in Cuba as Steven."

Grace flushed. "I don't deny it. The military... all the talk about national security... I thought I was doing the right thing. Besides, Steven's my *son*. I hope you understand where David and I are coming from."

"Forgive me if I don't. *My* sons are out there, wandering the world. If they're caught by the authorities, they'll be dragged home in handcuffs to face charges of treason. They'll be convicted of a crime they didn't do!"

"Patrice, you can't say Brad was completely right, can you? You're also blind to your children's faults." Placing her hand on Patrice's arm, Grace continued, "I'm sure everything will be all right. Even if Mr. Temple cannot help them, his friend—that Mr. Andersen—is working on a pardon for Brad. Your boys will be back home, safe and sound."

"How can you imagine everything will be all right?" Patrice snapped. "For one, Brad was tricked. For another... what happens once he and the rest return? Everything will be forgotten?"

Tone earnest, Grace said, "I hope so. Look, life goes on. In a few months, Steven will be married. He'll have a wife, children... he'll forget this silly vendetta thing he has going on with Brad." She laughed. "I think he already has. He and Charles are going to Thailand on vacation. With Richard. It's going to be a bachelor party. They've been talking about it since New Year's Day!"

A bachelor party in *Thailand?* Did Grace not know the place was famous for sex tourism? Or did she think her sons were going there to take in the sights? Shame attacked. Patrice's son, too.

After the conversation, she didn't stay long. On her way back to Aaron's apartment, she debated letting Andersen know about the planned trip to Thailand. The place was near China. Patrice had looked up all the countries her sons could've taken shelter in, and China was one such. She shook her head. It wasn't as though Steven could simply walk into such a large nation and zero in on his cousins. The Kingsley men were rich and always traveled a lot. She couldn't drive herself crazy any time one of them ventured outside the States, imagining them locating her boys. Plus, this trip to Thailand was clearly a stag party. Nothing to do with Brad's problems.

Patrice wondered if Andersen would want to know, anyway, if at least to keep track of Steven's location. *But Richard will also be there. In Thailand.* Patrice refused to think about it. There were things a mother didn't need to know about her children. Andersen didn't need to know about it, either. If he did, he'd consider it another black mark against Richard despite the trip having nothing to do with the exiles.

Her boys were surely safe. Mr. Temple couldn't do anything to help them, but there were others working on a pardon. Someday, their innocence would be proven. Somehow, Steven would be made to pay for his crimes, and with him gone, Richard would be free of the bad influences in his life. Grace was wrong. It was hardly blindness when Patrice knew her children were blameless.

Part XII

Chapter 34

A week later, April 1989

Mae Klang Luang, Thailand

After the New Year's Eve conversation in the Kingsley mansion, it took months of painstaking legwork to arrange a meeting with Prince, the drug lord from Burma. Not as though Steven was involved much in said legwork. He simply showed up where Richard asked him to.

In early January, Richard contacted a Danish journalist who'd done a couple of interviews with Prince. The writer had since been banned by the Burmese government from entering the country but still maintained his connections in the area. Persuading him to cooperate took a couple of trips to a bar in Copenhagen and the promise of an exclusive once the fugitives were caught with Prince's help.

Leaving the newspaper's offices after arranging matters with the reporter, Steven was beginning to feel uneasy about all the deals they were making. Deals they already knew they'd break. "Rich, we don't plan to... Brad and Lilah are not going to be *caught.*" All Steven wanted was for Prince to finish off the exiles, but at a time convenient to the Kingsleys.

Richard shrugged. "Even if the reporter fellow suspects something, he's not going to snitch. He could get into legal trouble for being an accessory. Also, if someone else does blab we met Prince, the reporter will vouch for us. Trust me... he knows what's good for him. All that the cops will hear is we were trying to smooth the way of justice." The blame for the demise of the exiles would fall solely on Prince.

More weeks passed after Steven and Richard's trip to Denmark... the journalist kept trying to convince Prince into forming a temporary alliance with Steven. With each delay, the plans for Harry got pushed further down the road. Godwin got more agitated with each passing day. Thank God Richard was in the pilot's seat with this part of their campaign. He was better at dealing with the Kingsley patriarch than his own grandsons.

Also, thank God Godwin was faced with his own roadblocks to maneuver. Turned out Temple's son, the Harvard professor, did not have authority to sign over his father's care to Godwin. Noah Andersen was given power of attorney by Temple years ago. Godwin didn't mutter a word in anger on hearing the news, simply thanking the professor before hanging up the phone. The old man's silence scared Steven more than the usual opprobrium directed his way. Who knew what new plot the former justice was brewing in his mind and who'd end up taking the fall for it? The one silver lining was the fact Temple showed no signs of improvement at all no matter how much time passed.

Then a call came from the Danish correspondent. More than three months after Steven and Richard made the decision to contact Prince, they were in Thailand. No bodyguards, obviously. Or the drug lord wouldn't show. Neither Steven nor Richard believed Prince would be fool enough to buy trouble by tangling with the network's CEO.

The driver parked the car in the village and pointed his charges toward the dirt path winding up the tree-covered hill. The chilly wind carried the faint smell of smoke, and it pierced through Steven's shirt, providing welcome relief from the sweltering heat of the city. He only wished he could transport the mountain weather into the civilized world.

"Are you sure this is where your contact asked to meet?" he muttered to Richard, making sure Charles couldn't hear. Luckily, he was a few feet away, gawking at a group of local women in long, shapeless dresses.

"Prince has business in the Golden Triangle, and the reporter fellow says the drug route goes through Taunggyi in Burma to Chiang Mai in Thailand, then Bangkok," Richard mumbled back, his eyes on the driver waiting for them at the mouth of the path up the hill. "I'm not surprised by the choice of meeting places."

"The journalist... how trustworthy do you think he is?"

"His job runs on trust, Steven."

Steven and Richard followed the driver to the small clearing near the top, Charles huffing behind. The valley below was a messy brownish-green, not at all the lush emerald rice terraces the guidebook told them to expect.

"Planting in May," the driver said, clearing up the confusion without being asked.

The breeze brought the unexpected smell of coffee with it. The driver pointed in the direction of a hut, its roof and walls made of bamboo.

"Prince's place?" Steven asked.

"No," said Richard. "Just a coffee shop. But this is where my contact asked us to go."

The inside of the hut was as rustic as the outside, and the Thai couple running the place were pleasant and welcoming. The coffee grinding was manually done with mortar and leg pestle. The three

Americans waited at the long wood table with a couple of bikers while coffee simmered in an iron kettle hung over a wood fire. Steven looked around. No signs of a drug lord's minions.

They spent a couple of hours in and around the coffee shop, wandering, taking pictures, and ordering more freshly brewed Arabica. The vigil yielded nothing.

"We need to return to civilization," Steven muttered, irritation mounting by the second. "I don't think Prince is interested."

Richard shook his head. "He's waiting for something."

"For what?"

"I don't know," Richard said. "Let's get back to the village. I need to talk to my contact and figure out what next."

"I hope we don't have to stay here another day," Steven said. "I'm a creature of the concrete jungle, not..." He waved his hands in the air. "...trees and mud. All this nature is making me nervous."

Richard grinned. "We need to get this done in one trip if possible. Which *might* mean staying longer. Steven, I've heard some stuff from contacts in China. Political trouble."

"The communist party secretary who died?" Steven asked. "He was pro-reform. Very convenient death for the party elders. I hear student groups are marching to protest."

"It's going to escalate for sure," said Richard. "The communist bloc is already in turmoil... good chance the situation in China might destabilize further. It could spread to other countries in the region. If we delay our plans, who knows when we'll get another chance? We need to locate Prince and make arrangements before we leave."

They stopped at the telephone booth in the village where Richard tried to place an international call.

"Phone take long time," the driver said. "We go to restaurant?"

"Meet us there, Rich," Steven called out. Since there was only one such establishment in the neighborhood, there was no chance of confusion. Plus, it was merely one street down. Perhaps he could get started on beer while waiting for Richard.

The Toyota stopped in front of another thatched building, its engine still running. "I really need to get back to Bangkok," Steven muttered, jiggling the lock. "Hey... driver, I can't get out."

Without warning, the back door swung open on the left side, where Steven was. A Thai man bent low.

Valet? Not bad for a hillbilly place. A weight landed on Steven's right shoulder. "Charlie?" Steven twisted around to confirm it was indeed his idiot brother who was pressing against him. "What the hell are you—"

From the left, something cold and metallic pushed against his neck. He stilled, not daring to check if it was what he suspected. The "valet" shoved him toward Charles and climbed in, slamming the door shut. Steven didn't move, but out of the corner of his eye, he could see a second Thai man doing the same to Charles. The "valet" said something to the driver.

"Stop," a voice shouted.

Rich!

The car jerked forward, slamming Steven's body into the seat. Fingers gripped the hair on the back of his head and yanked painfully. "Don't move an inch," the "valet" said in perfect Hollywood gangsta accent.

Chapter 35

"Stop," bellowed Richard, chasing the speeding car. There were backpackers in his way. Pushing them aside, he ran. Human bodies tumbled. Curses in a couple of languages followed. When the car disappeared around a bend, he stopped, looking wildly up and down the road. The tourists were still heaving themselves up from the asphalt. "Hey," Richard yelled, his voice hoarse. "Do you know where the police station is?"

A chorus of shouts rose from the group. "Bloody bastard," said a man with a bright-red beard.

"Someone kidnapped my friend," Richard said.

Disbelieving mumbles and a "hold on, mate" followed.

Twenty minutes later, Richard was in a car to Chiang Mai, the nearest town, having agreed to the hundred U.S. dollars demanded by the driver. The cops took the details down.

"Your friend, what kind of business was he in?" asked the officer, leaning back in the squeaky chair across the plywood desk. Outside the small room, chatter went on, accompanied by typewriters and the occasional coarse laughter.

"Oil services," said Richard, trying to ignore the sweat trickling between his shoulder blades. "We're wasting time. I gave you the license plate number. You should be putting out an... APB or whatever you call it here."

"Oil, heh?" the officer asked. "Not heroin?"

"*What?*"

"We've had smugglers here before."

"Look, my friend..." Richard resisted the urge to plant his fist on the jaw of the smirking cop.

The police were clearly not going to be of much help. Higher-ups needed to be forced into acting. If the feds were to be informed, they certainly would move for Steven Kingsley, CEO of the network, but they'd want to negotiate with whomever was responsible. The longer the talks went on, the chances of getting Steven back in one piece would crater. Also, who knew what claims Prince would make about the setup?

On the other hand, contacting the officials in DC from this little precinct meant the news would hit the press before Richard left the building. The media furor... governments would cry about damages to the global oil market, but it would also prod the Americans into necessary compromises to shorten the financial trauma.

"The man who was kidnapped is Steven Kingsley," Richard said. "He's the heir to one of the wealthiest businesses in the world and the CEO of a large oil company network. He doesn't need to smuggle drugs. We came here on a small vacation before his wedding... nothing else."

"Let me verify the information," said the cop, disbelief evident in his tone. "And don't worry. My staff has already started looking for the car."

"Nothing else?" Richard asked. No contacting the U.S. embassy? No Thai military to organize a search? No world-wide alerts?

"Not right now... except stay around town. Notify us if you get a ransom demand."

It was already night by the time Richard found himself a hotel room. Huffing out a breath, he picked up the phone and asked the operator to connect him to Godwin Kingsley's private number. In the ten minutes it took for Richard to relay the details, the Kingsley patriarch stayed completely silent. At the end, he asked, "How did *you* avoid getting snatched?"

"Huh?" Richard shook his head. "Why would anyone kidnap me? I'm not a Kingsley... only a regular member in the network... not much money in getting me." In fact, the kidnappers were likely waiting for him to step away before grabbing the other two. If Richard had been there, the bastards would've paid for what they tried. "We need to move fast... have the state department contact the Burmese government—"

"No," said Godwin, tone cold.

"We don't have an option," Richard explained. "I don't believe we can rely on the cops to find Steven. Burma can tell us if Prince is the one behind the kidnapping. He must be... he wants something in return. Cash, most probably. As soon as he gets it, he'll let Steven and Charlie go."

Godwin asked, "Have you seen the news, Mr. Armor?"

"Not yet... I'm hoping the financial turmoil will force the U.S. government to ask Burma to contact Prince—"

"Every channel here is carrying reports of Steven's kidnapping. They claim he was on a 'pleasure' tour to Bangkok when he got snatched. The press says it's why he didn't take any bodyguards. You'd better hope your real reason doesn't leak."

"I didn't say anything about Prince to the cops, but it doesn't matter," Richard said, trying to keep the impatience out of his voice. "We need to let the feds know we were trying to enlist Prince's aid in capturing the traitors for the American government. U.S. authorities can then ask Burma to locate Prince. As soon as we know what the ransom is, we'll pay—"

"I told Steven—and you—this was a bad idea. You decided to go ahead, anyway. You captained this mission; you crashed it. So *you* take responsibility. Both you and Steven need to learn a lesson. A week or so in Prince's prison will do the trick. I'm sure the network's board can hold the fort for a few days. The markets will recover sooner or later."

Richard shouted into the phone, "Prince is a drug smuggler! Steven's not going to stay alive long enough to learn—"

A high-pitched sound rang in his ear. The former justice had hung up. Cursing, Richard dialed the operator a second time and asked for the U.S. Army Garrison Wiesbaden, the German military district captured by Americans toward the end of WWII. Richard asked his acquaintance in the base to take a trip to Copenhagen to "talk" to the Danish journalist.

Prince was going to be located one way or the other. He was going to hand Steven and Charles over. Then, the drug lord would do exactly what he promised and do away with Brad and Lilah.

Part XIII

Chapter 36

The next afternoon

Macau

The punk goth proprietress of the Naughty Girl Salon and Tattoo Parlor informed Alex and his companions she did brisk business all times of the day with no room for walk-ins. "Make appointment, come back," she said, her jaw working hard on a wad of gum. The air conditioner whirred behind the reception desk, bringing slight respite from the muggy heat outside.

An elbow on the counter, Alex leaned forward. "I'm hoping you can squeeze my friend in. Since we're neighbors." Sort of. The salon was right next to their hotel.

After more than three months of caging herself in her room to evade detection, Lilah finally conceded she needed daylight like everyone else. Alex harbored a sneaking suspicion her decision was partly due to the behavior of their landlords, the Wus—George and Christine.

Brad usually went to the reception desk to pick up newspapers and struck up a friendship with the couple. The three of them often played dice games in the office behind the tiny lobby with pennies as stakes. Of course there were the occasional personal questions. And of course there were no secrets revealed. The establishment was meant for guests who didn't want to talk, after all. But the couple was curious about the woman traveling with the group, especially since she never left her room. Brad admitted Lilah was his wife. Since the bankruptcy of the family business—the nature of which remained unspecified—she'd been giving him the silent treatment. The group was waiting for some money to come through in a court case before returning to their home country in South America.

The news triggered frequent visits from Christine Wu to Lilah's room under the pretext of delivering food. Sometimes, George went with her. Detailed lectures on appropriate behavior for wives would follow, replete with examples of saintly figures from Chinese culture. Three months of haranguing... Lilah couldn't tell off the owners of the hotel and risk getting all of them evicted, but it was no surprise she finally wanted out during the times the couple usually showed up.

To brave the public, her hoodie and glasses were not enough camouflage. Hence, the visit to the salon. She'd asked Neil to accompany her, but Alex and Victor were her self-assigned guards, and they insisted on one of them going along.

"It's an emergency," Neil said to the salon's proprietress, the punk goth.

The goth—a thirty-something Chinese woman—studied Lilah, standing stiff and silent between Alex and Neil. "Makeover emergency? Boyfriend beat you up? I don't see no bruises."

Before Lilah could respond, Neil exclaimed, "No."

Eyes narrowed in confusion, the goth asked, "You the boyfriend? Or him?"

Alex held up his hands. "We're not her boyfrien—"

"Pimps?" The goth clucked. "Girl, if you gonna whore, work for yourself. Be independent."

Alex didn't dare look at Lilah, but he sincerely hoped the gurgle he heard didn't mean she was choking to death on shock.

Enthusiastic, the goth continued, "I used to be like you. All the time shooting up, too." She extended her arms, gesturing at the track marks with her head. "See? I got out. I help you if you want." Halting her evangelization, she glared at the men. "Don't think you're gonna come after me for talking to her. I got my friends."

Of course she did. Her business couldn't operate in this neighborhood without paying the gangs for protection.

Neil cleared his throat. "She's not... we're not... she's *auditioning*. For the new strip club, Eden. *Ouch.*"

"Oh," said the goth, looking mildly disappointed. At Neil's sudden squeak, she added a grumpy "Whassa matter with you?"

"Just something on my foot," Neil said, voice high. Something like the heel of Lilah's right boot.

Dismissing him, the goth turned back to the aspiring stripper. "You won't make it," the goth pronounced. "You too skinny."

Alex winced. The woman who was heralded as the most beautiful in America... Lilah had resumed eating healthy portions after the first night in Macau, but the clothes she bought in Quito at the beginning of their exile were still too loose on her. "We'll pay double. Please... do your best."

The goth pocketed the money and left to find a stylist, telling them there was space for only one of the men in the air-conditioned waiting area.

"Neil, please stay," Lilah requested, her tone low. "I'd like you to make sure everything's sanitary."

As though a medical degree conferred some kind of x-ray vision! Lilah couldn't deny she needed muscle around, but she was making it clear Alex would have to stay outside her comfort zone.

"You don't run out of excuses, do you?" he asked, not bothering to hide his bitterness. "Never mind. I'll be by the door if you decide you do need me."

He stalked to the street, intending to visit the café on the other side. He needed something to drink. Or a bucket of ice to dump on his head. The temperature was high enough, and the humidity made it unbearable. He didn't know which was worse, the clamminess or the dark storms pelting the city nearly every day.

A car honked and took off. Alex leaped back to the curb, cursing fluently. High-pitched voices joined him as two painfully thin women in Spandex minis chased futilely after the fleeing vehicle. A tiff over payment for services rendered, no doubt. Ignoring the fracas, he got himself a can of Coke and returned to pace the pavement in front of the salon.

Neil stepped out after fifteen minutes to update Alex on the progress of Lilah's disguise. "Two hours is what they said... Alex, you know it's only because she's still hurt by what happened in Cuba, right? It *was* a big miscalculation on our part."

"I *know*, Neil. None of us ever imagined..." But Alex was the one who made sure her access to any kind of help was blocked off. "I just don't know how to make it up to her without disowning my own brother. How do I get her to forgive me?"

Neil's eyelids flickered. "Her forgiveness is important to you?"

Irritated almost beyond endurance, Alex snapped, "Dude, how many times do I have to say it? I'm not in love with her. Nor she with me. Yeah, I love her, but there are forms of love beyond romance. Lilah is... she's *family.*" As much family as Brad. They should've found a way to work around Brad's weaknesses.

Even with Lilah's public and ongoing rebuff, Brad had not repeated the insane accusations of an affair. Alex knew why. Her rejection of her marriage on all but paper was far outweighed by her rejection of her so-called lover. Even so, Alex could only feel pity for his brother, not anger. Besides, they couldn't afford dissension. Not with their lives at stake.

"You'd better get back inside," Alex said to Neil. "She shouldn't be left alone." After Neil disappeared into the salon, Alex resumed his patrolling. "A miscalculation," he mumbled, staring at the pavement. A mild word for the events which ended in their exile.

"What happened now?" asked Victor's voice.

Looking up, Alex asked, "Did you decide to get a haircut, too?"

Victor muttered, "I need air. Can't stand—"

Alex nodded. Of all of them, Victor was the one most affected by the confinement. Physically, everything was too small for him: the room, the bed, the shower shared by the occupants of the entire floor. Mentally, the inability to do anything about their situation was taking a toll. The troubleshooter was now in trouble, waiting for others to help him out.

"What miscalculation?" Victor asked.

Alex slashed the air with his hand. "Lilah didn't want me to wait with her. She's... difficult... as usual."

"Bro!" Victor exploded. "Don't you think we've done enough to justify her behavior? I know I have. Poor girl. Because of me... us, she's..."

If Neil still suspected Alex of harboring an illegitimate affection for Lilah, where Victor was concerned, the pendulum had swung all the way to guilt. Something in his tone... Alex said, "Careful. Lilah is not one of your rescue projects. For whatever reasons, she's decided to stay married to Brad. You're married, too. Hell, I shouldn't have to tell you this. Only a few months ago, *you* were accusing *me* of romancing her."

Victor flushed. "I'm not an idiot. It's just... I'm..." He groaned. "I did talk you into ditching her right when she needed you. If I didn't..."

"Yeah, well," Alex muttered. "Doesn't look like she's holding it against you. Not the same for me, though."

"Goddamit, bro! You find it easy to blame her for not forgiving you. Can't you see she's half the size she used to be?"

At least she was eating again.

"At least she's eating now," Victor echoed Alex's thoughts. "But I don't think she sleeps."

She didn't. Alex had lain awake many nights, listening to the creaks on the other side of the thin wall.

He shoved his fingers into his hair. It wouldn't be much longer before he went out of his mind if his conscience didn't stop constantly reminding him of what he'd done. Not only to Lilah, but to the wife he left behind, to the son who must have waited for his daddy's phone call on his birthday. Alex almost smiled. Sabrina had wanted another child, a girl. Before they could try, he'd... guilt squeezed Alex's heart. Out loud, he said, "You'd better stop before people start to think you spend all your time watching Lilah."

Victor's accusatory silence lasted a few seconds. Finally, he said, "Guess I deserved it."

Alex huffed. "Sorry, dude. I know you didn't mean—"

"This exile business is getting to all of us," Victor said, holding a hand up. "Wish we could do something instead of just sitting around."

"I know. Unfortunately, there is nothing we *can* do. Any move we make has the potential to reach Steven. All our lives will be at risk. Keeping our heads down is our only option."

Victor mumbled a curse. After a couple of moments, he said, "I'm going to get something to eat. See you back in the room."

Not long after Victor left, a coy voice called, "Mister, have a try?"

Not again! Alex had been subjected to the same invitation from countless sources over the last five months. As had all the Kingsley men. As had every tourist wandering down the street. "No, thank you," he said, taking care not to look the prostitute in the eye. He couldn't bear to see the desperation.

Alex considered walking away. Neil was in there with Lilah, but he was a surgeon, not a soldier who could protect her from miscreants. However, if Alex stood around in the street corner much longer, there would be more lewd propositions to fend off. There was the coffee store across, but it was frequented by young abusers with heroin cigarettes. Alex had spotted boys who couldn't be more than thirteen.

If he walked a bit, he'd reach one of the main streets where all the glitz was. Where Macau Eden opened the week before.

Alex grimaced. He'd seen the tabloids and read all about Harry's supposed romance with Lupe Valdez. There was also a strange section on him carrying on with a waiter in the same establishment, some boy called Ira. It was the first Alex even realized something had gone wrong between Harry and Verity. This dalliance with Lupe and Ira and whoever... Harry wasn't out partying as the yellow press assumed. Alex had a bad feeling about it. He handed the magazine to Lilah, but she didn't comment at all. She'd have realized just as he did how Harry's latest game was very dirty and very dangerous.

Fetching himself a bundle of newspapers from the salon, Alex leaned against the wall and read every single one. The disintegration of the Soviet Union was in progress, and trouble was brewing in mainland China. He selfishly hoped it didn't spread to Macau. If it did, there was a good chance the communist government would ask all non-natives to get out. They needed to prepare for the eventuality... just in case. Alex bit back a groan. What other nation could they flee to, and how would they get there? Mentally, he went over the list of safe countries. China was one but out of the question since the problems were centered there. India... the country did have an extradition treaty with the U.S. Where else...

Sweat soon plastered Alex's shirt to his chest. His back turned stiff from staying in the same position, and his neck hurt. The cops in the car cruising by gave him narrow-eyed looks. Victor sauntered back from the other end of the street, raising his hand in a casual salute as he walked into the hotel. He was done already? Victor didn't waste time over food, but he also usually relished every morsel.

Taking a quick glance at his watch, Alex swore. He knew salon visits usually took longer than intended. He was a married man, after all. But they were on the run, dammit! He couldn't afford to assume things were okay in there. Alex was almost ready to risk Lilah's wrath and barge in when the door swung open.

Alex gaped at the woman with Neil. The long hair was gone, replaced by a bob. The glasses were the same, and the eyes behind them were large as always, but they were brown, not the hazel he was used to seeing. Lenses? A tiny ring glinted on her left nostril. The boots, the faded denims, and the shapeless, black hoodie added to the impression of a rebellious adolescent rather than the thirty-two-year-old only recently celebrated as one of the most powerful women in North America.

"You cut it all off?" he accused, pointing at her head.

"I begged her not to," Neil said, tone mournful. Brightening, he added, "She did buy a couple of wigs."

Alex smiled, feeling grateful. He'd been afraid they sapped all positivity from her. "No one's going to confuse you with Lilah Kingsley, so I guess it's all good."

A sharp whistle cut through the air. At the door to the hotel stood Victor, gesturing them closer. Scott and Brad were right behind.

When Lilah squeezed past them into the hotel lobby, Victor stared, apparently lost for words. Scott peered closely at her hair, muttering, "Nice." Brad was silent, fortunately. Alex couldn't imagine Lilah's reaction if her husband dared offer an opinion.

"What's up?" Alex asked Victor.

Making sure no one was near enough to overhear, Victor said, "We've been found."

In five minutes, Alex was on one of the sagging twin beds in the room he shared with Victor, reading from the *International Herald Tribune*. There was the most recent update on the trouble in China. Plus, something else. "Where's the kid who brought it to the room?" Alex asked.

"No idea," Victor said, pacing the tiled floor. "She caught me by surprise, so I didn't think of detaining her." The others were also present and were silently digesting what happened.

Alex flung the newspaper to the side. "Someone kidnapped Steven. What for?"

"The same someone made sure we saw the news," Victor said, nodding. "Time to move on from Macau."

Alex shook his head. "We can't. Not until we know what's going on."

Brad agreed, "Whoever it is didn't report us to Macau police. They want something from us. If we leave, it might mean trouble."

"If we stay, it will definitely mean trouble," Victor argued.

Alex said, "The minute we walk out of here, the cops will get us. The person behind this will have made sure of it."

"We have no option but to wait," said Lilah.

So they did. Bags packed, they stayed together in Alex and Victor's room and waited for their unseen foe to make contact. Alex kept his gun ready. On the side table was a wad of notes, the rent to date for their lodgings. If they were forced to leave in a hurry, their hosts would not be left unpaid. Their destination would depend on what they learned in the next few hours.

Time crawled. Pacing up and down the creaky floor, Victor muttered, "Whoever it is, he's making us sweat." Literally. The stench was suffocating. Oh, all their rooms were air-conditioned, but the cheap units did a piss-poor job of keeping the heat out. Even over the annoying whir, sounds penetrated into the building. At every shriek of laughter from the street, at every honk, they jumped.

Not daring to step out of the room, they skipped dinner. Not as if any of them could have actually eaten. Outside, thunder rumbled. Stars disappeared from the nighttime sky as dark clouds rolled across. But it didn't rain. There was no respite from the punishing weather or from the tension.

"We should try to get some sleep," Neil said. "Only one of us needs to stay awake at a time." No one responded. No one slept.

Midnight passed by the time their landlady told them there was a phone call for Adrian Cooper, Alex's alias in Macau. At the reception desk, Neil covered Alex while he picked up the phone and waited for the landlady to leave. "Hello?" he said once Christine Wu was out of earshot.

"Alex Kingsley?" came a polished voice. "Or should I call you Mr. Cooper? It's your old friend, Jùn Wángzǐ."

Under his breath, Alex cursed. *Prince.*

Chapter 37

Fifteen minutes later

Macau

"I don't believe this," Alex said, his knuckles beating a rapid tattoo on the small desk in a corner of the room. "How could Steven be fool enough to get himself kidnapped by Prince? And what happened to the son of bitch, Major Armor? He was with Steven and Charles according to the news. How the hell did the kidnappers manage to get past Armor?"

Two feet to the right of the table, Victor rested his hip against the windowsill, but the twitching muscle in his cheek belied the casual stance. All of them were tightly wound, not only Victor. On the plastic eyesore of a chair next to him was Lilah, looking ready to bolt. The twins were on one of the two cots lined up along the walls with Brad on the other.

Snorting, Victor said, "Armor probably ran at the first sign of trouble. The sniveling little—"

"Don't underestimate the major," reprimanded Brad. "He's dangerous, and all of us know it... or should know. Prince probably waited until Armor was away precisely because he's dangerous."

"Armor's not the main problem at the moment," Scott said. "What I don't understand is why Prince expects *us* to negotiate for Steven's release. Why not the American government? Why not *any* government?" Markets everywhere would be going haywire, and political types would be shitting their pants. They'd be begging for some clue as to what happened. "Why call us?"

Neil agreed, "I'd be happy to let the bastard die."

Alex threw a glance at Neil. "Prince's men will talk only to Brad and Lilah. Not you or me or anyone else."

"His men?" asked Brad. "Not him?"

"Since Prince is wanted in many countries," Alex explained, "he directs his proxies from his home base in Burma. Supposedly, as soon as you and Lilah get to the meeting place, Victor and I will be 'escorted' to Steven's location. I presume they're holding him somewhere in Macau. We'll be allowed to leave with him once Prince gets whatever he's after."

"What *is* he after?" Victor asked. "What do we have that he could possibly want?"

"Maybe he's planning an ambush?" Brad asked. "Revenge for breaking up his drug ring in India?"

Tone emphatic, Neil said, "I bet he's working with Steven. They're splitting us up, hoping to pick us off one by one."

"Could be," Alex said. "But why this charade of kidnapping and negotiation? Prince obviously knew where we were all along. He could've simply had us killed. He didn't need Steven and still doesn't. No, I doubt Steven has any idea what's going on. He's only a hostage for Prince to get us to do what he wants."

Driving a fist into the window jamb, Victor asked, "What *does* he want? And why does he think we'll do anything for Steven?"

"Could Prince be planning to hold *us* hostage to get concessions from the American government?" Brad asked. "As you said, he's a wanted man."

"Why?" Alex countered. "He could use Steven."

"Steven's the acting CEO of the Peter Kingsley Network," Brad said, tone bitter. "Using him would be considered blackmail. *We're* traitors. Prince can pretend to be a friend of the Americans by capturing us."

Alex said, "Which brings us back to the same problem. He doesn't need to twist himself into a pretzel to do so. He could pick up the phone right now and call Macau police."

There was silence for a couple of minutes.

"How did Prince figure out we're here?" Lilah asked.

"Someone saw us?" Scott hazarded a guess.

"I don't know, Scott," she said. "If you were Prince, and you wanted something from us, wouldn't you have kept an eye on where we went from Panama?"

Scott said, "But after Quito, we used—"

Victor groaned. "Our fake passports."

"Exactly," Lilah said.

"What?" asked Neil.

Alex explained, "The place which made us the documents was not exactly legitimate, Neil. I'm betting the local gangs tracked us there and got our new names. Prince has connections with many of the criminals in Panama. Why not in Ecuador, too?"

Scott exclaimed, "So Prince has been keeping an eye out for us since our exile began. He knew Ecuador was one of the places we'd head to. Thanks to the new passports—or maybe even before—he located us in Quito. He knew the fake names we were traveling under and tracked us to Macau. He probably had his people watch us all these months in this city, merely waiting for an opportunity. Which Steven provided."

"Opportunity for what?" Victor asked.

"Not to kill us," Lilah said. "Or we'd have already been dead. That much is obvious. So it's highly unlikely Steven's working with him."

Smoothing a hand over his head, Brad said, "This is going nowhere. There's only one way to find out. Go to the meeting."

"Are you crazy?" snapped Victor. "Let Prince do what he wants with Steven."

"Even if Steven gets killed?" asked Brad.

Victor snarled. "Lemme ask again. Why should we give a damn about what happens to Steven?"

Brad explained, "At our trial, it was implied we were working with Prince, and if he's accused of killing Steven, by extension, we could be, too."

"We're a thousand miles from Burma!" said Victor.

"Steven was kidnapped from Mae Klang Luang," Alex corrected. "Thailand, not Burma. If we're supposed to 'pick him up' after negotiations, I bet he's already been brought to Macau."

"We traveled from Ecuador to Macau under false identities," said Brad. "In less than four months, Steven got kidnapped by one of our supposed allies in the region. No, Victor. No one's going to give us the benefit of the doubt."

"There's no proof," Neil said.

"Suspicion is sometimes good enough to get you convicted," Brad said. "I'm the best example of the fact. All I did was shake someone's hand. A third party took a picture of the one moment and used it to drive me out of my own home. But now, there are actual threads connecting Prince to Steven and us to Prince. Even the phone call Prince just made to Alex will be used as evidence against us." Doggedly, Brad added, "We cannot afford to have even a single misstep while we wait for a pardon."

"Bro," exploded Victor.

From the chair, Lilah spoke up, "He's right."

The rhythm Alex was rapping out with his knuckles faltered. At the window, Victor straightened. The twins exchanged glances.

"I agree." Scott adjusted his glasses, flushing slightly.

Lilah continued, "Prince knows where we are. If we refuse and walk out, he will call the authorities to get us. We will be caught and be blamed for kidnapping Steven and Charles in addition to everything else. Prince and gang have us over a barrel. We have no choice but to go where he wants and listen to his demands."

"Prince wouldn't have set up this elaborate scheme if what he had in mind was something simple," said Alex. "We're not going to like what he says."

"What it boils down to is this," Lilah said. "Prince knows we're going to show up and negotiate. When we go to the meeting, it will need to be with an escape plan in place. Not only for us. We'll have to rescue Steven, too, to avoid getting blamed for the kidnapping. Even if we manage to somehow evade Prince and get out of Macau, we simply cannot afford to have abduction charges thrown at us."

"Imagine if Prince kills Steven and Charles..." Alex mused. "We could be accused of the murders."

"What are our options?" Brad asked. "For an escape route, I mean."

"When I dealt with Prince before, the CIA and the Indian military worked with me," Alex said.

Victor said, "Not gonna happen now." The Macau government was also not likely to help. "Hell, the cops here would probably hand us over to the U.S. the minute they realize who we are and how we got here."

A germ of an idea was sprouting in Alex's mind, but he needed information. When they encountered Prince and his gang in India, Harry got it for them. But now... "In India, Prince relied on local gangs to move merchandise across the border. He's repeating the same pattern... perhaps the forgers in Ecuador, locals spying for him in Macau... we could, potentially, use his *m.o.* as our weapon."

"How?" Neil asked.

Alex explained, "In my experience with the army in Pakistan, there's never only one gang around. If Prince is using one group—"

"We can use someone else against him," Victor finished, his shoulders suddenly bunching with purpose.

"Who does Prince work with in Macau?" Neil asked.

"It's the part I don't know," Alex said.

"*I* do," said Victor, pacing the room. "I was the damn troubleshooter for our business. There are probably not a whole lotta lowlifes I don't know in Panama. The first time I met Prince was when he was working with Noriega's pals. Those men had their connections to Asian gangs which ship heroin from the Golden Triangle to Latin America for transport into the U.S."

Alex hissed. "I bet Prince contracts with the same gang."

"I'm sure of it," Victor said. "There are two I know of operating along the Pacific route to Panama. The one which deals almost exclusively with drugs is called 13BC. The other is Peace Guard."

"Peace Guard?" Scott repeated, face confused.

"It's what they call themselves," Victor said. "They insist they keep peace in the underworld. Unlike 13BC, Peace Guard has fingers in many pies: money laundering, gambling, counterfeiting, prostitution, and of course, narcotics."

"Diversification," Lilah added, a tinge of humor in her voice.

Neil smiled. "Since heroin is Prince's main business, I'd guess he's a 13BC man."

"No," Alex said. "Remember, Prince wanted us to arrange a little exchange of clean cash for dirty funds during the episode in India."

"Money laundering is mostly Peace Guard territory," said Victor. "Since Peace Guard is also involved in counterfeiting, it would explain how Prince tracked us through the forgers."

"What happens if we're wrong?" Scott asked. "What if we end up contacting the same gang Prince uses?"

"We'll be done for," Alex said, tone cheerful. "I need to make a couple of calls. First, to our lawyer... Grayson."

Chapter 38

Next morning

Macau

"No refunds," called out the goth, treating Lilah to a hostile eye.

It was only after eleven in the morning, but the Naughty Girl Salon was already packed with... er... naughty girls.

"No, no," Alex soothed. "We... ahh... came here to ask you a favor. You said you could help my friend."

"Yeah?" said the goth, curiosity replacing wariness in her tone. "But why she needs help? You say you not her pimp."

Alex winced. If they ever got out of this mess, he was going to ban the word from his hearing. "Ms. Go—miss, you said you know 'people.' Can your people put in a good word for my friend? At the strip club, I mean."

She pursed her jet-black lips and stared unblinkingly at him.

Almost holding his breath, Alex waited. The phone call he placed to the States earlier was the crucial first part of their escape plan—the favor he asked Grayson Sheppard to organize. If it were something impossible, Alex would've heard by now. Regardless, any arrangements made by people back home wouldn't work without the cooperation—unwitting though it might be—of the goth girl.

"I'm sorry," Lilah said. "Maybe we shouldn't have bothered you. Only, I thought as a woman you'd understand..." She turned to Alex. "You were right. It's better to ask your boss when you start your new job. They'll know someone in the business."

Way to go, Alex cheered in his mind, nearly treating her to a raised brow of appreciation.

The goth's eyes narrowed. "He work for a triad?" she asked Lilah, gesturing at Alex with her chin.

"Triad?" Lilah asked, her voice full of innocence and ignorance. "You mean, gang?"

Impatiently, the goth said, "That word, not good. Triads are business. They give security for my store."

"Sorry," Lilah said. "Al... Adrian is interviewing with one of the triads. Peace Guard."

"What?!" said the other woman. "Peace Guard is recruiting on this street? This is not their territory!"

"Oh, really?" Alex asked. "But they can still recommend my friend to the strip club, right?"

Chewing her lip, the goth negotiated, "How about we make a deal? I get *my* friends to recommend her for the job, and you tell us about Peace Guard's plans."

"Snitch?" he asked, tone dramatically high.

"Look at it this way," the goth suggested. "You want to stay alive? You help us. *And* your friend gets a job."

Not a bad bargain. "What do you want to know?" Alex asked.

"Where is the interview?" Black-lined eyes glinted. "And when?"

Yes. Out loud, Alex admitted, "We don't know yet. I'll update you as soon as they call."

Walking back to the hotel, Lilah muttered, "Phase one, check."

Like old times. Alex grinned. All six of the exiles were highly likely to be under surveillance by Prince. Hopefully, the drug lord would hear of their moves and draw the conclusions they wanted him to. The next step would involve the twins, Neil and Scott.

When Prince called back in the evening for their decision, Alex brought up two conditions of his own. "Steven cannot be allowed to recognize us."

"Done," said Prince. "He's going to be... shall we say, 'heavily sedated'?"

"Also, Brad and Lilah won't go inside the meeting room until Victor and I see Steven alive. They will have to stay on the phone with us while the negotiations are going on."

Tone amused, Prince asked, "You don't trust me, do you?"

"Can you blame us?"

Prince laughed. "Alex Kingsley, my friend. It wasn't I who started the feud."

Stonily, Alex said, "It was no feud. You tried to force your way into our business in Panama and in India. What we did was self-defense."

"Let me assure you there's no trap. I simply want to discuss business with your brother and his wife."

Chapter 39

Next day, 6 PM

Central Business District, Macau

Dark clouds hovered threateningly over the city streets as they had for the last two days, leaving the air saturated with steam. Casino Lisboa glowed golden against the late evening sky. Chattering crowds streamed around Brad and Lilah as they stood outside the famed gambling hall. Prince's associates were in the casino, while the drug lord himself would deal with Alex and Victor.

All very straightforward, but... stomach churning, Lilah reminded herself there was no option for her except to trust these men. She would walk into the casino with the same gambler who wagered her life and liberty in Cuba. Brad never ventured anywhere near the gaming houses in the months they were in Macau, but he spent hours playing the owners of their hotel for pennies. Still, he wouldn't be stupid enough to succumb to temptation tonight, would he? At least all five brothers agreed there would be no asking Steven for reconciliation if the mission went well. He was not to be trusted.

Shoving the lingering bitterness to a shadowed corner of her mind, Lilah told herself to focus on the present, or the mission *wouldn't* go well. There was also the other thing... her personal future.

The bright-red hair of her wig was held in a twist by crystal spikes, and her brown contact lenses were left in place as was the clip-on nose ring. She smoothed out the *qipao*. The long, body-hugging mandarin gown in deep green had a delicate gold pattern worked into it. It didn't come cheap, but she couldn't afford to stick out among the glamorous crowd visiting Casino Lisboa's VIP rooms. Inside the Louis Vuitton clutch hanging from her right wrist was a paper clipping. The article on Harry and Guadalupe Valdez.

Lilah held onto it like a talisman the last couple of weeks. It wasn't the first time an outsider was persuaded to help them. Eugene Bishop, who owned *The Big Apple Reporter,* played a huge role in bringing about the fall of Jared Sanders. In return, he got his interviews with certain movers and shakers of society. Lilah couldn't imagine what Harry promised the strip club owner, but he was working on something to bring his friends back home. It might be dirty, and it certainly was dangerous, but he'd do whatever it took. Once he did... she winced in remorse, remembering the mention of Verity at the tail end of the article. Apparently, Harry and his wife were in the process of getting a quick divorce. There was a lightness inside Lilah she hadn't experienced for a long time—hope.

All she needed to do was get through this exile, and everything she wanted would be within reach... her plans for the business empire, her own *self,* the personal happiness she thought was lost forever. They *would* reclaim the network. Lilah would destroy it. She would also get back the ability to hold her spine straight and direct her own destiny, and the future awaiting her appeared sweeter than she imagined possible.

Lilah chanced a glance at her husband, standing silently at her side. He was dressed in a suit, and his hair and beard were neatly groomed, but he was still unrecognizable as Brad Kingsley, ousted CEO of the Peter Kingsley Network. He'd be chief executive again, but only after they brought him so close to getting his property back that he'd agree to dismantle the network and keep only his own business. Surely, Brad would also agree their marriage was over and done with.

None of it would happen if they couldn't stay out of Prince's clutches. Turning to the twins, Lilah said, "Time for the two of you to go."

Both had donned department store suits for their parts in this elaborate play. Neil pulled his customary bandana more securely over his blond head, looking strangely chic in it. "Remember, wait in the main casino until Alex and Victor call and tell you they have Steven and Charlie," said Neil. "Don't let anyone get you into the private rooms until then."

She smiled. "We won't. *You* be careful."

"We're going to get this done," Neil said. "C'mon, Scott. Showtime. We need to reach the club by six-thirty."

"Don't let Prince's people catch you," Lilah warned.

"He's never met us," Neil said, tone confident.

Dryly, Lilah said, "I highly doubt Prince has forgotten your existence. Make no mistake, he's keeping an eye on you."

"I'm sure," agreed Neil, "and we'll do exactly what we discussed. Let's go, Scott."

"Wait," said Scott, adjusting his glasses. Unblinkingly, he stared at Lilah for a second or two before pronouncing, "Your red hair... it's like fire. You look good. Like a princess."

Lilah laughed in bemusement. Temple once called her a fire-borne princess, a woman who was forged by the flames at the Egypt-Libya border. Except for Alex, the Kingsley brothers knew nothing about that part of her life.

"I mean it," Scott said. Clinically eyeing her top to bottom, he added, "You're thin now... but still symmetrical."

Lilah laughed again, feeling lighter by the minute. Reaching out, she patted his cheek. Or rather, the brown fuzz covering his face. "Thank you."

Neil groaned. "Let's go, Romeo."

As they walked away, Scott said to Neil, "Nine. I have nine. You have only four."

At Neil's pithy curse, his twin snickered. Lilah frowned, wondering what it was all about.

#

6:20 PM

Naughty Girl Salon & Tattoo Parlor

"I told your partner before," said the salon owner, spitting her gum into the trash can. "We always busy. Make appointment."

"My brother," Scott corrected, voice quiet. "We're not gay." It was vital for the lady to know this for their plan to work. He'd pulled the same trick a few times before, but this time... it was exciting. Scott pushed his glasses up his nose. "We may have to leave tonight. But before we go, I... ahh... I need to... do something."

"So?" snapped the salon owner—goth lady as Alex called her. "Not my problem."

Neil interjected, "But he has one... a problem, I mean. A girl problem."

With her index finger, the goth outlined a circle in the air around her face. "Do I look like I care?"

Ignoring her avowal of disinterest, Scott drew a much-abused pamphlet from his pocket. "My brother told you... I don't know what's going to happen with all these gangs... we may not have much longer to live."

At his side, Neil muttered something that sounded like, "Keep it cool, man."

Placing the pamphlet on the desk, Scott smoothed it out. "Your First Time," it read. When he bought it years ago, he never imagined it would come in handy to actually save his skin someday.

The goth shot him an annoyed look. "You're not first boy coming to Macau to lose virginity. Like I said... not... my... problem."

"I know," Scott soothed. "But I want... ahh... I want..."

"I got it," she said. "You want to get laid. Sorry, not in the business anymore."

"No," exclaimed Neil. "All he wants from you is a haircut. Then, he's going to Eden. The strip club. They have *nice* girls there. Clean."

The salon owner drew herself up to her full height, her form quivering in outrage. "What you trying to say?"

Hurriedly, Neil said, "I didn't mean... those girls are young."

The goth growled, her hand grabbing the paperweight next to the phone.

"Let's go, Nigel," Scott said, using the alias his twin picked. Scott tucked the pamphlet back into his pocket. "She's upset."

A hand held to his heart, Neil said, "I swear—"

Scott shoved his twin toward the door. "We'll find another barber."

They had the door open when something whooshed through the air.

"Duck," shouted Neil.

The paperweight flew past and into the street, shattering on the pavement. Someone screamed. "Barber?!" shouted the goth.

Scott and Neil ran, the salon owner's abuses following them into the evening. Pushing past tourists, they wended their way around parked cars. By the time they got to the next block, Scott was struck by the urge to laugh uncontrollably, but he didn't dare.

Halting to take a breath, Neil asked, "You think she believed us?"

Scott thought back to the woman. Cheeks flushed, pupils dilated, nostrils widened. Feet planted apart, hands fisted at her side. The paperweight-missile. He allowed himself a small grin. "Yes."

Prince would know exactly where Neil and Scott were headed while the rest of their group was occupied, dealing with the drug lord's demands. The exiles could only hope the enemy would make the assumptions they wanted him to.

In ten minutes

Macau Eden

Scott stared at the neon goddess on the signboard, welcoming passersby in with an apple in hand. Just like every other establishment in the city involved in the entertainment business, the outside glittered gold.

"Membership card, gentlemen?" The doorman was a Chinese gent of gigantic proportions. Almost as big as Victor. With his accent, he could have been at Buckingham Palace, serving tea to the queen.

"We don't have one," said Neil.

The doorman nodded. "Macau Eden has a special arrangement for tourists." The entry fee he quoted would have fed a family of four for a month.

"Ahh, no," said Neil. "Your manager's expecting us." The twins produced their fake IDs.

The doorman's eyes widened. "The Coppersmiths?"

Scott nodded, recognizing the weight in his belly only when it lifted a little. Alex had assured them this meeting would happen, but schemes like this could not be expected to go precisely as planned.

Inside, the Macanese hostess led them to a table where a group of men was gathered. Mostly Chinese, some Slavic, one or two with Latino features. All in black suits.

"Nigel Coppersmith," Neil introduced himself.

"Sebastian," said Scott.

One of the Chinese men stood. "We're from Triangle Enterprises." Known to Interpol as the Triangle Triad.

Not 13BC. Not Peace Guard. They'd just walked into a leadership meeting of a third gang.

#

7: 55 PM

Macau Maritime Ferry terminal

The yacht docked in the slip past the bulky passenger ferry was named *Olympus*—the abode of ancient gods—but it was nothing spectacular. Nothing to draw the eye of the police. Night had almost settled on the city, anyway, rendering the craft nearly invisible.

Standing back from the chattering crowd pushing along the well-lit ramp, Alex and Victor waited their turn. The smell of diesel fuel mingled unpleasantly with the salty heat of the ocean air. Thunder rumbled.

"C'mon," Alex said, tugging at his sweat-soaked collar. "Rain already."

"At least we didn't have to dress up," Victor pointed out. Unlike the rest, they'd stayed in their cotton tees and khaki shorts. "I hope Prince's boat is air-conditioned."

Alex laughed. "You sound ready to beg him to take you along."

Grinning, Victor said, "I might. Anything to escape this heat... is it eight yet?"

"Almost."

"Can't get in until the Hong Kong ferry leaves," Victor said. "Too many witnesses."

Alex nodded. "Prince would need to show us Steven and Charlie are alive and well, which will create more delay. Then, we need to speak to Brad and Lilah on the phone. Scott and Neil should get enough time to negotiate the rescue."

Victor mused, "Brad and Lilah... bro, was it my imagination, or did she seem sort of happy?"

"Did she?"

"Happy might be the wrong word," Victor allowed. "Not as tense. I hope they work it out. Brad's not a bad man. He's simply got his weaknesses like everyone else around. I wish Lilah could see it."

"Ain't our place to decide whether they should work it out or not," Alex said, tone firm.

"Yeah," Victor acknowledged. "Still... he's our brother no matter what he's done. Family first, right?"

"Family first," Alex agreed automatically. "But let's focus on the mission."

"I hope this goes the way we planned. Hell, *Steven* better hope this goes the way we planned."

"He would if he knew," Alex said. "Plan B wouldn't end well for him." If the twins failed, Brad and Lilah would have to reject Prince's demands and leave Steven to his fate. The exiles would be blamed for his death, but it would still be better than actually getting involved with the drug lord.

"Plan C wouldn't end well for *us*," said Victor. If Prince succeeded in detaining any of them, they'd have no option but to agree to work with him.

With a smile, Alex suggested, "We could always opt for plan D."

Victor started. "We didn't talk about any plan D."

"You never need to talk about plan D. It goes like this..." Alex took a deep breath. "We run like hell."

Before Victor could retort, the passenger boat blew its horn, signaling it was pulling away from the slip. When Alex and Victor made their way to Prince's yacht, two men patted them down and led them to the short flight of stairs to the cabins.

Cool air hit them in the face when they walked in. Alex sighed in blissful relief, relishing the breeze penetrating his clothes. Roses... the faint fragrance soothed his raw nerves. When he took a look around, it was all he could do not to let his jaw drop at the sheer luxury of the interior as opposed to the unimpressive exterior of the yacht.

The meeting room could have been inside any hotel, except for the mild roar of the Pacific and the rocking motion of the craft. Four armed guards stood two on each side of the entrance, the two who'd just greeted Alex and Victor having returned to the deck. So six guards in total. Slumped on a couch in the far corner were two other men. With his brown hair disheveled, eyes closed, and a few days' worth of hair on his face was Steven. His chest was moving up and down, indicating life. Next to him snored the worthless pile of shit called Charles.

Alex's hands itched to thrash the bastards to death. At his side, Victor growled, his giant form shaking with sudden rage. "It would only take a couple of minutes," the boxer muttered. "One twist of their useless necks..."

Taking a calming breath, Alex said, "We'd be in worse trouble. Stick to the plan, dude."

After a few seconds, Victor nodded jerkily. "Where's Prince?"

"He'll show soon, I'm sure." Alex glanced around. "Damn... I wouldn't mind living here." Unconscious occupants aside, the room was impeccably decorated. The leather chairs perfectly matched the gleaming mahogany of the U-shaped table. Windows lined the wall to their right. The wall on the left was wood-paneled, and a console in the center held bound books. Magnificent paintings hung on both sides of the bookshelf, the glamor of the artwork shown off by yellow lighting.

Alex took two steps toward the one closest to him and peered. A nude woman lounged on a couch, a posy of roses in one hand.

"The goddess of sexuality," said a voice, the words precise in a manner someone not born into the English language could make them sound. "*Venus of Urbino.*"

The figure walking in from somewhere inside to stand with a hand on one of the chairs was familiar to both Alex and Victor. Boyishly handsome face, typical Southeast Asian features, the build of a pugilist. Jùn Wángzǐ, a.k.a. Prince.

Gesturing at the painting with the glass in his hand, Prince said, "I acquired her from an old enemy who thought he'd gotten away with killing my second-in-command."

"Nothing more?" Alex asked. "Only a painting for a life?"

"Ahh," said Prince. "You don't understand. My enemy was a collector. He adored her. The loss of his *Venus* hurt him more than the loss of my friend affected me. To be honest, I can empathize. It's hard to have owned a beauty like her, then watch someone else claim ownership. Look how confident she's in her nudity. What a coquette she is to tempt the viewer in such a manner. I've never seen—"

"Hmph," said a girlish voice, an incredible amount of indignation infused into the one syllable.

When Prince shifted to the side, Alex saw the woman who'd been hidden by the drug lord's figure. Platform heels, smooth legs leading up to gorgeously rounded hips clad in a high-waist bikini with blue and white stripes. Above the impossibly tiny waist, full breasts nearly spilled out of a white halter-top bra.

"Hi, handsome," she said, fingertips held to her red-painted lips. "Remember me?"

Jet-black curls tumbling down her back, kohl-lined, large eyes. Somewhere... somewhere... he'd met her... but where? With Prince?

She giggled. Her shoulders shook almost as though she were laughing in time to some internal rhythm, swaying her torso to a song only she could hear—

In a blink, Alex remembered. She'd been with the Indian politician back when Alex was helping intelligence agencies trap the drug-smuggling ring. "Priya," he said, smiling. "I didn't expect to see you here."

She pouted. "What could I do? After you got everyone caught by the police, I couldn't stay in my own country."

"The Indian government has an arrest warrant out on her," Prince explained.

"I lost all the films I signed," Priya said. "Unfair." Turning to Victor, she explained, "I used to be a movie star. In Bollywood. They were going to give me the Urvasi Award. Only talented actresses get it, and I am very talented."

Face thoroughly bemused, Victor nodded.

Priya linked her arm with Prince's and rubbed her cheek on his sleeve. "I'd have starved to death if not for him. He's a great philatelist."

"Philanthropist," Victor corrected, his eyes somewhat dazed at this curious bundle of naïveté and seduction confronting them.

Laughing, Prince said, "Go on. You were waiting for them to get here."

Priya sashayed to Alex and in one sudden move, threw her arms around his neck. He stumbled, only just steadying them both with his hands on her hips. "What are you—" he said, voice strangled.

Her fingers dug into his hair, and her curvaceous body nestled closer. Pursed and ready to be kissed, her mouth hovered only a whisper beneath his. The scent of roses once again walloped his senses.

"Stop," Alex said, "we're gonna—ahh." He skidded, taking her backward with him. His elbow collided with the wall, breaking his fall. A bolt of electricity ran up his arm.

Her breasts were crushed against his chest. Summoning every ounce of willpower he possessed, he stopped his hands from curling around her buttocks and used them to unwind her arms from around his neck.

"You didn't want to in India, either," she complained.

"Priya, I'm a married man. I have a child."

With genuine puzzlement in her eyes, she asked, "So?"

Alex gently pushed her aside. Searching for a way to let her down without being hurtful, he blurted, "You remind me of my mother."

There was astounded silence from everyone around for a few seconds, broken by a gulp from Victor. Brows drawn into a single line of fury, Priya snapped, "I think you're gay." With an affronted twirl, she pranced out, going farther into the interior of the boat. Her hips still seemed to be swaying to whatever song was playing in her head.

"Mother?" asked Prince, laughing. "I must confess to being surprised by you. Priya's quite a tempting piece of art."

Alex cocked an eyebrow. "Art? *I* must confess, my wife will never buy the excuse."

"The problem with marrying clever women," commiserated Prince. "I made the mistake with my first wife. But she did me a favor and died in childbirth. I was very careful in choosing the second one. Unfortunately, she, too, didn't live long. A military raid at the village."

"Priya's number three?" Alex asked. "So why are you letting her—"

Prince pulled out a couple of chairs, gesturing at Alex and Victor to take seats. He walked around to the other side of the table. "Haven't you ever collected things, Alex Kingsley? Stamps? Coins? Priya is one of those stamps I can do without, but someone else may think otherwise. So I'll exchange her for something—someone—*I* want."

Irritation welling, Alex said, "She's a woman. Not a stamp."

"Come on, Kingsley," said Prince. "Don't be a hypocrite. Your sister-in-law, Lilah Kingsley. From what I hear, her family made a deal with your brother to build your alliance using her. Although..." He sat deeper into his chair. "...she *is* your CFO. So perhaps Brad Kingsley made the same mistake I did. Married the smart one instead of the pretty one."

Neither Alex nor Victor said a word. Alex knew Lilah never met the drug lord face-to-face. Not in Panama, not during the sting operation in India. In Panama, it had been deliberate. Lilah only took part in those negotiations they saw as going somewhere, and the Kingsleys wanted to make it very clear to Prince and his dictator buddy, Noriega, that all they'd hear was no. Victor, their troubleshooter, could convey the message with appropriate levels of forcefulness.

"The papers say she's quite a looker," Prince continued musing. "I've seen pictures. Not bad, I suppose."

Alex cleared his throat. Prince was right. The photographs weren't bad. Only, nowhere enough to convey the impact of the actual woman.

Echoing his thoughts, Prince said, "But photographs can lie. Funny thing, lighting. Even the most unattractive of women can be made to look good." He smiled. "Simply an observation, of course. I'm not calling her unattractive." When neither of the Kingsley men responded, Prince said, "I wish I could've been at the casino to meet her, but with the arrest warrants the Chinese have out for me, it was too risky. No matter. I'm sure I'll meet the mysterious Mrs. Kingsley another day. We're going to be business partners, after all."

Lightning flashed in the dark sky outside the windows, followed by a loud crack of thunder. Pellets struck the glass panes. No, not pellets. Rain. Blessed rain. Alex heaved a sigh of relief.

Frowning, Prince said, "I was hoping to be done before... no stopping Mother Nature I suppose."

A speakerphone was placed between the two parties. When the dial tone broke off, a cautious voice answered, the sounds of Casino Lisboa in the background. Jangling music, whirring machines, clinking coins.

In less than a minute, the subdued tones of Brad Kingsley came over the crackling line, "Hello?"

"We're here, bro," said Victor.

"Steven?"

"Alive," Victor spat, his eyes going to the barely conscious men on the couch in the far corner of the room.

Somberly, Brad said, "Prince's men are waiting for us to go into the conference hall. They're using one of the VIP gambling areas for the meeting."

"Go ahead but stay on the phone," Victor said.

Outside, a horn blew, loud even over the tumult of the squall. When both Victor and Alex looked up, Prince explained, "The ferry operates every quarter hour, so things can get noisy." In the next few minutes, Prince laid out his plan. "I have my contacts in your country. If I request, they will help you with your pardon."

"In return?" asked Lilah, the caution in her voice very clear to those in the boat.

Prince said, "There are rumors going around—strong rumors—about your president's plans to invade Panama. If and when it happens, my friend Noriega will either be killed or thrown in prison. My business in the region will be severely affected. I'm going to need new partners."

Brad started, "Mr. Prince—"

"Prince will do. Before you object, let me tell you how I plan to structure it. I no longer need you to transport my merchandise. I'd prefer *you* to remain legitimate." The craft rocked, gusted about by the wind. Something metallic tumbled on the deck. Someone shouted. The frown returning to his face, Prince grumbled about global warming making life difficult.

"Who's taking care of shipping for you now?" Victor asked. "13BC or Peace Guard?"

Prince eyed both the Kingsley men. "You think you're clever, don't you?" he asked. "Contacting 13BC for help?"

Victor visibly started.

"Did you really believe I wouldn't have you watched?" Prince asked. "Would you like to know what your little brothers are getting up to as we speak?"

Both Victor and Alex leaped from their chairs. Shaking a finger in Prince's face, Alex warned, "If you touch them—"

"Relax," said Prince. "I don't shed blood if I can possibly help it. Very messy and altogether too much trouble. They're safe enough in the strip club."

"Strip club?" Alex parroted.

Prince smiled. "Are you going to pretend you don't know what I'm talking about? Your brother-in-law, Harry Sheppard, is supposedly seeing the owner. Don't tell me he's suddenly developed an affection for the lovely Ms. Valdez. Don't tell me your little brothers' sudden trip to Macau Eden has no connection with any of it. You wanted the doctor and the scientist safely out of the way and stashed them there."

A pulse pounded in Alex's ear, dizzying him momentarily. Prince believed the youngest two were hiding in the club for safety.

A heavy thud sounded on the deck, causing the craft to shudder. Except for the two drugged hostages, everyone in the room stiffened, but there were no sounds following. No more thumps to suggest an intrusion.

Prince snapped out an order in his language. One of his men wheeled around and jogged up the stairs to check. Turning back to the Kingsleys, Prince continued, "I'm not fool enough to let you trick me again. Both 13BC and Peace Guard will have equal participation in my business. So neither group is going to help you. I've also had my contacts in Macau police department watching out for unusual activity. I've even had American military movements in Asia-Pacific watched. There will be no rescue today."

Almost afraid to believe what he heard, Alex briefly closed his eyes. So far, everything was going according to plan. Now, it remained to see if the help he sought came through.

Prince added, "Harry Sheppard is in New York City... in your former president's house, no less. I've had him watched, too."

Victor muttered a curse. Alex didn't dare say a word.

"You see," Prince said. "You have only two options before you. Either you agree and leave with your cousins, or you decline my offer and watch them die. So sit, please. Let's have a serious discussion."

Two of Prince's men strode forward. A hand on Victor's shoulder, one of them shoved the former boxer back into his chair. Without waiting for similar treatment, Alex sat.

The storm picked up speed, the rain violently lashing the windowpanes. Someone called down the stairs—the guard who'd left to check on the noise. Annoyance passed over Prince's face. "It's hard to get decent help," he said to the Kingsleys. Turning to the remaining guards, he said, "Tell them to fix it instead of wasting my time."

Over the speakerphone, Lilah asked, "What do you want us to do?"

Prince explained, "My law firm has set up a network of shell corporations through Delaware. The innermost layer of these shells will be an entity which will buy gas stations across the U.S. But the point will not be to sell gas."

"No," Alex said, "It will be to sell heroin."

Prince shook his head. "If you don't understand how the financial world works, ask your sister-in-law."

"Service stations do a lot of cash business, Alex," Lilah reminded him.

"Money laundering," said Alex, catching on. "Like you tried to get me to do in India. You will mix in the dirty money you get from the drug sales with legitimate cash and move things about. What do you need *us* for?"

"I will need the Peter Kingsley Network—upon your return—to purchase part of the gas station chain," said Prince. "It will obviously be after the pardon... once you have authority to sign papers on behalf of the network."

"Thereby giving you legitimacy," Victor said. In complete silence, the Kingsleys contemplated the plan.

What Alex didn't get was why Prince couldn't ask Steven if he'd agree to the same damned deal. The Kingsley patriarch wouldn't cooperate, but Steven carried the powers of the CEO—

Harry, of course! As chairman, he'd scrutinize Steven's doings and start trouble for the criminal partnership. Prince would know it. He would also imagine Harry Sheppard was less likely to kick up a fuss when the undertaking involved Brad and his brothers.

"What happens to us if we don't agree?" Alex asked. "Other than Steven dying, I mean."

Prince shrugged. "Nothing."

"Nothing?" Victor asked, tone disbelieving. "You'd let all of us walk out? You wouldn't try to kill us?"

"He wouldn't have to, Victor," Lilah explained over the phone. "Once we get blamed for Steven's death, even Harry won't be able to get us pardoned. We'll eventually have to beg Prince to put up an alternate explanation for Steven's death, one the Kingsleys cannot refute."

"I could say one of my men did it," suggested Prince, smiling. "Unlike a denial, a confession to a crime is rarely disbelieved even coming from someone on FBI's wanted list."

"But if we agree," Alex said, his thoughts whirling, "we'll become party to one of the biggest criminal enterprises in the world."

"One way or the other, we'll get there," Brad said. "Only, Steven will die if we decide to take the long route. It will add to the time we spend on the run before we get back home."

Once more, Prince smiled. "Practical man, your brother," he said to Alex and Victor. "Face it... your only viable choice is to work with me. My men at the casino have the papers ready... both the CEO and the CFO will sign them now. The documents won't be dated until you're back in charge of the network... they wouldn't be valid at this time, but after the pardon goes through, our partnership will be made public. And yeah, if you later claim coercion, remember Mr. Brad Kingsley and his wife walked voluntarily to the conference hall. The casino specifically checks for weapons before they let anyone enter their VIP rooms. My men there are not armed."

"But the ones here are," Alex said. "You're holding *us*, along with Steven and Charles. This *is* coercion."

Prince laughed. "I couldn't have the two of you in the casino with your brother and his wife without actually arranging armed guards. You two are too damned dangerous. I couldn't leave you free to roam the city, either. Here, you're outnumbered and outgunned. If you claim you were threatened into this... who'll believe you came here to save the same cousins who got you exiled?"

There it was—Prince's plan. The desperate exiles would have no choice but to agree. Yet another reason the drug lord couldn't make the same deal with Steven. Prince simply wouldn't have the same kind of leverage.

"So what is your decision?" Prince asked.

Alex exchanged glances with Victor, knowing exactly what his brother was thinking. Neither dared look at their watches, but at least half an hour passed since they jumped onto the deck. If Neil and Scott had succeeded in persuading the Triangle Triad, it was way past time for them to have shown up.

"Can we have a day or two to think about it?" asked Lilah, the tremulousness in her voice evident only to those who knew her well.

Incredulity on his face, Prince said, "Mrs. Kingsley, what do you—"

Heavy footsteps thundered down the stairs from the deck. The olive green of the guard's uniform pants appeared, the fabric wet from rain.

Dismissing the reappearance of his employee, Prince continued, "I'm not a fool, madam. You'll give me your decision right here and right now."

Pop-pop-pop. Shoving his chair back, Alex whirled to see the guard who returned riddle the two who'd remained.

Prince leaped up. "Wha—who?"

"Are you the Coppersmiths?" the shooter asked Alex.

Cooper was the name Alex adopted, leaving Coppersmith to the twins, but he nodded.

"Take your cousins and get out."

Brad's voice came over the speakerphone. "What's happen—"

Pops sounded over the line. Screams, instantly muffled. "We got them," someone shouted. "Hell, one of them's 13BC's second."

"Good," said the shooter in the yacht. "Let the Americans go." He turned to Prince.

The drug lord froze.

"We don't want trouble with you," said the shooter. "Our problem is with 13 BC and Peace Guard. You can leave as soon as the Coppersmiths—and the two people in the casino—get out. Your boat driver—or whatever he's called—is still up there."

Mentally, Alex cursed. It would have been a clean ending to the saga if Prince got killed. At least with him held hostage by Triangle members, Brad and Lilah would be able to safely exit.

Victor and Alex hauled the deadweights of the kidnapped duo to the deck. They were drenched in seconds. Through the water pelting down, Alex could barely make out the three corpses strewn around. A fourth form—the helmsman, presumably—was cowering next to the mast.

"Who?" slurred Steven.

"Shut the hell up and walk," said Victor. "Alex... what about Priya?" Chortling, Victor added, "'Mother'? You couldn't find anything else to say to a pretty girl?"

It took Alex a couple of moments to remember his awkward rejection of Priya's advances. With a pithy curse, he admitted. "It was the first thing which came out." Alex glanced back. "She'll be fine with Prince. It's not like we can cart her around with us."

Making sure the ramp was deserted, they got out of Prince's yacht, *Olympus*. As soon as they dumped the two drugged men under the bright lights, Victor and Alex moved to the shadows and waited for the next ferry. It wasn't long. With a loud horn, the boat arrived. Passengers streamed out, stopping short at the sight of the two bodies on the floor. Someone screamed.

"Are they dead?" shrieked a feminine voice.

"Call the cops," shouted someone else.

Alex and Victor merged into the crowd, mingling with the departing passengers. Before reaching the immigration counter, they worked their way back to the ramp and again concealed themselves in the shadows. From their hiding place, they couldn't see either the yacht or the spot where they dumped Steven and Charles, but that was no longer important. Patiently, they waited for the rest of the Kingsleys to arrive as arranged.

Neither noticed the tall, blond man sprinting in, stopping short at the sight of them. Neither saw the sheer terror on his face as he rushed past toward the yacht, only to halt by the two bodies on the ground.

Part XIV

Chapter 40

9:30 PM

Macau Maritime Ferry terminal

From the cab, Lilah peered at the brightly lit entrance to the ferry terminal. The twins were already there, Neil waving enthusiastically. Alex and Victor would be at the ramp, waiting for the rest to join them after getting tickets and going through exit procedures.

As soon as the two passengers were out, the cab vroomed off, nearly scraping the back of Lilah's ankle in the process. She yelped. Cabbies... they were the same everywhere, New York or Macau. Ready to launch into outer space from streets barely wide enough to accommodate a horse cart.

Neil came jogging. Laughing uproariously, he said, "We did it! Gimme five!" There was a grin on Scott's face.

"Careful," said Brad, eyes darting around. "And great work, both of you."

Scott shrugged, a mild flush on his face. "The Triangle Triad was already curious why Lupe Valdez called them for a meeting. We told them we could help them get the other two gangs. A business opportunity."

"They didn't have any questions about how you got mixed up with the gangs?" asked Lilah.

"We told them the truth," said Scott.

At her side, Brad goggled. *"What?"*

Lilah struggled to speak. After all this trouble, Scott had revealed their identity to a new group of criminals?

"Only that we are Panamanians in trouble with both 13BC and Peace Guard because of Noriega's problems," Neil explained. "Triangle believes we couldn't make payments or something. They're happy we showed them a way to get their rivals, and since they think we're broke, they're not going to chase after us."

"God," breathed Brad. "You almost scared the life out of me."

With narrowed eyes, Scott scrutinized Lilah's face. "You're all red. Your breathing rate... are you getting the flu?"

Still unable to say a word, she shook a fist at him. As Neil exploded into laughter, she took note of Scott's capacity for subterfuge. With a straight face, too. The astrophysicist was not as innocent as he appeared at first glance.

"Everything went okay with you two?" Neil asked. "No bad moments?"

Brad smoothed his hair back. "We weren't sure you'd be able to convince them, obviously. I have to admit I was regretting the plan until I saw the gunmen rush the room."

"The hotel staff?" asked Scott.

"Staff wasn't allowed in while we were negotiating," Brad said. "So likely no collateral damage." He grimaced. "One of the men from Triangle hustled us out as soon as the shooting started. I thought we might have to sit there through it all. Anyway, they said they'd take care of things and leave us out of it."

"I doubt Triangle would've hurt the staff," said Lilah. "The gang leadership would want businesses to feel they'll be kept safe by cooperating. If not, the police will eventually get dragged in."

"So things went as we hoped," said Neil, immense satisfaction in his tone. "We won!"

They certainly did. Lilah almost couldn't believe it. Flanked by the twins, she followed Brad into the ferry terminal. Alex and Victor spotted them easily, and as soon as they got near, melded in next to them into the stream of passengers walking toward the waiting boat. Alex eyed her, a quizzical expression on his face.

"What?" she asked, helplessly smiling. He'd delivered on promises this time... poor Alex. He almost always kept his word. Even in Cuba, he'd only done what he thought was best for everyone.

"Told you so," Victor said, his words puzzling her.

Alex frowned, then sniffed. "I don't smell any alcohol." After a few seconds, he added, "Must be the adrenaline rush."

Oh, no. That was not it. Lilah wanted to throw her head back and laugh. "I missed you," she said to Alex. She'd also missed a certain coffee-eyed man. Badly.

The look of approval on Victor's face suddenly faded. At her side, Brad stiffened.

Flushing, Alex said, "I've been gone only an afternoon."

This time, Lilah did laugh. "It felt like you were on *Olympus* for months... *years*. Now, it's finally over." Not quite. She never imagined anything could be worse than their arrest and the subsequent interrogation, but the last few months... they'd been horrible. No matter. The ordeal *would* be over as soon as Harry arranged a pardon. He was working with Lupe Valdez to do it. Lilah would return home and assume charge of her own life, of her own destiny. The personal happiness she'd taught herself not to expect would be hers for the taking.

Through the glass windows of the boat, she watched the rain mercilessly pelt the sea. The waters of the ocean rose up to meet the storm. Her eyes drifting shut, Lilah murmured, "Hurry up, Harry."

Chapter 41

A few hours later, 11 AM

Long Island, New York

When Grayson Sheppard, lawyer to the exiles, called Harry a couple of days ago to request the presence of "Miss Valdez" at a meeting in Temple's home, everyone knew it was surely about Lilah and the rest.

As the network's chairman, there were a million things Harry needed to attend to... Steven Kingsley's kidnapping for one. Harry didn't know what to make of it, and the feds weren't inclined to talk. It didn't mean the cops didn't have questions for *him*. So did governments across the planet. There was even speculation about the hand of the Panamanian strongman in it, given the friction between him and the U.S. political establishment. The few sources Harry had left claimed Pentagon was strongly pushing for military invasion. Thankfully for the network, Lilah and the Kingsley brothers had already moved the base of operations to New York when signs of trouble first started, maintaining the Panama office mainly for legal purposes. Still, markets went wild following Steven's abduction, and business executives were panicking. Harry's phone stayed in use day and night. One of the calls he made was to Lupe, and Liam came along to New York City at her request.

Confusing all three of them, Grayson asked Harry to figure out which was the hungriest gang—or triad—in Macau, after 13BC and Peace Guard. Speed was of utmost importance, Grayson stressed. He requested Lupe to send the gang's leadership an invitation to her club. Oh, yeah, there would be a couple of men visiting the club the same night: Nigel and Sebastian Coppersmith.

Harry and Liam eyed each other. Grayson had to be talking about the exiles. They were in Macau? Where Eden opened only recently? Did they pick the city after learning about Harry and Lupe's supposed relationship from the yellow press? Or was it simply coincidence? Anyone in the entertainment business—like Lupe—would consider Macau a prime target, *and* it happened to be a good place to hide from the U.S. government. But why were they meeting a gang? That, too, right after Steven was kidnapped from Thailand?

Grayson did not answer Harry's unasked questions. Harry, Liam, and Lupe stayed put in New York to know the outcome of whatever it was Grayson arranged between the exiles and the Triangle Triad. If any calls came through about what happened, it would be to Temple's line.

When it was time for the meeting in Macau, Harry turned his cell phone off. Those who wanted to talk to the network's chairman would be forced to wait a couple of hours. Eyeing the clock on the wall, he gulped ice-cold Coke. It did nothing to soothe the fear knotting his guts. The other occupants of the library in President Temple's home were equally tense, waiting for the phone on the coffee table to ring.

Liam was in the chair on Harry's right with Lupe on his left. On the couch, Noah Andersen and Grayson Sheppard conversed in muted tones, Temple silent between them. He'd returned home from the hospital weeks ago, his doctors having said there was nothing more to be done except speech therapy which might or might not help. The worry in his companions' demeanor was reflected in his eyes, mixed in with confusion and the frustration at not having a clue what was going on.

"This is killing me," Liam muttered.

The shrill ring of the telephone interrupted the relative quiet. Picking it up, Grayson greeted the caller and immediately handed the device to Lupe.

Lupe's side of the conversation was stilted. Her eyes were worried when she hung up with a terse "Thank you." Turning to Harry, she said, "The Triangle Triad left a message with my manager that the Coppersmiths are fine. Their kidnapped cousins have been rescued."

Hand to his forehead, Grayson muttered, "Phew." Noah laughed in relief. Eyeing his friend, Temple smiled.

"Wait a second," Liam said. "Cousins? This was a rescue mission? For *Steven and Charles?* What the hell for?"

Computing quickly, Harry said, "I'm beginning to get the picture. Whoever kidnapped Steven dragged our group into it. They would've been blamed for anything happening. Thanks to Lupe—" Harry threw a quick glance at her face and noted the pallor. "Something wrong?"

"The Triangle boss asked the manager to convey his gratitude to me for helping them in their 'business' with the other two gangs," she said. "What if—"

"If 13BC or Peace Guard starts problems, we'll deal with it through legal channels," Harry assured her. "The Chinese are in the process of taking over Macau. They're not going to want any trouble. If the cops can't help, I already told you I'll cover any losses."

"Which brings us to the other little matter," Grayson said, standing. "Miss Valdez, do you need to freshen up?"

Lupe stood to face him and smoothed the jacket of her cream-colored skirt suit. With gloved hands, she straightened her shoulder pads and adjusted the matching hat with the little veil. "No, I'm as ready as I'll ever be."

"You, Harry?" Grayson asked.

"I'm good," Harry responded, taking his place next to Lupe. Business suits worked for most occasions.

The rest clustered around. Liam muttered but didn't raise further objections.

"I still think your sister should be here," Noah said to Harry.

"Need to know, only," Lupe interjected. "It's bad enough she overheard me talking to Harry... I was upset at the time. If word gets out, it won't be good for business." Lupe had explained it to Harry before. The proprietress of Eden could not be seen as "taken."

Grayson began, "Dearly beloved, we're gathered here today..."

Part XV

Chapter 42

Late April 1989

Upper East Side, New York City

Patience wearing thin, Richard repeated, "I couldn't wait to follow Alex and Victor at the time." Godwin Kingsley was pacing up and down his office room. Steven and Charles, their faces still pale from the recent ordeal, were silent in their respective chairs. "My first priority was to make sure Steven and Charlie were still alive," Richard explained. "Then, I needed to get them to a hospital. I couldn't wait around to check on Alex and Victor."

"Macau police would've taken Steven and Charlie to the hospital," Godwin thundered. "Mr. Armor... first, you arranged this trip against my advice. Next, when Steven was kidnapped, you got your friends in the military to threaten some Danish journalist into revealing Prince's location. Through dumb luck, you ended up getting exactly what you wanted, which was the hiding place of the exiles. What sense did it then make to *let them out of your sight?*"

"We can find them again," Richard said.

"How?" asked the former justice. "I'm sure they left Macau the same day. They'll have new identities by now, which means we're back to where we started. All thanks to your poor judgment."

Did Richard ever imagine Godwin's recent affection would be anything but fleeting, dependent entirely on doing what the former justice found pleasing? At the same time, if the safety of his heir didn't matter to Godwin, what was the son of a chauffeur to expect?

Richard shook his head. "They would've had to use the same passports to exit Macau, or the immigration officials would've wanted to know why there was no entry stamp. We know they likely arrived in Macau not long after they left Ecuador. All we have to do is cross-check entry records for the time with the exit records for the day they left. The first place they would've gotten to is Hong Kong. It is also under China now, so they would've had no choice but to use the same passports at the entry port, or again, the officials would ask how they traveled between Macau and Hong Kong with no stamps from either place. So on and on. I assure you we can easily figure out where they're headed."

"Mr. Armor," bit out Godwin. "You keep assuring me of this or that. Harry escaped the man you appointed to take care of him during the mess in Cuba. Lilah walloped you in court during the interrogation. Brad's stupidity was what won the day for you then."

Lilah Kingsley argued successfully against the former supreme court justice as well, but Godwin would never acknowledge it.

"You and Steven insisted you could find Brad and Lilah after they left Quito," the Kingsley patriarch continued raging. "They beat you a third time. My sources tell me Harry and the Valdez women were in Temple's home during the entire fiasco in Macau. There's no question they were all involved in it whatever it was Alex and Victor were doing with Prince. Armor, you're simply not as clever as you imagine yourself to be. Harry—an enlisted man—outsmarted you. Again! West Point made a mistake with you."

Impotent... there was no word more suited to describing how Richard felt at the moment. The media reports of the Thailand incident were bad enough. Newspapers ran stories about Steven and Charles harassing local women and Richard running away when the group got into trouble. The rumor started on the pages of *The Big Apple Reporter*, Petty Officer Sheppard's go-to tabloid. Tossing every damned magazine which carried the tale into the shredder did nothing to assuage Richard's humiliation, his fury, the feeling of utter powerlessness. Neither he nor Steven could contradict the fabricated narrative to defend themselves without risking the real story leaking via any of the parties involved.

Even the feds believed most of it, and Steven's rescue was assumed to be the chance outcome of an encounter between Prince and the triads which ran Macau's streets. A lucky break for the network. Major Armor, decorated officer, allegedly sat on his hands while all this was happening. Then, to be told he was inferior to a trickster like Harry Sheppard!

"I will find Brad and his brothers," Richard vowed through clenched teeth. "It's not going to matter what Sheppard does. I *am* going to find them. It won't take long."

"It had better not," said Godwin.

"Grandfather," Steven spoke up, voice still fatigued. "Prince cannot travel to China or India because of all the drug-smuggling charges on him. Since Brad and the rest are going to have to keep out of Prince's way, those countries are our best bet."

Richard leaned forward in his chair. "China has no extradition treaty, but your cousins will face problems there... the recent political troubles. They won't want to take the risk. India does have an extradition agreement, and they have stricter border control, but it will be easier for all the Kingsleys to blend in if they pick one of the big cities. Plus, Mrs. Kingsley has relatives in the country. The CIA report on Alex's trip to India mentioned a General Mittal... he's her cousin. Either China or India, but I'm betting on India. We'll have them in a week or two. A month at the most."

It took less than a month.

Chapter 43

"We need a few days to finalize some arrangements on this side," Richard said to his contact over the phone. "Let them overstay the visa, and you keep a close eye on things. If they try to leave, have them arrested, but under no circumstances should they be identified as Kingsleys. Let them continue to think they've fooled everyone."

When he hung up, Steven asked from the couch, "I thought our plan for Harry is ready to go?"

"It is," said Richard. "Will Luce is going to do exactly as asked. McCoy will make sure of it. What's remaining is for us to decide on a convenient date."

"Poor Lilah," Steven muttered. "I feel kinda bad for her. She's the only one who never signed on to Brad's... wish there were a way out of this which didn't involve her."

"Stupid Lilah," Richard corrected. "Don't forget she laughed at you for falling into the pool. Despite it, you did offer her a way out. You asked her to come to our side. She refused to be reasonable."

"Got any more of the Scotch, Rich?" Steven asked. "I want to get so wasted I don't remember any of it. Wake me when everything's done."

Watching Steven chugging down whiskey, Richard dialed another number.

"No excuses this time," Godwin warned over the phone.

"I'll get it done," swore Richard. It was no longer merely for Steven. Sheppard might have outsmarted Richard a time or two, but the final triumph was what counted. Major Richard Armor would win the war.

"At least Temple's out of the game," said Godwin. "Count yourself lucky. Of all the pieces on the board, he'd be the most difficult to manage. But I don't expect you to understand."

Richard gritted his teeth. Yeah, the chauffeur's son had been too busy making his own way in the world to indulge in chess. Still, he understood real-life games well enough.

"Lilah is boxed in," continued Godwin. "She doesn't have the power to move around as she pleases, but Temple still has clout. He might have helped them get to a different place. Fortunately for you, they made a few mistakes."

Petty Officer Sheppard approaching Lupe Valdez for assistance turned out to be a major unforced error. Now, the woman he trusted to help him would watch mutely while the woman he was fighting for walked unwittingly to her death.

"A blunder," mused Godwin. "The Beijing Blunder."

Part XVI

Chapter 44

June 2, 1989

Crown Heights, Brooklyn, New York

The roach crawled across the countertop toward the empty pizza box. His two mates were not far behind. Chewing the last bit of the sausage pie, James McCoy slapped the insects hard with the rolled-up newspaper. Satisfied, he noted that the latex gloves he'd been instructed to keep on at all times didn't affect his grip.

Home, sweet home, he thought, looking around. The peeling paint on the living room walls, the grease-stained stove in the open kitchen, the cracked vinyl on the floor—all reminded him of his childhood in Hell's Kitchen. Outside the window, he could hear an argument going on. A couple of young punks were fighting over some girl when they should have been in school. The dumpster across the street overflowed with rotting garbage, its stench seeping in through the ill-fitting window sashes.

A combination of grit and gray matter and dumb luck had taken McCoy from a slum similar to this to the top spot in one of Morocco's oil trading companies. The first step involved working for a bookkeeper, learning all the best ways to break a limb. He'd been so good at his job he was offered a position protecting the gang boss. McCoy vowed he was ready to take a bullet for the man, but his poor old mother needed financial security in the form of a gas station in Jersey. The boss laughed, knowing McCoy's mother had been in prison for years. He got the gas station he wanted *and* the job title of Assistant Security Officer.

Somehow, McCoy managed to stay below radar sweeps by the cops. Through the gas station, he branched into counterfeiting. From there, he bought more gas stations. Life was good. Then, the boss and his immediate circle got arrested on racketeering charges. McCoy's name found mention as a person of interest, and he decided it was time to get out of the country.

He sold his chain of gas stations and was looking around for a worthwhile investment when he heard about Gateway. The company was expanding, looking for partners outside the United States. McCoy jumped at the chance. The business in Morocco was owned partly by him and partly by Gateway.

To this day, McCoy couldn't tell why he decided to steal from the Sheppards when everything was going so well. He could pinpoint the exact date, though. He talked to Will Luce, the man who'd been reduced from one of Gateway's biggest shareholders to a clerk in the accounting division, working for Hector Sheppard. Curious because he'd heard the story of the downfall, McCoy asked what happened once Will's daughter married Harry Sheppard. A litany of complaints followed.

Luce played cards his entire life. In fact, Will, the youngest of several children, was kept on a short financial leash until his old man kicked the bucket well into his nineties. Almost all the money Will inherited immediately went into Gateway, a new business at the time. The gamble paid off, and Will Luce got himself plenty of loose cash to play with. If he weren't stupid enough to get drunk and agree to the dumb poker game with Harry... Will had his suspicions on what exactly was in the drinks. Thanks to the one bad decision, he was branded a loser even by his own son and daughter. The tirade ended in a hopeless mutter about missing the big game with his old friends.

McCoy's offer to lend money had been done on purpose... out of an urge to start mischief. Will won the pot. And the next one. When McCoy heard about the third game, he agreed again to lend cash, but this time, for a percentage of the winnings. Unfortunately, Will lost.

McCoy made some rapid calculations. He could forgive the debt without missing much. Or even wait until Will paid him back from the small salary he earned. But McCoy knew gamblers like Will were never really able to quit. He would at some point end up stealing to feed his habit. Most likely, from his employer.

When McCoy called Will with a better plan, he didn't even hesitate. In Will's mind, taking from the Sheppards was justified since Harry Sheppard took his stock from him. Only, *Will* wouldn't be doing the stealing. McCoy would with a small percentage going to Will for covering his tracks through the accounting division.

Then, Will surprised McCoy. He listed the names of a few other partners of Gateway who'd lent him money to gamble. Thus, their enterprise grew.

When Harry Sheppard decided to expand, Will was the one to tuck the names of his coconspirators into Hector's list of executives to warn against accepting. This sent Harry careening in the wrong direction, suspecting his brother of crimes he didn't have any part in.

The punks, Neil Kingsley and Daniel Barrons, had still shown up to negotiate. Unfortunately, if McCoy agreed to sell a percentage to the network as Harry wanted, he'd have to open the books. All the discrepancies would be revealed. The poisoning attempt might have worked, except for the Muslim friend of theirs who didn't take a single sip of the wine. McCoy was arrested and extradited.

He didn't say a word to the cops about Will Luce. What would have been the purpose? Also, it was satisfying to learn Harry accused Hector of orchestrating the murder attempt. Still, being in prison was really not McCoy's style. Over the years, he'd grown accustomed to the comforts of a good life. Unfortunately, he couldn't see a way out of it. Until Rickie Brennan showed up at Rikers, claiming to be an old buddy from Hell's Kitchen.

Garbed in shiny black leather and metal accessories, the man gave all the appearance of being enamored by McCoy. It didn't take him long to understand good old Brennan was no idiot fag. If he were actually from McCoy's old neighborhood, he would've been the king of hell.

Brennan declined to share how he figured out Will Luce was involved in the embezzlement, but the fag gave the pathetic defense lawyer enough financial incentive to get moving on the appeal. If it weren't enough, McCoy was now out on bail, a rare thing to happen after conviction as the defense attorney told him in awe. McCoy was sure Brennan—whatever his real name was—possessed money and clout. His target was Harry Sheppard. Which suited McCoy just fine, since he too harbored a hankering to see the bastard dead. Will Luce was the key to it all.

Wiping his mouth off with the rough napkin provided by the pizza place, McCoy threw it to the side. He checked his watch. Almost time. When he went to the window, the man he was expecting was already turning the corner into the street, hesitating before the large building which housed low-income tenants.

The knock came, and McCoy jerked open the door, taking care to keep his gloved hands hidden. With a gleeful smile, he greeted Harry's former father-in-law. "William Luce, we finally meet."

Chapter 45

Later in the day on June 2, 1989

Eden, Washington, DC

Pausing at the door between Paradise and Oasis, Lupe muttered a particularly foul curse under her breath. The loathsome insect, Charles Kingsley, was in the club. Why? He never approached her for sexual favors on his own before and not at all after her contract with JD ended. Charles was a Kingsley, but he followed JD's orders on most things. The politician's wariness about being seen too often with Lupe was surely behind Charles keeping away—which meant his presence tonight was also authorized by JD.

She eyed Charles, now jovially conversing with a couple of businessmen.

Lupe fought the urge to turn to the side and spit. Briefly, she considered having him thrown out. But no, she couldn't do it. JD would most certainly retaliate. She'd already created enough enemies with the mess in Macau. What she needed was to figure out ways to somehow keep JD from attacking her. The wedding, for instance.

Mrs. Harry Sheppard. Lupe still couldn't believe it. If there was a time in her life when she'd dreamed of being Mrs. Somebody, she couldn't remember it. With the cheat who'd taken her virginity, it was just a matter of two lonely souls turning to each other. Or so *she'd* thought. For him, she'd only been an easy lay. There was Alex, but her ideas on the matter never progressed to any wishes for permanence. Never got the chance to.

JD's threat of deportation made the marriage necessary. Liam raised every objection he could think of. Why didn't Lupe simply take Harry on as partner? If anyone tried to deport her, she could move someplace else—Canada, perhaps—until the case went through the legal system. They could hire the best possible lawyers to represent her while Harry kept the clubs running.

"No way," Lupe had said. The clubs were her own. Harry was going to sign an airtight pre-nup giving up any claims to Lupe's business but could act as her representative in case she was left with no choice but to leave the country. There would be no such conditions the other way around. It meant if Harry decided to take advantage of her absence and do something nefarious—like sell the clubs to a proxy or such—he still couldn't force her out financially. Half of his would be hers... half of any proceeds from the clubs *and* the rest of his holdings. Other legal partnerships... who knew how the courts would rule if it ever came to a tussle between Lupe and Harry? But American law took financial agreements between married couples very seriously.

Yes, she was aware Harry was unlikely to cheat her out of her property. Yes, her argument had more holes in it than Swiss cheese. But it was the best way she could think of to save her clubs if she got deported.

All Harry said was if it was what she wanted, he'd make it happen. Liam finally agreed to hurry along the divorce process between his sister and Harry without revealing the reason behind it. The sooner Verity was out of the mess, the better, said Liam. He did ask Lupe one last time if she were sure.

Lupe was damned sure. She still didn't want the matter to be public knowledge. There was the most obvious reason of marriage being bad for business, but there was also something in her which grated against pretending undying love for a man so clearly enamored of someone else. She wondered irritably why no one else seemed to recognize it... except of course perverts like JD and Charles who reduced everything to sexual depravity. The rest of the world apparently couldn't see the depth of Harry's feelings. Lupe remembered the wedding night she'd never dreamed of.

Immigration required proof marriages were real, and though hers wasn't strictly a green card marriage, they'd thought it better to have pictures and receipts ready. Just in case. The guest bedroom in Mr. Temple's room was occupied by the lawyer, Noah Andersen. Harry's sister was in his apartment, so they opted for The Plaza.

Chapter 46

A few weeks ago, April 1989

New York, New York

Horse-drawn carriages waited on Fifth Avenue, drivers attired in top hats and waistcoats. Catching an errant tendril of hair dancing in the mild breeze, Lupe decided she would have to take a ride. Someday. It didn't seem to have occurred to Harry his brand-new wife might enjoy a romantic trip through Central Park. He was waiting for her at the top of the short flight of stairs to the front entrance of The Plaza, the doorman having collected the couple of bags from the limo driver.

There was no delay at the reception desk. In fact, they didn't even get to the reception desk before a young woman brought something for Harry to sign. Then, they were escorted to the suite. Such was the life of the privileged.

Crossing the threshold behind the valet but ahead of Harry, Lupe needed to try very, very hard not to let her jaw drop. She'd seen luxury before, but this... *this!* The spacious hall boasted of walls upholstered with blue silk damask, and an antique chandelier hung over the seating area around the fireplace. The furniture was so elegant that it could have decorated the palace of French kings.

Leaving Harry talking to the valet in muted tones, she walked from room to room, enjoying the sheer opulence of it all. The bedroom was equally magnificent with more chandeliers and a large, canopied bed.

The *pièce de résistance* was the bathroom in white marble and gold leaf. There was a step-up tub, the window next to it looking down on Central Park. Miniature bottles of toiletries were arranged aesthetically on the platform, and a dish of potpourri weighed down the pile of pristine white towels on the table next to the tub. Lupe breathed deep, letting the faint smell of roses fill her lungs.

The Astor Suite was made for lovers. Not just any kind of lovers. Ones who yearned to cocoon themselves in a world of their own, wanting to see, touch, and taste only each other. Ones who would drive each other to the brink of madness in that tub, tumble into the soft bed to tear each other apart. Ones who would cherish the memory of their wedding night for the rest of their lives together.

Half an hour later

Wearing only a short bathrobe, Lupe stood in the luxurious bathroom and soaked in the romantic sounds of saxophone drifting from the radio. Cinnamon-scented water foamed in the circular tub. A champagne bottle rested in a bucket of ice next to the tub, two flutes lined up alongside.

Tying her hair into a loose top knot, Lupe made her decision. "Harry, I need a hand in here." She grimaced. How wifely!

Silence greeted her request. Last she checked, Harry had been right outside. She'd almost given up when he appeared at the door, blazer and tie discarded, the collar of his cream, silk shirt unbuttoned. "What can I do for you?"

Dark hair and eyes, even features melding into a classically handsome face, chiseled body. Power radiated from him, and recklessness added an edge to his charm. Intense sex appeal, just like his brother-in-law, Alex, but Harry's allure was different. Raging inferno to Alex's volcanic eruption. Both equally destructive. Both irresistibly tempting to Lupe.

Her hands went to the belt of her robe. Untying it, she shrugged out of the plush, terry garment and let it fall to the floor. "I'd like some help with the bath."

Euphoria hit as she watched him take in her nudity: her full breasts, the gentle curvature of her belly, the smoothness of her limbs. Without waiting for an answer, she turned and sashayed up the steps, dipping a toe into the warm water in the tub. When she threw a glance over her shoulder, he was still at the door. His eyes were still on her body. *Phew*. At least, he wasn't running back to the living room.

"Don't simply stand there," she teased. "Or you're going to give me a complex."

Harry smiled, making her heart tumble around in excitement. Water splashed as Lupe put one foot in. He took a step forward into the bathroom. Then, another. With each of his steps, she lowered herself further into the tub. When he sat on the marble platform, her body was fully immersed, soap suds glittering on her breasts.

"Lupe, you're a beautiful woman," he stated, still smiling.

"I don't like the sound of that," she muttered.

His smile turned into a short laugh. "I find you attractive... *very* attractive... what I'm trying to say is I have a past. Things I've done and people I've hurt... and I already tried using a woman to forget all about it."

"Didn't work?" she asked, mightily curious.

"Spectacular failure," he admitted. "Ended up hurting yet another person."

"Your ex-wife," Lupe guessed.

Harry looked out through the fifth-floor window. Night was rapidly falling over Central Park. "Verity deserved more than I had in my power to give."

Cupping her right hand, Lupe picked up foam and blew on it. "The heart of a handsome and wealthy husband who by all accounts indulged her in every way possible. What more did she expect from you?" At his silence, she sighed. "You didn't, did you? Give her your heart, I mean. Because you'd already lost it to someone else?"

Without answering, Harry turned to the ice bucket and uncorked the bottle.

"Men," Lupe muttered. "Did you tell her... what's her name... Verity... before you got married?"

Harry snorted.

"I'm not joking," she said. "If you'd been honest with her from the beginning, she wouldn't have been so hurt."

Eyes crinkling, he poured champagne into the two flutes and handed her one. "I'll remember next time."

Smiling, she took a sip of the bubbly and placed the glass to one side. "You did."

"Huh?"

"You told me, didn't you? I know what to expect."

He straightened, the mirth on his face fading. "Lupe—"

She placed a soapy finger on his lips, leaving suds on his cheek. "Look at me! I'd never planned to get married, but you managed to get me to the altar. You know what they say. You break it; you own it. Time to pay up, broker man."

He surprised her by softly kissing the finger across his mouth. "I didn't come prepared, Lupe."

She laughed. "I did. Everything we need is in the bedroom. No more excuses."

When she stood, water sluicing down her limbs, he heaved himself off the steps. Then, to her shock, he swept her into his arms.

"Your clothes," she squeaked.

But Harry paid no mind. He carried her to the bedroom, dripping puddles on the floor. When he set her down right next to the canopied bed, it was to let her naked body slide down his fully covered one.

"You smell of cinnamon," he murmured, voice muffled against her neck.

He smelled of sandalwood.

His warm hands cupped her bottom, urging her closer. Her breasts grazed the silk of his shirt, and little jolts of electricity blasted through her body. Her knees suddenly weak, she asked, "You don't like my perfume?"

"Love it," he said.

"A couple of drops of oil to bathwater," she said, her soap-slick fingers leaving wet patches on his sleeves. "My whole body has the scent."

Harry drew back. Laughter in his dark eyes, he said, "You can't possibly be sure. Let me check it out for you."

So he did. They tumbled into the soft mattress. His fingers sought out every inch of her body, followed closely by his mouth. His focus was on her and her alone. His mission, to bring her pleasure. It was as though once he made up his mind about Lupe, everything else was banished from his thoughts.

Each time he paused to take a breath, her hands went to his clothes... to his pants to return the favor. But each time, he renewed his sensual assault, giving her no chance to seize control.

Through a wild haze of lust, she was aware of him stripping himself. There was the ripping sound when he opened the box of condoms on the side table. Gaze going to the silver chain he always wore around his wrist, Harry stilled. He murmured something in a language Lupe didn't understand.

She didn't intend to make any sounds, but a noisy breath escaped, somehow coming out questioning. Harry glanced up. One blink, and the lost look in his eyes was gone.

When he reached again for her, she gasped, "Lights."

"Leave them on."

Sweaty arms lifted her torso off the bed. The sudden fullness inside left Lupe gasping in pleasure. The room spun as they rolled across the bed. Shrieks of desire set the air reverberating.

When she drifted back to reality, music was still playing overhead. Right next to her, Harry sprawled on his stomach, his face buried in the pillow. Against the white sheets, his naked body gleamed.

"So vanilla," she teased, turning to lie on her side. "Not what I expected from you."

He laughed into the pillow. "Oh, yeah? I was not the one screaming loud enough to bring the roof down."

Pouting, she punched his shoulder. "You gave me no chance to... where's your tie?"

"What?"

"I prefer having men at my mercy." Her hand wandered all over his muscled back, now slick with perspiration. "I'm going to tie you up and have my way with you."

Harry stiffened. Lifting his head to look at her, he asked, "Lupe, I hope you did this with your eyes open?"

"What do you mean?" she asked, tracing the tops of his buttocks with the tip of her finger.

"I was not a good husband to Verity," he said. "I used her to forget someone else, but I also tried my best to remember who I was with in the bedroom. She was never a substitute. Are you sure it's not what you're doing with me?"

Lupe stilled, her nails digging into his flesh. With a muffled yelp, he shifted away and sat up.

Humiliation, shame, embarrassment. Feelings tumbled around in her brain, muddling her thoughts. Staring at the thin scar on his left chest as though her life depended on it, she stammered, "I... ahh... how? He told you?"

"What do you... who told me?"

"Alex!" At the prolonged silence from the broker, Lupe stared. "You tricked me," she mumbled in dawning realization. "Again!" She *let* herself be tricked into the admission. Clothes. She needed her clothes. Wild with rage, she looked about the large room.

"I didn't," Harry swore, hand over his heart. "I thought... Lupe, I was talking about something completely different."

Spotting her suitcase in one corner, she scrambled across the bed and hurried over. "Yeah, right!" With shaking hands, she yanked the zipper. It wouldn't work. After a couple of attempts, she screamed in frustration.

Harry dropped to his haunches next to her, now dressed in his pants. The belt buckle was undone. Offering her his shirt, he said, "Here."

She tugged it out of his unresisting hands and shrugged herself into it. Glaring defiantly, she used the silk sleeve to wipe the snot off her nose.

He didn't exactly laugh, but his shoulders shook with the effort to hold back amusement. "You remind me of—"

She snarled.

"Hear me out, please?"

"I am not staying here another minute, *Señor* Sheppard. I don't normally sleep with con men, and I never sleep with men who think I'm a joke!"

"I'm not a con man, and I definitely don't see you as a joke," he said. "Look, Lupe. First, let's get out of this..." He looked around wildly as though blaming the romantic décor for his behavior. "Neither of us can go anywhere tonight without risking being found out. So why don't we talk in the living room?"

They *were* stuck in the suite for the night. Sniffling quietly, she let him cajole her to the sitting space and the semicircular window seat overlooking the city streets. Stars twinkled in the summer night sky. Romantic melodies continued to play on the overhead radio. When Harry excused himself for a minute, she drew her knees up to her chin and hugged her legs. Still in his dress pants, he reappeared with the champagne from the bathroom and two fresh glasses. The tiny Eiffel Tower dangling from the silver chain around his wrist struck a glass. The scratch was so soft Lupe shouldn't have heard it, but she did.

"Bottle's already open," Harry said, tone cheerful. "If we're going to pay for it, might as well drink it all down."

"What brand?" she asked, voice hoarse from crying.

Collapsing next to her, he handed her a flute, froth bubbling off the brim. "Hmm? Krug."

"Krug?" She grabbed the bottle by its neck. "Idiot man, do you have *any* idea what it costs? Nobody's getting out of this room until the last drop is done."

It was only after they were well into their second glasses that he said, "I wasn't asking you about Alex."

There was a mild buzz in her brain, infusing her with pleasant lethargy. She didn't respond.

"I try to get as much information as possible on the people I work with. When I first met the Kingsleys, I found out Steven's sister married Jack Drummond. Then, I got to the stories of his habits in the bedroom."

Lupe mewled.

"Do you want me to stop?"

"Obviously, you already know about him and me," she said, voice tired. "Might as well finish what you want to say."

"When you said you preferred men at your mercy, I thought perhaps it was a reaction... Lupe, how badly did he hurt you?"

Stricken, she stared. Her mouth opened. She tried to tell him it hadn't been like that. She'd gone to JD, offered her body in trade. Whatever he'd done, she'd deserv—

A loud wail interrupted the radio music. It took Lupe a couple of seconds to realize the sound was coming from her throat. Weeping uncontrollably, she rocked back and forth.

Harry took the glass from her fingers and set it aside. Wrapping his arms around her torso, he let her sob against his chest. She told him about the chokeholds, the punishments for disobedience. The casual wrenching of an arm until she screamed in pain. The beatings, the cigarette burns. But each time JD called, she agreed to go with him. She never said no to anything. Not from JD and not from his pal, Charles.

"You know what I am?" she asked, voice breaking. "A whore. Just like the witch said."

"No," said Harry, tone firm. "What witch?"

She laughed, struggling out of his arms. "Is there a dictionary in the effing room? Pick it up and read the definition of whore. Someone who sleeps with men for money. That's me, get it?"

"You did what you needed to survive."

"Excuses," she spat.

"Reasons," he countered. He looked out the window, his gaze unseeing. "What if I told you I once asked a woman to marry someone else only so I could get access to his business?"

Her tirade of self-loathing sputtering to a stop, she asked, "Lilah Kingsley?"

His jaw tight, he nodded once.

"She could've said no," pointed out Lupe.

"She could've," Harry agreed, "and lived with the guilt the entirety of her life."

"Guilt?"

Then, it poured out of him. The friendship which started in their swaddling clothes, the budding romance. The deaths of her parents. The kidnapping... Harry trailed off, not elaborating on what happened between the time they were snatched and the day they finally escaped Libya, but it wasn't difficult for Lupe to guess. A woman as beautiful as Lilah—a mere girl at the time—with only her equally young boyfriend for protection. Lupe had been on her own at the same age, too. The men around saw her as fair game.

God, no, Lupe murmured in her mind, pain welling.

The years after the escape, the rekindling of a sweet, sweet love. An enemy in the shadows. A world crushed under his foot. Harry witnessed for himself the extent of the horror unleashed by a monster with power and money, but his outrage alone wasn't enough to accomplish anything. "Truth without valor is useless," he said, his tone so low it was almost a whisper. "And valor without sacrifice is meaningless." His soulmate would be the sacrifice.

Lupe shook her head, her heart breaking. "No," she murmured again.

Harry explained, "Without Lilah's help..."

Without her help, Jared Sanders would have continued his tyrannical reign, condoning the sale of children into sex slavery, propping up despots friendly to his business. Lilah agreed to give up her own self to destroy the enemy.

Harry poured himself and his audience of one another glass of champagne each. "Then, she met Alex."

Lupe could tell Harry hadn't liked it one little bit. Whether it was because of the threat to his plans or because he considered Lilah's heart exclusively his was anybody's guess. But eventually, it worked out exactly as he wanted. Alex was thrown out of the family, his exile culminating in marriage to Harry's sister. Unknown to Harry, Alex had met Lupe.

Tone grim, Harry talked about their trip to Argentina. The unintended genocide.

"The Puelche?" Lupe asked, sitting up. "In Neuquén?"

"Yeah. You're from around there, right?"

She swallowed hard. How much did he know?

"Told you already," Harry continued. "I investigate everyone I work with. You lived with your mother in the city. It's only a mile or so from the Puelche village. Are you familiar with the tribe?"

Familiar? She was... "Did the old woman die? The machi?"

"You *do* know them. And no, she didn't."

Damn. The witch was going to outlive everyone around her. Lupe pursed her lips, willing herself not to blurt her disappointment. "As you said, I happen to be from the neighborhood. My family kicked me out when I was fourteen." She picked up the bottle and emptied the contents into their glasses.

"You then made the trek to the U.S.?" Harry asked.

"Yup," she agreed. "Never looked back."

When she showed no signs of wanting to elaborate, he continued with his own story and took her through the brash plan to beat the triad of Temple and Godwin Kingsley and Noah Andersen.

"But Mr. Temple and Andersen are with you now?" she asked, confused.

"They changed their minds. Unfortunately, the damage was done by then."

The empire building, their adventures around the world. Rekha, the transgender woman who'd propositioned Alex and announced to the world she was Harry's lover.

Lupe laughed.

The board meeting in Panama. The encounter with a colonel... someone Harry and Lilah first met during their ordeal in Libya... once again, Harry didn't explain, but Lupe understood without a doubt the colonel was the rapist who assaulted the child Lilah. The attack on the evening of the conference, the gunshot.

"By the time I recovered, the Kingsleys had her arrested. She was dragged to the interrogation room bleeding and sore, assaulted, threatened with being stripped naked, and finally, exiled." His voice broke.

The pain in his eyes... the agony of that poor woman, Lilah... Lupe couldn't bear to contemplate.

"Truth's always worth sacrificing for," he stated. "Unfortunately, I was too fixated on my bright idea of a permanent solution to the problem children of the oil sector to spot the lies. Hell, I lied to myself. Each time something happened to make me uneasy about what we were doing, I'd rationalize it away. Because of me..." Taking a deep breath, Harry vowed, "I will never forget. Armor and the Kingsleys will pay for what they did to Lilah."

"Who's Armor?" asked Lupe.

"Steven Kingsley's bosom buddy. I told you about him before... the lawyer who was arguing against Lilah. He asked the thug—Charles Kingsley—to drag her naked to the court."

Harry talked about Steven's suggestion that Lilah switch sides.

"She refused?" Lupe asked. "I don't get it. Why didn't she try to make the same deal with Steven she had with her husband? Maybe not marriage... but a partnership? From what you said, Steven would've known his grandfather wouldn't be happy about it but still offered. To me, it suggests he was thinking she would be a stronger ally... him, Lilah, you... your brother already likes Steven, right? And Lilah's family would've supported her."

"Godwin would then team up with Brad," Harry pointed out.

Lupe shrugged. "Didn't you just tell me Brad trusted his grandfather too much? Doesn't sound like it would've been a problem for Steven. The oil deal scam wouldn't have worked on him. Except for Brad and his brothers, the rest of you could've lived in peace."

"Peace?" Harry asked. "How can we call it peace when the entire argument was about power? How can there be peace with someone like Steven who was willing to have his own family killed only to make sure he got to rule the oil sector? Yeah, we could call a ceasefire, but it wouldn't be the same as actual peace... only a compromise borne out of fear and cowardice. It wouldn't even be a true compromise. Steven would still get to be the CEO, *and* he wouldn't have to answer for his crimes. In fact, he'd be rewarded with a way to slither out from under Godwin's thumb. Lilah would never get justice for what happened. The network was meant to ensure stability, but it would end up being another tyranny." Shaking his head, Harry added, "True peace is not possible without justice and liberty and equality."

He talked about Lilah's determination to demolish the monstrous empire they created. His audacious plan to bring the exiles back. The danger they were in. The fact she was still with the same loser husband who'd been prepared to see her imprisoned or put to death than admit he was wrong.

"Half the world calls her a whore," Harry murmured.

Lupe would never shame another woman for her actions, yet she'd believed the stories about Lilah Kingsley. Guilt sent blood rushing to Lupe's cheeks, but Harry didn't notice, his mind lost somewhere in the past. In a husky whisper, she admonished, "Don't say that. Lilah did what she did for a greater cause. Whereas I..."

"What other options did you have?"

"None," she admitted. "I had—have—no formal education. I read whatever I could get my hands on and taught myself to speak well. But none of it would've guaranteed a decent living without the legal right to be in the country. I could've continued as a stripper, but age catches up."

"See? What you are is a survivor. Your club is partly a halfway home for society's misfits." He laughed. "Nikki being the prime example. Which other boss would put up with her?"

"Okay, okay," Lupe grumbled. "We're a pair, aren't we?"

"In the spirit of this newfound friendship, let's finish the champagne."

Heaving the bottle up by its neck, she peered through the dark glass. "All gone," she announced, tone mournful.

A tweet from the level of her elbow startled her. Outside the window, a brown bird perched on the sill, the breeze ruffling its feathers. The sky was turning pink. "It's morning," she said.

They staggered to the bedroom. Chandeliers flooded every corner with brightness. Crawling under the soft comforter, she complained, "Turn off the lights."

Harry was already sprawled on top of the sheets, loose-limbed and smiling. He stilled for an instant. "I prefer to keep them on. Do you mind?"

"Really?" She laughed. "You didn't want them off when we had sex, either. Afraid of the dark or something?"

"Or something," he muttered.

A giant yawn attacked Lupe. "Wha'd'you mean?" she asked.

"I like to see the lady I'm with."

"To make sure you don't get them mixed up?" she asked, laughing. "Not good, *Señor*." Her eyelids were heavy. Too heavy to hold open.

Tone steady, Harry said, "Go to sleep, Lupe."

When she woke, Harry's heavy arm was around her midriff, and the worst headache of her life was pounding away at her temples. But she couldn't wait to spring out of bed and face the day. The sordidness of her year with JD had finally been put six feet under.

Her bladder throbbed. All that champagne... she crawled out and was about to tiptoe into the bathroom when Harry stirred.

Blinking his eyes open, he grinned. "'Morning."

Her eyes went to the digital clock. "It's after twelve."

"In which case," he said, flinging aside the covers. "Let's get some lunch, and you can tell me the rest of the story."

"What 'rest'?"

"Alex... I want to know why his name was the first to occur to you."

Every pleasant feeling drained out of her. The ache in her chest returned. The broker was reaching into the deepest recesses of her heart, yanking out the sharpest pain. The story of a love that had never faded in one soul, never kindled in the other. Curiosity... was it what last night was about?

Suddenly, shame attacked. She'd confessed everything to this man. All the horrible things she let JD do to her. The money she took. She'd forever be a whore in the broker's eyes. She'd slept with him.

"I'm returning to DC today," she said, keeping her voice abrupt. "One night should be good enough evidence for the immigration people."

His smile faded. "Lupe, what—"

"I'd appreciate it if you keep your visits to a minimum. Let Liam talk to my girls for you."

After a few seconds of silence, the broker nodded. "Whatever you say. I'll be at my apartment if you need me."

Chapter 47

Back on June 2, 1989

Eden, Washington, DC

Lupe shrugged herself out of the reverie. It was all right that Harry obeyed her instructions for once and didn't call. Forever after had never been part of her plans and certainly not with Harry Sheppard. In the present, there was JD's pal and brother-in-law to deal with.

Forcing a politeness she didn't feel into her smile, she glided toward the table where Charles Kingsley was talking to the businessmen. There was barely concealed annoyance on the faces of Charles's companions, but they'd tolerate him for at least a few minutes before excusing themselves. The family name carried such clout.

"It's good to see you back here, Mr. Kingsley," Lupe said with none of the coquettishness she showed around JD.

One of the businessmen stood and with polite charm, held out a chair for her. Lupe's arrival also gave him and his colleague pretext to escape Charles's company. Once the businessmen left, Charles didn't wait. Blowing a smoke ring, he asked, "JD wants to know how things are going with Sheppard."

A phone call from Charles asking the same question would've sufficed instead of imposing his vile presence on her. She managed half a nod. "Ahh... Harry still visits."

Sparing a moment to leer at a passing employee, the Kingsley idiot returned his attention to Lupe. "What did he tell you about his plans?"

"I... nothing. I haven't heard anything."

His eyes narrowed. "JD said Sheppard took you to visit Temple and Andersen."

Of course the politician was having her watched. At least her marriage wasn't public news, since only the four witnesses in the know besides the bride and the groom. "They were talking about Mr. Temple's health... that's all."

With a near-giggle, Charles said, "I don't believe you. You went to the house and spent all the time there discussing the old man's health?"

"Maybe they didn't want to bring up anything in my presence." Poor excuse, but it was all that occurred to her.

Charles blinked at her for a couple of seconds. "You know JD wouldn't like it if you lied, don't you?"

"I wouldn't dare," Lupe said, allowing a trace of bitterness to creep into her voice.

"But you did go with Sheppard to the hotel." Charles laughed, repugnant excitement in his demeanor. "The Plaza! He's trying to diddle things out of you."

Her stomach clenched, threatening to upchuck its contents. Trust scum like Charles and JD to turn even the sweetest of memories into something sordid.

Charles laughed maniacally once again. "I gotta admit Sheppard has style. Even when he's screwing someone over. *Literally.*" Adjusting himself in his chair, he mused, "JD and I were talking about

Sheppard and Lilah. Maybe he's done her. He say anything to you about it?"

Quickly, Lupe countered, "They're friends."

"Friends." Charles giggled. "JD's seen her only a couple of times. He talked about having a go at her."

As though a woman like Lilah would have given the bastard the time of day! Not that using force had ever been beyond JD. "What stopped him?"

"Are you kidding me?" asked Charles, his tone shifting to morose with lightning speed. "Did you hear what the woman did when she was arrested? No respect for authority. She got me into trouble. Imagine if JD tried anything before the arrest. Also, Mr. Temple. He was the president. He could've finished JD's career. Now..."

A jolt of fear ran through Lupe. Now, Lilah's connections had abandoned her. Temple was incapacitated.

"Excuse me, Ms. Valdez," said a voice.

She looked up to find a waiter hovering by her elbow, a cordless phone in one hand. The boy's face shone with sweat.

"There's a call for Mr. Sheppard."

"What?" she asked, confused. Why would anyone try to reach Harry at the club? His friends and family would call his home, not Lupe's place of business. As far as the public knew, he was only one among Eden's many patrons.

The waiter's fingers trembled as he handed Lupe the device. She frowned. He was a recent hire, but even recent hires were expected to present a polished manner. She'd have to talk to the manager about the kid.

Ignoring Charles's strange smirk, Lupe put the phone to her ear. "Hel—"

"Harry, m'boy," said a bluff and hearty voice. "Where have you been hiding? I've been trying to reach you."

"This is Lupe Valdez," she said, keeping her tone short. "Who's this?"

"Oh, pardon me, Miss... ma'am. This is Will Luce, Harry Sheppard's father-in-law."

No, he wasn't. Not anymore. But she let him continue.

"Er, may I speak to Harry, please? It's important."

"He's not here."

"When do you expect—"

Words dripping ice, Lupe said, "This is a club, sir. Not Mr. Sheppard's home or office."

"But he and you... you must have some idea..." The voice at the other end rose.

Once again, Lupe frowned. There was a note of desperation in Will Luce's words.

The man was Liam's father. Gentling her tone, she said, "As far as I know, Mr. Sheppard is at home in New York City."

"I tried the home number," said Will Luce. "No one's picking up."

Lupe rolled her eyes, remembering the promise Liam extracted from Harry not to even talk to Will Luce. Neither Harry's sister nor Liam's picked up the phone these days, only returning messages left on the answering machine if they needed to talk to the caller. Harry had also adopted the same *m.o.*

"Please, you have to help me." Will Luce's words ended on a sob.

What the— Gambling, of course. She'd heard enough of Liam and Harry's conversations to know Will Luce harbored a weakness for cards. Like every addict, he'd probably gotten himself in over his head. *Poor Liam.* "Have you tried your son?"

"He refuses to talk. My daughter, too. There's no one... no one..."

Enough was enough. She needed to extricate herself from this soap opera of a conversation. "What's the number you're calling from?" she asked. "I'll see if I can reach someone."

"Oh, thank you much, ma'am," Will Luce blubbered. "But I need Harry, not my son. Liam doesn't have the... *Harry* knows people."

"Okay," she said, trying to keep the impatience out of her voice. "I'll try to reach Mr. Sheppard. Give me your number."

"Er, this is a friend's phone. Can you tell him where I'm at?" Will Luce rattled off the address to some apartment in Brooklyn. Crown Heights, to be precise.

Lupe waved the waiter to her, mouthing, "Paper." Quickly, she scribbled the address on a Post-It note. "Fine. And good night." Without waiting for a response, she hung up.

Charles was staring at her, a peculiar look in his eyes. "*Mister* Sheppard? I thought you called JD and me that only because of politics. Aren't you supposed to treat your other patrons like they're close friends?"

"*He* is not a patron," Lupe said, gaze darting toward the phone.

"Luce is rich," Charles objected. "I bet he'll be happy to visit this place once he gets his stock back. You should treat him nice. Also, I meant the way you talked about Sheppard. Why are you calling him mister? Did you have a fight?"

"No, we didn't have a fight," Lupe said, wishing she could smack the smirk off Charles's face. "I'm simply trying to keep business and personal lives separate. That's all." The band switched to a dreamy melody, Lupe's girls inviting patrons to sway along. Toto Cutugno's *"L'Italiano."* She smiled. Her introduction to the romance of jazz.

"How about a dance?" Charles asked. "For old times' sake?"

Her stomach clenched. As though she'd let the bastard taint the sweet memory. As though she'd dance with him even if all her memories were suddenly wiped out. "I promised to call Harry, so I'd better get to it. Please give my regards to JD."

When she glided away from her table, the Post-It note with the address held between her fingers, her thoughts were turbulent. There was a restlessness in her limbs as though—

"Oops," said a high-pitched voice. Nikki giggled. "Sorry, Lupe. Guess we both weren't watching where we were going."

Lupe looked around, surprised to find herself backstage.

Smile fading, Nikki asked, "Are you okay?"

Nodding, Lupe said, "Yeah, I was thinking... go onto the stage or wherever you're supposed to be. I need to catch up on some paperwork."

Something about the brief meeting with Charles... she was missing something... but what?

Chapter 48

Early hours of the morning, June 3, 1989

Her office door shut, Lupe rocked in the swivel chair, irritable and on edge despite the relative quiet. Yes, Charles made his unpleasant presence felt, but he showed up on JD's orders to make sure she toed the line. Will Luce's call was unexpected but not unexplainable. So why on earth... *I'd better let Harry know before all the Luces pitch camp on my doorstep. Maybe then I can put all these people out of my mind.*

Sighing, she reached for the phone, eyeing the Post-It note with Luce's address on it. When the machine came on, she said, "Harry, this is Lupe. There was a call for you from—" Maybe she was jumpy because she was feeling guilty about her abruptness to a man she'd come to like and respect. If morbid curiosity were the only reason behind his question about Alex, he wouldn't have confessed his own past. Perhaps talking to him would clear her mind. "Call me back, please? It's important."

Sliding the side drawer open, she eyed the carton of Virginia Slims. Lupe quit smoking in her early twenties but always kept one pack as an emotional crutch. Thankfully, her will turned out to be stronger than the call of nicotine. Tonight, though... her fingers itched with the need to hold a cigarette to her lips.

The phone rang. Slamming the drawer back in, Lupe grabbed the handset. "Hello?"

"Are you all right?" Harry asked, not bothering with a greeting. "You sounded anxious."

With a relieved little laugh, she sat back. "I've been the same all evening. Harry, I'm sorry about walking out on you the way I did. At The Plaza, I mean." Innocuous enough phone conversation between supposed lovers, and Harry didn't raise objections about security.

"Morning after regret?" he asked, voice teasing.

"Don't say such things out loud," she admonished. "The pocket Venus might hear you."

There was surprised silence from the other end, followed by, "Sabrina?" He guffawed. "She's my baby sister, not my babysitter."

"Whatever," Lupe said. "She doesn't like me."

"You got her pegged from one meeting? She's merely worried about all the gossip and what Li—"

"What some other people are going to think," Lupe finished. "Do *you* have regrets?"

"No," he said. "Yes. I don't know... Lupe, some questions are better left unasked."

"You warned me already," she said, unsure if she were irritated or amused at the sudden wariness in his tone. "You're crazy in love with someone from your past."

"'In love,'" he mimicked. "There should be another word for it."

"Okaaay. A woman you have feelings for. How else should I have put it?"

"Verity—my ex-wife—asked me more or less the same thing. Do I love... uhh... her? When we were young, I thought I needed to tie her to me, body and soul. Since then... it doesn't seem to matter whether she's married to someone else, whether *I'm* married. It's enough to know she exists. Without her, I'd probably wither away. Is it what everyone calls love? Seems like there should be a stronger word to describe it."

Lupe's eyebrows rose. "She feels the same about you?"

Chuckling, Harry said, "She once called me a bad habit."

"Poor lady," Lupe muttered.

"What's that supposed to mean?"

"It means you, Harry Sheppard, have a thick head. She was telling you her feelings for you are so strong she has little hope of breaking free. No matter how much you hurt her."

Harry admitted, "I've done plenty of hurting." He laughed. "Not like she doesn't have claws. She could rip me into little pieces if she wanted to. She's done it a couple of times. You remind me of her now and then."

Lupe's lips quivered in a helpless sputter of laughter. "I have a feeling you think it's a compliment."

"Why not?" Harry asked.

"Idiot man, never compare your current to your ex."

"Can't wait until you two meet. Then you'll see."

"How did you *ever* get any woman to go out with you?"

"They felt sorry for me," he said, tone appropriately humble.

Lupe exploded with mirth. Wiping tears of hilarity from her cheeks, she said, "Thank you for making me feel better."

"Glad to be of service. Now, let me get some sleep. I have a morning meeting with... uhh... a couple of important people."

"Wait," she said. "I almost forgot. Your father-in... *ex*-father-in-law... called."

"He called the club?" Harry asked, surprise and irritation in his voice. "Sorry, Lupe. I'll make sure he doesn't bother you. You already have enough to deal with."

"No, Harry, hear me out. The man—Luce—sounded strange. Some kind of trouble, I think. He didn't even want to talk to Liam... said only *you* could help... some emergency."

Harry huffed in annoyance. "Cards, probably. All right, I'll check it out."

She read off the address for him, wishing him a good night before hanging up.

Lupe didn't feel like leaving the peaceful solitude of the office, so she sat spinning the globe on her desk with her finger. A club in Paris in a few years, one in Sydney... she'd come a long way from Neuquén. *God knows where I'd be if I followed orders and stayed.*

Lilah had obeyed orders. Her life was vaguely similar to Lupe's, both of them half-breeds in a white man's world. Lupe was regarded as an outsider by both sides while Lilah... her family background and money made sure race didn't matter. The fact she was stunning to look at of course helped, but the only color which really counted was the color of cold hard cash.

Still, her initiation into adulthood was similar to Lupe's with the death of her parents. Just like Lupe, Lilah survived the assault on her body and emerged triumphant. Like Lupe's own family, those around Lilah also made demands on how she ought to live her life. Everyone used her as a pawn. She let them. She willingly sacrificed her heart to destroy a monster.

Not Lupe. She'd have laughed in the face of any lover who asked her to take on so much pain. Harry was a nice man, but he'd offered up his soulmate as sacrifice. The constant torment Lilah must be living with... her spine was surely made of steel. After the mess in Cuba, she could've chosen the easy way out. She could've stayed back in the U.S. with Harry, safe in the circle of his arms. *Lupe* would have. Instead, Lilah took on the weight of atoning for the mistakes of the past. What kind of resolve did it take? How could any human volunteer to go through such hell?

Lupe hoped they did get to meet someday. The first thing she'd do was poke at Lilah's arm to make sure she was flesh and blood. Lupe was having a hard time believing Lilah was not one of the mythical goddesses from the Native American stories she heard in Argentina.

Silly child! Reprimanding herself for the unexpected flight of fantasy, Lupe heaved herself off the swivel chair. Her eyes snagged on the Post-It note. The itchy feeling in her chest returned. Lupe growled in frustration. What the hell was wrong with her tonight?

Charles's visit, the phone call. On top of all that, the annoyance of having a waiter lacking in waiterly skills! He didn't even remember to tell her who it was on the line. What if the caller had been someone she intended to avoid? What if he or she were someone who wanted to discuss something private? Some even demanded Lupe avoid mentioning their names where others could overhear. *I have to talk to the manager. I want to know how the kid got hired.* A lot of the young men who applied for jobs in Eden were no more than spoiled brats who were there to ogle at strippers without paying for the privilege. They invariably messed up.

In front of a patron, too! The fact that she loathed Charles was immaterial; they still needed to live up to the club's reputation for smooth sophistication. Instead, the waiter thrust the phone at her without—

Her thoughts screeched to halt. Something had been off in that whole encounter. Sitting back down, she closed her eyes, trying to visualize what happened.

Excitement flared in Charles's eyes when he talked about Harry. That was to be expected. The waiter's arrival... the hitch in the boy's breath, the sheen of sweat on his face... the phone... the peculiar look in Charles's gaze. *Why?*

The conversation with Will Luce. Her offer to call Liam and/or Harry. Writing the address on the note. Charles's admonishment to treat Will Luce better.

Lupe's eyes snapped open. How had Charles known the identity of the caller? Her mind rewound another time through the evening's happenings. The waiter never mentioned the name, but did *she?* Lupe had been distracted by memories at the time, but she didn't think so.

The chair squeaked when she shoved it back. Heart thundering, she stood. Stiletto heels clicked rapidly on hardwood. Securing the deadbolt, Lupe ran to the phone and dialed Harry's number.

"Harry, call back, please. Right now. It's an emerg—"

A click sounded in her ear. Sabrina Kingsley's curt voice asked, "What do you want, Ms. Valdez?"

In the background, the answering machine said something in Harry's voice. Ignoring it, Lupe asked, "Where's Harry? I need to speak to him *now!*"

"*You* called and sent him someplace."

"He left already? Never mind, I'll ring his cell."

"He's not driving," Sabrina said. "My brother didn't get around to switching to the new flip model, and there's no point taking the DynaTAC on the train. There would be very little charge left by the time he gets where he wants to go."

"Heh?"

Sabrina's impatient huff was audible. "Harry doesn't have his cell phone on him. When he gets home, I'll let him know you called."

Lupe screeched, "You don't understand—"

"What?" snapped Sabrina, brusqueness morphing into outright rudeness.

Briefly, Lupe contemplated telling Alex's wife about her suspicions, then discarded the idea. It would accomplish nothing good. Sabrina would either go chasing after her brother, or she'd send the fellow who was supposed to be guarding her and her son. What if the enemy had someone watching Harry's apartment? They were clearly keeping an eye on Lupe. If the Kingsleys realized Sabrina and the baby were alone and unprotected... no. The pocket Venus was related by marriage to JD and Charles, but she didn't have a clue what they were like in the dark, and Lupe didn't want her finding out. "I'll ring Liam," Lupe said.

She still tried Harry's cell, but the call didn't go through. It took her trembling finger three attempts to get the sequence of numbers right to Liam's phone. The answering machine told her he was out of the country for a couple of days. *"Merde!"* This would be the one night! But he lived in DC, anyway. Not New York.

Who else? Who else? The cops? There was a good chance they'd only laugh at her, especially when a congressman was involved. Maybe the lawyer, Grayson Sheppard, could call them? No, Noah Andersen was a better bet.

A thought occurred to Lupe, and she eyed the phone in fear. *My God! What if it* is *bugged?* She hadn't said anything so far which could get her into trouble, but if she did manage to reach Andersen, she'd have to be very specific. If JD, somehow, got to know...

There was a phone booth at the corner of the street, and she could take one of the security guards with her. Grabbing a fistful of quarters from the coin dish on her desk, she hurried outside. No Charles in Paradise or Oasis. *Gracias a Dios.* The bastard probably thought having the phone bugged was enough. Lupe sprinted toward the security desk by the front door, not bothering to pretend sophistication. Waiters gaped at her; customers stared openmouthed.

An arm shot out, blocking her way. "I don't think you should leave, Ms. Valdez," said a voice. "It's dangerous outside at night."

In shock, she stared at the new waiter leaning casually against the wall by the door, a sneer on his face. The nervousness from earlier in the evening was nowhere in evidence. *A spy? In my own home?* How had he been allowed in without the manager's knowledge?

"Wait for the morning," the spy advised. "Everything will be back to normal."

The extra security she hired... they were involved in this plot? Her girls, her staff? She refused to believe it... but someone had broken her trust and helped the spy get the job. The walls of the room converged on her. Without a word, Lupe wheeled around and returned backstage.

The club she built with her sweat and blood had turned into a prison. If she obeyed orders, she could get it back. The spy said so, didn't he? Everything would go back to normal if she did nothing and let Harry walk into the trap waiting for him. He used to be in the military and even won medals for whatever he did. He'd know how to fight off an ambush, and he wouldn't be caught by surprise given the kind of enemies he was up against. Also, Harry said over and over he didn't want Lupe to risk herself or her girls. He'd understand... if he remained alive after tonight. If he didn't...

All of Lilah's sacrifices would be in vain. If Harry had it right, Lilah wouldn't even be allowed to survive long after his death. The Kingsleys would win. Men like JD would rule the world. JD... oh, God. JD had said he wanted a "go" at Lilah. Was it why Charles came to the club alone tonight? Was JD someplace else, licking his chops at the thought of Lilah?

Lupe made one more trip to her office. First, she took every single bit of paper concerning Alex and fed it to the shredder. If the criminals broke into her office while she was away, they wouldn't find anything to link him to her. Then, she scribbled a quick note on her personal stationery and folded the paper multiple times. Tucking it neatly under the statue of Virgin Mary, Lupe crossed herself. "Hide it from them," she admonished the mother of God. The votive candle glowed brightly.

The front door was guarded by the spy, and she was quite sure the trade and emergency exits would also be manned. She took the stairs to her apartment and opened the sash window to stare down at the small plot behind the building. There was no one there. *Madre de Dios!* She never realized she was up this high. Well... she hadn't pole-danced from the time she was sixteen for nothing. Even if Lupe no longer stripped for money, she was actively involved in coaching her girls.

"Looks so damned easy in the movies," she grumbled, tying sheets together and fastening the rope thus fashioned to the leg of her bed.

Somehow, she managed to slither down. The difficult part was squeezing sideways through the unlit gap between the club building and the next. Bricks scraped her back, tearing through the silk of her gown. Her skin burned. She could swear she stepped on something dead. The stench was so thick she gagged more than a couple of times. She'd have to throw away the stilettoes after this rescue mission. Pity. They were Manolos.

There would be plenty of people on the sidewalk, so Lupe didn't worry about walking all the way to the corner where the telephone booth was. She hadn't taken a step out to the pavement when a force landed on her shoulder, shoving her back into the gap.

Her face hit brick, sending pain blasting into her skull. The light from the street disappeared as a shadowy form moved into the gap.

From the side, the assailant slammed his hand over her mouth and nostrils.

No, this isn't happening, Lupe thought wildly. She clawed at the fingers but struck only rubber. Desperately, she bit as hard she could, but the hand didn't budge. Her legs flailed, but she wasn't allowed to fall, held up against the wall by her chin and neck.

Time lost all meaning. It could have been a minute or an hour when she heard a familiar voice on her other side. "You thought you were clever," said Charles, giggling.

"Charles, please..." she begged, her words muffled by the gloved hand.

"Shut up," her captor said.

"*I* wanna do it," said Charles, and jerked her toward him by the elbow.

Her captor released his hold. Lupe had taken one big gulp of air when Charles's arm circled her neck from behind. *God, oh, God!* Was he going to kill her? She opened her mouth to scream.

Something glinted in the darkness; steel hissed. Heat shot across her throat.

"JD doesn't like disobedient women," said Charles. "I don't, either. You've been bad, Lupe."

Gurgling, Lupe slid to the ground, blood gushing from her severed carotids. Her last thought before she succumbed to death was strangely of two women, neither of who she'd ever met. *Hide, sister!* Lupe screamed at Lilah. Dios te salve, María, llena eres de gracia—

Part XVII

Chapter 49

June 3, 1989, just before dawn

Crown Heights, Brooklyn, New York

The A train shuddered to a stop, and a few occupants staggered out. There was the homeless man with his shopping cart stuffed full of clothes headed for God only knew where. A middle-aged nurse, dressed in scrubs, hurried toward the stairs. Following her was the tall, dark-haired man in jeans and a light-cream Polo shirt, eyes vigilantly scanning the narrow platform.

The conductor shouted something incomprehensible, and the doors swished shut behind Harry. As if the muggy heat weren't enough, stale cigarette smoke mingled with the stench of rotten food spilling over the sides of the tall garbage can. Graffiti covered the walls.

By the time he jogged up the stairs, Harry's shirt was drenched in sweat. The deli across the street was still doing brisk business. Chasing away some teens with fake IDs, the storekeeper turned to Harry. "Dumb kids," the man grumbled in thick accents strongly hinting of Caribbean origins.

"Bottled water," Harry requested, cursing Will Luce in his mind. The man was pushing sixty, but he was as irresponsible as the boys trying to sneak alcohol. With all the other things to juggle, Harry certainly didn't need to add Luce's card problems. Unfortunately, ignoring his messages was no longer an option if Luce was desperate enough to call the club. Still, if he weren't Verity's father, Harry might have left him to sort out his own mess. He owed it to his former wife to help, but the old fellow deserved the boot to the backside he was about to get.

Gulping ice-cold beverage from the plastic bottle, Harry walked at a rapid clip between the steel fence bordering an empty lot and a row of parked cars. There were very few people on the streets. He frowned mildly, wondering yet again why Will Luce was in this particular neighborhood when he lived in Connecticut. Liam would've said something if his father managed to gamble away his home.

Luce was going to have to agree to a deal. Money in installments, contingent upon him getting counseling for his addiction. A tightly controlled monthly budget would help him pay off his loans.

The tall buildings of Albany House loomed in front of Harry. What the hell was Will Luce doing in this place meant for low-income residents? The salary he drew from Gateway should've been more than adequate for a single person's needs. Exactly how much money had the man lost?

The one functioning bulb at the entrance flickered as Harry marched up, and shards of glass from a broken beer bottle crunched under his shoes. Mild pressure from his fingertips opened the main door. In the lobby, cigarette butts littered the linoleum around the small trash can, and an empty box from a fast-food joint lay next to a toppled plastic chair. He dropped the bottle of water into the garbage.

The elevator was not working, so he took the dimly lit stairwell. The building stank of cheap alcohol and stale junk food. *And drugs,* Harry noted, kicking aside the empty syringe. New York's poor couldn't seem to catch a break, with crack cocaine tightening its grip on those of the city's inhabitants least equipped to battle it.

His destination was the corner apartment on the ninth floor. Skin prickled as Harry noted the small gap between door and jamb.

Drawing the SIG-Sauer he'd taken to constantly carrying on his person, he stood to the side and delivered a hard kick to the door. It bounced off the wall.

Silence. Dark silence thickened the air in the apartment... along with the metallic scent of blood.

Harry cursed. *Will Luce? Or someone else?* Groping along the wall, he found the light switch.

In the middle of the living room was a man lying on his stomach, draped partly across the coffee table, his feet dragging on the floor. Dark-red blood pulsed out from around the knife hilt projecting from his upper back. The viscous liquid dripped down the man's bulky torso, forming ever-expanding circles below. Will Luce, Verity's father, gave every appearance of having been knifed while Harry was on his way up.

Weapon at the ready, Harry strode forward. The body slid when he tried to check for a pulse at the neck. An arm fell across Harry's sneakers, smearing the shoes and his jeans with blood. Luce, Sr. was quite dead.

The phone... as Harry looked around for one, there was loud clattering outside. He whirled.

Footsteps thundered toward the apartment. The front door was kicked open for the second time in five minutes.

"Police! Drop your weapon!"

Chapter 50

(13 hours ahead of New York City)

June 3, 1989, in the hours before midnight

Beijing, People's Republic of China

Darkness was on the city, but Tiananmen Square remained brightly lit. Close to the Monument of the People's Heroes, student protestors thronged the south end, singing songs and chanting slogans. At the north end stood the Goddess of Democracy, a huge white structure built to resemble the Statue of Liberty. She held her torch aloft with both hands and defiantly faced down the portrait of Mao Zedong.

Inside the crowded medical tent, Lilah perspired. As soon as she was done helping Neil, she was going to kick off her sneakers and scratch the soles of her feet. If she could, she would peel off even the jeans and the cheap tie-dye tee.

It wasn't merely the heat that was overwhelming. The students had been on the streets for months, protesting the lack of true democracy. Disagreements escalated. The Chinese capital was sitting on a powder-keg, primed to explode any moment. Everyone in Beijing was sweating the next couple of days.

The exiles wouldn't have picked China to hide in if they got enough time to contact any of the lowlifes they knew to arrange clandestine entry into India. Travel to Beijing was easier, and not only because of the less stringent border controls than the nation's southern neighbor. There were the passports already stamped by officials at the Macau and Hong Kong entry points. But the political situation... Lilah hoped to God they hadn't just made the mistake of their lives, a monumental miscalculation which could get them killed.

In some ways, the chaos benefited the exiles, because the authorities were too distracted to track down visitors who overstayed the seventy-hour limit allowed for air passengers on their way to another country. Even the hotel didn't find their lengthy stay remarkable, dismissing them as yet another group of American journalists. It allowed the Kingsleys to secretly meet Dan's contact in the city. New travel documents were an absolute necessity since Prince was likely aware of all their old aliases. Unfortunately, also thanks to the ongoing turmoil, the fake permits to visit Tibet were taking longer than expected. Only once the papers were ready could the trek to India begin.

When Neil spotted the medical tent today, no one could stop him from running to help. Lilah accompanied him purely from a need to get out for a few minutes. Alex was also with them, on bodyguard duty at the door of the tent.

She knelt on the ground and handed a pair of scissors to Neil. "You really miss it," she commented.

"Yeah," Neil admitted, bandana still in place, the white smock lent to him by one of the Chinese doctors now smeared with blood. "I never dreamed I'd be working in the oil sector. It was always medicine for me."

"Your father was the heir to one of the biggest oil services companies in the world."

Snipping off a stitch, Neil dabbed disinfectant-soaked gauze at the college student's forehead. "Perfect," he proclaimed. "It's not even going to leave a scar." Once the student left, he said to Lilah. "Father died when Scott and I were six. He had no impact on anything we did. I don't remember him, you know. What about you? Didn't your parents die in a crash?"

"Yes," she said, not elaborating.

After a few seconds of expectant silence, Neil said, "Guess you don't want to talk about it. Lilah, I was waiting for the right time. I mean, I wanted to apologize to you for my part in the... I didn't expect Brad would—"

"Neil, Lilah," called a voice, tone urgent.

Alex. Behind him was Scott.

Throwing the forceps in her hand in a kidney dish, Lilah scrambled up and strode to the two men. "What happened?"

431

Scott pushed his glasses up his nose. "There was a message from the Indian embassy."

"What?" asked Lilah, her heart speeding unpleasantly. "How did they find us—"

"Addressed to the Coppersmiths," Scott said. "Says, 'Package arriving at Beijing airport tonight from Kathmandu; get out of China as soon as you pick up.'"

"Grayson would be my best guess since the alias was used," Alex said. "He probably contacted your cousin in India, Shankar Mittal."

"Shankar asked the embassy to bring the message around to the hotel?" Lilah frowned. "Grayson would call the hotel if it was an emergency. He knows our location."

Tone moody, Alex said, "Communications are being restricted. The journalists at the hotel were complaining. But diplomatic messages might still be going through."

"I suppose it's possible," Lilah acknowledged. Also, Grayson might have thought it more prudent to contact her through Shankar. After all, the exiles' calls to their lawyer were made from different lines, but if he rang the hotel, it would give away their exact location to any potential listener. "But what does he mean? What package?"

Alex shoved his fingers through his hair. "Victor's gone to the airport. Him and Brad and Scott going there all together... situation's not good on the streets. Also, there's a possibility it might be a trap." After Macau, Alex and Victor had stated they would return to round-the-clock guard duty. If the exiles were forced to split up for whatever reason, either the boxer or the sniper would go with each splinter group. But Grayson's cryptic message meant one of them needed to show up at the terminal to find out what was going on. In case it did turn out to be a trap, Victor could best deal with it alone without having to worry about protecting his brothers. Brad was apparently told to barricade himself in the room with weapons, and Scott was sent to collect the rest. It took the mild-mannered astrophysicist close to two hours to navigate the mayhem and reach the medical tent. "Victor should be back soon," Alex said. Unless it was a trap.

The chop-chop sound of helicopter engines had them all peering out through the tent flap.

"Military," said Alex. "They've been doing fly-overs for some time. It's not looking good."

"Yo," hollered a familiar voice. Victor squeezed through the narrow space between two trucks and beckoned to someone behind.

Before Alex could complete his huff of relief, a face came into view, one Lilah never expected to see in Beijing. She goggled. "Oh, my God. Hema!" The Nepali girl was supposed to be safe with Patrice. Lilah ran to her former intern, Alex following closely. "What are you doing here?!" she asked. Hema hugged Lilah with a little sob. Patting the young woman's shoulder, Lilah inquired, "Victor?"

He shook his head. "No clue what Grayson was thinking."

In thickly accented English, Hema snapped, "Don't blame Mr. Grayson. Lilah, I told him I wanted to come to you. He dropped me off with someone he knew in Nepal. He couldn't bring me himself because he believed he'd be..." Thinking for a few seconds, she concluded, "...tailed."

Victor spat out, "And he booked you on a flight to Beijing. What were you planning to do if we'd already left China?"

"Mr. Grayson bought me a round-trip ticket," said Hema. "If I didn't see any of you at the airport, I'd have returned to Kathmandu and called him."

"You should've stayed in Nepal," Victor insisted. "It's your home, and you'd have been safe there."

"I haven't been to Nepal since I was ten, Mister Victor," said Hema. "I don't have any family there. I grew up in India at the orphanage, and I'm too old for the place now." Turning to Lilah, the girl added, "I promise I won't be any trouble. I could even help."

A panicked screech erupted directly in front, interrupting the argument. A bicycle rickshaw rolled toward the medical tent, carrying a young man with blood gushing out of his chest.

Victor stared after the vehicle. "He's not going to make it." There were other rickshaws following, carrying more wounded. "The army's out on the streets. They're opening fire. Not as if it's stopping anyone. People are making human chains and trying to block tanks and trucks. Rocks, Molotov cocktails, you name it... they're using everything. It's not going to end well." Wiping the sweat off his forehead, he said to Alex, "We need to get back to the hotel. Brad must be going out of his mind." He would know the crowds would slow his brothers. Still... "Let's pick him up and leave the city like Grayson said. Pronto!"

"I agree," Alex said. "At least let's get out the square. Some of the wounded reported tank movements in this direction."

A voice blared over the loudspeakers in the square, announcing that the government would take "any measures" to enforce the martial law imposed just two weeks prior.

The group pushed through the throng and went to Neil. "We have to leave," said Victor.

"In a few minutes," Neil said, eyes on the stitches he was putting on yet another patient.

Victor scratched his jaw. "Hurry."

The night sky lit up without warning. "What's that?" Hema asked.

"Illumination rounds," Alex said. "Neil, *enough*. Let's go." It took the young surgeon another two minutes to complete what he was doing.

Screams and angry shouts echoed from every corner as the group shoved through the mob. "Keep close," Lilah said to Hema. Panicked young men and women, bicycles, rickshaws... it seemed to be forever before they were finally out of the square. The crowd wasn't any less thick on the streets, either.

A shadow loomed in front of Lilah. "Excuse me," she said and attempted to go around the person. The shadow moved with her, blocking her path. A blade glinted under the lamps. "Alex," she screamed, her hand darting to the pistol tucked into her belt.

Before she could get the weapon, the assailant jerked her around by the elbow, holding her as a shield. She struggled to get free but found the tip of the knife pressed against the underside of her chin. Warm blood trickled down her neck. The blade caused her head to tilt to an unnatural angle, forcing her to stare up at the large Chinese man holding her prisoner. She heard Hema's scream and Victor's roar but didn't dare take eyes from the assailant. The man said something to Lilah in Chinese. She didn't even dare shake her head in incomprehension. The knife dug painfully into her skin.

"Let her go, you son of a bitch," Alex bellowed. He would have his gun as would the other men, but no one would fire a shot at the assailant when Lilah was his hostage.

In a louder voice, the man repeated what he said earlier. Around them, the melee continued, no one paying attention to the subplot involving the Americans.

"What the hell is he saying?" Victor asked.

"King want you," the man said in English this time, his voice guttural. "Yaa, yaa... king." He shuffled back a step or two and pulled Lilah along.

"Look out," shouted Victor.

The man jerked his head instinctively to check behind. His grip loosened. Lilah barely registered the large form shoving the man to the side as Victor. Grabbing her arm, Victor rammed into the crowd and dragged her to where the others were. Her glasses tumbled off her face.

Victor snatched them off the ground and continued onward.

"Move," Alex yelled. Pushing aside protestors with each step, bending low to avoid the flying bottles, they made for the hotel.

Her heart thudded, trying to figure out the implications of the latest attack. King as in Kingsley? Harry... but the press conference... would the Kingsleys dare go after him this soon?

Victor came to a sudden halt. "Battle taxi," he said tersely. Their way forward was blocked by a tank. He looked both ways and grunted in frustration. "Too many people; the thug will catch up easily."

"We could use guns, but..." Alex said.

"Last resort," huffed Lilah. "Too many people around." A shootout could injure one or more of the protestors, perhaps kill someone.

Victor ordered the others, "Get behind me and wait. But make sure Lilah remains visible." He handed something to Alex. "Give her the glasses."

Alex nodded and stood right behind his brother, his weapon drawn and ready. "Can't wait around too long. The armored vehicles are running over the tents on purpose. I don't want to risk all of us being crushed to death."

Without taking his eyes off the man getting closer, Victor told them, "Stay put. On my order, try to run left... into the crowd."

"Got it," Alex said.

"Ask who sent him," Lilah said, pushing the glasses up the bridge of her nose. A crack ran across one lens, but there were more critical problems for her to worry about now. If the Kingsleys were behind this attempted abduction, then there was a chance Harry was also under attack. Her stomach churned.

"No time," said Victor. He wiped the sweat off his top lip with the back of his hand and beckoned to the pursuer. "C'mon. You want to get to her? Let me see how you're going to."

The assailant sprinted toward them. The crowd continued to yell and scream and throw broken bits of concrete at the armored carriers. Everyone was pushing and shoving. Victor was jostled about by the protestors running back and forth. The assailant got so close Victor could reach out and punch him. Only the ugly blade stopped the former boxer. With the street in utter chaos, no one paid attention to their little tableau.

Breathing harsh, the Chinese man growled, "King." He looked over Victor's shoulder and spotted Lilah. Knife raised, the thug rushed at the man between him and his target.

Victor yelled, "Now," and sidestepped the thug at the last second.

The exiles went left as ordered, but the disordered throng made it impossible to move more than a couple of feet at a time. Lilah glanced back at what was happening.

Momentum had carried the knife-wielding assailant forward. Before he could recover, Victor hooked a foot around his ankle, making him stumble. Off balance, he was easily forced to one side... right under the wheels of the oncoming tank.

Victor caught up with the rest in seconds and took over the lead, thrusting aside a couple of journalists to clear a path.

"Look," Alex said. He'd turned around to check on the attacker.

Through her cracked glasses, Lilah watched as the armored vehicle was set ablaze by enraged protestors. The assailant was still trapped under the wheels, the crowd around roaring.

It took the group more than an hour to get to the hotel when it should've taken them under fifteen minutes. Anxious guests were standing around in the lobby, talking excitedly.

"Alex," Lilah whispered, taking care to hide the conversation from potential listeners. They fell a little behind the rest. "Call Mr. Temple's phone, please."

Nodding, Alex said, "I know. The man said 'king.' You think he meant Kingsley."

"Also, what Uncle Gray said about getting out as soon as we picked up the 'package.' I want to know what's happening with Harry."

"Getting out could be about the political situation here, not necessarily something about Harry," Alex muttered back. Uncertainty was clear in his eyes, but like her, he was hoping there was no new trouble. "Another possibility is Grayson might be worrying about someone following Hema. So getting out fast makes sense, right? I *will* try to call, but getting through..." To the rest, Alex called out, "You go ahead. Let me see if there's new info on what the Chinese government plans to do."

Victor led them up the stairs rather than wait for the elevator. In the suite shared by the twins, they updated Brad on what happened.

"What was he talking about?" Brad asked. "What king? Kingsley?"

"Or Prince," Victor said succinctly. "He does have a lot of connections in China."

Lilah started. The possibility hadn't occurred to her.

The door opened, letting Alex in. Tone grim, he said, "The army was already moving into the square when we left. The journalists downstairs say they expect a total crackdown." When Lilah eyed him, he shook his head. The call to Temple's home didn't go through.

You'd better be okay, Harry! Lilah fretted. No, she didn't buy Victor's theory it was the drug lord. If so, why wouldn't the assailant in the square use the Chinese version of his boss's name, Jùn Wángzǐ, instead of King? If the assassin felt free to admit who hired him, it meant the Kingsleys were sure there would be no repercussions from Harry.

"We have to get out of the city," Victor said, drawing Lilah's attention back. "Maybe even the country. Tonight. For one, the man tried to attack Lilah. For another, the situation is not merely unstable any longer. There's a good chance the Chinese will round up foreigners and start evacuating. If we stay, we're going to get caught in the net."

"Do we leave right now?" asked Scott, blinking rapidly.

"The streets are too damn dangerous," Neil said. "There's no option for us but to stay at least until tomorrow."

Brad nodded. "Pack everything," he ordered. "We'll stay put for now but be ready to leave at a moment's notice."

Lilah didn't bother to change out of the grime-covered jeans and tie-dye tee and sneakers. While Neil and Alex stood guard at the door to her room, she threw her belongings into the luggage. Hema picked up a piece of clothing or two and added them to the pile in the box. "Can I talk to you?" the intern asked in a whisper.

"Later," said Lilah. "No time right now." They simply couldn't afford to slow down and chat before they got to someplace safe. *Harry,* Lilah agonized. *What is going on with you?* He escaped Kingsley traps thrice—the chemical fire in Argentina, Parker at the board meeting in Panama, and the hired killers in New York City. Yeah, he knew how to take care of himself, but what if—

"Lilah," Neil called from the door. "Are you ready?"

When the two women reached the room shared by the twins, everyone else was already there, bags packed. Victor had managed to get food for the group. "Eat up," he said. "With everything going on... chances are we're not going to be able to stop for anything."

Hema kept making gestures at Lilah, signaling they needed to talk. The Nepali girl also nodded insistently a few times in Alex's direction. Lilah huffed out a breath. She couldn't imagine what the girl wanted to discuss with both her and Alex, but dragging him out at the moment for a private conversation could very well trigger another scene with Brad. Not something they could afford under the circumstances. Surreptitiously, Lilah raised a hand, asking the girl for patience.

Alex and Victor took turns going to the lobby to gather updates from reporters. The news kept getting worse. Violence was escalating. The tumult inside Lilah's mind spiraled along with the chaos on the streets.

Toward dawn, Victor returned, a hopeful look on his face. "The government says it's ready to negotiate with the students."

Before anyone could respond, Scott exclaimed, "Look... the lights went out." When they rushed to the window, the square—visible at some distance—was completely shrouded in darkness.

"What's going on?" asked Brad. "If the government is negotiating, why would they turn the power off?"

Suddenly, the rousing notes of *"Internationale"* rang through the night. The sounds from the street continued unabated... the singing, the screams, gunshots, noises from military vehicles.

"What *is* going on?" Neil echoed his older brother, but no one came up with an answer.

The lights in the square powered back on after some time. Every one of the watching exiles gasped in shock at the sight on the streets. The students were running for their lives, pursued by soldiers on foot and in tanks.

Unable to help while young blood spilled on the streets of the city, the group at the window turned away one by one and paced the room. With fingertips on the glass pane, Lilah stared unblinkingly at the scene. Only a few months ago, she'd cradled her friend's bleeding body, praying desperately for him to live. These students also had friends and lovers. Their parents, their siblings... Dan... while Lilah was being arrested at her home in Panama, her enemies tricked the Belgian police into detaining her twin on suspicion of terrorism. What would the Kingsleys have done to Dan this time around? *Oh, God,* she prayed. She couldn't lose her brother. *God,* she prayed for the families who were waiting for their beloved sons and daughters to return home.

Alex soon returned to the window. Together, he and Lilah watched in silence as the young people taking their first faltering steps into adulthood were butchered mercilessly. They watched the hope for freedom dying a brutal death in the early hours of dawn.

"Bastards," Neil said from somewhere behind. "Killing their own this easily. I hope the international community—"

"The international community will do *nothing,*" Lilah said, turning to face the room. "Blinded by ego... all of them... what they care about is power. No one bothers about minor things like doing their darned jobs. They won't even admit they had a hand in letting matters get this far. I mean... what if the citizens toss them out? Nuh-huh. Which politician will risk it?"

Neil objected, "The press—"

"Oh, the media will cry and carry on for a few weeks," agreed Lilah. "Riots are good for their business. Eventually, they will also play along. A few noises will be made by government types—

cosmetic changes. Then, things will return to where they were. The poor students will be told to move on. There will be some scholar showing up on TV, some military officer, some diplomat, to lecture the victims on consequences and peace and compromise and God knows what."

Friends and families of the dead would live with their pain, never finding closure.

"No matter who does or doesn't do their job, *we* need to get out," Victor stated. "I wish we could leave right now, but after what we just saw... I don't know... Neil's probably right. We might have to stay for a couple of days."

"Lilah," burst out Hema. "Can I talk to you *now?* And to Mr. Alex? Since Mr. Victor said we can't go anywhere at this time... please! It's important."

#

A few minutes later

Seated in the narrow armchair in her room, Lilah played with the switch, clicking the table lamp off and on. The yellow pool of light blinked in and out. The noise outside the windows continued unabated, but the occupants of the small chamber paid no attention to the tumult. Lilah simply didn't get what Hema was saying.

"Wife?" Alex asked incredulously.

"Shh!" said Hema, sitting on the bed. "It's supposed to be a secret."

Alex paced the room, his fingers making a mess of his hair. "Which makes even less sense. A secret marriage for a Green Card? Couldn't Harry find some other way? I mean... he could very well have set himself up as a partner in the clubs even if Lupe needed to move someplace else like Canada. It would've made sure she didn't lose anything while the mess got sorted out."

Flicking a glance at Lilah, Hema said, "Only you two are supposed to know about the marriage for now. Mr. Grayson said he didn't want to risk calling you directly, and the phone lines were anyway—"

"—not working," Alex completed.

"Mr. Grayson is supposed to explain better when he can talk to you," Hema finished.

"*He* married them," Lilah murmured. Grayson Sheppard officiated the private ceremony attended by the former president, Noah Andersen, and Liam Luce in the capacity of bride's friend.

"Are you okay?" Alex asked.

Leaving the table lamp on, Lilah glanced up. "Yeah... just confused." She could've been mistaken about the strength of Harry's feelings for her. He could've fallen head over heels for the temptress who ran Eden, enough to wed her even in the midst of the chaos involving the network. After all, Lilah offered no promises when she left, extracted no vows from him. The one thing Harry wouldn't have done was casually send her a message informing her he found someone else. Would he?

Lilah shook her head. She needed to focus on the practical for now. Did Harry's clandestine wedding relate at all to the Kingsley assassin? Hema would've known if something happened to Harry or Dan or anyone else dear to Lilah, but the Nepali girl flew out of New York more than a day ago. A lot could transpire in the space of a few hours.

Dropping to his haunches in front of her chair, Alex said, "Lilah, c'mon... there's no reason to be confused. You know Harry... he's not stupid enough to go chasing after women right when things are going south. He's got his reasons for doing what he did. We might not know them right now, but it ain't undying love for Lupe."

"Probably not," agreed Lilah. There was a sound within her brain—a droning noise. Shaking her head again, she glanced aimlessly around. "But everything else... none of it is adding up. This wedding... Grayson... Hema..."

Alex nodded. "The thug who showed up in the square... he might have followed Grayson. Natural assumption would be Grayson was taking Hema home to Nepal. But only until he booked the ticket from Kathmandu to Beijing."

"Mr. Grayson *was* worried someone could be spying on him," said Hema. "Also, he kept saying China is dangerous right now. He really wants you to leave."

"Still too many loose ends," Alex objected. "If the fellow in the square was hired by Prince and not Steven, I don't see how Grayson figures in the picture. If Steven did send the thug, why would he attack unless—"

Harry was accounted for, Lilah finished mentally. The image of his body, lying broken and bleeding on her lap... *Please,* Lilah whispered. *Let him be alive.* Her twin... when the enemy tried to have her charged with treason, they might have hoped to eventually persuade Dan that the problems he faced getting to her were merely coincidence. They might have expected to show the Barronses irrefutable evidence of her guilt, thus stopping them from seeking other answers. No way would Dan ever believe any such excuse, and the Kingsleys would've realized it by now. What could they have planned for him? What did they plan for the others... Sabrina... Michael... Patrice... Temple... everyone else who swore fealty to the exiles? The droning in Lilah's head got louder, more urgent. "I wish I could go," she whispered.

"Go where?" Alex asked. "Back home?"

"Yes... no." She bit her lower lip hard, trying to get her brain to focus. "To the mountains, maybe. Stupid idea, but I need to think clearly. It's hard here... too noisy." Too crowded. Too *much.* "Could you give me a few minutes? Hema and I will stay in the room until it's time to leave. We'll be okay." After all, Lilah slept alone all these months with one or the other of the men in the rooms on either side keeping awake to watch for problems.

"No way," said Alex. "Not after what just happened."

"Alex—" Breaking off, Lilah sighed. "Look, we've been here with Hema for almost half an hour. Brad's going to... any longer, and both of us will be in for a miserable time right when we need to focus on getting out of China. You could go to his room just for a short while. It will make him happy, and I... I swear I'll lock the door and stay inside until you return."

Alex's eyelids flickered.

"Please?" Lilah beseeched. "We could use the break to chew things over separately, then team up on a plan of action."

After a moment, he inclined his head. "Promise not to run off to the mountains without me or Victor."

Lilah mustered a smile. "I won't."

She remained in the chair, but the clamor in her mind continued, matching the commotion outside the windows. The door closed behind Alex.

"I'm sorry," Hema mumbled.

Lilah looked toward the bed where the Nepali girl was sitting cross-legged. "For?"

Flushing, the girl said, "For bringing you trouble."

"Trust me... this particular trouble would've found me whatever you... Hema, as long as you're around me, you'll be in danger, too. These are not small-time criminals we're dealing with. If they feel you're a threat somehow, they *will* kill you. First thing we should do once we're out of Beijing is find a way to send you back to the States."

"I'm not leaving," Hema said, shaking her head. "You didn't leave *me* when the horrible man attacked, did you?" The rapist who assaulted the young intern during the corporate event in Panama happened on her first in his search for Lilah.

With a sigh, Lilah said, "It's not a life debt, my dear."

"You don't understand," Hema said. "Lilah, you... you're the only one... I mean... if the only family you have left is in trouble, would you be okay if you don't know what's happening with them?"

"C'mon, girl. Patrice and Sabrina and Harry—"

"Mrs. Patrice doesn't talk much, and Mikey and Sabrina don't like coming to that house to visit. I couldn't even go to them. Mr. Grayson said the less I'm around Mr. Harry, the better for me. Too many reporters... umm... all kinds of stories."

Yet another female hanging around Harry's apartment *would* have drawn media attention. Lupe Valdez, some artist fellow, the women of the strip club... who knew what tale the press might have cooked up about Hema?

Lilah bit her lip again. "What *is* going on with you, Harry?" she muttered out loud.

"I'm sure there's an explanation," offered Hema. "For the Valdez lady, I mean. If you could talk to Mr. Harry—"

The phone rang, startling both women. Lilah didn't wait to think. She grabbed the receiver. "Hello?"

Static... a distant voice calling. "—lah?" Static... a buzzing sound... more static. "—are you—"

"Hello?" she hollered into the phone, straining to listen over the relentless din. "Who's this?" A wide-eyed Hema looked on, hands folded as though in prayer.

Static, again. "Can you hear—"

Who? Who? Lilah almost sobbed in frustration. It was a male voice but not Grayson's elderly speech. Was it Harry? Dan? His contact in the city could've informed him she was in China. He might be worried enough about the news from the country to risk direct contact with her. Or was someone else calling with an update on one or both men? Shawn, perhaps? "Hello—"

"—wnstairs." The buzzing sound stopped. The line went dead.

Tossing the phone back to the table, Lilah stood. "Hema, please get Alex and tell him to meet me downstairs at the switchboard. Someone's trying to call us. It might be Harry or one of my brothers."

"But—"

Before Hema could complete whatever she was about to say, Lilah was at the door, yanking it open. She sprinted to the elevator, only to stop short at the out-of-order sign. This time, a sharp sob did escape her lips. Pivoting, she ran toward the emergency stairwell.

Lilah tore down the stairs, taking two steps at once. Shrieks and shouts and the sounds of gunfire continued to echo in from the streets, but without windows, the decibel level was lower. Thank heavens, there were no other hotel guests to dodge in her race to reach the telephone operator. What the person on the line said... he surely meant to call back. She needed to be at the switchboard when he did.

God! Phones seemed to stop working whenever she was desperate to reach Harry or Dan or anyone dear to her. With the arrest in Panama, the Kingsleys made sure—Lilah stopped dead in her tracks.

Before she could turn, before she could even think of bolting to the safety of her room, heavy treads sounded behind. A hand gripped her shoulder, and her arms were wrenched to the back. A metallic click. Steel shackles fell into place, locking her wrists together.

"Alex!" Lilah screamed. The name ricocheted around the stairwell. A hand clamped over her mouth. Silence fell.

Chapter 51

(13 hours behind Beijing)

June 3, 1989

77th Precinct, Crown Heights

Brooklyn, New York

In the small, windowless room tucked into the far corner of the building, two detectives sat facing the detained suspect. Fluorescent lighting made the chamber unnaturally bright. Outside the door, there were the usual sounds of a workday, phones ringing and the clatter of furniture and employees talking. A painful pulse drummed away in Harry's ear, fear sharpening his vision. He could see every crack in the concrete walls, smell every odor in the place from the coffee to the sweat to the stench from the latrine not too far away.

"Please," Harry begged. "Let me go. By the time Andersen gets here, it might be too late. You said I'm not under arrest, so how the hell can you keep me here?"

"Mr. Sheppard," started the senior detective. "The law allows us to temporarily detain persons suspected of criminal conduct. A man has been found dead—your former father-in-law. You were standing over the corpse with a weapon in your hands. Yeah... but no. Any court will tell you we're being more than reasonable under the circumstances. You were allowed one phone call to your lawyer. Everything else must wait until he arrives, including the questions we have for you."

"I was lured there," insisted Harry. He was trapped, which meant Lilah was also under attack. The predator in him roared, wanting to rip the cage apart and charge to his mate's rescue. "I *need* to go."

The two detectives exchanged glances. "Sorry, Mr. Sheppard," the senior officer spoke again. "You will not be going anywhere at this time."

THE END of Book 4

For a sneak peek at the next book in the series, please head over to www.JayPerin.com

Want to know what happens next to Harry, Lilah, and Alex? Order *The Indian Defense* today to continue with this exciting tale!

Afterword

As mentioned in the afterword to the prior books, the One Hundred Years of War series is an adaptation of the *Mahabharata*, the Indian epic mythology.

A few comments (some are repeats from prior books):

1. My thanks to the writers whose works on *Mahabharata* I've enjoyed and learned from and to fellow myth enthusiasts from various discussion groups. Thanks to my friends who have patiently sat through my arguments on various plot points, especially Amrita Talukdar and Preeti Gopal.

2. For the purpose of this story, Temple was president from 1979 to 1986. Reagan-Bush (take your pick) from 1986 to 1992. Yes, I realize that doesn't make it eight years, but it can't be helped because I want to end the story the year I want it to end, so Temple's presidency had to come at this time. Also, I didn't want Temple identified with either a real president or with one of the political parties. Right now, he straddles Carter (D) and Reagan (R) administrations.

3. I did not use real characters except peripherally. That, too, only for things they were actually accused/guilty of doing.

4. I tried to stick to historical facts throughout the story, including the minor details, but some changes were inevitable.

5. Citations for the maps are in footnotes.

6.   As far as I can figure out, the U.S. Supreme Court did not have an internship program in the 1940s. Please consider it literary license. Columbia did have female students in their law school.

So that's it. See you again when *The Indian Defense* releases.

Sincerely,

Jay Perin

P.S. As always, if you liked the story, do tell others about it. Also, writers thrive on reviews. They help us figure out what worked and what fell flat. They help other readers make up their minds. Please do leave a comment on any of the sites.

Visit www.EastRiverBooks.com for a bunch of interesting stuff.

———————————————